The Apostles of Satan

F. Scott Kimmich

First in the trilogy *Ordeal By Fire*

ISBN 1495813023
ISBN 9781495913020

Cover: The expulsion of the Albigensians from Carcassonne,
© The British Library Board, Cotton Nero E. II

To
Michel Roquebert,
whose painstaking research, enormous industry and passionate commitment to historical accuracy have stripped away the myths to reveal the beating heart of the Good Folk in their beloved Midi.

Contents

Acknowledgement

The historical setting is based first and foremost on Michel Roquebert's monumental *L'Epopée Cathare* (2008) in five volumes; his earlier work, *Histoire des Cathares* (1999); and *La Religion Cathare: Le Bien, le Mal et le Salut dans l'hérésie médiévale* (2001). The theological discussions and descriptions of Cathar ceremonies in the novel are based closely on the latter book and upon Walter Wakefield's and Austin Evans's *Heresies of the Middle Ages* (1999), which contains English translations of medieval sources of inquiry into heresies, including writings by the heretics themselves. *Les Catharismes* (2008), by Pilar Sanchez, argues persuasively that the Cathars' return to the pious morality and simplicity of the early Christian church probably preceded and out-weighed dualistic dogma in winning adherents.

Nicolas Gouzy and Charles Peytavie's magnificently written and illustrated *Cathares in Languedoc* (2009) and Jonathan Sumption's sweeping chronicle, *The Albigensian Crusade* (1999) provided a convenient and highly readable 'forest,' without ignoring the 'trees.' *The Occitan War* (2008)by Laurence Marvin supplied additional details about the first nine years of the French invasion of the Midi, as well as insight into the fragility of Occitan society. Thomas Bisson's *The Medieval Crown of Aragon* (1986) shone light on the count-kings of Aragon.

I am very grateful to Veronique Marcaillou of Le Centre des Etudes Cathares in Carcassonne for her help in channeling my inquiries.

I would like to thank Doug Brown, Chantal Rode, Elliot Danforth, Tony Morley, John Sharpe, Joan Kelly, Judy and Hans Copek, Mabel Dudeney, Regina Krummel, Ann Pettus, Allan Hobson, Rod Lopez-Fabrega, my son Erlend, my late brother Bob and his partner Billie Bem; my daughter Daniela, my grandsons Nic and Dieter; and my wife, Kate, for their encouragement and suggestions.

This book could not have been published without Kate's assistance and without Nic's formatting, and preparation of the genealogical tables and the maps. He and Russ Gilfix helped format the cover design.

Song Credits

The 13th century *trobar* (poem), *The glance that my lady darts at me must slay (Mort m'an li semblan que madona·m fai)*, is by an anonymous *trobador* (troubadour). The translation by A.S.Kline, © Dawn to Dawn (2009), faithfully reproduces the themes, rhythms and rhyme schemes used by 12th and 13th century *trobadors*, writing one century before Dante's birth, and two centuries before the birth of Chaucer. *Cansos* (songs) in the *lenga d'oc* were composed and performed throughout the Midi, from Poitou on the Atlantic to Die in the foothills of the Alps.

Map Credits

Figure 1. The Midi, rivers and selected towns.
Figure 2. Feudal holdings in the Midi, 1209 Adapted from Figure.2, Lawrence, W. Marvin: *The Occitan War*, Cambridge University Press, 2008.

Prologue

Jerusalem, 32 AD

As the two men carried the body into the tomb, the women stopped just outside, wailing and keening and racked by sobs. The brawny giant had passed his arms under the dead man's armpits, while his comrade had locked one arm around the knees. In the flickering light of a small oil lamp perched in a wall niche, the big man nodded toward the stone bench that formed one side of the sepulcher. They were lifting the body to place it on the chiseled surface, when a voice called, "Simon, wait!"

The big man looked around at the two men clad in the robes and headdresses of the *Sanhedrin* standing behind him. One of them took off his outer robe and spread it onto the bench.

"Good thinking, Nicodemus," Simon said, and nodding again to his partner, lowered the body onto the robe. Except for a loin cloth, and a circlet of thorns on its head, the corpse was naked. Its skin was mottled with bruises and crisscrossed with welts caused by scourging. Dried crusts of blackened blood on its wrists and ankles marked where the dead man had been nailed to the cross. A wound gaped between the ribs of the left chest.

"Maybe we can remove the thorns before we start," the other *Sanhedrin* said, just as the women, their eyes red with weeping, burst through the doorway and threw themselves down by the corpse. The veil of one of them had slipped down to her shoulders, revealing a pretty woman with dark brown ringlets gathered into a Roman-style chignon. She was clearly pregnant.

At the *Sanhedrin*'s words, she lunged at him, grabbing his upper arms and digging her finger-nails into his flesh. "Joseph," she cried, "how could you let this happen? You said it was utterly safe and foolproof!"

"I know," Joseph began, "but…"

v

"You know? You *know?*" She spat on his robes. "We trusted you; we thought you were one of *us!*"

"But I *am,* Mary. It just went wrong. I'm as sorry…"

"*Wrong?* Is that all you can say? *Sorry?* And who's to blame?" she cried, her dark eyes ablaze. She wheeled around to the motionless figure stretched out on the bench. "Oh, my darling," she sobbed, and bent over and cradled the head in her arms. "Alas, my poor love," she murmured, kissing the pale lips and caressing the ashen cheeks streaked with dried blood.

The older of the other two women picked up one of the dead man's hands and held it against her cheek as she spoke. "We must get on with preparing him for burial. Tomorrow's the Sabbath."

At that moment, Joseph touched her on the arm. "Gracious Lady, I've got everything you need just outside."

She gently laid the hand back down on the bench and followed Joseph out of the tomb.

"I'm so terribly sorry," he said, wringing his hands. "We brought along medications he would have needed—myrrh and aloe, bandages, too. And plenty of oil. We thought he would…"

She touched her fingers to his lips. "I know you didn't mean to harm him, but what's done is done. Now I must help his wife with the *taharah,* the ritual cleansing. We need plenty of oil. Where did you say you put it?"

"Right here, my lady." Joseph pointed to a large amphora beside the entrance, just as Simon emerged.

"Let me give you a hand," Simon said, and picked up the amphora as if it were as light as a feather, and put it at the dead man's feet.

"Thank you, Simon, you've been a …a rock, a true rock, as my son used to say. And you, too," she said to Joseph as she patted him on the arm before going back inside.

Emerging from the crupt, Simon rounded on Joseph and grabbing him by the folds of his robe, pulled him up off his feet. "I ought to tie your balls around your neck! How did this happen? We had a plan, may David curse you!"

"We had a plan," Joseph gasped, "but how could we have known they would replace the centurion we bribed?"

"Can a camel be born to an ass? How did that happen, after all the money we spent?"

"I don't know, I swear, but..."

"You don't know?" He shook Joseph like a rag doll. "They were supposed to take him down before noon, but they left him up there for hours. Tell me why I shouldn't knock you all the way back to Arimathea."

"Simon, I swear I don't know how it happened," Joseph sputtered. "First, the centurion refused to use ropes instead of nails. He went on and on about regulations. That's when they brought out the hammer and nails..."

"Why in the unutterable name of God didn't you say somethin' to me? I might have..."

"But you were right *there*. You *watched* them nail his wrists to the beam. I *saw* you."

Simon set Joseph down and let go of his robes. "Methought they were just foolin,' like we planned." he said and hung his head.

"So did I..."

"And then, when they nailed his other hand, it was too late." Peter groaned and pounded his breast with his fist. "I wasn't armed, and they *were*. I would have been food for the crows."

"And when they nailed his legs to the stipes ..."

"Yeah, the only hope after that was the drugged sponge."

Joseph relived the ordeal once again. The three crucified men -- the Rabbi in the middle -- moaning and crying out; the soldiers playing dice. The women and Simon and John, all weeping. His own tears coursing down his cheeks. The Rabbi and the other two heaving their chests upward for every single breath, time after time after time, and -- as the day wore on -- the grimaces of agony, with or without the pleading and the groans; the knots of muscles in visible spasm; the incessant begging and wailing for water; the soldiers responding by swigging water then spitting it out on the ground, taunting the crucified men, whose lips were crusted with dried spittle.

He had quietly assured Simon and John that, as agreed, the sponge in the bowl at the foot of the middle cross had been soaked in a solution of opium, madragora and hemlock and would render the Rabbi unconscious as planned. The problem had been to get the soldiers to administer it when he called out for water. Instead, the soldiers kept on taunting the dying men.

After midday the Rabbi's breathing became more and more labored and he began losing the ability to raise his chest. The centurion looked up at the Rabbi and cocked his head to one side. This one was not going to last much longer. He spoke to one of the soldiers. The legionnaire jammed the sponge onto the point of his spear and was lifting it up to let the Rabbi suck it, when he stopped and lowered the spear.

"Smells funny," he said, looking over his shoulder at the centurion.

The centurion shrugged. "Maybe it's wine. Don't people drink wine at funerals?"

"Could be," the soldier said and put his nose into the sponge and inhaled deeply. In the next moment, his knees buckled, the spear clattered the ground and he fell on all fours, his forehead resting on the stony ground.

"Jupiter's asshole," cried the centurion, kneeling by the stricken man. "What's wrong?"

"The sp—sponge. It's...it's...."

The centurion picked up the sponge and sniffed it gingerly.

"It's been drugged, by the gods!" The centurion glared at the little crowd of disciples and leveled his forefinger at them.

"Now I see your game. You been pestering me to go easy on 'im and all the while conniving to fake his death! Well, know this: your friend's going to croak, that I can swear to. Any more tricks, and I'll nail you all up there along side of him."

With sinking hearts, the disciples had accepted the grim truth. The plan to feign a crucifixion and a simulated death had been thwarted by a bureaucratic change of command. Now instead of spiriting their Rabbi out of the country alive, they were faced with entombing his corpse on the eve of the Sabbath. It was unbearable!

Joseph had hurried over to the governor's palace to get permission to take charge of the Rabbi's body after his death. Returning to Golgotha, he had seen the Rabbi's head slumped on his chest, and the women at the foot of the cross holding onto each other and wailing. As the full meaning of the scene hit him, he heard the centurion order one of his men to make sure that the prisoner was dead. The soldier thrust a spear through the Rabbi's ribs. It happened so fast that none of the disciples had time to protest, and afterwards they just hugged each other in despair. Never, Joseph reflected, had he felt so utterly crushed, as when he watched the mostly clear fluid gush forth when the soldier removed the spear. The unthinkable had just taken place. The Messiah, the hope of the people, was no more.

Joseph swore under his breath. Was Jawveh inveighing against their scheming? In His eyes, it must assuredly look like fraud. And yes, of course, it had been planned as a fraud, but now it had become an ugly reality. At midnight, they would follow the original plan, and go to Joppa, where a boat would be waiting. It was almost as imperative to prevent the

Rabbi's body and his pregnant widow from falling into the wrong hands as it had been to save his life in the first place!

As he grappled with the logistics of getting the group to the coast, it occurred to Joseph that the centurion he had bribed had not only failed to fulfill his part of the bargain, but had disappeared with the bribe. What a fool he'd been to trust a Gentile! He cursed again, and kicked at the large stone used to seal the sepulcher.

Part I

Besièrs, 1207 AD

The goldsmith's wife turned the big key in the lock, and hurried off toward the market place, cradling her baby in her arms while her small daughter skipped along by her side. The thief watching them from across the street smiled. All week long he had been slouching in the same spot, posing as a lame beggar and observing the comings and goings at the shop. The couple never left the shop untended, and he had been on the verge of abandoning his vigil, when that very morning the goldsmith had ridden away on a hired mule, and now the rest of the family was disappearing around the corner!

The thief rubbed his hands together. His moment had come. Up to now, his pilfering had paid for vinegary wine and bad meals and aging whores at third-rate inns. After today, he would be wearing silk and fine leather boots and he would mix with rich merchants. A saddle horse would be at his disposal. He nodded in anticipation.

Rising slowly, like a cripple, he picked up his crutch and squinted right and left. Two women passed by, their wooden shoes clacking loudly on the cobblestones, but once they were gone, the street was empty. Hobbling across the pavement, he entered a narrow passageway of packed earth that separated the smithy from a small chapel. It ended at a stone wall pocked with square mortises that had once held the ends of beams in the distant time of the Romans.

Dropping the crutch, he reached up and found a handhold in one of the recesses. He heaved himself up, stuck his foot in a mortise a bit lower down, and using other recesses, worked his way up the wall until his knees were level with the tile roof of the smithy. Like most roofs in the region, it had a very gentle slope. Carefully transferring his weight, he put his left knee on the tiles and reached out for another purchase. Once he found it, he pulled himself the rest of

1

the way onto the roof and crept up the slope to the ridge line, where he scuttled along in a crouch until he reached the smoke vent over the forge below.

He kicked in the shutter over the vent and it clattered into the room below. Lowering his legs into the opening, he eased himself down and dropped onto the broad rim of the forge. He looked around in the half-light. Bins of charcoal, crucibles of all sizes and shapes, bellows, cast-iron dippers and molds lay on the floor and small shaping tools were scattered about on trestle tables. The walls were lined with shelves filled with jars of agents used in processing gold into gold plate or gold leaf.

Where did the smith hide his unworked gold? The thief slowly circled the room, looking for telltale signs of loose paving stones in the floor He turned over the bins, but found nothing. Then he turned his attention to the walls. Most of the mortar had fallen away from cracks around the snug stones, but when he tried to move a few with his poniard, they did not budge.

Passing through the doorway into the living quarters, he ransacked beds, opened cupboards and studied the stone floor. Nothing. Then up on one wall, he noticed one stone block with slightly wider spaces than its neighbors. Using the smith's tools, he shifted the stone slightly and his heart leapt. Prying first one side and then the other, he coaxed the stone outward, a quill's breadth at a time until at last he could grip it with his fingers. Then, with a grating sound, he drew it out and set on the floor. His forehead was beaded with sweat, and his fingers trembled. He had found the hiding place, and now the question was, how *much* gold would he find?

He thrust his hand into the hole, hoping to find an ingot, or a coffer filled with metal, but all he felt was a soft cylinder. He pulled it out: it was a quiver for cross bow quarrels, but it contained neither gold nor quarrels. Just a thick coil of parchment scrolls. He threw it on the floor and reached back into the hole. Nothing! Wherever he poked, the compartment was empty. He inspected the other walls and ran his hands over them frantically, to no avail.

He'd been outsmarted! He hammered the wall with his fist. May the bastard trip over his own testicles! He craned his head toward the ceiling and shook it violently, muttering more curses. Finally, he looked down at the quiver that the goldsmith had taken such great pains to hide. Perhaps the scrolls had some value, after all?

Drawing them out of the quiver, he saw the parchments were covered with writing. What kind of whoremongery is *this*, he wondered? He shook his head and sighed. If only he could read! Ah, well, the scroll looked ancient. Perhaps a monastery might purchase it, and Fontcaude Abbey was but half a day's walk away.

He wrenched his mind back to a more pressing concern; he needed to get out of the shop before the blasted woman came back. Raising the latch of the door, he peeked out. Not a soul stirring. Sticking the quiver under his arm, he stepped out, shut the door behind him and started off in the opposite direction than the one the goldsmith's wife had taken. All was not lost.

Fanjaus

Olvier de Mazan stood on the fringe of a crowd of men and women, nobles and peasants, artisans and merchants chattering like a large flock of magpies. Children darted about playing tag, their piping voices shrieking with excitement. Here and there, colorful gowns and kirtles were punctuated by the black robes of more than two dozen Good Men and Women. He and Micaela had arrived the day before, after a leisurely, four-day ride from their home in the Comtat Venaicin.

Good Woman Ermengarde, the Count of Fois's sister, was in deep conversation with Geralda, the castellan of Lavaur, a well-known benefactor of dozens of Good Folk. Among the Believers, as well as the friends and relatives of the postulants, Olivier had counted at least thirty knights, many with their ladies. Like many so-called True Christians who had taken vows in the Church of the Friends of God, most of the Good Folk were of noble birth, and Olivier had met some of them at the time of his wedding with Micaela. These acquaintances had been renewed when he had accompanied his mother back to her ancestral home after the death of his father two years earlier.

Beyond the crowd, an ivy-covered limestone escarpment that served as a fourth wall for many of the habitations in Fanjaus jutted up, and at its base yawned the mouth of a cave, broader than it was deep. At its back stood a small table covered with a white cloth, on which a thin book rested. Dozens of lamps burned in niches chiseled into the stone.

To Olivier, the cave evoked the Holy Land, where he had served as his father's page in the Fourth Crusade. He remembered many such man-made caves, and he had even slept in some of them. When his father decided to return home after Richard the Lion Heart's unsuccessful campaign to retake Jerusalem, he had persuaded Olivier to stay on and attend the Templar school at Acre and become a squire. Many of those five years were spent studying Greek and Aramaic and he learned to speak French and Arabic fluently, by necessity. When not exploring the Templar fortress and the bazaars in the town, or strolling along the waterfront, he and the other pages and squires developed skills at swordplay and the handling of other weapons.

Then there was the incomparable sea. Even today, he missed the blue swells dashing against the breakwater, the screeching of the gulls and the muezzin's plaintive calls to the faithful outside the walls.

At Olivier's elbow, Micaela was in deep conversation with his mother, Aude, and the other two postulants who would soon receive the Consolation and become Good Women for the rest of their lives. Micaela was as dark as his mother was blonde, and as he stood watching, his heart swelled with love for both of them. To his mother, he owed his deep faith in a God of love and kindness, and to his wife he felt he owed his very breath.

From the moment the two women had met, two years before, they seemed to enjoy a kindred spirit that they shared as if he had never existed. When they were together chatting and laughing, he felt like a clumsy, tongue-tied intruder. Perhaps his mother saw Micaela as the daughter she never had. Or perhaps they simply hit it off, as it all too rarely happens in family life. Whatever it was, Olivier was grateful that their relationship was such a positive force. He had seen so many marriages where issues between in-laws had led to deep divisions and estrangements that tore families apart.

With the death of her husband, as a result of a hunting accident, Aude had become determined to seek investiture as a Good Woman, and to join her own mother in Fanjaus, where there was a thriving community of Good Folk.

As much as she had appreciated life with her husband in Provença, Aude had never lost her love for her native land. Her decision to move back had been hastened when, on a trip to see her mother, she learned that two childhood friends, Faye de Durfort and Raimonde de Saint-German, had independently resolved to take the same sober step. Having spent almost two years fasting and living frugally and ascetically to demonstrate that they could abide by the dietary and social restrictions of life as Good Women, and having become skilled weavers and spinners of thread, the three friends had arranged to be ordained together at the same time and place.

As Olivier took in the scene, a burly man with jet-black hair and beard emerged from the crowd and came over to him. "Is that you, Ollie, come hither all the way from the Comtat?" he cried, clapping Olivier on the shoulder. "Ready for two falls out of three?"

"Whenever you are," Olivier grinned back. "How are you, Camille? Good to see you!" and he grasped the man's head with both hands and gave it a friendly shake before they hugged. During his last visit to Fanjaus, Olivier had wrestled with Camille, at the harvest festival and had bested him in a long, drawn-out match watched by a huge crowd.

"How fares the forge?" Olivier asked the Camille, who was the village blacksmith.

"'Twere witless to complain," Camille said. "I've got an apprentice, and you'll never guess who."

"All right, I give up."

"'Tis Pierre Raimond de Cuq."

Olivier gave a low whistle. "The castellan of that bonny castle over in Cuq?"

6

"Tis the very one. But since he became a Good Man, it fell out that he's living in my old supply shed."

"'Tis rather old to be hammering horseshoes on an anvil, methinks."

"Forsooth, but by my beard, he's a strong one! I must heed not to provoke him, else he'd dust off the floor with me," Camille said with a wink, and elbowed Olivier in the ribs.

Olivier chuckled and slapped Camille on the back. "I'll wager."

"Turn not about, but here comes Good Man Gilhabert de Castras," Camille said. A tall grey-haired man clad in a black robe had reined in his horse and swung out of the saddle. Handing the reins to a varlet, he strode toward the cave. "Now we can get the cantaloupes to market, as they say, and let the ceremony begin!" Camille continued in a low voice, "Castras is the Bishop Gaucelin of Tolosa's Major Son. He's to perform the Consolation."

The crowd parted as Castras acknowledged greetings left and right. When he reached the table at the back, he turned to face the throng. Other Good Men and Women threaded their way through the crowd to join him, and once the three postulants had taken up their positions next to Castras, the crowd surged into the cave after them. Olivier worked his way to Micaela's side and took her hand. She looked up and smiled and he winked back at her. As a hush descended over the onlookers, he heard the insistent calls of swallows flying to and from their nests in the cliff.

Castras raised his palms to the crowd and then began to speak. "Dear friends and neighbors, Believers and Good Men and Women, we are gathered here today to solemnly witness the investiture of three exceptional women as guides and helpers to those seeking salvation through the Church of the Friends of God. Today, they formally sever all family ties and give up worldly practices to help save the souls of those

7

around us, and they have proved that they can abide the rigors of their calling."

"As they embark on their journey of redemption, they wot well that the Roman Church and its secular allies will oppose their ministrations by every possible means, including harassment and persecution. Not so long ago, Good Folk here in the Midi -- and many more in the North -- were burned at the stake! But these, our postulants, would fain brave these material difficulties and dangers and employ their deep stores of faith to overcome such obstacles, just as generations of Good Folk before them have done, and just as the Holy Apostles did so long ago. That Spirit will sustain them and will enable them to help others break through the darkness and see the light. 'Tis that Spirit, that inner voice of our Lord God, that makes our faith flourish."

Castras paused and turned his gaze on the postulants. "Now, Aude de Fanjaus and Faye de Durfort and Raimonde de Saint-German, each of you wots well that as you stand here before the Church of the Friends of God, you also stand before the Lord our Father and the Holy Spirit of Jesus, as the Scriptures teach. For Jesus said in the Gospel according to Saint Matthew, *wheresoever two or three are gathered together in my name, there I am in the midst of them.*"

"Wherefore be it understood that your presence here confirms the faith and teaching of the Church of the Friends of God, as the Holy Scriptures tell us. For you stand here before the disciples of Jesus in the place where the Father and Son's Holy Ghost have their spiritual abode, to receive that Holy Prayer which Jesus gave to His disciples, so that your prayers may be granted by our Heavenly Father. Therefore, if you would receive this Holy Prayer, you must repent your sins and forgive all men. For as Jesus

8

said, *if ye forgive not men their trespasses, neither will your Heavenly Father forgive your trespasses."*

"Hence, it is meet that you be resolved in your heart to keep this Holy Prayer all your life according to the custom of the Church of the Friends of God, in purity and truth, and in all other virtues which God would bestow upon you."

Castras bowed his head to the three postulants and began, "Our Father...." Pausing to let the postulants repeat each phrase of the prayer, he also explained how each phrase fit in with the dogma of the Church of the Friends of God.

When the postulants loudly cried Amen at the end of the Prayer, the Good Man continued. "We all agree with every thing that Jesus Christ said in this prayer and make it our own so that our spirits may join his in the afterlife. We deliver this Holy Prayer to you from God and our Church to empower you to repeat it as long as you live, day and night, alone or in company, and that you must never eat or drink without first saying it. If you omit doing so, you must do penance."

"I receive it of you and of the Church," the three postulants chorused, sinking to their knees before him.

Looking slowly from one to the other, Castras asked, "My sisters, must needs you give yourselves to our faith?"

"Yes," they responded in one voice. They bowed their heads to the ground, then wormed forward a few inches on their knees. "Bless us; pray to God that He will lead us to the good end."

Castras looked down at them fondly. "God bless you and make you good Christians and bring you to the good end. Do you give yourselves to God and the Gospel?"

"*Yes!*" They cried in unison, and inched ahead again.

"Do you promise that henceforth you will eat neither meat nor eggs, nor cheese, nor fat; that you will subsist only on vegetables, fruits and fish; that you will not lie; that you will not swear; that you will not kill; that you will not abandon your bodies to any form of luxury; that you shall not give in to carnal urges from hence forward; that you will never venture alone when it is possible to have a companion; that you will never sleep without kirtle; and that you will never abandon your faith for fear of water, fire or any other manner of death?"

"We do!"

"Aude, Faye and Raimonde, you have indicated a wish to receive the spiritual baptism whereby the Holy Spirit is given in the Church of the Friends of God with the Holy Prayer by the laying on of hands. And if you wish to receive this power you must keep all the commandments of Jesus and the gospels according to your ability.

"And know that He has commanded that you shall not commit adultery or murder or lie, that you must not swear any oath, that you shall not seize or rob, nor do to others what you would not have done to yourselves, that you must forgive whoever wrongs you and love your enemies, pray for your detractors and accusers and bless them; and if anyone strike you on one cheek, turn to him the other also, and if anyone takes away your cloak, leave him your mantle also; and that you should neither judge nor condemn."

"Also, you must hate this world and its works and the things of this world. As Saint John said, *O my beloved, love not the world, neither the things that are in the world. If any man loves the world, the love of the Father is not in him. For all that is in the world, the lust of the flesh and the lust of the eyes and the pride of life, is not of the Father but is of the world. And the world passeth away and the lust thereof, but he that doeth the will of God abideth for ever.* And as Christ said unto the Gentiles, *the world cannot hate you, but me it hates because I bear witness of it that its works are evil.*"

"By these witnesses, must you hate the world. and heed the commandments of God. If you continue well to the end, your soul shall have life eternal."

The three new Good Women chorused, "I will pray *to God to give me His power!*"

Now the three Good Men who had supervised the women during their abstinence stepped forward as witnesses and declaimed in unison: "Spare us. Good Christians, we pray you by the love of God that you grant this blessing, which God has given you and to our friends here present."

The three women then spoke again: "Spare us. For all the sins I have ever done in thought, word and deed, I ask pardon of God, of the Church, and of all of you."

The crowd recited in unison: 'By God and by us and by the Church, may your sins be forgiven and we pray God to forgive you for them. "

Castras picked the Gospel off its white napkin and each of the three Good Men serving as witnesses stepped up behind a kneeling woman and placed his right hand on her head. Slowly and in succession, Castras touched the Gospel to Aude's head, then Faye's and finally Raimonde's. He then led the congregation in three repetitions of *Let us adore the Father and the Son's Holy Spirit.* The three Good Men attending the women helped them up, and when they were standing, Castras prayed, "Holy Father, welcome thy servants in thy justice and send upon them thy grace and thy Holy Spirit." After three more repetitions of the adoration and another recitation of the Lord's Prayer, he opened the Gospel and read the first seventeen verses of the first chapter of John.

As he came to the end of the last verse, Castras gently closed the book and beckoned to Ermengarde and Astorgue, the two Good Women who had been flanking the postulants during the ceremony. They girded each of the new Good Women with a sacred purple thread under the breasts of her kirtle, and then helped each into a black gown, kissing each in turn.

Castras and the other Good Men exchanged kisses, and then went into the crowd kissing the male believers, while the five Good Women, old and new, fanned out and kissed the female believers, bringing an end to the ceremony.

The throng surged to congratulate the new Good Women. As Olivier and Micaela tried to penetrate the whorl of the faithful, they found themselves edging along next to Camille.

"Good day Madame Mazan, methinks you are especially beautiful today," he said, smiling at her, "Your presence honors the village, as does your husband as well."

"Master Smith," Micaela responded with a slight blush, "your tongue is pure gold. Why do you limit yourself to working with base iron when you are so facile with the most precious of metals? Why not become a goldsmith?"

Camille answered without hesitation. "Because, fair lady, up to now, I've had too little gold to work with, but now that you are here among us, I must needs make haste with yours."

Olivier, inwardly pleased with this typically bold and inventive praise of his wife, spoke up. "Camille, old friend, methinks I shall have to take up your challenge after all. But I warn you, I will try to pluck out that agile tongue of yours instead of trying to put you on your back."

"But have I said aught short of the unalterable truth?" Camille opened his eyes wide in feigned innocence.

"By my troth, you haven't," Olivier chuckled, "but mayhap if I could boil your tongue, slice it and wash it down with a good rosé, I might achieve the same eloquence and expect an equally provocative response from my wife."

"Fair lady," Camille said to Micaela, "in the face of such a threat, I should hold my tongue, although I would much prefer to engage it in your service."

"You do me honor, Sir, but I fear 'tis too deeply ensconced in your cheek to be extricated." As she uttered the words, she found herself face-to-face with her mother-in-law, and threw her arms around her.

"How did I do?" Aude asked Olivier, beaming at him over Micaela's shoulder.

"You were magnificent, mother!" Olivier said, hugging his mother in turn. "I suppose I shall have to genuflect to you from now on."

"Go on with you, Olivier, darling. Nothing's changed except that now I have a ministry to perform."

"'Tis meet, for I have the perfect candidate for you to proselytize: Master Camille here," and Olivier flung out an arm toward his friend.

Aude burst out laughing. "Olivier, my sweet, I became a Good Woman precisely because I needed to fend off the many advances of Master Camille, and I hope he heeds the depth and breadth of the moat that protects me now that I'm a Good Woman and safe within my vows."

"My dear Good Woman, many congratulations on your investiture," Camille said, and raised an eyebrow. "But surely you would lower the drawbridge for an old friend?"

"That's exactly the trouble, good sir; you may be a friend, but you are not old. Tsk, tsk," she clucked. "But, Master Camille, if you contemplate putting me under siege, you should know that my battlements are impregnable and that I am now protected by an indestructible donjon of faith. From now on, I fear, you must find weaker fortresses to invest."

Olivier put his hands on Aude's shoulders. "Before he lays siege to your daughter-in-law, I'm afraid I must deliver her from temptation and beat a hasty retreat to the Comtat."

"By my troth, I would hate to have her become a Good Woman just to escape Camille's clutches," Aude laughed.

Before the two men could engage in more banter, Aude begged off, blaming her 'emotional exertions.' Camille headed for the festival in the market square, while Olivier and Micaela accompanied Aude to the small house that she shared with three other Good Women. Half of the room that they entered was occupied by a small horizontal loom surrounded by sacks of wool. On a table next to the loom, Aude had laid out a small feast. As he caught sight of the victuals, Olivier rolled his eyes in view of her vows of austerity and deprivation.

Following his glance, Aude clucked, "Have no fear, my darling, I shan't be taking aught but bread and water. I'd fain have you both dine well to celebrate this momentous day, and I must needs hear all about my granddaughters. I was so disappointed that you didn't bring them along."

"We fain would have, but we feared 'twould be too much for them," Olivier said. "They both have wet nurses. Isabel for almost a year and Margarida for about two months. Micaela had mastitis and had to quit nursing Margarida after only three months."

"Oh, dear, Micaela darling, I wot well it must have been terribly painful! You poor thing." Aude pursed her lips and drew her daughter-in-law into her arms.

"'Tis like most things, Maire," Micaela shrugged, "if you be not peevish, belike 'twill fall out well. Once I stopped nursing, 'twasn't long before the swelling and the pain disappeared. I'd forgotten all about it until Olivier brought it up."

"Well, please fill your beakers with some wine, and try some of this lamb."

Olivier ate with great relish as the two women rattled on and on about virtually every day of his daughters' lives. The inexhaustible subject was limited only by their ages: Isabel was a two-year-old toddler, while Margarida was only 5 months old. By the time Olivier poured his third beaker of wine to wash down an excellent local *brebis*, the talk had already switched to the weaving that Aude had been doing for more than a year. The very robes she was wearing -- including the dyeing process -- were her own work, she stated proudly, and she gestured to several wicker baskets full of rolls of material. By visiting the markets in the nearby towns, she had been able to earn enough to sustain herself in food and fuel.

Her work had put her on a good footing with everyone in town, Aude said, and now she was far more aware of the economic forces that drive commerce -- the lifeblood of a town -- than she ever had been as a castellane in the country.

"Nevertheless, running a household as you do is not unlike being the mayor of a town," she told Micaela. "I'm sure you would make a very good Mayor, don't you agree, Olivier darling?" Aude looked over to Olivier for support.

"Maire, Micaela excels at aught she puts her mind to, I trow, and even some things she doesn't put her mind to."

"Just as long as she's not a dreamer like you, Olivier!"

"Be of good cheer, Maire, one dreamer in the family is enough," Micaela said. "I simply plod along without exerting myself. Sometimes, Olivier deems that I'm idle, when to say truth I'm actually getting a lot accomplished. Methinks you understand, Maire."

"I wot only too well what you are saying and it makes me glad of heart. I'm also glad that you both are fairly safe in

Provença, where there's less petty warfare. Hereabouts, some baron is always a trying to swell his fiefdom. After biding a month here, I ween, you'll be thrilled to get home safe and sound and see your babes again."

"I can't wait to see them again, I trow, but we'll miss you very much. We are very proud of you." The women hugged and Olivier stood by beaming, proud of his mother's prowess and industry and besotted with his beautiful, able wife.

Aude placed her index finger alongside her nose. "I almost forgot. Is it possible for you two to bide one more week? Some of our Good Men are going to debate the Roman clerics at that time."

"Here in Fanjaus?" Olivier asked.

Aude shook her head. "No, in Montréal a league or so away. 'Tis on your way home."

Olivier asked. "Methought you said the debates will be in Servian and Besièrs. What's to be gained by going over the same ground?"

"Mayhap naught, but if they avail to dispute toe-to-toe with trained and highly placed prelates before different audiences, 'twill be a victory for the Friends of God, I trow, and the people know it.

"Maire, 'tis what I fear. If you embarrass or humiliate them, they will seek revenge, which eventually will mean trouble for you and me and Micaela; to say truth, is that what you'd fain have?"

"Well if the Good Men can show them that we are their equals, maybe they will back down."

"Remember what happened when King Peire of Aragon presided over that debate three years ago in Carcassona? When it was over, the Church announced that its prelates had won and they denounced the Good Men. What good came forth from that? When you lose, you have to carry the blame."

"Here in Fanjaus 'we heeded them not. When the King went home, everyone carried on just the same as before. 'Twas scarce a ripple."

"Forsooth, But I'll wager the Holy See felt that ripple. Aught that draws attention to Good Folk will fall out bad for us."

"What do you mean?"

"When that Roman lawyer became Pope, one of the first things he did was to decree that heresy is *lèse majesté*: treason against the Holy See itself, and, by extension, against secular rulers as well."

"How does that affect us?"

"Whoever defends, harbors, supports or believes in what they call heresy is subject to disinheritance and seizure of property as well as heavy punishments. And by heretics, he means you. 'Tis intimidation, I trow."

"But, Olivier, 'tis scarce cause for grief. Has anyone ever enforced that decree? If so, I'm not aware of it. Not the King of Aragon, methinks."

Olivier shook his head. "Maire, greedy people may try to have the decree enforced. Better not to provoke them, say I."

"Think you that there should be no debate?

"No, forsooth. I fain would attend. If you can persuade Micaela, then, we will bide with great pleasure. However, methinks 'twere well done not to bite off more than one can chew."

17

Narbona

At midday the tavern was deserted; the regulars were not expected before nightfall. Other than the seedy looking man sitting opposite Brother Pascau, the only person in the room was a drunk sprawled senseless in a far corner. Sunlight streamed through the open window onto the table upon which Pascau had spread out and flattened a half dozen parchment scrolls. The lighting was perfect for the task before him, certainly better than the dim recesses of the library at Fontfroide Abbey.

A brief perusal had told him that the scrolls documented more than sixty generations of a single family, the longest family record he had ever heard of, let alone seen. Maybe comparable to that of the Egyptian Pharaohs? He stared at the oldest entries in disbelief. What astounded him was not only the extreme age of the document or the fact that the first dozen entries were written in Aramaic, but that the name of the progenitor was *Eshoa*, which was Aramaic for Jesus! And that the name of his wife was Mary...*Magdalene*!

He fought to control his emotions as his skin crawled and his scalp tingled. Could the record be authentic, or was it some kind of hoax? Had those names really been recorded more than eleven centuries ago? He checked the dates. They were written according to both the Hebrew and the Roman Calendars. He recalculated both dates and concluded that if they were correct, the scrolls were almost twelve centuries old! He raised his eyes to the man sitting across the table, but found nothing reassuring in the man's face; indeed, it radiated suspicion and distrust.

If the names on the scrolls were authentic and referred to the historical Jesus, Pascau gasped, it would mean that Jesus had progeny, and that some of his descendants were alive. The promulgation of this knowledge would mean the end of Christianity as currently practiced. He leafed

18

through the flattened scrolls and selected the one with the most recent dates. The last two names, recorded in the *lenga d'oc*, were a sister and a brother, born in 1203 and 1208. The father's name was Jacob Ravanel, and the mother's was Ruth. The children's names were Rebecca and Isadore. The family was apparently Jewish and the place of birth was Besièrs.

He looked across the table at the bearded seller, who had introduced himself as Thibaut, although giving a false name was not unusual under the circumstances Thibaut said he had first taken them to the Abbey at Fontcaude, but they could not decipher the language and had recommended Brother Pascau here at Fontfroide.

Was his real name Jacob Ravanel? Was he a Jew? Pascau couldn't tell. If the man wasn't Ravanel, then how did the scrolls come into his possession? If he stole them, he ran the risk of being given away by the false name. Why would he take such a chance? Perhaps he hadn't read the last entry.

Alternatively, perhaps he was illiterate. That was a strong possibility, given the fact that few people could read. Thibaut certainly didn't make the impression that he was among that elite.

Pascau turned the parchment so the man could read it and pointed to the name Ravanel. "Is the spelling correct?"

The man shrugged. "I don't read,"he said, and glared at Pascau defiantly.

"Can you tell me where you got the scrolls?"

The man hesitated for a moment. "From my father, but I know not whence he got them."

The answer did not definitely prove that the man was *not* Ravanel, but certainly made that possibility very slim. "Do you have aught idea what it is?"

19

"Methought that you would tell *me*!" Thibaut shifted in his seat and smirked. "I watched you studying it. From the expression on your face, 'tis like you know."

Pascau knew he had a fish on his line and didn't want it to throw off the hook. "'Tis a list. A very old one. I must needs study it some more because I can't make out all the words. Let me say that, speaking for my abbey, we are very interested in ancient texts like this, no matter how insignificant their contents. Have you a price in mind?"

Thibaut's face worked and his eyes shifted away from Pascau's. Then regaining his composure, he said. "I am asking three pounds fifty."

Pascau struggled to control his surprise and relief. Such a sum could buy a fine horse. Or a very good sword. Even if the true significance of the scrolls had been lacking, he would have been ready to pay ten times that amount. But, with their earthshaking revelations, they were priceless! It would still be necessary to verify their provenance; someone would have to go Besièrs to check on the Ravenel family. In the meantime, he had to play his fish.

He clasped his hands on the table and pursed his lips in a whistle. "That, my friend, is a lot of money," he lied. As he watched Thibaut scowl, he hastened to add, "but, mayhap my Abbot will pay it. Unfortunately he's still away at the moment, but I expect his return within the month."

Thibaut's face contorted with anger and he rose from his stool. "I was told he was coming here with you. Clearly we're wasting each other's time. I'm sure I can find a buyer who appreciates real value." Thibaut started squaring the scrolls as he prepared to roll them up.

"I wish you luck," Pascau said. "Not everyone can read the language in the oldest scroll. Isn't that why you came to me?" He was gambling that the fish was still on the hook. Thibaut was inscrutable, but was he bluffing? "I'll tell you what," Pascau said. "I'll take the responsibility, and risk the wrath of the Abbot. I'll give you two and a half for all six."

Rolling the scrolls together, Thibaut paused. "Three and not a sol less."

Pascau took out his purse and counted out thirty Tolzans. "Done!" he said.

Thibaut scooped up the coins and put them in a mantle pocket. Then he stuffed the rolled-up scrolls into the quiver and tossed it on the table." Farewell," he said, and touching a finger to his cap, strode out into the sunshine.

Pascau watched him out of sight. Then he turned to the man slumped in the corner. "He's gone, Olivier."

Olivier de Mazan rose up and grinned. "I'm glad there was no trouble. Did you get what you want?"

"I fain would let you be the judge. Take a look for yourself," he said, and removing the scrolls from the quiver, spread them out on the table again.

Olivier bent over them. "Aramaic," he muttered. After a few moments, he straightened up and stared at Pascau. "Impossible. I don't believe it. It can't be true!"

"But what if 'tis? 'Twill be easy to prove if at least part of it is true."

"You mean by checking the latest entries?"

"Forsooth! Does a family named Ravenel live in Besièrs?. Jacob and Ruth? 'Tis like they are Jews. Brother Aurelh can run them down."

"Can you count on him?"

"He's a Believer, like me," Pascau replied. "'Tis why I trusted him to fetch you from Fanjaus.'Twill only take him a day or two. Scarcely eighteen leagues back and forth."

"No need to hurry, because I'll be coming back through here on the way home." Olivier assured him. "If this record is real, 'twill shake the earth."

"'Twill certainly sound the knell for the Roman Trinity."

"I was curious why you sent for me, but this...*this* is incredible! Did you have any inkling of their content?" Olivier asked.

"Not at all. Methought mayhap more than just Latin or Greek were involved. I figured maybe Arabic, and I am totally lost in that tongue. Then methought, what if 'twere Aramaic? I'm can read it a bit, but far less proficiently than you. So, with a manuscript possibly in Arabic or Aramaic, I knew right away that I needed your help."

"If it had been Arabic, would you have roused me a while ago? I was supposed to be drunk."

"God wot, there are drunkards a-plenty within our order. I would have done what we planned; introduced you as a lay brother who had overdone his merriment."

"Speaking of drinking, where's the innkeeper?" Oliver asked. "A cool draught of cider will help me believe this isn't some wild dream."

Citeaux

The old Castilian smiled over the rim of the horn of wine that shook in his palsied hand, and nodded across the table to his companion, who bobbed his own horn in reply. From their dusty grey mantles and caps, one would never have guessed that the elder was a bishop and the younger was a subprior. They had just arrived at Citeaux Abbey more than five weeks after an audience with the pope in Rome. The orchards outside the monastery were in bud, although the surrounding peaks were still covered with snow.

Their attempt to persuade Pope Innocent III to support a missionary effort to the pagans on the Baltic Sea had fallen on deaf ears. The Pontiff was far more interested in having them help staunch the tide of heresy in the land of *lenga d'oc*, which lay just across the Pyrenees from their native Castille. He had given them a letter of introduction to his chief legate there, Arnaud-Amaury, who was also the Abbot of the Cistercian monastery, and here they were, sharing some wine with him in the refectory. The letter asked the legate to help the Castillians launch a new attempt to bring heretics back into the fold. He was to assign as many monks as necessary to save souls that were risking hell's fire.

Arnaud-Amaury was a massive man in his prime, who, but for his hooded white *cappa*, a full-length black scapular, and a large golden crucifix dangling at his waist, looked more like a laborer than like the august Abbot of perhaps the most famous monastery in western Christendom. A brown tonsure framed a fleshy face that bore the red nose of a tippler.

He had read the letter and tried not to let his face betray his anger. Innocent's letter constituted a veiled reprimand for the Abbot's lack of success in rolling back heresy in the

23

Midi. He was to be subservient to the two Castilians. Well, let them try and good luck to them! From what he had observed over the last three years, they hadn't a chance in hell.

"So, you've come almost four hundred leagues," he said, squinting at the two Castillians as if they were some kind of exotic animals, "and still many lie ahead of you. I grow weary just thinking about it."

"That four hundred is the least of it, by my troth," the bishop responded. "We've been on the road for almost three years. Altogether we have gone more than 2,500 leagues."

"No!" Arnaud-Amaury smote his forehead. "You must have traveled to the ends of the earth!"

"That we did. Twice. All the way to Denmark and back."

The Abbot's jaw dropped open. "Why, in Heaven's name? What was the attraction?"

"The attraction, as you say, was to secure a bride for our Crown Prince Ferdinand. Our first trip accomplished the betrothal, and the second was meant to bring the young lady back to Castile. But when we arrived in Copenhagen we found that she had died of a fever."

"'Tis a pity," Arnaud-Amaury exclaimed. "All that way for nothing. 'Twas that the time that you encountered the pagans you wished to convert?"

"One of the times."

Arnaud-Amaury grunted and scowled. "Well, you won't find any pagans down in the Midi, where His Holiness would fain have you preach. 'Tis totally overrun by heretics, who are far more dangerous than pagans."

"So we've heard, in our travels back and forth across the Midi. But, full sure am I that the local clergy will give us the support we need."

Arnaud-Amaury stared at the bishop as if he had gone mad. "The local clergy? You're joking, of course. Why, bethink you, does heresy flourish down there? There's no sorrier Church in the whole wide world; the clergy are corrupt, inept, and indolent. And worst of all, they are complacent, if not complicit, in letting heresy flourish under their noses." Arnaud-Amaury shook his head at the enormity of the southern clergy's depravity. At the same time, he felt a new flood of resentment against Innocent for continually going over his head and second-guessing him in the struggle against heresy. More preaching was the last thing that was needed.

"But how does it happen that the clergy down there are so weak and corrupt?"

Arnaud-Amaury smiled in derision. "Ignorance. Lack of education. In the North, where they practice primogeniture, younger and ambitious sons go into the priesthood. They are literate, and so they set a high standard for clerics as a class. Not so in the Midi, where no noble would ever dream of becoming a priest. Thus, the Church gets the dregs of society, not the standouts."

Diego placed his elbows on the table and brought the tips of his fingers together. "But can't your bishops discipline the priests and bring them into line? Dedicated bishops should have no problem in controlling their priests."

"'Tis not always easy, my Lord Bishop," Arnaud-Amaury answered. "The bishops themselves are a large part of the problem. Not a single one has mounted a real effort to systematically eradicate the heretics. In fact, His Holiness had tasked us with the responsibility and authority to dismiss any bishop who allows heresy to expand in his bishopric."

"And have you?"

"I sacked the bishop of Besièrs, suspended the bishop of Viviers, and forced Rabastens, the bishop of Tolosa to resign," Arnaud-Amaury said. "We caught Rabastens red-handed selling church property for his own profit. He had also used bribery to achieve his office in the first place. Can you believe it?"

"On the other hand, Berenger, the incredibly corrupt archbishop of Narbona, is a horse of a different color. His nephew is King Peire of Aragon, and that renders him untouchable, because the pope is grooming Peire to lead the secular battle against heresy. Moreover, Berenger's a past master at manipulating the bureaucracy of the papal curia in his favor and so...." The Abbot shrugged.

Although Arnaud-Amaury's lieutenant – Peire Castelnau –had actually sacked the bishops on his own initiative, the Abbot felt no compunction about presenting the deeds as if he had had a hand in them. As the senior and chief legate, he felt that Castelnau had taken undue credit for disciplining the bishops. He tossed down a half horn of wine, and poured himself another. Castelnau needed a come-uppance.

Diego furrowed his brows. "Have the bishops no recourse to secular power to combat the heretics directly?"

Making a wry face, Arnaud-Amaury pushed his stool away from the table and stretched out his legs. "Secular power? That's an even greater joke. The local nobles not only protect the heretics but in many cases, especially in the smaller towns, they embrace the heresy themselves. And these very same nobles are often related to the corrupt or do-nothing bishops that I was talking about," he said, tossing his head.

"But can't the heretics' liege lords pressure them to give up their heretical practices?"

Arnaud-Amaury rolled his eyes again. "Well nigh all the counts in the Midi tolerate the lassitude and inaction of their vassals in this regard, or even condone the heretics' vile behavior. Take Raimond- Roger Trencavel, Viscount of Besièrs and Carcassona. He oversees a vast domain and openly sympathizes with the heretics!"

"The same or worse can be said of the Count of Fois, or that master schemer, Count Raimond of Tolosa, who can't be relied upon to combat heresy. He minds naught about the Holy Church. His lackadaisical attitude can't compare to the diligence with which your Castilian nobles uphold the faith against the Moslem infidels."

The two dusty Castilians raised their horns in salute.

"To say truth, King Peire lured some of the Cathar leaders into a debate with us," the Abbot continued, "and when 'twas done, he denounced them as heretics, and then we excommunicated them. But the Cathars openly mocked the interdiction, and since then, Peire has done naught to discipline those vassals who sided with the heretics."

Diego raised his eyebrows. "Strange. In our country, the King is deemed a virtuous and pious member of the Church."

'Mayhap 'tis true there," Arnaud-Amaury said, "but in the Midi, the Church is a mockery. In towns where word spreads that a papal legate – Castelnau, for example -- will hold a mass, fewer than a dozen people show up. People even shut their doors in our faces, or drown out our sermons with their noise. All this outrageous conduct is encouraged by the local nobility. A year ago, Brother Castelnau was so discouraged, he begged His Holiness to let him resign, but the pope persuaded him to bide a while longer."

"Well, then, 'tis like that we have our work cut out for us," Diego said. "I trow His Holiness has asked you to lend us the services of some of your monks to aid us in our task. We are anxious to get on with our mission and make some conversions. We'd like to start as soon as possible. Are your monks used to traveling? Have they ever performed pastoral duty?"

"I'm full sure they can meet the challenge," the Abbot replied, trying hard not to groan. These Castilians had no idea what they were getting into. For two years, he and his other legates had crisscrossed the Midi, preaching to all kinds of people with a singular lack of success. They had been scorned and ridiculed and borne humiliations at the hands of the heretics and their sympathizers. As far as he was concerned, the only way to defeat these Apostles of Satan was to draw the secular sword from the scabbard. In the North, scores of heretics had been condemned and burned. 'Twas the only way to cure the fulminating infection.

However, the Holy See had clearly made its wishes known, and Arnaud-Amaury would obey, to the letter. But he would also do everything in his power to satisfy the pope's equally strong desire to involve the King of France in a Holy War against the Midi and rid that land of heresy.

"'Twill require two days to organize the journey. We have one hundred fifty leagues to go. For you, 'tis but a stroll, but I fear some of my brethren may become footsore," Arnaud-Amaury chuckled and winked at the Castillians. "Actually, we'll be in boats much of the way," he reassured them. "Come, let me fill your horns."

Frontfroide Abbey

An hour after leaving the inn in Narbona, Olivier and Pascau were riding along a trail that wound through heavy woods toward Frontfroide Abbey, hardly two leagues away. Pascau was mounted behind Olivier, with his monk's habit pulled up, revealing bony knees and hairy calves. Olivier wore a tradesman's brown tunic and grey trousers encased in leggings. Suddenly a man stepped out of the thicket with a palm outstretched. Olivier reined up and the man stepped forward and grasped the bridle.

"Remember me?" he asked. It was Thibaut, the man who had sold Pascau the scrolls.

"Let go there," Olivier cried, his face flushing with anger.

"Only when you hand over what the scrolls are really worth. I know you were cheating me," the man said, and pulled his mantle aside to reveal a sword hanging at his waist. "Get down, both of you, and throw me your purses."

Pascau slid down off of his horse, but as Oliver swung his right leg over the saddle, he eased his left foot out of the stirrup and, locking his fingers in the mane of his horse, in one smooth motion he drove both feet forward hard into Thibaut's chest. Knocked to the ground, the thief writhed around, gasping futilely for air. Olivier circled him in a crouch and when the thief recovered his breath and rose to his knees, Oliver kicked him hard in the crotch, tumbling him forward into the dirt again, where he rolled in agony. Leaning down, Oliver, unbuckled the man's belt and handed the belt with its sword and scabbard to Pascau who was looking on aghast.

Olivier drew his dirk and placed its point under Thibaut's chin. "Hold your peace, else I'll pin your tongue to your skull," he warned, his eyes flaming with loathing.

29

With his free hand, he searched the man and found a purse tied around his waist. He untied its strings and tossed it to Pascau.

"There, good brother, our friend here fain would make a donation to your abbey. And as a reward for his generosity, I am granting him his life," Oliver said as he sheathed his dirk. Then he leaned down and put his nose within a thumb's width of the thief's. "I give you life, but I will reclaim it if I ever find you in these parts again. Now get you gone before I change my mind."

Montpelhier

The sacristy of Nòstra Dòna de Taulas was alight with a dozen lamps and even more candles in honor of the two Castilian clerics, to whom Arnaud- Amaury introduced his two colleagues, Peire Castelnau and Raoul de Frontfroide. Even after the week of traveling with the Abbot and the dozen monks who accompanied them, the Castilians still wanted to hear more details about the people they expected to convert, especially from colleagues other than the Abbot.

"What about the heretics themselves, are they Waldensians? Cathars?" Diego asked, deliberately turning his head toward Castelnau.

"Too many of both, I fear, but the vast majority are wicked Cathars," the Abbot boomed, before his colleague could answer.

"Their dogma is Manichean, is it not?" Diego asked.

"Most certainly," Arnaud-Amaury agreed. "They believe that every thing that exists under the sun and the moon is evil and will one day disappear. God is perfection, and because nothing in the world is perfect, God didn't make the world: the Devil did. He created the visible material world and God created the invisible spiritual world."

"Do they believe in the Lord Jesus?"

"Yes, but he is neither incarnate, nor the Son of God, they ween. Instead, they deem he is some sort of angelic, heavenly messenger."

"Then they reject the Trinity?"

"Most assuredly. They deem not that the Lord died on the cross or was resurrected, or that He ascended to heaven, but rather *descended* from heaven."

"To say truth, they heed not the Holy Scriptures."

"Aye, they revile the Old Testament and much of the New Testament, too. Paradoxically, all the Perfects — the

31

ones who have taken vows – carry a copy of the Gospel of John attached to their belts."

"'Tis strange indeed, to follow a gospel, yet reject most of its dogma," Diego said.

Arnaud-Amaury leaned back and threw up his hands. "They heed the Gospel out of context! Their interpretations are utterly contrived, and their ranting is antithetical to the positions of our Holy Church. For example, they reject the sacraments, including infant baptism, marriage and the Eucharist. They don't even believe in Hell or Purgatory! They believe everyone will one day be redeemed!"

"Then they have a dogma that they agree on?"

"Not exactly," Arnaud-Amaury replied. "Most believe that the Devil, the evil force, has always existed, but a minority believe, as we do, that the Devil is a fallen angel. But which ever it is, it doesn't alter their heretical claims or their fanatic hatred of our Holy Roman Church!" Arnaud-Amaury hit the table with his fist.

The beakers jumped, and Bishop Diego flinched. "How do you explain their popularity and success, Brother Castelnau?" he managed to ask.

"Two main reasons." Entering the conversation at last, Castelnau held up two fingers. "First, many Catholics regard the so-called Perfects as very holy men, and call them Good Men because of their vows of chastity, their asceticism, their ability to care for the sick, and their production of goods."

The Abbot forced himself not to frown and betray his disdain of his outspoken colleague. Why doesn't Castelnau just become a blasted Cathar? What's he waiting for, Arnaud-Amaury wondered.

"Goods?" The bishop looked perplexed.

"Yes," Castelnau answered, "they support themselves through industry. They occupy themselves with weaving,

32

carving, cobbling, coopering, and many other crafts. They are part of daily life in towns and villages."

"Remarkable!" Diego pursed his lips and turned his head toward Dominic, nodding. "They are catering to the people's needs."

Arnaud-Amaury felt as if he might explode. He pointed a finger at Diego. "*You* may think so, but *I* most certainly don't!" He jammed a thumb into his chest. "Along with many others, methinks these fine-feathered, so-called Perfects are perfect *perverts!*" He smacked the table with his palm.

"Forsooth?"

"Aye, I wot it well. According to their dogma, marriage is evil, by reason that the outcome is children, whom they see as just more vile matter. Hence, they frown on sexual intercourse with the intent or even the possibility of bearing children. To slake their carnal lust, the Perfects -- who are vowed to chastity -- engage in sodomy among themselves. Why do they always travel in pairs? I'll tell you why: so they can satisfy their vile impulses with a person of the same sex! Such unnatural sexual acts are not what are usually meant when one talks about chastity, so they can claim they are not violating their vows." He shook his head in revulsion.

"But methinks that the people..." Diego began.

"Begging your pardon, Your Excellency," Castelnau interrupted, "my colleague is surely correct, I trow, but the problem is that the Perfects *do* perform good works. It is their service to the community in caring for the sick and needy and the aged that has won the hearts and minds of the people. Even dedicated Catholics revere them for their works."

Arnaud-Amaury could hardly believe his ears. He looked at his colleague to see if a gospel was attached to his belt.

33

The old bishop let his rheumy eyes wander over the stonework of the sacristy. "What about their houses of worship? Can *they* be the attraction?"

Castelnau shook his head. "They don't have churches as such. Instead, they preach in houses, castles, or without doors, in woods, or fields, or anywhere people gather."

The bishop raised his eyebrows. "So they don't need to maintain churches? Or to raise the money to pay for them?"

"Right."

"Methinks that for many, 'twould be a great relief not to pay a tithe," Diego said, pulling on his chin. "Belike that helps them recruit adherents."

"Decidedly. Especially among the nobility and the merchants," Arnaud-Amaury broke in. "'Tis a huge problem. It means much less revenue for the Holy Church."

"What about administration? Do they have a hierarchy?"

Arnaud-Amaury scowled. "A handful of bishops, but 'tis like they lack authority. Then there are the so-called deacons and major and minor sons."

"Major and minor sons? What does that mean?"

"They're senior perfects," Castelnau explained. "When a bishop dies, the major son succeeds him and the minor son becomes a major son. But all these titles may be merely honorific, because they all seem to continue to engage in pastoral duties in addition to their craft work."

"What about religious orders and monasteries? What about women?"

"They don't have any orders as such, but they have refuges. As for women, they can also become perfects, and most of these are of noble birth. I fain would add that, compared to women in other countries, those in the Midi have always enjoyed a high degree of independence. It's the way of life here," Castelnau said, and took a swallow of wine.

"With all that, I'm fed up with these disgusting, heretical freaks!" Arnaud-Amaury thumped the table with his fist. "A century ago, hundreds of these same heretics were burned alive in Flanders and the Rhineland. 'Twas done then, why not now? Here in the Midi, roughly one in three believes in the heresy and another one out of three supports them and protects them. They are not deserving of human kindness or respect, nor can we win them with words. We must exterminate them, as if they were vermin."

Dominic Guzman broke his long silence. "I won over a Cathar in a discussion on the way here. The bishop and I were staying at an inn, and I fell into conversation with a committed Cathar, a Believer, I trow. It took me most of the night, but in the end he recanted his belief, confessed and asked for my blessing. So it can be done."

"And I can vouch for that conversion," said Diego.

"But I just told you how heretics swarm here in the Midi and what powerful connections they have," Arnaud-Amaury said, his face beet red. "With so many Perfects of noble birth, they have ties to secular power. We would need an *army* of clerics to persuade and influence so many people."

"Also, as I keep telling you, the clergy down here are lazy, inept and corrupt, not to mention completely unlearned and illiterate. They are useless. We need the pope to preach a crusade against these heretics, just as he does against the infidels in the Holy Land and in Spain." Arnaud-Amaury threw up his hands again in frustration.

"Methinks you need to mobilize an army of a different kind," Diego said. "In truth, these heresies seem to have sprung up because of the same failings within our Holy Church that His Holiness Gregory VII tried to rectify, and alack, many of those reforms have yet to be fulfilled. In our travels, we have witnessed a mounting public dismay with the profligate misconduct of much of the clergy, in varying degrees, in every country we came to. Clerical excesses are not confined to the Midi, I trow. Abuses throughout the ecclesiastical hierarchy are at the heart of the Waldensian heresy, whose theology remains very orthodox. And although the Cathars have a heretical dogma, by my troth, it sounds as if they behave like the Apostles of the New Testament. Methinks the way they go about their preaching attracts those who are angry with the corruption they see in our Holy Church."

"But they want to *destroy* the Church and its hierarchy, not to reform it," Arnaud-Amaury said, pounding his fist on the table. "Forsooth, they are expanding in numbers and power. Their wickedness makes them the very apostles of Satan. "

"Exactly!" Watching Arnaud-Amaury out of the corner of an eye, Diego smacked the flat of his own hand on the table. "People would forego the heresy if they were offered a viable alternative, I trow. What if, instead of preaching down to people from a pulpit, the clergy were speaking up to them from the street? What if, instead of albs and the finery one sees at mass, the canons were clad in the garb of simple monks and shod with simple sandals, or better yet, barefoot? What if clerics were constantly mingling with the faithful in humility and fellowship, taking no advantage of their priestly prerogatives, but persuading by example? If these kinds of behavior have enabled the Cathars and Waldensians to make the inroads as you describe, why not try to emulate them or even surpass them? By purveying a new kind of Roman clergy that returns to apostolic simplicity and compassion, we can fight humility with humility! I wot well it helped Christianity spread like wildfire in ancient Rome, and full sure am I that such humility lies at the root of the spread of heresy."

Arnaud-Amaury struggled to keep his hands from strangling the old bishop. He and Castelnau had spent almost three years trying to preach to people who refused to listen, nay, who even made fun of their sermons! "Where can we get enough trained and dedicated prelates to carry out this evangelical mission," he asked.

"What about the dozen monks you brought along? They are perfect examples of learned and incorruptible churchmen," Diego smiled.

"'Tis a perfect opportunity to establish other orders of teaching friars," said Dominic. "By my troth, 'tis not by the display of power and pomp, cavalcades of retainers, and richly caparisoned palfreys, or wearing gorgeous apparel, that the heretics win proselytes. They achieve it through zealous preaching, apostolic humility, austerity, and by conveying the impression of holiness-- which belike may be false, 'tis true-- but nevertheless appears genuine to the people. Zeal must be met by zeal, humility by humility, false sanctity by *real* sanctity, and preaching falsehood by preaching truth. Look at the success of your own order."

Arnaud-Amaury had grown tired of listening to such nonsense; he knew it wouldn't work, but he would let the Castilians learn the hard way, because the Holy See expected him to support them. Their failure would teach the pope a lesson.

He shook his head. "You're dreaming, both of you! These people need the scourge and the stake, not sermons. However, I do not intend to impede your zeal." He rose. "I'll tell you what; I have to get back to my abbey to hold the general chapter, but when I return, I'll bring three dozen monks and you can take them on the road. That is, if you want to bide and help us. Now I must take my leave," he said, giving thanks to the Lord on high that he could get away from these misguided do-gooders.

The others stood.

"I fain would take you up on your offer," Diego said. "'Twould make up for not being able to convert those pagans. Our vocation is saving souls, and saving those who have left the Holy Church is perhaps the noblest task of all."

"We are indeed very grateful for your handsome offer," Dominic said, "and we wish you Godspeed on your journey home. Come, let us drink to the great cause we have in common."

Beakers were drained and hands were shaken all around. As Arnaud-Amaury stalked off, Castelnau snapped his fingers at one of the young acolytes serving them.

"Take the Bishop and the Subprior over to the bishopric," he commanded, and then turned back to the Castilians. "While you wait for the Cistercian monks," Castelnau said, "you may wish to help us win converts in a different way. We have proposed debates between Cathar Perfects and ourselves, and our adversaries have accepted. When you arrived, we were in the process of settling the rules for the debates, and we would fain have you participate. Methinks your *Catalan* is so close to our *lenga d'oc* that you need not fear that people here won't understand."

"Where will they take place?"

"The first will be next week in Montréal, in the Lauragais; then three weeks later in Servian; and a month after that, in Besièrs."

"By my troth, we'd be delighted to take part." Diego said as he rose. "Isn't that right, Dominic?"

"With the greatest pleasure." Dominic said. "There is naught more satisfying than converting heathens or heretics.

'Tis what I live for. Thank you so much for arranging this."
The Castilians bowed to Castelnau and went off with the
young monk.

Fanjaus

The two men had arrived separately after nightfall, having purposely taken different paths to make sure neither was followed. The shepherd's hut had barely enough space for a man to lie down, but as he entered, Olivier dropped to his knees and uttered the words of the *aparelhament* rite.

"Bless me, Lord; pray for me and lead me to a good end."

Out of the dark came Castras's answer, "God bless you. May God make a good Christian out of you and lead you to your rightful end."

"'Tis a pleasure to meet you again, my friend," Castras said, as Olivier rose. "How fares your mother?"

"Very well, thank you, Good Man. Word has it that you are going to take part in the debate with the Roman clerics tomorrow, and I wish you luck."

"Thank you, my Brother. 'Tis like I may need it. But now, methinks you have some news for me."

"Forsooth. The other day at Fontcaude Abbey, someone tried to sell some old scrolls to the monks. 'Twas a very long list. Apparently, 'twas a, very old family tree. The problem was the Fontcaude monks could not read the language in which the first few generations were listed. So they sent the seller to Fontfroide, where the monk in charge of the library is actually a secret Believer and a friend of ours, Brother Pascau."

"Ah, yes, Brother Pascau. A fine man, and a real Friend of God."

"When he inspected the scrolls, Pascau realized that the earliest entries were written in Aramaic, the language spoken in the Holy Land at the time of the ministry of Jesus."

"Extraordinary!"

"Indeed, but just wait: the record starts out with the marriage of Mary Magdalene to Jesus, and then records a birth in the same year Jesus died!'

Castras was glad that it was so dark that Olivier could not see the consternation in his face. He tried to control himself. "'Twould mean that Jesus was a man, not a spirit. If 'twere true, 'twould do much harm to our dogma. You wot well that we hold that Jesus has always been a spiritual being, like an angel."

"If you deem it harms *your* dogma, Good Man, bethink you what it does to the Roman Church! If Jesus and Mary Magdalene lived as husband and wife and had children, then the Trinity becomes absurd."

"By my troth, 'tis overwhelming! Is it possible to have a copy made for me? Tell Pascau I will gladly pay for it."

"He's already working on one. 'Twill take him at least another day or two."

There was a long pause before Castras spoke again. "Does anyone else at Fontfroide know about this other than Pascau?"

"No. The others were told it was a simple list of little value except for its age."

"'Tis very interesting, seeing that Pascau has two papal legates as colleagues. If 'twere leaked, 'twould lead to a huge crisis for the Holy See, and indeed, the whole Roman Church."

"Right, but don't you think they'll squelch the story before that happens?"

"'Tis like," Castras nodded. "However, until we can verify its authenticity, I would fain not inform any of our Good Folk. What if 'tis but an elaborate forgery?"

"Mayhap, but 'twould have to be a very clever one. The age of the parchment is undeniable. Those who work with ancient Greek and Roman texts know what aged parchment looks like. They can't be fooled. And what would be the purpose of such a hoax?"

"I wot not," Castras answered. "To say truth, it doesn't serve the Church of the Friends of God, so who benefits? 'Tis impossible to say! But this I wot well: it must bide a secret. Will the copy look like the original?"

"Not to a scholar. The original was written by many hands, whereas the copy is all in Pascau's. Any expert would notice that. Also, the parchment he used is much lighter in color and far less worn."

"Is there a way to make the copy look more like the original?"

"Pascau said he was going to darken it with tanning liquor."

'Tis a good idea. And I believe 'twould be best if the original were returned to the goldsmith. Probably no one will look for it there."

"There's a problem," Olivier said. "Both Pascau and I deem that if ever the Romans discover the truth, they fain will go looking for the goldsmith and his family and eliminate them. That they be Jews makes it all the easier. Belike this will befall no matter where the original is."

"You're right. I hadn't thought of that. Where could the family go?" Castras asked.

"Carcassona? Tolosa maybe? Wherever he can find the biggest market for his jewelry, I trow."

"They can still be traced. All you have to do is look for goldsmiths…but wait a moment." Castras paused. "What if Pascau doesn't copy down the entries concerning the goldsmith's family? What if he simply omits them? Then no one would know about them and they would be safe, even if we give the original back to them."

"By my troth, 'tis a bonny solution! I will tell Pascau. My wife and I are returning to Provença right after the debate, and on the way I can deliver the originals to the goldsmith."

"Excellent. We've tended to the material matters, but if the revelation is true, then we Friends of God have a huge spiritual matter to contend with. Methinks you know how much depends on your discretion."

"Good Man, I'm not only a Believer but I'm a son of the Midi. I have my *paratge*. You can put your trust in me."

"I have faith in you, my son. Give me the Kiss of Peace." The two men embraced and kissed each other on the lips.

"After you leave, I'll tarry here and recite five *Our Fathers* before I go back. Good night, and have a safe journey," Castras said, and Olivier stepped out into the brilliant starlight.

Craning her neck to see the men on the stage, Aude bumped Faye de Durfort who was sitting next to her. "Oh, excuse me Faye," she blurted, "I'm so sorry. I fain would catch a glimpse of the Castilian clergy. There's some kind of a giant sitting in front of me.

"Would you fain change places?" Faye asked.

"No, thank you, silly woman, you're even shorter than me! I'm dying of curiosity because they've opened that convent in Prolha."

"The one for True Christian women who have converted back to the Roman Church?"

"'Tis the very one. I hear they have a half-dozen such women. Word has gone about that two were once Good Women. I wonder whatever made them leave us?"

"I wot not. Methinks I could not do that," Faye said, shaking her head.

The two friends were sitting on one of the benches that had been built for the much ballyhooed debate between The Friends of God and prelates of the established church; the entire inner courtyard of the Montréal castle was jammed with some five hundred people jabbering away at the same time. Aude spied Margarida and Olivier waving at her from several rows away. She chuckled and waved back. They had obliged her and postponed their return to the Comtat in order to attend the debate.

Together with the other Good Women from Fanjaus, only three leagues distant, Aude had been looking forward to the debate for weeks; now at last it was about to take place. They had taken the opportunity to preach along the way and had visited two families with sick children on whom they had lavished attention and herbal remedies.

Entering the courtyard, Aude had spotted several Good Men and Women, as well as many Believers who were her personal friends. She sensed that the majority of the crowd was of her persuasion, but she knew full well that many others supported the Roman faith. Were they the ones frowning with lips grimly pressed together? The ones who either stared or looked away when they saw her black robe? Would she ever know, she asked herself, as she took her seat?

At that moment, upon the square stage that had been erected against one of the walls a scant pace above the pavement, a man stepped forward with outstretched arms gesturing for silence. One of six members of the town watch standing below him on the courtyard cobblestones loudly rapped the butt of his spear on the wooden platform three times. As the hubbub died away at last, the man on the stage coughed into his hand, and began to speak.

"Good day! My name is Bernard, Chivalièr de Vilanau and 'tis my pleasure to be presiding over this debate. There's a long-established custom of debating religious issues here in the Midi. Many years ago, the first such debate took place in Lombers, and just recently, they have been held in Verfeil, Servian and Albi. We are very grateful to the Lords of Montréal, who have graciously lent us this perfect setting."

"Please permit me to introduce my fellow arbiters: Bernard, Chivalièr d'Arzens; Raimond Got, miller of Laurac; and Anradu Rivièra, merchant of Preishan. 'Twill be our task to make sure that the debaters abide by rules that they themselves helped formulate and have agreed to. If there is any departure from the rules, 'tis our duty to intervene."

"For you in the audience, 'tis your privilege and for your edification that you listen quietly without comment, or applause, or other sounds of approval or disapproval. Any outbursts will not be tolerated, and the men of the watch will expel those who violate these rules and any

45

other troublemakers as well. What we ask, and what you should expect, is to let our distinguished guests argue their beliefs. They, themselves, submitted their main arguments to us three days ago. After careful review and discussions with the participants themselves, we have narrowed the debate down to a single proposition: is the Roman Catholic Church a force of evil?"

There were murmurs of consternation among the crowd, and again, Vilanau held up his hands until the noise had died down. "The proposition agreed upon is a proposition for debate, not a conclusion. The distinguished prelates of the Roman Church will oppose this proposition, while the Good Men of the Friends of God will defend it."

"Let me now introduce the opponents of the proposition from the Roman Church, if they would please rise here beside me." Aude watched the church men get up from their bench and stand next to Vilanau as he introduced them, one after the other.

"His Excellency Diego, Bishop of Osma in Aragon; Father Dominic Guzman, the subprior of Osma; Brother Peire of Castelnau lately of Fontfroide Abbey, and Papal Legate of the Holy See; and Brother Raoul, another papal legate from the Abbey of Frontfroide."

To Aude, Dominic made a more determined, authoritative impression than his colleague, but she put it down to the very apparent difference of age between them. Dominic was barely thirty years old and had an extremely youthful face, while Diego seemed old and frail and somewhat tentative. Born and raised outside of Montpelhier, Castelnau was no stranger and indeed was one of the most hated men in the entire region. He had been the archdeacon of Maguelona before joining the Abbey of Fontfroide near Narbona. As a legate of the Holy See, he was well known as a bitter foe of those among his countrymen who preferred the heretical church to the ancient and universal institution. Aude had seen him several times in the last two years, but she had never heard him speak in public.

As she studied the four Catholics, who had sat back down, Aude remembered how surprised she was when she heard that the Roman prelates had condescended to debate the upstart heretics. She recalled what the confessor of one of her Catholic acquaintances had said: there was not a chance that ignorant artisans could possibly rise to the level of theology that was commonplace among the higher levels of clergy. She had heard more or less the same smug predictions from other sources: that the Roman Church regarded the debate as a God sent opportunity to hold up the leaders of the Good Folk as bumbling fools full of hot air. Yet she had always been impressed by the erudition of many of the Good Men and Women she knew.

Pondering the enigma, she became aware that Vilanau was introducing the four Good Men. She knew them all: Major Son Guilhabert of Castras; Pons Jourda, from Verfeil; Deacon Roger Hot of Cabaret; and Bishop Benoit of Tèrme.

"As is the custom," Vilanau was saying, "those who support the proposition will be the first to speak. The rules of the debate stipulate that the speakers will take turns in responding, so that no speaker shall speak twice in a row, and neither side will speak in succession."

"Deacon Hot will begin the debate by stating the case for the proposition." Vilanau took a seat on a curule at the corner of the stage.

Hot, the very image of an ascetic, rose and came forward to the edge of the stage and looked out over the audience. His face was pale and drawn, but resolute, and his voice was strong and steady. "The Roman Church presents itself as holy and as the so-called Bride of Christ. On the contrary, 'tis the church of the Devil; 'tis the whore of Bablyon."

A gasp rose from the crowd, then voices shrilled in anger. Others shouted the protestors down. The watch waved their cudgels and Vilanau jumped up, arms spread, and bellowed, "Men of the watch, stand ready! One more commotion like that and I'll ask you to remove the troublemakers! We be here to listen and judge, not to complain or comment." Then he nodded to Hot. "I apologize for the interruption, Deacon, please continue." He glared around the courtyard once more and took his time returning to his seat.

Hot gave no sign of being the least bit cowed. "In the words of the Apostle John, the Roman Church is the mother of fornication and abominations, and 'tis drunk on the blood of saints and martyrs. Its dogma is demoniacal. The mass and other so-called sacraments it practices are neither those of Christ, nor those of the Apostles. They are superstitious gibberish."

"The priests who conduct the vile services and perform those sacrilegious rites, and who by rights should minister to the congregations and teach the love of Christ, are very often common drunks and fornicators who are illiterate and cannot possibly be expected to perform sacraments of any kind."

"They profit from selling indulgences, including baptismal water, and land for the burial of the dead, and oil for the sick; and then they extort tithes from the parishioners they swindle. They and their bishops parade at the alter in gold and silver raiments, brandishing gold and silver implements, while honest yeomen, who wear woolens and toil in the earth with hoes are expected to give up a tithe of their labor to the church."

"Instead of *giving*, in the name of charity, they *take*, in the name of licentiousness and avarice. 'Tis blatant iniquity. There is no other word for it but *evil*."

"During the course of this debate we will show exactly how this cursed institution deviates from God's truth and the words of Christ our Lord." Hot's eyes swept over the audience once again; then he returned to his place among his colleagues.

Bishop Diego slowly got up and walked to the front of the stage.

"The heretics are employing their heaviest siege weapons to try to besmirch the Holy Church, but their missiles fall short of the target. In the first place, when the Apostle John spoke of the Whore of Babylon, he was referring to the ancient, imperial city of Rome. He was using Babylon as a metaphor for Rome, where many evil rites were performed by the pagans who lived there. We proudly call our church Roman because the Apostle Peire went to Rome and converted the pagans and founded the Church there, as our Lord Jesus had wished."

"Before the Passion, Jesus had asked, *But who say ye that I am?* And Simon Peire, whose name means rock in Greek, answered and said, *Thou art the Christ, the Son of the living God.* And Jesus answered and said unto him, *blessed art thou, for flesh and blood hath not revealed it unto thee, but my Father, which is in heaven. And I say also unto thee, that thou art Peire, and upon this rock I will build my church; and the gates of hell shall not prevail against it. I will give you the keys of the kingdom of heaven.* As you wot well, that 'rock' became the foundation of our Church."

"What constitutes the Roman Church of God, you well may ask? What is its essence? 'Tis the congregation of the faithful. Just as a tree is rooted in the ground, so the

Holy Church has its roots in faith. Hence, in his letter to the Romans, Paul wrote, *the just man liveth by faith.* Faith is the foundation of the spiritual edifice. Hence, in his letter to the Hebrews, he wrote: *Faith is the substance of things to be hoped for, the evidence of things that appear not.* In our Church, which works for the good, faith precedes good works; thus the essence of the church originates from faith, and thereby acts in harmony with good work."

"By means of faith, the Church of God is distinguished from the malignant church of our opponents. John said, *faith makes the sons of God.* In the Holy Roman Church of God, faith produces purity, justice and glory. Purity restores us, justice leads us onward and glory guides us to overcome obstacles and find the way from exile on earth to our homeland in heaven. For that reason, Paul said in Corinthians, *the only foundation that man can have has already been laid.* Christ Jesus is the foundation of our faith and He lives in the hearts of the faithful."

"Obviously, the Holy Roman Church of God has good works as well as faith, as supported by the Holy Gospels, and the heretical Cathar church cannot even come close to finding such support. That is because for more than a millennium, our Holy Church has accomplished the ultimate good by saving souls. In contrast, the Cathar church is a brief flame in a weak lamp and cannot begin to compare with the good works of the Holy Roman Church. Certainly there is little hope and even less proof that they have ever saved a single soul." With a small wave of the hand, Diego returned to his bench.

Benoit of Tèrme rose and came forward. He was a big man with a beard almost as black as his cassock and he began in a voice that was very high pitched for a man his size. "The Apostle James said, *thou hast faith, and I have works;*

show me thy faith without works, and I will show thee, by works, my faith."

"One glaring difference between the two churches is the true service performed by each. Throughout the Midi, 'tis a commonly accepted practice to call for the Good Men or Good Women when one is sick or in trouble, even if one worships the Roman faith. This is not only because of what the Good Men and Women believe, but because they serve dependably and competently. They care for the sick and the lame without recompense, in contrast to priests too lazy or too inebriated to respond to a call for help. Indeed, the Roman priesthood greedily lays heavy financial burdens on people's shoulders but will not move a finger to help them when they need it. They do not serve; they *oppress.*"

"A tree is known by its fruit, and the fruit of the Roman Church -- its priesthood-- is corrupt and evil; therefore the Church itself is evil. How can such incompetents be expected to administer to their congregations? How can a hierarchy decked out in priceless robes and jewels be expected to respond to the needs of its congregations, who have been impoverished by the avaricious and predatory greed of these very same high-placed prelates? What possible bond can such fops have with the people? Like the money changers in the temple, they unabashedly *sell* indulgences to their parishioners! As Jesus said to the moneychangers, *my house shall be called the house of prayer; but ye have made it a den of thieves.* Aye, the fruit of the Roman faith breeds avarice, and its Church is a den of thieves, not a force for good."

"The Church of the Friends of God believes that God is supremely good, holy, just, wise and true, and stands above all praise. The Lord God is the creator of all good things, and being goodness and purity Himself, He is incapable of creating evil. Let me repeat. He is incapable of creating evil."

"But we all wot well that evil exists. It exists right here among us. There are famines, and disease and illness and there is death. That is the human condition, and by its very nature, humanity has the capacity for evil. However, the human soul is the creature of God, Who is so supremely good that He cannot create evil or tolerate it and could not possibly have created it in the past."

"Yet my opponents have said that 'tis God who is responsible for *all* creation and that He is also all-powerful and all-knowing and all-merciful. If God did not create evil, where did it come from? Why did he allow it to exist? Why does it plague us today?"

"Let's look at it logically, using two divergent arguments. First, let us say, God would have liked to suppress evil, but could not. If that were true, He cannot be all-powerful. Surely you'll agree that proposition is clearly false."

"Second, let's say God could have suppressed evil, but didn't want to; if that were true, then He enjoys seeing his creatures suffer. Therefore, he can't be all-merciful or infinitely good. You'll agree this is also patently false.

"Forsooth, our infinitely good God wants to choke evil and, being all powerful, is capable of doing so. So therefore, why doesn't He do it? Does any of our opponents dare answer this question which lies at the heart of our differences?" Benoit looked over at the prelates, challenging them with his sternest expression before he retreated to his seat.

Dominic rose. He wore no cap, and his raven locks fell down to his shoulders. He had a strong face with a prominent nose, and walked briskly to the front of the stage even before Bernard had sat down.

"Very well," he said, and turned and bowed to Bernard. "I'm glad you asked that question. God is omnipotent, but doesn't suppress evil even though He can. He allowed evil to come about, not because he likes to see people suffer, but because he gave us the great gift of wisdom, a gift that brings us infinitely more good and joy than any conceivable trouble brought by evil, because it permits us to know God and to achieve immortality through his Grace, which is the supreme, unsurpassable Good, the essence of our faith.

"In addition, the perception of evil necessarily enables us to recognize and distinguish it from virtue, which we desperately need to endure and overcome the onslaught of evil. Thus, without God's gift of knowledge, 'tis true that we might not know evil, but that is only a paltry burden compared to the immeasurable advantage of achieving the supreme good that is eternal life. Thus it has been arranged that man must know evil as well as good."

Benoit rose up off the bench. "But you didn't answer my question! Why didn't God suppress evil? Why did he allow it to come about as you say?"

Vilanau rose with a scowl and started toward Benoit wagging his finger, but Dominic put out a hand to stay his progress. "'Tis well, Chivalièr, 'tis a good question, and I welcome it." Then he turned back to the audience. "There is only one infinitely good and omnipotent God. If evil exists and God doesn't suppress it, He has His reasons. His infinite goodness exists at a completely different level than where we reside. 'Tis utterly inconceivable that we, who deplore the existence of evil cam divine His reasons. We have faith that God has only the best interests of his creations in mind. As a mere, fallible mortal, man has nothing to say, he only needs to have faith. Faith is the answer to your question."

Benoit rose once more and asked, "But excuse me, if keeping the best interests of God's creatures in mind is a matter of faith, then where does evil come from and why should we mortals be fallible?"

Dominic shrugged. "God's infinite wisdom did not obligate Him to make His creatures necessarily incapable of doing either good or evil. But He did provide them with free will. But because they were envious of God's stature in heaven, some of the angels became demons and evil beings by their own volition. Instead of remaining saintly and treating their Lord with respect and humility, they allowed their own willful pretensions and sinful pride to spite Him."

"Besides, God created the angels imperfect, He could have made them perfect and incapable of sinning if He had wanted to. However, He didn't want to make them into marionettes, reacting mechanically. If they had lacked the ability to do evil, they could not have proved their loyalty to God, and God would not have had to acknowledge it."

"Therefore, God, from the very beginning, created his angels in such a fashion that they would be disposed, depending on their individual inclinations, to do either good or evil. He endowed them with free will, thereby retaining the possibility of judging his creatures in all fairness: they all were capable of sinning, so He was grateful when they didn't, and disappointed when they did." Dominic smiled at the audience as he returned to his seat.

Pons Jourda, an older man who wore no cap over his white hair, came forward slowly and when he reached the front of the stage, he looked around at Dominic. "Methinks you are saying that God set up free will as a loyalty oath rather than trying to make noble creatures in His own image of incomparable goodness. From such pure creatures He need ask nothing because He lacks nothing."

Then he turned toward the crowd. "When a man does something meritorious, God is acting within him, and thus should not expect praise for something the *Lord* did. All we can really do is to open ourselves to the Word of God, so that He can act within us. By heeding God in this way, we assure absolute love and humility. God, being absolutely Good, can only proceed from good. Why should He suspect disloyalty among the angels that He Himself had created? The mere suspicion would be evil and hence impossible coming from God. An infinitely good God would not have allowed the angels to consort with evil or to be sullied by evil."

"Being Almighty implies that if God made any creatures, he created them to reflect his Goodness. In the voice of Jesus Christ, He asks that His will be done, especially when people act with charity toward their neighbors, but we know that this has not yet been accomplished."

"If there were only one infinitely good principle, namely God, sinning and malevolence would not be possible. If He were the *only* principle, without any opposing power to limit His will, then the things he created would have been perfect. God would not have been vexed by the wickedness of His creatures to the point of regretting their creation. He wouldn't have had to ask men, through the mediation of Jesus Christ, to follow good rather than evil. He wouldn't have needed that help; everyone would have obeyed Him by absolute necessity. They would have had no other choice."

"We ourselves have absolutely no strength. All that is good in His creatures comes absolutely from Him and by Him. 'Tis He who is responsible for the existence of Good and 'tis He who is its root cause. Being the primary and unique principle, He and He alone was completely responsible for the angels' behavior."

"Therefore, as our opponents' argue, the disposition to commit evil could have come solely from God; they claim He wanted his creatures to have that potential for evil. If 'twere true, this means that God, from the very start, and with full knowledge, endowed his angels with a flaw that would prevent them from evading evil and would banish them from heaven."

"My opponents thus maintain that evil can come from good. But a flawless God can't create a flawed creature. Just as the Ethiopian can't change his black skin to white, and the leopard can't get rid of its spots because of the disposition given to them by their Creator, so with Hs creatures in heaven. The flaw must therefore be the effect of an evil cause. Does this mean that God is evil?"

"Of course not! We, the Friends of God, reject this false reasoning. We deny that the God we call good, holy, just and wise and straight, who is above all praise, would even remotely be responsible for evil. 'Tis why we insist that there are two principles: one infinitely good, and one infinitely evil. This evil principle was the cause of disharmony among the angels and the root of all evil."

He turned to the bench where the prelates sat, and slowly shook his head. "The stand taken by the Roman Church on the origin of evil is untenable. 'Twould mean that Almighty God tolerated evil, which is impossible. 'Tis therefore a faulty premise, one that promotes evil and therefore corrupts the dogma of the Roman Church, which, therefore, cannot be a force for good, but one of evil."

Peire of Castelnau jumped to his feet and strode to the front of the stage, coming within a hair of shouldering Jourda out of the way. Instead of taking his seat, Jourda stopped, and looked askance at Vilanau, who stood up and took a step toward Castelnau.

"Anyone who can read knows that the book of Genesis clearly states that God made everything, visible and invisible," Castelnau began, spitting his words out in anger. "Being omniscient, God knew exactly what his creatures would do throughout eternity, but he did not, I repeat, did not direct them toward evil rather than good. He created them free to choose evil or good on their own. The angels that fell from heaven, as well as Adam and Eve and their progeny, were at fault. 'Tis written in Genesis. Mayhap our opponents are reading some other book, or perhaps they are illiterate, and are taught by some renegade canon, who, being dismissed from the Church, is spitefully seeking revenge," and he glanced over at Jourda with a sneer.

Vilanau spoke to Castelnau in a low voice, "You are out of line. You must wait until your opponent finishes and sits down, your Excellency."

"Well, Sir Legate," Jourda addressed Castelnau, "if, as you say, God is the only prime mover, then the creatures owe their dispositions entirely to God and no one but God. If they are flawed, and able to choose evil rather than good, then according to your reasoning, 'tis because God made them imperfect. He wanted them to have the disposition to do evil. Now all of those within these walls see the impiety of this argument, which must be rejected; for, if only one prime principle exists, then God the good, omnipotent and omniscient becomes the prime cause of evil. We of the Friends of God do not accept this implausible argument. In contrast to the Roman Church, ours is the Church of Good, not Evil." With this, Jourda turned and took his seat.

Castelnau's sallow face had reddened and he slammed one fist into the palm of his other hand for emphasis as he spoke. "We, of the Holy Roman Church, firmly avow and affirm that there is only one true god, the unique principle of all things, creator of all things visible and invisible, spiritual and corporeal since the beginning of time. The scriptures say that God is the creator of all things. A sole God, creator of all things. *All*, did you hear that, *all!*" Castelnau's voice had become shrill.

"As John wrote in the Apocalypse, He who lives for centuries of centuries created heaven, and *all* which is in heaven; the earth, and *all* that is on the earth; the sea, and *all* that is in the sea. And Paul wrote there is only one single God, which is the Father from whom *all* things proceed, and who made us for Hmself; and there is only one Lord, Jesus Christ, by whom *all* things have been made. *All* things are from Him, everything is by Him, and everything is in Him. *All* things have been made by him, those in heaven and those in of the earth, the visible and the invisible. All, all, *all*," he cried.

"Evil originated from free will. To reject that belief is to risk ascribing human behavior to some horrid fatalism, and consequently the denial of any human responsibility for malevolent behavior. With his omnipotence, God has made spiritual creatures like the invisible heavenly angels, as well as material, visible creatures in the terrestrial world; and of course, we humans are composed of both spirit and matter."

Castelnau nodded and managed a thin smile before he continued. "As for evil, it originated from the wicked use of the free will, first in angels, then in man, as endowed by God. By itself, free will is innocent and blameless! The commission of error, or fault, stems directly from its misuse. Pride pushed an angel to try and make itself equal to its Creator. Thus, the willfulness of pride is the original sin. The penance that we all must undergo comes to us indirectly as the punishment for that first willful and sinful step of pride."

"St Augustine believed evil was purely a non-being not something existing positively in itself. If a sole creator, who must be a being, were supremely good like God, he reasoned, then the opposite would consequently not only be the absence of good, but a non-being. It would be a nothing."

"Evil only comes about because of a break in the natural order and there has to be a thinking subject who becomes aware of this rupture and of its disorder. When the integrity of the body breaks down, we suffer. When the rules of human conduct fail or are missing there is inequity. Investigating evil and sin, St. Augustine found that Evil was not a substance, but only a breakdown of volition, that is, a failure of *will*." Castelnau slammed a fist into the palm of his hand.

"Anselm said that evil is the privation of a good that has been endowed. That man is weaker than a lion is not evil. Man isn't endowed with such strength. But blindness is evil, because God made man to see. Making evil unreal demands a divine plan. If God is not the origin of evil, and if a principle different from God cannot be found, then God has merely rendered evil *not* impossible, otherwise creation would become a total absurdity."

"Therefore, we must accept that even if we mortals can rarely perceive how evil will contribute to the supreme order of things, much good will be suppressed if God permits that no evil is produced. Fire would not burn if air weren't destroyed. The life of the lion would not be assured if he couldn't kill the wild ass. Everything that has been, is, and will be belongs in an inalienable fashion to the work of the divine. It is faith in this divine order of the world that my opponents – the apostles of Satan -- utterly lack, and they want to impose their faithless doctrine on unsuspecting and innocent members of the Roman Catholic flock." He thrust his chin out and glowered at the crowd, daring someone to show disagreement, before he went back and sat down.

Guilhabert Castras approached the front of the stage. "Everybody within these walls can attest to the fact that evil persists in the world. 'Tis a part of our existence. Our opponents say that evil is due to free will that the Good Lord allegedly endowed us. We, of the Friends of God, say the evil that is spread throughout the world can only be imputed to a principle other than God. Let's take it one step further. Evil exists in the world because the world itself was created by an evil force!"

Castras paused to let his words sink in. "Let me quote the scriptures to support what I am saying, although all of you have at one time or another been touched by evil."

Matthew wrote, *an evil tree bringeth forth evil fruit.* A good tree cannot bring forth evil fruit, neither can an evil tree bear forth good fruit. And James wrote. *doth a fountain gush forth sweet and bitter water out of the same hole?* Can the fig tree, my brethren, bear grapes; or the vine, figs? Neither can salt water yield sweet. Evil is begot by evil.

"When man does good, my friends, there is no merit in it for him and no glory to draw from it, for it is God who is acting within him. Man serves God by accomplishing his good works, because through us God consummates what he proposes and wishes to be done. We serve Him when we fulfill His will with His help. We ourselves do nothing good unless God is the cause and principle. So when we worship Lord Jesus, we do it by God's grace, not our own."

"I say this by the authority of the Holy scriptures. Paul said to the Philippians, *for it is God who worketh in you both to will and to accomplish according to his good will.* And to the Corinthians, *The steps of a man are guided by the Lord....* If evil is found in God's people, it does not truly come from God Himself or Lord Jesus, nor does He bring it into being, nor was He ever, nor is He now, its cause."

"No evil can come from a creature of God, itself good, unless there be a *source* of evil, another principle that is the cause of all pride and wickedness, of all defilement of the people and all other evils. In other words, when we are doing something good, we wot well that we are in God's grace, and when we do something wicked, we wot well we are doing the Devil's work. We cannot serve God by freely willing to do good because we lack the power to do so, Castras said, shaking his head.

"If anyone listened attentively to the argument put forth by Rome's legate, he would realize 'tis impossible to wield two contrary powers simultaneously, or to be capable of doing both good and evil for all time. 'Tis especially true for God, who has complete knowledge of the future and whose wisdom of all things take place throughout eternity. And so 'tis particularly puzzling," Castras scratched his head for effect, "how the good angels that He created could have been capable of turning away from their very own natural goodness, which had existed from eternity, and instead took delight in wickedness, which did not yet exist and which is the exact opposite of goodness!

"And 'tis even more puzzling to make such a choice if, as the unenlightened say, a principle or cause of evil did not exist! 'Tis especially true because 'tis written that every beast loveth its like, so also every man loveth him that is nearest himself. All flesh shall consort with the like to itself and every man shall associate himself with his like. Clearly, the angels would have chosen the good like unto themselves, which had existed from eternity, rather than spurning it to cleave to evil, of which they knew naught. Yet, according to my opponents, lacking any cause or impetus, the angels chose the unknown

"'Tis written that whatever has a beginning must have a cause. Yet, my opponents claim that what existed, namely God, had less effect than what did not exist, namely evil; despite the fact that to have an effect, a thing must exist. 'Tis also logical that if a cause remains unchanged, the effect will always be the same. In order to produce a new effect, there must be a new causal factor. Just as diversity yields differences, so uniformity produces sameness and conformity.

"If the angels could not have sinned without free will, God, the all-knowing, would in no wise have granted it to them, since He would have known that it would corrupt His kingdom. Moreover, 'tis most wicked to suppose that such corruption could have come from God who is far above all praise. It follows that a principle of evil exists that must be the source and cause of the corruption of the angels and of all wickedness."

"To the wise, 'tis obvious that God never gave the angels the choice of either doing good, or evil, for all eternity. Without such a choice, they would have continued to do good forever. They could never have done evil.

"Therefore, how can my unenlightened opponents claim that once given the choice, the angels could have avoided evil? For God, who knows the future completely, would have known that they would choose evil. An all-merciful God never would have stooped to that. That is why there must be another source of evil to cause the angels to sin and fall from heaven. To believe they exercised free will is both absurd and evil in itself, because it assumes that God was solely responsible for inflicting eternal punishment on his angels. To any wise man, it is utterly preposterous that God, who is good and holy, should condemn any of his angels for all time by giving them free will. And the same applies to man." Castras bowed to his opponents and sat down.

Vilanau turned to the prelates, who were huddled together, and lifted his eyebrows. "Do you wish to speak in rebuttal to this argument?"

Diego stood, and advanced to the front of the platform. "'Tis our humble opinion, and we are confident that 'tis widely shared by the congregation, that Father Dominic and

Brother Peire skillfully anticipated Senhor Castras's arguments, and reduced them to naught even before they were spoken. Once again, the heretical church is trying to befuddle the audience by denying man's fatal flaw, the existence of free will, and how it brought about death as described in Genesis. Try as they might, they cannot elude the words of the Holy Scriptures, and so they must invent another principle to explain evil. Without this invention, their entire argument founders into nothingness. However, no such principle can be found in the Scriptures, because none ever existed. The heretics have spun it out of thin air."

"As we have repeated over and over, faith is the strength of our religion, and this faith is reinforced time and time again in the Holy Scriptures. With faith, we overcome the evil of death and with faith, we will all mount into the heavens to see our Lord Jesus. We will therefore wait to have the final word, thank you."

Vilanau turned to the Good Men. "Do you wish to continue?"

Roger Hot stood and drawing his slight frame together, smiled at the sea of faces. "Having disproved that man sins of his own free will, which the Lord God most certainly did not give him, and which is not even mentioned in the scriptures, let us turn to the rituals of the Roman Church.

"First, let us address that keystone of their faith, the Eucharist. When Jesus said, *He that eateth my flesh and drinketh my blood hath everlasting life, and I will raise him up in the Last Day,* what did He mean? That we munch on His body and gulp down His blood to render ourselves immortal? No, forsooth! He was speaking metaphorically."

"When He said, *if any man eat of this bread,* he meant for people to heed His way of life. When He said, *the bread that I will give to him is my flesh, for the life of the world,* He meant the lives of the *people* in that world. *If you eat the flesh* means if you keep the commandments of the Son of God -- *and drink His blood*—if you accept the spiritual intent of the new testament—you will live forever. By his *'flesh',* He meant the will of God, which stays within Christ as it does in him who accepts Christ. Truly, therefore, false priests eat not the flesh of our Lord Jesus Christ, nor drink His blood, because they abide not in the Lord Jesus."

"Moreover, 'tis impossible that the substance of bread and wine can, through the ministry of any man, wicked or no, be transubstantiated into flesh and blood. Can you imagine the sacrilege that would be taking place if the Host were really Christ's flesh and blood? People chewing up the Lord's body, and gulping down his blood like some horrid form of leech? Imagine when the flesh and blood of Lord Jesus Christ reach the latrine of the bowels. 'Tis utter sacrilege! It makes one gag! The whole idea of transubstantiation is ridiculous. If the bread and wine really were Christ's body and blood, were it as big as the biggest peak in the Pyrenees, 'twould have been consumed centuries ago by the many who blindly followed this fraudulent practice."

A few titters broke out in the audience, and Hot went on.

"And what is the Host? 'Tis but a batter of flour and water that has been baked in an oven. Purely and simply, 'tis bread, and not the body of Christ. 'Tis but a simple piece of food no better or no worse than a radish or a turnip. No matter how much the priest consecrates it at the altar, it remains bread the same as before. You see it with your own eyes, and you taste it. Mice have probably been eating consecrated hosts for a thousand years! Once more there was scattered laughter in the crowd.

"Because the Roman church teaches that God and the Son are united in one, to eat the host is to eat God as well, which is impossible nonsense In fact, to believe or make believe that you are eating Him is scandalous. If God were in the sacrament at the altar, would He let Himself be eaten? If 'twere the body of God, He wouldn't put Himself in a place so shameful as a man's intestines. In short this sacrament is a mockery of the Lord our God, and as such 'tis an evil and condemnable practice."

"One more thing. If God, who is totally spirit, sent his Son Jesus into the world, what makes you think Jesus was ever flesh and blood, or even mud like Adam? God made Jesus like he made the angels. The term 'son' is strictly an honorific term, not a genealogical term. Jesus was not flesh and blood, but an angelic spirit who carried God's message to the creatures of the earth that had been created by the Devil, not by God in heaven."

"Briefly, just as God, the infinite Goodness, could not create an evil being, neither could He create an evil world. Instead, the Devil created the visible world, the tangible world that we see and feel and hear around us, a kingdom plagued by evil catastrophes such as drought, hail, floods, and land-slides that beset us, full of evil creatures such as wolves and vermin and spiders and lice. It is also burdened by war and strife, disease and death, all brought about by the Devil. This world is transitory and someday will end. 'Tis the evil world of the Old Testament."

"But the kingdom of God is eternal. Jesus and the other heavenly creatures are eternal, as are the souls that Jesus has saved with the help of the Holy Spirit. Since Jesus is spirit, not flesh, 'tis impossible for anyone, Roman or otherwise, to eat His flesh or drink his blood. That is why we believe it is fraudulent of the Roman Church to base its most holy sacrament on impossibility. By being a fraud, the Roman Church is not a force for good, but of evil."

As he finished, Hot stood nodding at acquaintances in the audience who had caught his eye, and gave a start when Brother Raoul, who had come forward, tapped him gently on the shoulder, whispering. "'Tis time for my rebuttal," Hot flushed and begging the monk's pardon, went back to his seat.

"With much vanity and deceptiveness, Senhor Hot, you are in error about the body and blood of Christ," Raoul began. "Although all of Christendom relies on the words of the Lord which the Apostle also followed, that say the transubstantiated flesh and blood of Christ are swallowed, you -- representing a pitifully small group of heretical dissenters – would gainsay it with numerous untruths and with sophisticated and vexatious scoffing. After years of watching the faithful take the Host, I can vouch that it is not gulped down like pig swill at a trough. 'Tis consumed with great delicacy and reverence, a mode of consumption that is unique, and as unnatural and faithful as 'tis commendable."

"Among your many other errors, you say Jesus enjoined his disciples to share a *meal* in His memory, but actually 'twas only a piece of bread and one cup of wine. He commanded that all drink from it and that they do this in commemoration of him. As the faithful well know, what is consecrated today in the Mass by a priest in the Church is not the Lord's last supper, not even symbolically; it is rather that which the Lord taught His disciples to do for others in memory of what He Himself did for them, blessing and giving them the bread and the chalice of benediction, saying *Take, eat and drink of this, all of you, this is my body and my blood*, and so on.

"The Mass is the most holy and well-considered office established in the Holy Church of God: the sacrifice of the Lord's body and blood which is celebrated at the end of the Mass transports him who participates therein. Nor is the ministry of any unworthy priest who may very rarely administer the Mass, an impediment in respect to those who take part. As the Apostle says, *neither he that planteth, nor he that watereth is anything, but God alone who giveth the harvest,* which is the effect itself. Thus, God hath no fellowship with the unclean. If wicked men minister daily before God, may one say that God is the companion of the wicked?"

"As for Jesus being some kind of a wraith, or a phantom, the testimony of many witnesses who saw Him daily as recorded in the gospels clearly refutes such a proposition He was born in a manger by His mother Mary and was wrapped in swaddling clothes. He forcefully ousted the moneychangers from the Temple; He bore the Cross to Calvary; He bled where the nails pinned Him to the cross, and blood and water came out of His chest when it was pierced by a spear. He died, was wrapped in a shroud and placed in a tomb and was resurrected in the flesh. There is absolutely no hint that He was not flesh and blood. My opponents are going to have to do better than this, if they expect people to take them seriously." The bishop inclined his head to the crowd, and made his slow way back to the bench, a small smile playing on his lips.

Benoit of Tèrme made his way to the front of the stage, shaking his head.

"Your Excellency," he asked, looking around at the legate, "what about the time Jesus walked on water? For an angelic being, 'twas easily done, but not if He were really flesh and blood. Remember when Peire tried it and sank like the rock that he was?"

"And how, when the disciples met Jesus, they mistook him for a spirit and became afraid? In the Gospel of Luke, Jesus passed right through the bodies of the disciples and 'went away.' That would have been impossible had He been flesh and blood. And in Luke, He spent a whole day in the company of the apostles before they recognized Him. In his letter to the Romans, Paul himself said that Christ had been made, and I quote, *in the image of man and in the resemblance of man.* All through the New Testament, His celestial appearance evokes comment. He seemed other worldly and came or descended from heaven; and looked like a shadow or an outline. There is every indication that He was not flesh and blood, and therefore could not have suffered on the cross, or been transubstantiated, let alone be eaten and drunk. Thus the whole idea of the Eucharist is a sham."

"So, too, is the Roman baptismal ceremony using actual water. Like the blind leading the blind, the wicked Roman church quotes Christ as saying *and he that believeth and is baptized shall be saved, but he who believeth not shall be condemned.* Yet, the Roman clergy mock Christ's words by baptizing infants who do not believe and who can have no knowledge of good or evil."

"If baptism with water was really effective in saving souls, then God would not have had to send Christ here, because the means of saving souls was right at hand. But, forsooth, it wasn't. As John the Baptist himself said, *I have baptized you with water, but He shall baptize you with the Holy Spirit.*

"Luke says that when Paul came to Ephesus, he found certain disciples and asked them if they had received the Holy Spirit when they became believers, and they replied they hadn't and knew nothing of the Holy Spirit. Paul put his hands on them and the Holy Spirit came upon them. These were middle-aged men who believed with all their hearts and knew good from evil. Baptism by water had not brought the Holy Spirit to them, proving that the ritual is useless, especially for infants and children. In contrast, the apostles Peire and John journeyed to Samaria and baptized new believers by laying their hands on them, and Paul baptized Timothy in the same way, saying *I admonish thee that thou stir up the grace of God which is in thee by the imposition of my hands."*

"In conclusion, we have clearly shown that the Roman Church has strayed from the teachings of Christ and His Apostles, and is founded on the false premise that God gave His angels and men free will, and the power to sin. By using the scriptures, we have proved that the Lord our Father would never have made them the conduits of evil, and that another principal must exist that has created the evil world in which we live, and 'tis this principal that leads us to commit sins. To make God the bearer and giver of evil is ridiculous, yet that is the concept of the Roman Church, which we have shown to foist preposterous and fraudulent sacraments on people and bilk them out of their hard-earned possessions. Such a Church cannot be a force of good, and instead must be a force of evil." Benoit bowed his head and went back to his seat.

Dominic had risen during Benoit's summation, and now stepped forward. "The heretics assail the Mother Church, which has been in existence for more than twelve hundred years after the death and resurrection of Lord Jesus Christ. During this enormous span of time, the Holy Church has helped millions of people achieve salvation. You can see the monuments of our faith and good works in every village, town and city throughout Christendom. We stand on our achievements over time, and no amount of bluster and acrimony can alter the reputation of the Holy Church or its potential for salvation."

"Our heretical opponents have used quotations out of context to try to besmirch the core elements of our Holy Church: our dogma and our sacraments. You have heard us set the record straight, again and again. You also wot well that the majority of your countrymen are loyal, faithful members of this Holy Church. By their actions, they are

69

assuring their salvation in the same way as the generations who preceded them. If that isn't the ultimate good, then I don't know what is. Clearly, the Roman Church is a force for good."

Bernard de Vilanau stepped forward and shook Dominic's hand, then turned to the crowd.

"You have heard the arguments both for and against the proposition debated today, and you are the true arbiters of what was said here. On behalf of my colleagues, I would fain thank the representatives of the Church of the Friends of God and those of the Roman Church for having presented their points of view for the benefit of all who attended. Also, I must needs give special thanks to the Senhors of Montréal for having provided the venue. May you all return to your homes with the Lord's blessing."

As Vilanau finished speaking, people rose from their benches and created a hubbub as they spoke with their friends and neighbors.

Shuffling toward the castle gate with the rest of the crowd, Aude turned to Faye. "Think you not that our Good Men were marvelous? Methought they shamed the prelates."

"They did, I ween, but, alack, that Dominic had the last word."

"Aye, but methinks it failed to weaken the Good Men's arguments. How can any Catholic go away satisfied?" Aude said.

"Deem what you list," Faye answered, "but full sure am I that many still agree with the churchmen. Faith and logic are like oil and water."

"We must wait to see how 'twill fall out. Mayhap time will tell." Aude said. 'But the Roman prelates were at pains to make the Good Men look sackless and they utterly failed.

All our side had to do was to make a respectable case. And they did, by my troth!"

"Forsooth. Let's see how your son and daughter-in-law deem it went."

Fontfroide Abbey

Ruminating about his role in the debate earlier that day, Raoul decided to take a midnight turn in the cloister to clear his head before retiring. As he strolled, he noticed a faint glow coming from the cracks around the door to the library. Who could be there this late, he wondered.

Crossing the courtyard, he pushed the door open. At a table illuminated with two lamps and a candle, Brother Pascau sat bent over a page of parchment upon which he was writing.

Taking pains to make no noise, Raoul slipped up behind the monk. Raoul was aware of Pascau's task to copy the old scrolls and now and then had chatted with him about his progress. But what caught his eye was that the job was almost finished. Pascau was literally putting down the last few flourishes.

Raoul cleared his throat and Pascau jumped in his seat. "Sorry to have startled you, Brother, I was just passing by and thought I'd see how you are getting along. Is the job finished?"

Pascau rose hastily, and stood blushing before his senior colleague. "Aye, at this very moment." Could he continue to dissemble or should he tell Raoul the truth?

Raoul gestured to him to sit down. "Were you able to comprehend that strange language at the beginning of the original?" Pascau looked away and sat down heavily without answering. He looked sick. "Well, did you?" Raoul asked and folded his arms as he waited. He was contemplating tapping his foot, when Pascau finally spoke.

"Aramaic," he said, so softly that Raoul had to lean forward to catch it.

"Aramaic? Never heard of it," Raoul said. "Where does it come from?"

Pascau became more uneasy than ever. If Raoul took the scroll away now, the truth would soon come out. As he sat there, one of his knees began jiggling uncontrollably under the folds of his habit.

"Are you all right?" Raoul asked.

"Oh, yes, thank you, Brother," Pascau said, lifting his eyes to Raoul's. "Aramaic is a language spoken in the Holy Land when Our Lord Jesus walked the earth. And this scroll records the births and deaths of a family that goes all the way back to the time of the Gospels."

"That long ago? What family could possibly be that important?"

Pascau looked down at the parchment and slowly shook his head. "The family of Mary Magdalene," he said in a cracked voice without looking up. His knee was jerking so hard that he feared his sandal would start tapping the floor.

Dumbfounded by what he heard, Raoul stared at the monk open-mouthed. When he recovered the power of speech, he said. "The Magdalene of the Gospels? Then who -- who in the world was her husband?"

Pascau rose from his stool and placed his palms together as if in prayer.

"I fain would spare you this. But someday, some other scholar will find out the truth. The husband was Jesus. *Jesus Christ!*"

Raoul believed he hadn't heard right. "Did you say Jesus Christ, our Lord and Savior?"

"That is correct."

"This is a list of his descendants?"

"Yes."

Raoul tried to imagine the ramifications of this information, but gave up after a few fearful moments. "You realize what this means, don't you?"

Studying the floor at his feet, Pascau nodded.

"Sit back down, Brother Pascau. Does anyone in the monastery know about this?'

"No, not a soul.

"Good. You are not to tell a soul, on pain of...on pain of dismissal or worse, do you understand?"

Pascau nodded.

As he watched Pascau roll up the parchments and place them inside a quiver, Raoul's mind was racing ahead: how would he break the news to Peire Castelnau? One thing was certain; he would be relieved to share the responsibility with someone else.

"Do you have them under lock and key?" Raoul asked.

"Forsooth. I wear the key around my neck."

"Good! Brother Peire will be here tomorrow so I will want to show them to him.

"I shall have them ready." Pascau genuflected, and Raoul answered in kind, then turned on his heel and strode to the door and let himself out.

Pascau sank down and breathed a sigh of relief. Raoul had never examined the original set, thus it was possible that he could pass off the copy that he had so painstakingly "aged" as the original, which he had given to Olivier for delivery to the goldsmith. A month earlier he had made the first copy. Now he had to convince the two legates that one of the fake sets of scrolls was authentic.

At twilight the day after leaving Fanjaus, Olivier and Micaela rode through the massive gates of Besièrs, and Olivier found a room at an inn and a stable for the horses. During the journey, Olivier had pondered what he would say to the goldsmith when he returned the scrolls. There was the slight chance that the man would not believe him and hold him responsible for the theft, but once the scrolls were in his hands again, how could he complain? Olivier decided that the easiest approach would be to tell the truth.

After making sure Micaela was comfortable, he asked the innkeeper for directions to the goldsmith's shop, and a few minutes later, found himself standing before the door, the quiver of scrolls in his hand. After a slight hesitation, he knocked. Through the door, he heard footsteps approaching.

A woman opened the door. From under a cap, jet-black curls framed a pretty face with enormous blue eyes.

"Yes?" she asked. "May I help you, sir?"

Expecting the smith, Olivier was momentarily flustered. "I – uh – I'm looking for Senhor Ravanel. I have – uh -- something for him. May I speak with him?"

The woman's eyes fell upon the quiver in his hand, with the brown edges of parchment peeking out, and she took a step backward, her face blanched with apprehension. "Who are you?" she blurted, "what do you want?"

"My name is Olivier de Mazan and I've come into possession of something that belongs to Senhor Ravanel that I fain would return to him. Is he here?"

"I'm his wife. He's not here but I expect him any moment." She frowned suspiciously and nodded toward the quiver. "How did you…where did you …er…find it?"

Olivier's fear of being mistaken for a thief seemed justified, and he blushed. "'Twas bought by a monastery outside of Narbona. From the latest entries, we surmised that it belongs

75

to you and your husband. We deemed 'twas dear to you, so I've brought it back."

"Dear?" she exclaimed. "You have no idea what we've been through. My husband is almost out of his mind." She tried unsuccessfully to blink back tears, and one or two ran down her cheeks.

"I'm terribly sorry, and I can imagine how painful it has been for you. That's why I wanted give it back to you as soon as possible. I never…"

"What's going on here?" boomed a voice behind him in the street. Olivier wheeled, and found he was facing a man of his own height, wearing a broad-brimmed hat and a long mantel over his tunic. The man was staring with astonishment at the quiver in Olivier's hand.

"Where…?" he shook his head in wonder.

"The gentleman says he got it from a thief," the wife said.

"I take it you are Senhor Ravanel…" Olivier said. The man nodded, eyes still fixed on the quiver with its precious contents. "…in which case I believe this belongs to you." He handed Ravanel the quiver.

Ravanel took it and looked at his wife in the doorway, flooded in tears. Turning back to Olivier, he said," please Senhor, please come in. I cannot begin to tell you what this means to us." Putting his arm around his wife, he led them inside.

He gestured at a stool by a table. "Please have a seat, while I put this away," he said, and disappeared into the other room. His wife opened a cupboard and brought out a pitcher and set it on the table.

Sitting across from the Ravanels, a beaker of cider in his hand, Olivier recounted the details of how the scrolls had come into his possession, and then told the couple how the thief, who had no idea of its contents, had been warned to stay away from Besièrs on pain of death.

"Had the ecclesiastical authorities learned what the scrolls contain, 'twould have meant our death warrant. 'Tis why we were so frightened when it disappeared. In the wrong hands…" Ravanel's voice trailed off, and he drew a finger across his throat.

"Belike it has occurred to you that 'tis a huge liability, no matter where you hide it? Bethought you never to simply burn it?"

"Of course, but then I think how painstakingly it has been kept up and preserved over all these years, and I can't bring myself to do it."

"I agree," Ruth said, her eyes glowing, "I can't imagine anything as precious as these records. We owe it to our ancestors, even if it remains a secret."

There was a loud knock on the door.

Ravenel stood. "Excuse me, good sir, belike an impatient customer." And he went to the door and slid back the cover of the peephole.

At that instant, the door shook with two heavy blows, and a voice cried "Open up!"

Ravenel slammed the cover shut, and turned to his wife and Olivier. His face was drained of color. "'Tis a monk with some men from the watch."

"Is there another way out?" Olivier asked, looking around the room.

"No," Ravenel answered, and bit his lip.

Two more thunderous knocks were followed by a shout. "If you don't open up, we will break it down."

"Let them in," Olivier said. "'Twill go better if we do."

Ravanel slid back the iron bolt, and opened the door. Two red-faced watchmen wielding cudgels gaped at them and then stepped inside. A monk emerged from behind them.

Olivier recognized him immediately. It was Peire de Castelnau.

"Which one of you is Ravenel?" Castelnau said, looking from Ravanel to Olivier and back. "I have a warrant to arrest you for the possession of stolen goods." He waved a leaf of parchment in their faces.

Olivier stepped in front of the goldsmith. "Who are you? What are you talking about? Let me see that warrant."

The watchmen leveled their cudgels at Olivier. "Back off," said one, a burly man with black hair peeking out from under his cap.

For an instant, Olivier imagined wresting the cudgel away from one and knocking the other weapon out of the other's hand before they knew what was happening, but he stayed his hand and took a small step back. "I repeat. What does the warrant say? On whose authority have you entered this shop?"

"My name is Brother Peire de Castelnau. I am a legate of His Holiness the Pope. The warrant says that this... this *Jew* possesses an ancient scroll that was stolen from the Abbey of Frontfroide. But who are you to question the authority of a deputy of the Holy See?"

"My name is Olivier de Mazan and Master Ravenel has commissioned me to buy back some scrolls from Brother Pascau of Fontfroide. He had unwittingly bought the scrolls from the thief who stole them from Mr. Ravenel in the first place. I just returned them to their rightful owners a few minutes ago."

"I know nothing about any theft except the one that took place at Frontfroide," Castelnau said. "Now, stand aside."

"If I can prove that the scrolls belong to Mr. Ravenel, will you leave us in peace?"

"Perhaps, but how could you possibly do that?"

"What if Brother Pascau tells you how the scrolls came into his possession?"

"Brother Pascau cannot do that."

"Why?"

"He's dead. Fell into a well and drowned, God rest his soul."

Olivier winced at the news. Healthy young men like Pascau did not fall into wells. The bastards were committing murder! "I warn you, Sir Legate," Olivier said, "I'm not without resources or influence. If you insist on legal niceties, I will truss you up with so many attainders you'll think you're a Christmas goose. This isn't Montpelhier, where your Church runs the city. 'Tis Besièrs, where my relatives number among the consuls. Unless your warrant is signed by the secular authorities, 'tis an extravagant waste of ink and paper."

"You dare threaten a legate of the Holy See? Do you have any idea how difficult I can make your life?"

"Stop posturing and show me the warrant."

Castelnau's eyes narrowed, and his jaw worked. "You insolent swine, I know your kind all too well. You haven't seen the last of me, I can assure you;" Passing through the door, he called to his two retainers. "Come, let's be gone from this foul nest of enemies of Christ. and breathe the Lord's clean air again!." The watch men stomped on out. after him.

Although thankful to be rid of the monk, Olivier realized that he had only increased the danger to the Ravenels. When he got back home safe and sound in Provença, who was to prevent Castelnau from threatening or even harming the Ravenels, with their young children? He thought of his own daughters and how he would react if *their* lives were threatened.

He ran into the street and called out to Castelnau, "Wait. Senhor Legate! Wait!"

Castelnau was mounting his horse, but took his foot out of the stirrup as Olivier caught up with him.

"I lied," Olivier told him. "I had the scrolls in my mantle all along." Out of the corner of his eye, he could see the astonishment in the Ravanel's faces. "I will part with it only on one condition: you must give me your sacred word that from this day forward you and your Church will not harass the Ravanels. Otherwise, I'll tell the authorities that you were harassing citizens with a bogus warrant. Then mayhap you will be able to tell us what kind of air you breathe in a dungeon!"

He reached into his mantle and pulled a bulging quiver out of his pocket and waved it in front of Castelnau's nose. "Swear, or else be gone."

Castelnau's eyes blazed with fury, but he swore, under pain of hell's fury, that he would never visit the Ravanels again, and that no one from the Roman Church would ever disturb them again. When he finished, Olivier slapped the quiver in Castelnau's hand.

"Take the cursed parchments and get out of here and stay out! We don't like meddling prelates!"

Castelnau glowered and his jaw worked, then he swung into the saddle and rode away. When the prelate had gone, Olivier turned to face the bewildered couple. "'Twas a copy," he said, "a very clever copy made by a dear friend of mine but your names are not on it. He paid with his life. They probably tortured him to reveal your names before they killed him. Castelnau never saw the original, so I'm full sure 'twill fool him. He was obviously bluffing about the warrant, so I believe you'll be safe now." Olivier didn't add that he believed he had made a relentless enemy.

Mazan

From the arrow slits high up on the wall, two sun beams filled with motes of dust played on the table around which a dozen men were debating the best way to handle their liege lord, Count Raimond VI of Tolosa, who ruled the March of Provença, where all of them dwelt. As host of the meeting, Olivier nevertheless found he was at odds with the opinions of most of his guests, who were Roman Catholics. Indeed, five of them were members of the League of Provença, a group of nobles who wanted to purge the region of Cathars. The others, like Olivier, either found fault with the Count's high-handed treatment of his Provençal vassals, or were kindred with Baron Hugue of Les Baux, an implacable foe of the Tolosan dynasty

Olivier believed they could persuade Raimond to improve relations with his vassals to the benefit of all concerned, but Azalbert of Vaison, who had been nervously grinding his teeth, saw otherwise: "'Tis high time we stood up to this tyrant and taught him a lesson. He's sacked our Bishop and now, by my troth, he would fain *tax* us! 'Tis one thing to pay tithes to the Church, but pay them to our lord? He's mad!"

"He did the same in Carpentras," Amaldric of Venasque exclaimed, throwing up his hands. "Why does the Church let him get away with such antics? Old Gregory must be turning in his grave."

"Raimond's insecure and jealous of our privileges." Olivier looked around the table from one face to another. "He's still smarting from our refusal to support him in his wars with Trencavel. Surely 'tis understandable. When all is said and done, he's still our lord, after all, and we're his vassals. By opposing him, we're breaking our feudal contract."

"Rubbish! He's in the wrong, and won't admit it," Rotger de la Sorgue put in. "Besides, the Church has a host of wrongs they could charge him with, and to say truth, I see not what they are waiting for."

"Why wait for the Church?" Amaldric cried. "Are we paralyzed? The next time he sends his seneschal with those wild Aragonese mercenaries to collect taxes, let's teach 'em a lesson. That might make him see the light."

"But then he might raise an army against us." Olivier said. "Methinks the taxes are not that high. By my troth, is it really worth risking your life in such a petty feud?"

"Surely you're not afraid to fight, are you, Mazan? 'Tis a matter of principle, I trow, and if we let him ride rough shod over us, we will much sorrier in the long run," Amaldric said .

"'Tis a matter of principle, forsooth, and that's why we should present him with our grievances," Olivier answered. "We should try to reason with him, not attack him. He has the means to overpower us if we make war. Why risk lives, when we might be able to persuade him to drop his demands?"

"Because our letters have gone unanswered," said Germail of Courthezon, "and because he sends all those mercenaries to dun us. He resorts to force to make us pay. Therefore, we refuse to pay by fighting back, as Amaldric says. Count Raimond deems he can overpower us one at a time, but we can surprise him with a concerted effort."

There were murmurs of agreement around the table. "Am I the only dissenting voice?" Olivier said. He waited for a reply but none came. "Then I accede to the wishes of the majority in the spirit of unity." As he sat listening to their plans to resist their liege lord with force, he pondered the folly of it all. Why do men back away from negotiating their differences and prefer to solve them with brute and, often, lethal force? Is life so worthless, that you risk it for pride's sake? He shook his head in disbelief.

Olivier told Micaela about the League's decision made in Vaison, and she immediately voiced her opposition to his participating in any military action against the Count's men.

"If you disagree with them, 'tis not your affair, I trow. To risk your life for stupid decisions made by cousins twice removed is incomprehensible to me. Would they do it for you?" Micaela arched her eyebrows.

"We're not discussing *them*. 'Tis me. Me and my *paratge*. Even if they're mistaken, I've no choice. They are my kinsmen."

"Yes, and if they had your sense of *paratge*, they would insist on fighting the Count *without* your help. Either that, or they could abandon the dim-witted idea, as you say you suggested."

"Do you doubt my word?" He tried to control an unexpected surge of anger.

"No, but sometimes people embellish their stories. 'Tis only natural."

"Mayhap, but I *did* disagree and as I told you, I was the *only* one who did so! And I used the very same arguments you're making." He glared at her.

She met his eyes without flinching. "Then if 'tis so, all the more reason not to take part in it."

"How can I? They'd accuse me of cowardice!"

"But why? Clearly, you disagreed. If so, then why in the world go along with them? I just don't understand!"

"I wot well you can't. And nothing I say can change your mind. That is clear." He shrugged, and shook his head.

She held his gaze with her eyes. "If you really love me, you won't take part in this witless struggle."

"I love you more than words can say."

She tossed her head and left the room.

Olivier peered through the blades of grass at the distant horsemen approaching on the road ahead. Lying on the bank of a sunken cattle trail that met the road thirty or so paces away, he could see they were carrying the blood red shields of Tolosa. To his right, where the trail debouched into the road, three crossbowmen lay prone on the grassy bank, their weapons trained on the riders advancing toward them at a trot.

Behind Olivier, a straggle of dismounted knights and squires stood in the swale, holding the reins of their horses and awaiting the signal to mount and start the attack. Some of them—those farthest away from him – were going to ride up over the bank and take the enemy in the flank. Those closest to him would deliver a frontal assault straight down the road. It was a simple plan, and, depending how poorly trained the seneschal's men were, it should succeed.

Olivier tried to focus on the oncoming riders, hoping to overcome the trembling he could feel in his arms and legs. What was wrong, he wondered. Was he afraid? For a brief moment, he worried if he would turn tail and let down his comrades, but then he remembered a veteran's advice: "hit 'em as hard as you can the very first time and again and again and you'll prevail."

When he could make out the distinctive cross of Tolosa on the lead horseman's surcoat, he knew the moment had come and sprang down into the dry stream bed where his horse was cropping. Vaulting into the saddle, he seized his lance and waved it over his head. "*Por lo Comtat.*" he cried and spurred his horse into a canter. "Shoot to kill," he yelled as he rode behind the crossbowmen. At the intersection, he leaned into the turn and urged his courser into a gallop as the crossbows twanged on his left. Up ahead, a riderless horse veered off into the fields, while another reared and bucked, its rider struggling for control. A third rider shied away from the plunging horse. Olivier leveled his lance and went for him.

Seeing Olivier bearing down on him, the knight lifted his shield to protect his head and upper body, but Olivier's lance went under the shield and hit the Tolosan in the pelvis, knocking him out of the saddle and under the hooves of the milling horses. The momentum of the charge slammed Olivier's mount into that of another Tolosan mercenary and both horses staggered from the collision.

Dropping the lance, Olivier drew his sword and using both hands, swung hard at the Tolosan, who had just lifted his own. Olivier's blow knocked the sword out of the man's hand, and Olivier's backswing would have severed the man's arm just above the elbow had it not been covered in chain mail. As it was, the man howled and fell out of the saddle. All around him, Olivier's comrades engaged the Tolosans in a melee of lance thrusts, sword sweeps, and axe blows.

The flank attack had routed some of the Tolosans, but others were resisting ferociously. Olivier was working his horse toward the thick of the fight, when voices shouted, "We give up! Mercy! Enough!" The clang of steel on steel stopped along with the outcries, and there was a sudden silence. The Tolosans had dismounted and knelt, holding their swords hilt-first to the Provençals. The fighting was over almost before it began. The ambush had been a success.

Turning to pace back across the vaulted refectory, Arnaud-Amaury stopped and studied the stone wall just inches away. The masons had cut the smooth stone blocks so expertly that the mortar could hardly be seen. Placing his cheek against the wall, he sighted along the joints between the blocks that ran straight as an arrow. Uniformity, the miracle of uniformity, he marveled. If only he could achieve such precise and dependable results in trying to eliminate heresy in the Midi!

Although proud of his organizational skills as the leader of the Cistercian Order, he was chagrined at his failure to bring heretics back to the fold. He had known all along that those efforts were doomed, yet nevertheless he had hoped that – on a small scale – it would be a success, given the number of monks he had assigned to the task. Instead, he was forced to face the ignominy of watching his discouraged friars abandon the mission, one after another, and come slouching back to the Abbey. Conversions back to the Holy Church had been pitifully few. Some monks had not succeeded in converting a single heretic. He pounded his fist against the wall. If only he could get his hands on those Cathar sodomites!

Resuming his pacing, he remembered warning his colleagues that the only real answer to the problem was a bloody one. Unless the Holy See preached a Crusade against these Cathar libertines, the heresy would continue to spread. That's why he had sent Castelnau to bait a trap that might just trigger the Crusade, especially if Raimond reacted violently, as one would expect him to do. On the other hand, if Raimond submitted to the demands of the Holy See, he – Arnaud-Amaury -- would be back on the pawn row, trying to open instead of checkmating the enemy.

Early that morning he had received a copy of Innocent's letter to Philip of France, promising the king and his vassals all the indulgences of a crusade if they would descend the Rose and strike the heretic vipers in their southern lairs. At last, Innocent was acting! But would that letter suffice to persuade the northern barons to take up the sword against people like themselves? The heretics were not Saracens or Moors. Furthermore, the Capets of France were at war with the Plantagenets of Aquitaine and England, and Phillipe, the King of France, had made it plain that he opposed a war on two fronts. Clearly, the Abbot swore under his breath, 'twas stalemate.

What was needed, he reflected, was a horrible outrage against the Church that could be pinned on Raimond; an event so appalling that it would rouse the French king from preoccupation with his strife with England and Aquitaine. Assassination of Pope Innocent would obviously be such a transgression, but would rob the anti-heresy movement of its greatest champion and spokesman. Perhaps the death of an archbishop or a cardinal would do the trick. Even, he shuddered, a papal legate such as himself, or Peter Castelnau, or the late Raoul.

Ah, poor Raoul, he mused, with a shake of his head. Raoul should never have involved himself with those scrolls. He had stumbled onto a secret the consequences of which were almost too dreadful to contemplate. Its revelations were so terrifying that even the pope should be shielded from its infamous calumnies. It would poison the very throne of Peter!

The thought of poison jerked his mind back to the day in July when he placed a vial of it along with a fat purse in the hands of a man he had hired to make sure that Raoul never revealed what he had learned in the scrolls. After Raoul's death, people said he died of the shaking ague. But, of course, it was not the ague, but a strong dose of nightshade. Come to think of it, what a shame that he hadn't arranged it to look like Count Raimond's work! Such a murder could have sparked the Crusade that would change everything. In that way, the Abbot sighed, he could have killed two birds with one stone.

He stopped pacing and stood stock still in his tracks. *Two birds with one stone*! By the Holy of Holies, why hadn't he thought of it before? He had let the opportunity slip! Damnation! Utter and endless hellfire and damnation! Then suddenly it came to him: Castelnau! His colleague, Peire Castelnau. What about *him*?

For months, Castelnau had received one death threat after another, and had grown so fearful that several times he had asked Arnaud-Amaury to be relieved of his duties. In fact, at this very moment, Castelnau was in hiding in Provença, ostensibly organizing the League with which they would entrap Raimond. If Castelnau were to meet a violent end, Count Raimond would be the prime suspect, given his persistent and highly public antagonism toward the legate.

It was common knowledge that the Count hated Castelnau for having excommunicated him, and had not only failed to conceal his rancor against the legate but had broadcast it far and wide for all to hear. Arnaud-Amaury scratched his tonsure. The situation bore an uncanny resemblance to the legendary standoff between Henry II of England and Archbishop Becket only forty years before. If Castelnau was a marked man, no one would be surprised if he met a violent end.

Moreover, Castelnau was the only other person besides himself who knew the secret of the scrolls! Arnaud-Amaury felt his hair stand on end. *Two birds with one stone*! He smacked a fist into the palm of his other hand. By God, if Castelnau's death could be blamed on Raimond, it would be the provocation the pope had been waiting for! 'Twas as sure as sunrise. As for himself, he would not only become the clerical leader of the Crusade, but at the same time, he would become the only clergyman in all Christendom who possessed the secret of the scrolls. That knowledge could give him immense power. As the dogma disintegrated and the church hierarchy fell apart, he could become a new St. Paul. A founder of the successor church!

And Castelnau? He had long been a burr under the saddle. He had sought to advance himself in the eyes of the Holy See at Arnaud-Amaury's expense. Well, now Castelnau could achieve the pinnacle of service to his church by donning the mantle of a martyr in the eyes of the pope and the rest of Christendom. It was far too good for the sniveling bastard, Arnaud-Amaury conceded, but sometimes one has to put aside personal prejudice to promote the general good, which was the ruthless eradication of heresy throughout the Midi.

Impatient to get his hands on the scrolls, he had told Castelnau to bring them to Citeaux for safe keeping. But the more he pondered, the more he became suspicious of Castelnau's intentions. After all, Castelnau had more reason to distrust *him*, than vice versa. What if Castelnau took the scrolls to the Pope? Ah, that was a nasty thought, and wouldn't at all be surprising! That is why, Arnaud-Amaury decided, he must act quickly and decisively. He knew a squire in Beaucaire who could do the deed. The assassin would be wearing the arms of Tolosa, so the crime would be blamed on Count Raimond. Two birds with one stone!

As for the scrolls, he would bribe a bodyguard to make sure that if anything "happened" to the legate, God forbid, the scrolls must be delivered to Citeaux where a large reward would be waiting.

There was a spring in his step as Arnaud-Amaury went to change out of his clerical garments. Whether or not the Castilians succeeded in converting any heretics, he was full sure that the spiritual and material conquest of the Midi was possible. But first, just as he arranged for Raoul's demise, he must proceed with exquisite caution in bringing about the end of his other colleague. It was, of course, absolutely imperative that the murder not be traced back to that pillar of the Church, the Abbot of Citeaux.

Mazan

For weeks, Olivier had been aware that Castelnau was in the Comtat, making the rounds of the barons who comprised the membership of the League of Provença, most of whom were acquaintances, if not friends or kinsmen, of Olivier's. Dead set against the mission of the League, the only purpose of which was to put an end to the Church of the Friends of God, Olivier did not attend any of its meetings. However, as a frequent visitor to the various noble households, he had access to their servants, who were not adverse to accepting a coin or two for information about the papal legate. Did they ever see him carrying a quiver? What about scrolls?

Olivier was convinced that Castelnau, who was constantly on the move, did not keep the scrolls in some secret hideaway, but kept them close to his person, in a mantle pocket, or a saddle bag. At the castle of Almaric of Les Barreaux, his diligence was rewarded. Not only had the servant seen the quiver, but he had also seen Castelnau poring over some old, heavily discolored scrolls. This was an enormously important breakthrough, Olivier knew. But how to get hold of the scrolls was decidedly a horse of a different color.

St. Gilles

Count Raimond was clearly upset, when he met with his council. Pope Innocent had appealed to Philip Augustus, the King of France, to lead a Crusade against the heretics in the Midi. Apparently, the pontiff had decided that the efforts of his legates and those of the two Spanish prelates had failed to stop the inroads of the Cathars and that only armed intervention by French knights could resolve the issue. Innocent promised that those who took the cross would profit from the same indulgences as those who fought in the Holy Land. Infinitely worse, the Innocent had sent copies of the letter to his major vassals, offering up Raimond's fiefdoms as part of the spoils of war.

He scowled as he paced the floor awaiting the arrival of the loathsome Castelnau, whom he had invited to Mirapetra, his elegant castle in St.Gilles, the traditional seat of his dynasty. He was prepared to accept the legate's terms to lift the excommunication that cast him as the enemy of the Church and hence fair game for the prospective Crusade. The trick was to be able to salvage as much of his political independence as possible, while submitting to scourging by the Church, which was clearly seeking his humiliation as well as fomenting dissension among his barons. He bowed his head in desperation. His options had largely dried up.

A page came up to him and bowed. "The legates have arrived, your Highness."

"Legates?" He scratched his head. "I was expecting but one, Brother Castelnau of Frontfroide.

"He's accompanied by the Bishop of Couserans, as well as the Abbot of St. Gilles, Sire."

Raimond groaned. He would have to put up with three of these clerical jackals. "Have the chamberlain show them in," he said and sat down on the gilded throne that he had commissioned years before. He waved to the courtiers who surrounded him "Please, my good brethren, take your seats. We will await the Church mice together. I am afraid I must give them some crumbs to make them go away."

As Raimond crossed his legs and nervously stroked the carved knobs of the armrests, a rumble of conversation broke out among the vassals, but that did not distract his ruminations. If only he could arrange a solution like the one his father-in-law, Henry II of England, achieved with that old troublemaker, Archbishop Beckett. Who didn't know the famous line spoken by Henry, "Who will rid me of this meddlesome priest?" Who indeed? Who could ever forget the story of how the Archbishop was cut down at the very altar of his Cathedral? And yes, four years later, Henry wore sackcloth as he was scourged through the streets of Canterbury, but emerged more powerful than ever for the rest of his reign. *Good Lord, sweet Jesus, let history be repeated with the despicable Castelnau,* Raimond prayed.

His reverie was broken by the chamberlain's thin voice announcing the presence of the clergymen. He tried to stare Castelnau down, but it was he himself who finally yielded and looked away.

"Ah, brother Castelnau, how nice to see you looking so well. I must admit I had rather hoped that you had come down with leprosy." He watched Castelnau wince. "Just joking, of course," Raimond said, forcing a grin.

"And welcome to you, too, my Lord Bishop," he said, nodding to Couserans. "I am delighted to see you again. It's been several years, hasn't it? And you, Sir Abbot—what a pleasure to renew acquaintance with my neighbor to whom my family generously bestowed the very Abbey that you administer."

"I would fain settle the matter that has ruined my life over the last few months," he continued, turning back to

94

the legate. "I would fain get back in the good graces of the Eternal Church. What must I do to accomplish that?"

Castelnau coughed and cleared his throat. "Shall we begin with the proximal cause of your excommunication? By refusing to join the League of Provença, which was formed to eradicate heresy in your marquisate, you broke the Peace of God. I enjoin you to reconsider that decision."

"If I do, will the interdict be lifted?"

Castelnau shrugged, but his face was immobile. "Other transgressions must be rectified as well."

"Such as?"

"Sire, we have gone over all this before. You wot well the charges against you. Use of foreign mercenaries against your own people. Giving public offices to Jews. Pillaging monasteries; converting churches into fortresses; violating the feast days. Et cetera!"

"But I've been highly generous in my donations to the Church. Surely that should count in my favor?" Raimond was clearly annoyed.

"What good are those alms, when you despoiled churches in Espeyran and Sieurre; pillaged those of Casissargues and Estagel; hounded the bishops of Vaison and Agen out of office; imprisoned the Abbots of Moissac and Montauban, and confiscated goods from the bishoprics of Rodez and Cahors? 'Tis not a balance sheet in some ledger." Castelnau frowned and shook his head.

Raimond leaned forward in his throne. "'Tis no business yours or the pope's, for that matter, where I procure my troops. I see no ecclesiastic violation whatsoever. Are you quoting canon law, or are you just trying to load the dice? As for appointing Jews to public office, I have yet to see any proclamation from the bishopric, let alone from the Holy See, forbidding such action. Am I supposed to be a mind reader?"

Castelnau's face was impassive. "I am not here to argue with you, my lord. I was led to believe that you had made up your mind to throw yourself on the mercy of the Holy Church and were ready to accept the various forms of penitence that you must undergo to absolve the anathema. I see I was mistaken."

The Count flushed with indignation. "I am indeed throwing myself on your mercy, Sir Legate, in hope that you will lessen the charges against me. I am extremely anxious to get back into your good graces."

"If so, simply accept our terms for restitution and we can proceed."

"What about the charges I asked you to drop?"

"I'm sorry, Sire, the charges and the penitence are not negotiable."

"But how it that possible? Bethought you that I would acquiesce to every silly and capricious whim of yours? I fail to comprehend how you dare come here and spout such puke." Raimond looked at his courtiers and shook his head in disbelief.

"I came at your bidding, my lord." Castelnau said quietly. "'Tis not a question of daring. I accepted an invitation. And the wording of the charges comes from the Holy See Itself and therefore cannot be categorized as puke."

Raimond shrugged. "Well, you see how mistaken I was. Methought we could make amends. I am perfectly willing to pay for any damages my people may have inflicted on the monasteries you mention. Similarly, I could fund the restoration of the few churches I fortified. And I would use my mercenaries to hunt down heretics. But the League of Provença? I could never join that pit of vipers. They are my sworn enemies."

"Then you make yourself the sworn enemy of God in the eyes of the Holy Church. And that's the message I'll take to His Holiness."

"You concede nothing?"

"That is correct. 'Tis not up to me; 'tis you who must concede."

"Hell will freeze over before I do that."

"Then Heaven's doors will be shut to you for eternity, Sire. I fully rue that we could not persuade you to come back to the fold, but there appears to be no purpose to our tarrying any longer. We must needs take our leave."

Raimond rose to his feet. "You will leave when I want and not before! Now that you're here, I want to resolve this matter." Raimond glowered at the churchman.

"Am I then a prisoner?"

"No, forsooth. But I will not allow you to dictate how I manage secular affairs in my possessions. You have no authority here. If I employ foreign mercenaries or assign certain civil positions to Jews, that is none of the Church's business, let alone yours. Moreover, I have been a generous contributor to the Church as you wot well; methinks it should credit me for that. I admit responsibility for damage and alterations to a few monasteries and churches for which I am only too willing to compensate you. I will admit disturbing the peace on Holy days, and I will also pay compensation for that. If you are holding me to the oath I made last year to suppress heretics, then I will do so and do it with my own resources. However, as I've told you repeatedly, I will not join the League of Provença. I have no need of your so-called League. What is so special about the League?

"The League is made up of men..."

"...who seek to overthrow me and usurp my role as their lawful lord!" Raimond interrupted.

"…who are dedicated to ridding Provença of the Cathars." Castelnau made no sign that he had heard Raimond's interruption.

"Has any member of the League ever succeeded in converting a single Cathar? Have they?" Raimond laughed scornfully. "Good God, man, I have the very resources you need to banish the heretics. I'm even offering them to you. But my oath doesn't include joining that blasted League! Last month, some of those bastards ambushed my seneschal and killed two of his knights and wounded five others. 'Tis you who are aiding and abetting rebels and terrorists. Talk of the Peace of God! You should choke on those words!"

"The Holy Church does not see it that way," Castelnau said, and folded his arms across his chest. "In its eyes, you have waged war against some of the few vassals in your domains who are pledged to fight the heretics. Hence, you are guilty of lese-majesty against the Holy See itself, which is the equivalent of treason."

"There you go, spouting legalistic clap-trap at me. I waged war with no one. On the contrary, my men were attacked by a horde of rebellious vassals who have broken the feudal contract and behave like common outlaws."

"My lord, I did not come here to dispute with you. I came here to…"

"You came here to trick me, to entrap me!" Raimond flushed with anger. "Don't think you can pull the wool over my eyes, I know your game. I know your sort…"

"I bid you farewell, my Lord. You are beyond all hope of redemption." Castelnau spun on his heel and walked back toward the door.

Raimond stood up and glared after him. "If you weren't a prelate, I'd spill your guts on the floor," he bawled, shaking a fist at Castelnau's back. "Get you gone and tell your wretched master that he can send all of France against me. I will have crosses waiting on which to nail each and every one of the invaders. If somehow you survive to look on his Holiness -- and with your infamous reputation, I wouldn't give a sol for your miserable life for as long as you tread my land -- tell him what I say!" Raimond stamped his foot on the floor, and flung himself back in his chair, where he threw his head back and stared at the ceiling.

The bishop and the abbot gaped at each other, nodded quickly to Raimond, and hurried after their fellow prelate.

In the dwindling twilight, Olivier caught sight of Peire Castelnau, mounted on a mule and moving down the road at a walk with his small bodyguard. Olivier waited until the legate's party had proceeded several hundred paces before setting out to follow them. They had gone two leagues, when night fell, and as they approached the ferry dock on the Rose, a faint light streamed from a small inn nestled at the water's edge.

From the cover of some willows, Olivier watched while Castelnau conversed with the ferryman, who finally shrugged and walked away toward the inn. Apparently, the waterman didn't want to chance the fast-moving river in the dark. Most of the bodyguard followed him into the inn, while three others led the mounts to the stable. Before turning over his mule to them, Castelnau detached his saddle bags and carried them inside himself.

Olivier waited until the legate's party had gone into the inn, and then approached the hostler and paid for a stall.

He purchased a bushel of hay for his horse, and propping himself in a corner, tried to stay awake to make sure he didn't miss the churchmen when they left in the morning.

At some time, he dozed off, and awoke to the bustle of horses and men. Looking up through the stable door, he saw the evening star. Dawn had not broken, but Castelnau and his entourage were up and getting ready to cross the river at sunrise. All the horses were saddled, and Olivier noticed that the saddle bags had been put back on the mule. As the mounts were drinking water in the shallows, the ferryman emerged from the inn and began to haul the shallow-draft craft as close to the shore as possible to help board the animals. He heaved a wide platform made of two heavy planks onto the inshore gunwale and began telling the men how he wanted them to get the mule and the horses aboard.

Watching from afar as the party stood listening to the ferryman, Olivier was suddenly conscious of movement behind his back, and turned to see a horseman approaching at a trot. In the growing light, he saw the Occitan cross on the man's blood-red surcoat. As he swept by, the rider spurred his horse into a gallop.

"Castelnau!" the horseman cried. As the legate turned around, the rider leaned forward and thrust a lance through the churchman's middle. Castelnau staggered and fell back into the water, his head thumping against the gunwale of the boat as the horse splashed on into the river. By the time the guards recovered from the shock and jumped forward to pull the dying man out of the shallows, the rider had wheeled and was galloping away back up the road toward Beaucaire. In spite of the murderer's head start, three of the bodyguards caught their horses reins and sprang into the saddle in hot pursuit.

While the others huddled around the fallen legate, hotly disputing how to remove the lance, Olivier edged over to the mule and snuck a hand into the saddle bag. His fingers felt a familiar cylinder and screening the bag with his body, he pulled out the quiver full of scrolls and stuck it inside his mantel and under his belt. Looking back at the ferry, he saw the guards still crouching over Castelnau. Mounting his horse, he rode away at a walk. He had never imagined it would be this easy! Or that the legate would have to pay for it with his life. If everything turned out well, none of the scrolls, whether original or copies, would ever fall into the hands of the Holy See.

Part II

Before stepping into the audience room, Lottario dei Conti de Signi glanced at the mirror resting on the console that stood in the anteroom of the papal quarters. The bland face of a scholar, looking younger than his forty-eight years, stared back at him. His graying dark brown hair was largely hidden by the gold-thread-embroidered white cap he was wearing, but his earnest brown eyes framed a straight nose, a high forehead and round cheeks. His lips were full over a chin that he wished was a little stronger, but was by no means weak. He liked what he saw and he knew that it was a useful asset for the diplomacy in which he constantly engaged. It was a face that one could trust, evoking neither a stuffy prelate nor a wily advocate, and he was certain he would have reached the top of the legal profession had he not taken the episcopal path.

And now, here he stood, Pope Innocent III — "the vicar of Christ" in his own words--head of the Roman Church and certainly the ultimate arbiter in the western world! With a highly trained legal mind and years of working with canon law, he was certain that he had no peer in the ecclesiastic hierarchy, and not because he had ascended to Peter's throne. His self-confidence stemmed from his rich experience in the field of secular politics, where he had found few strong leaders, and where he now had ten solid years of positive achievements behind him. A man in his prime. A leader. Someone to whom virtually everyone deferred.

Of course, there had been challenges to his authority and power. The frown that now appeared in the mirror reminded him of the days following his investiture ten years before. Emperor Frederick had proved to be predictably contentious, but, in the end, he had managed to curb Frederick's power and solidify the role of the Holy See in approving and crowning all future Emperors. He had even won back papal lands in Sicily that the Normans had seized fifty long years before and he supplied crusading armies to fight the Moors in Spain and in the Holy Land. Yes, he had taken the Emperor's measure.

Then he had tackled the serious erosion of Church authority throughout the Midi, where lazy, corrupt bishops and ignorant priests had allowed the Cathar heresy to breed under their very noses. The Cathars —so-called because of the alleged purity of their leaders who were known throughout the Midi as Good Men — did not believe in the Holy Trinity or in the sacraments of the Holy Church! They endangered the Church not only because of such doctrinal disputes, but because those who believed in Catharism stopped paying their tithes to the Holy Church, forcing it to trim its budget. Innocent winced at the thought. That was why he had recently discouraged those Spanish prelates from their idealistic mission to the Danish heathens. It was far better to have them concentrate on heresy close at home.

One of the critical obstacles to eradicating the Cathar heresy was the recalcitrant behavior of the Count of Tolosa, who was notoriously lax about suppressing heresy and whose feudal power spread over much of the Midi. Although one of Innocent's legates, Peire Castelnau, had excommunicated Raimond, the Count remained unrepentant, and Innocent had already spent almost two years trying unsuccessfully to persuade the King of France to lead a Crusade against Raimond and the heretical Midi. Absent some terrible act against the church or the king, Innocent's hopes had languished unfulfilled.

Then, as if in answer to his prayers, one of Raimond's henchmen murdered Castelnau—and almost miraculously, the French had triumphed in their war with England. To Innocent, both events seemed heaven-sent, for King Philip

Augustus finally agreed to organize a crusade against the southern heretics, led by his son, the twenty-year-old Dauphin. Never underestimate the power of a martyr, Innocent reflected. Pity it had to be poor Castelnau, who had deserved so much better!

With hordes of avaricious Frenchmen poised to invade and despoil his territories, and with no potential ally in sight, Raimond had caved in and hastened to reconcile himself with the Holy See. Innocent was not surprised. At long last, Raimond would have to humble himself and submit to papal authority. For weeks, Raimond's emissaries had been cooling their heels in Rome, but today the pontiff deemed it was time to give them an audience.

Winking at himself in the mirror, di Signi opened the door and strode toward a handful of clerics standing in wait, each clad in his distinctive robes of office. They all bowed and Innocent's secretary came forward.

"Your Holiness, may I present Lord Raimond de Rabastens, erstwhile Bishop of Tolosa, and his Excellency Bernard de Montaut, Archbishop of Auch. They seek an audience on behalf of Count Raimond of Tolosa." The two men, their faces drawn with anxiety, approached Innocent and fell on their knees before him.

"Delighted to see you," Innocent said, and extended his ring for the ritual kisses, "Word of your accomplishments has preceded you, and I welcome you to the Holy See and to Rome."

Innocent's broad smile was genuine. He knew that both men were clerical hacks, with little to commend them beyond high-flown rhetoric and much to condemn them; his own legates in the Midi had dismissed the Bishop for bribing his electors, and had asked the Archbishop to step down for his utter failure to control heresy. They were buffoons. However, instead of being piqued by the Count's choice of such dolts, Innocent was amused and fought to keep his face straight. So, this is the caliber of the ambassadors that Raimond sends to negotiate with me, he gloated. Methinks he grossly underestimates me.

Buoyed by Innocent's kind words and benevolent attitude, both ambassadors lifted their heads, their faces shining with pleasure and relief. Bidding them to rise, Innocent led them to a marble table where he urged them to sit, and beckoned to his secretary and the scribes to join them. Engaging the ambassadors with small talk, he elicited accounts of their previous visits to Rome before he became Pope, despite his curiosity about the message they would deliver.

Would the Count continue to writhe impotently, or had he at long last decided to throw himself onto the infinite mercy of the established Church and more specifically onto the conditional mercy of the erstwhile law student in Bologna who now reigned over kings and princes from the Throne of Glory? Nodding to the scribes, Innocent asked the Tolosans to explain the purpose of their visit.

Montaut rose from his seat and bowed low to the pope before he spoke. "Your most gracious and extreme Holiness, we are come to you at the behest of Lord Raimond, Count of Tolosa to communicate his ardent wish to accomplish whatever you may require of him that would enable him to return to your good graces and to be once more welcome in the Holy and universal Church and to receive its sacraments. He most humbly begs you to forgive him his trespasses, and assures you that he will rule in a manner consistent with your attested policies throughout his realm."

"As a token of his heartfelt worship of your person and your office, he would fain present the Mother Church with seven castles and the county of Melgueil. He also declares and promises to uphold the Church and its Elect and to aid its endeavor to root out heresy wherever it is found in his lands, as he has sworn to do. He deeply regrets that your legates perceived any actions of his as being contrary to his oath or hostile to your office."

Montaut paused and shot a nervous glance at his partner, who nodded almost imperceptibly. Licking his lips, Montaut resumed his speech. "In this connection, Count Ramond humbly begs your Holiness to indulge him in a boon that he weens would do much to further the joint efforts of the laity and the Church in his domains to fight the scourge of heresy. The Count has been dismayed to find that your Holiness's legate, his Excellency Arnaud-Amaury, has allowed personal feelings to intrude into his relationship with the Count to the extent where meaningful discourse has now become impossible. The Count fears that this lack of accord greatly hinders the coordination and cooperation necessary to execute your Holiness's policies. Such personal rancor may actually lead to your Holiness misconceiving the Count's words and actions."

"For this reason, Count Raimond humbly and respectfully implores your Holiness to replace the Abbot with a cleric less sanguine in temperament and more cordial in manners, one who is more interested in carrying out policy than in holding personal grudges. In the name of the Father, the Son and the Holy Spirit who watch over us all, and who have made your Holiness His voice on earth, we thank your Holiness for your great patience and tolerance." Montaut bowed deeply again and took his seat, and cast his eyes down into his lap.

Although Innocent's face remained implacable, he bristled at Count Raimond's audacity of offering to return the county of Melgueil in earnest of his pledge to eradicate heresy in the Midi. It was the Count who had seized churches and turned them into fortresses! It was the Count who had encouraged the people of Melgueil, a papal holding, to wrest it from the Holy See! The cheek of the fellow, acting as if the return of stolen goods was the same as a bonafide concession!

Indeed, it was totally understandable that Arnaud- Amaury behaved obstinately and with outrage against a prince who had not only broken his sacred oath, but whose personal involvement in the murder of Arnaud-Amaury's fellow legate had never been satisfactorily resolved. One could hardly blame the embattled legate for taking a hard line with a man suspected of ordering the murder of his partner and who might very well be plotting his own.

Yet on the whole, Innocent was well satisfied. Raimond had yielded, like an insect in a spider's web that, -- by its own convulsions -- becomes hopelessly entangled and finally gives up struggling. Like the spider, the pope could now proceed at deliberate speed, assured that the prey was at last subdued. "Your Graces and dear brothers in Christ," Innocent said, "I thank you for the pains you have taken in the name of his Highness Count Raimond and in the name of the Holy Trinity to bring me this message. You may rest assured that I will give it my full attention, given the gravity, as well as the promise, of its content. I implore you to accept the hospitality of the Holy See by supping with my Secretary this evening. I will give you my answer tomorrow at the same time, so that you can carry my answer back without protracted delay."

Innocent rose up from the table and proffered his hand as the two ambassadors knelt before him. They kissed his ring fervently. "Brother Guido will show you out," he said with a pontifical wave, "and I wish you a pleasant evening in our ancient, but holy city." One of the scribes bowed to the Tolosans and led them out through a massive door.

As the sound of their footsteps faded away, Innocent broke into laughter, and rubbed his hands together Performing a pirouette, he said to his secretary, "'tis like catching trout in a brook. Dangle your hand in the pool and let the fish become used to your caress, then snap, you've clutched your dinner! Now, Andreas, please ask the notary and the canon to step in and join us. And Antonio, please have some wine brought in because what follows may take some time."

Antonio and Andreas leaped up from the table and hurried away on their errands. In a matter of moments, Antonio had reappeared followed by two stewards bearing flagons of wine and glassware, and soon after, Andreas ushered in the apostolic notary Milo and the canon Thedesius.

After the two clergymen had genuflected to the Pontiff and taken their places at the table, Innocent cleared his throat. "I have asked you here, dear brothers in Christ, to consider performing a very important and delicate mission for me, a mission that will tax your well-known talents of tact and diplomatic maneuver. Count Raimond is ready to submit to our authority and this means --at the best -- that he will aid us in our endeavor to eradicate heretics in the Midi. At the worst, he will not interfere with the crusade as it unfolds.

"The purpose of your mission, your Excellencies, will be to ensure that Raimond will come around to actively support the Crusade and not go back to his old ways. He is not to be trusted, no matter how hard he may try to persuade you otherwise. 'Tis a difficult mission, because the more you make him feel at one with the Holy Church and its leaders, the more you must be vigilant against any backsliding on his part. And so to avoid confusion and to be consistent in our communications with Raimond, you will take orders from my senior legate, Abbot Arnaud-Amaury, with whom I have spent many days working out an intricate plan to make sure that Count Raimond complies with the wishes of the Holy See. Do I make myself clear?"

The two clerics assured Innocent that they were at Arnaud-Amaury's disposal, and would follow his commands to the letter.

"Once you get to Montpelhier," Innocent said, "the Abbot will expand on the specific roles you will play. He will make the decisions and you will be his agents. You will keep this chain of command confidential, because by the time you meet with him, Raimond will be under the impression that I have dismissed Arnaud-Amaury and that you have replaced him. 'Twill be essential to maintain this deception in order to gain Raimond's confidence." Innocent stared fixedly at both men before continuing.

"Let me reiterate my profound belief, shared by Arnaud-Amaury, that Count Raimond will not be brought to heel without the constant threat of war, and it will be your task, guided by the Abbot, to make sure he feels threatened even while you try to win his favor. This is no bluff, because regardless of whether or not Count Raimond submits and the excommunication is lifted, I am determined that the Crusade shall proceed. The Crusaders will crush the heretics and their protectors in the Trencavel domains, which will further isolate Raimond. 'Twill do more than anything else to cleanse the entire region of heretics, with or without Raimond's help. If he subsequently chooses to rebel again, he will do so alone against the might of the North." Innocent searched the faces of the two legates and took another sip of wine. "*Capice?*"

"*Capice!*" they cried.

"I have given some thought to the ceremony in which Raimond will submit to the Holy Church. We'll do it at the Abbey of St. Gilles, and we will humiliate him publicly, complete with flagellating his naked flesh. I shall give you the agenda to take to the Abbot. How say you? Will you take on this mission for me?"

"Your Holiness," said Milo, falling to his knees on the marble floor where he was joined by the canon, "we are overjoyed and bursting with pride that you have chosen us for this crucial mission. We will follow your advice to the letter and carry out your policies expeditiously and faithfully. Thank you for having given us the honor to serve your Holiness and the Holy Church."

When they had gone, Innocent rubbed his hands again and picking up his wine glass, clinked it against that of his secretary.

Andreas sipped his wine and set his glass down. "Your Holiness, what will befall if the Count takes the cross and joins the crusade?

Innocent, who again was sniffing the bouquet, put his glass down and ran one finger around its rim until it rang. "'Tis a very good question, Andreas. If he becomes a crusader, the French cannot seize his land and at the same time he will try to take over some of the Trencavel lands that he has long been coveting."

"Bethink you that he should so profit?"

"Andreas, as long as he cleans out the heretics in his realms, I don't give a fig what he does otherwise. As a man of the law yourself, you wot full well that we have no right over his domains or any that he may acquire as long as he cooperates with the Church. To say truth, I am delighted at the possibility that he will be an ally, especially since neither Philip nor his son is taking part in this crusade. That could mean trouble, I fear."

111

"Trouble, your Holiness? But surely the Duke of Burgundy, the Counts of Nevers and Dreux..."

"Forsooth. I wot well they're powerful leaders. Know you how the Fourth Crusade foundered? It had too many leaders, pulling this way and that, and the upshot was that the idiots ended up fighting a stupid internecine war against fellow Christians in Byzantium instead of taking on the infidels in the Holy Land! We have much the same problem," Innocent said and leaned over the table, his eyes boring into Andreas's. "'Tis why, should Raimond turn out to be a leader like his great-grandfather, who conquered Jerusalem, I shall be glad of heart. In the meantime, the Abbot of Citeaux will lead the Crusade until a leader emerges."

The pope rose and pulled his hassock straight. Andreas sprang to his feet and bowed. "And now, Andreas, I fain would dine. You'll be entertaining our friends from Tolosa, I trow."

"Actually, 'twill not be until tonight, your Holiness."

"Ah, then; why not come along and dine with me, unless you feel the papal table is not up to your epicurean palate." Innocent winked at his secretary.

"Not at all, your Holiness," Andreas said, and blushed with pleasure, "'Twill be a delightful honor.

Montpelhier

Walking up the aisle of Nòstra Dòna de Taulas with the entourage of Viscount Raimond-Roger Trencavel, Olivier tried to keep from gawking at the pageant around him. On both sides of the aisle, their surcoats emblazoned with heraldry, Dukes of Burgundy and Nevers stood with their vassals and two dozen other nobles from France, Champagne, Flanders, Blois and Normandy. Olivier guessed that the large man standing on the dais behind the altar and wearing the white habit of the Cistercian Order must be Arnaud-Amaury himself, the overall commander of the crusading forces. That an Abbot who was also a papal legate with no military experience commanded the crusade was difficult for Olivier to fathom. However, given Arnaud-Amaury's bluster and domineering reputation, his assumption of overall command did not surprise Olivier. After all, it was a holy war. Why shouldn't a prelate lead it?

Before journeying to Montpelhier, Viscount Trencavel had explained to his retinue that he would submit to the crusaders in order to spare his compatriots from war, with its devastation and loss of life. He pointed out that Raimond of Tolosa had succeeded in sparing his lands from invasion and confiscation; therefore he, himself, was obliged to make a last minute attempt to procure similar terms. Precious lives and incalculable riches hung in the balance. Much as he hated to do it, he preferred to exile a few heretics rather than losing lands and chattel to the crusaders.

Not believing his ears, Olivier had exchanged glances with others and had seen they were equally dumbfounded. Did the Viscount really believe that the crusaders would turn around and go home without striking a blow? Would a zealot like Arnaud- Amaury tell his lay comrades that there was no need to go on, that the crusade was over and that no rich prizes would be seized and distributed? That the

113

time and money the crusaders had spent in coming this far was wasted? 'Twould be a miracle if the legate consented, Olivier concluded.

When he reached the altar, Raimond-Roger bent on one knee before the scowling Abbot, and made his case in a firm voice. He had neither harbored nor helped the heretics, and did not feel responsible for anything that his vassals had done, he said. He begged the Church to forgive him for what it may have taken to be an anti-clerical stance. As he spoke, the Abbot grimaced and wrinkled his nose, as if someone had farted. When the Viscount finished, the Abbot spoke, his voice dripping with venom.

"You should have made this submission eight months ago. Forsooth, you should have submitted when you came into your majority *ten* years ago. You have been sheltering heretics, nay, *encouraging* them. Ever since, despite constant pleading by your local prelates to bring the heretics under control, or to banish them, you come here all a-tremble, knowing that your lands are forfeit and that your friends, the heretics, are doomed. Once we march through your realm, 'twill be Roman Catholic from one end to the other, and your castles will be flying these colors," and he swept his arm toward the colorful heraldry around him.

"You ask us to accept your submission to the Holy Mother Church? My answer is but one word: no!" Then he burst into scornful laughter, and all the Northern nobility joined in.

Raimond-Roger seemed to hesitate as if he was going to dispute the Abbott's decision. Then he whirled and stomped down the aisle, his followers stepping aside to let him pass, and then falling in behind him.

Outside the church, where squires were holding the horses, Raimond-Roger mounted his charger and looked around at his men. "I hope you all agree that 'tis always better to avoid bloodshed and the risk of having strangers confiscate our lands. By refusing to accept my submission, the Abbot means he wants to spill our blood and steal our land, and we must act swiftly to make him realize that he is making a fatal mistake. We must ride through the night if we want to give Besièrs a day's warning. Let's be on our way! I can't endure another moment in this city of lying prelates." He spurred his horse through the gate toward Besièrs.

Olivier and Trencavel's other attendants hastened to mount and ride after him. As Olivier passed through the gate, a weight fell away from him. The Viscount was right. The orthodoxy of Montpelhier was stifling. Once outside, he filled his lungs with the fresh country air.

Across the fields to the south, campfires sent up plumes of smoke, and wagons and carts jammed the passages between hundreds of tents. Thousands of people were milling about, and herds of horses and oxen grazed in the fields beyond. Olivier had heard that the army had a thousand knights and six thousand spearmen, archers, crossbowmen, as well as at least an equal number of camp followers and those vagrants and brigands in search of booty who were called *routiers*. Although Olivier looked down at the routiers as a class, he also knew that they were often the ones sent into the thick of every fight. They were the poor devils who scaled the ladders, braved showers of arrows, stones and boiling oil, often armed only with cudgels and crude swords.

Olivier had never seen so many people in one place and he stared at the crowds with a sinking feeling. Here was the nemesis of the Good People. He had used this phrase to explain to Micaela why it was necessary to help his kinsmen in the Carcasses repel the invasion. However, he had continued, his Trencavel kinsmen were asking his help not to protect heretics, but because they felt their lands

115

were threatened. According to the Papal Bull, their land and property were forfeit to the Northerners; hence, it wasn't just a Holy War, but a war of conquest, one that might spill over into Provença. Their own possessions might be threatened if the crusaders were not turned back.

Besièrs

For a second time, Olivier found himself knocking on the Ravanel's door. When it swung open, Ruth Ravanel stood before him. Her eyes opened wide with recognition and her face flushed with pleasure.

"Senhor Mazan, what a surprise! We were just talking about you..." she interrupted herself to call over her shoulder, "...Darling, look who's here!" Then she turned back to Olivier. "Please come in, your coming is indeed propitious."

Jacob Ravenel put down the necklace he was working on, and after wiping his hands on his apron, he came across the room and took Olivier's hand in his. "Aye, we are extremely worried about the crusading army. Belike, you have no idea what they did to our people when they came through the Midi the last time. 'Twas long ago, but we have never forgotten."

"I see well what you say, and 'tis why I'm here. The crusaders are not even two days away. The fall of Besièrs would mean a blood bath and I am afraid that Jews will suffer the most. The crusaders will have no mercy for the Good Folk or Jews

"That's exactly what we've been worrying about," Jacob said. "The consuls of Besièrs are confident that we are strong enough to withstand a forty day siege. And by that time, they say, Raimond-Roger will come to our rescue with an army and the French will have to retreat. But if somehow that fails to happen, then my family..." Jacob broke off and exchanged glances with Ruth.

"To say truth, we've been talking about going either to Carcassona or to the Black Mountain," Ruth said, "but we didn't realize the crusaders were so nigh."

"It gladdens me that you realize the dangers," Olivier said. "Right now, as we speak, the Viscount is advising the town consuls to stand firm against the crusaders. Besièrs is impregnable. He will go back to Carcassona and levy troops from the Ariège, the Aude and up to the Tarn, and then he will come back with a much superior force to lift the siege

"Think you we should bide after all?" Jacob said.

"No, no, the Viscount agrees with you. To be on the safe side, he is advocating that the Jewish population leave immediately for Carcassona. The sooner you leave, the better the quarters you may find there. Have you any draft animals?"

"Yes, a mule."

"Good! Pack your children and your valuables on your mule, and you two can ride tandem with me and my squire. We should try to leave before the others start."

"What about the scrolls? I've found a new hiding place. No one will ever find them."

"I was coming to that. I don't think the crusaders can take this town, but if they do, anything might happen. Cities can burn down. It's up to you."

Jacob nodded grimly. "All right. Mayhap they'll be safer with us. Come on, Ruth, let's get started."

After a two-day march, the crusading army arrived before the walls of Besièrs late in the afternoon, and set up its tents in the fields east of the city. The river Orbe served as a moat to the western wall, so any attack would need to be made from the east. Following the evening meal, Arnaud-Amaury called a council of war with the ten most powerful nobles in the crusading army. They met in the Duke of Burgundy's pavilion.

Spies had told the Abbot that Trencavel had gone on to Carcassona, taking the entire Jewish population of Besièrs with him. That was disappointing news, because Arnaud-Amaury had counted on using their slaughter, along with that of the heretics, to terrorize the region and to persuade any remaining pockets of resistance to hand over their undesirables in order to save their own lives.

"Here's a list of 207 known heretics living in Besièrs that we want to get our hands on." Arnaud-Amaury said. "We will ask the consuls to deliver them to us."

"Your grace," the Count of Nevers said, "I'm sure we all want to punish heretics, but the Holy See promised that Trencavel's property was forfeit to our baronage. That was the motivation that made many of my vassals take the Cross. Our knights also expect to share in the treasure within the city, and, of course, the commoners all have high hopes of going home far richer than they came. Handing over a few heretics wont satisfy those expectations."

"Ah, thank you for that observation, with which I agree wholeheartedly" Arnaud-Amaury said. "I hadn't finished my thought. I will also tell them that if they don't surrender those heretics, then all the Christians must leave the city, otherwise they will have to share the fate of the heretics."

"But what if they refuse?"

"Well, then, we'll just have to carry on with the siege, as in any other campaign. Your men are eager for combat, I take it?" The Abbot swiveled his head, challenging the group with a haughty stare. "After all, we're not going falconing."

"Of course not," the Count of Nevers replied, "and we are itching to scale their walls and smash down their gates. But why parley, if they are going to refuse our terms?"

Arnaud-Amaury folded his arms across his chest and sighed. Why were these French so obstinate? Were they totally lacking in the knowledge of baiting traps?

"If you are aiming to pillage," he said, "then their refusal will give you the chance you are looking for. Besièrs is an enormously rich city. Its people are arrogant from top to bottom. They are insolent and have difficulty recognizing any authority, whether lay or clerical. Their history is rife with violence against the high clergy and against the various Viscounts as well. About forty years ago, a surprise uprising roughed up a bishop and killed Raimond-Roger's grandfather. His son Roger II stamped out that conspiracy, but today, bourgeois power -- mostly driven by heretics -- is plainly resurgent, and must be eliminated."

"Think you they will refuse?"

"Yes, but I pray that they won't. Call to mind, if they accept our terms, we will have all that booty without a fight, Otherwise..." The Abbot rolled his eyes and shrugged.

He did not go on to add what the others were thinking. A prolonged siege might be necessary. If it lasted too long it would jeopardize the crusade, because after forty days, the vassals and their men would no longer be bound by feudal law to remain in the field, and most would head back home. This would especially be true if they had been unable loot the town. As a result, the crusade would collapse and it would be next to impossible to mount another one. Arnaud-Amaury winced at the thought.

120

At midday, the city fathers sent their bishop, Renaud de Montpeyroux, to treat with the Abbot, who sent him back with the ultimatum and the list of known heretics. If, indeed, there *were* any Roman Catholics inside Besièrs, they were to turn over two hundred seven heretics to the Crusaders. But if they refused to surrender the heretics, they themselves would be obliged to leave the city and the heretics behind, or else share the fate of the heretics.

Not too long after going through the gate, the tired old bishop re-emerged followed by a few Catholic inhabitants, but not one member of its Catholic clergy or a single heretic. When Arnaud-Amaury pressed him for the answer to the ultimatum, Renaud hesitated.

"Speak up, man," the Abbot barked. "What did they say?"

"They said that they would rather drown in the sea than surrender themselves or the heretics."

Arnaud-Amaury ground his teeth in fury. The leaders of Besièrs had refused his generous offer; and even though it was no surprise, it was the curt and haughty way they responded that angered him. He told his valet to round up the high council, and within the time it took to say ten Pater Nosters, the same ten nobles were sitting around the table.

When Arnaud-Amaury told them about the rejection, the Count of Nevers raised his hand. "If we take the city, 'twill be next to impossible to control the men. What about the clergy who bide? And what about the unarmed population? How can we distinguish between good Romans and heretics? We might end up killing our own faithful"

"Maybe they could wear signs."

"The Romans could wear crucifixes."

"Put the people into pens and sort them out later."

The members of the council were all speaking at once and the Abbot hammered on the table with his beefy fist. "My lords, my lords! Order! Come to order! We have not lifted a single weapon, and yet here we are, arguing about the fate of the people of Besièrs. We don't need to make that decision now. 'Tis much more important to decide how we start to invest the city. I fain would hear from the Duke of Burgundy, and…."

A knight burst into the tent and pointed outside. "My lord, my lord, the enemy … they sally!"

As one, the members of the council jumped to their feet and rushed outside. A squadron of six or seven score of knights from the garrison of Besièrs had ridden out of a gate and were attacking the crusaders' wagon train. Trumpets blared from atop the battlements. From a distance of more than three thousand paces, the council watched dumbstruck as the routiers and the camp followers attached to the army reacted like bees in a disturbed hive. Those fleeing the sally ran headlong into a counterattack of hundreds of roaring men bearing cudgels, axes, scythes, and, here and there, a real pole weapon.

Soon, the horsemen realized they were being engulfed by sheer numbers and turned back toward the open gate. Too late, the riders in the rear were pulled down and sank under the human wave that churned inexorably toward the gate. Archers and crossbowmen on the walls loosed volleys of arrows point blank into the mass, but nothing could stop the human juggernaut. As the surviving riders passed through the gates, scores of *routiers* went in with them and soon a river of men was pouring into the city. In almost no time, they appeared on the walls in place of the archers and crossbowmen that they had undoubtedly slaughtered.

Northern knights milled about the camp, putting on their helms, seizing their weapons and calling for their chargers. "*Aux armes, aux armes*," they shouted. The walls had been breeched and the city was open for conquest.

The Duke of Burgundy shrugged. "We might not need a siege after all. We'd fain follow them in at once, or else no spoils will be left for us." Then he swung onto the charger his squire had brought up to him. Before the others had mounted, the Duke reined in his steed, which pranced on its hind legs.

"My lord Abbot," he shouted over the din, "what should I tell the men? How can we tell the heretics from the Roman Catholics?"

"Kill them all," Arnaud-Amaury screamed. "God will sort them out."

The July sun had begun its descent when Arnaud- Amaury stepped through the eastern gate into a scene straight out of hell. He had waited until the incredible crescendo of noise – men roaring and clamoring, women and children screaming and wailing -- had diminished to that of a few individuals shrieking as they were being put to the sword, or worse.

Inside the gate lay scores of dead men from both sides who were killed in the initial, desperate charge. Blackish pools and rivulets of blood had coagulated on the cobblestones. The enemy knights lay mostly naked, stripped of their surcoats, hauberks and helmets. As he progressed further down the street, he had to step over bodies—men, women and children -- some of them lying across thresholds they would never tread again. He looked through doorways and saw more bodies; the first was that of a child missing its head.

From then on, it was almost impossible to put his foot down without stepping on human flesh. Many of the corpses had been disemboweled and a foul stench rose from the purple entrails. He had to look away from the many mangled dead children who seemed to be as numerous as the adults. He met many routiers heading back toward the gate, their garments drenched with blood, laden down with bulging sacks of loot.

At last he arrived at the cathedral St. Nazaire. A hillock of corpses lay in front of its open doors from which wisps of smoke were emanating. He climbed over the bodies and gasped. The entire floor of the church was covered with the dead. The wooden carvings of the choir were ablaze. Here and there, *routiers* came toward him with sacks on their backs. He stopped one and instinctively put his hand on the pommel of his sword. Who could trust such people?

"Why is the church on fire," he asked. "Who set it?"

"I don't know your grace," the man said, "I don't have nothin' to do with it. All I know is that the gentry, the knights, have been takin' stuff away from folks like me, and so some folks is plenty mad. Some of 'em have been setting fires all through the city. They say if they can't get what they came for, nobody can, and they're going to torch the whole city."

The Abbot felt like drawing his sword and making an end of the man. Who would miss him in this charnel house? Meanwhile, the blaze had grown so strong that the clothes on the bodies lying in the choir were catching fire, and Arnaud-Amaury flinched, as he realized that some of those clothes were the albs and the cassocks of priests.

He followed the man back out into the street where more and more *routiers* were staggering under huge bags of booty. Here and there, a knight on horseback picked his way among the corpses, his horse laden with makeshift sacks full of loot. The smoke became thicker and the Abbot realized that many of the buildings on each side of the street were on fire. He quickened his pace and soon stood outside the walls again. Billows of smoke rose from different parts of the town, and the exodus of the crusaders grew heavier.

A young squire approached leading a horse with several large bundles tied to its saddle. He held the reins in one hand and in the other, he led a *routier* by a noose around his neck. The prisoner was bent over from the weight of the bundle on his back.

"Good day, your grace," the squire called out to the Abbot. "I've been looking for you, but I didn't believe that I would have the luck to find you so easily."

Arnaud-Amaury looked at the squire. He was almost as tall as the Abbot himself, and had a keen, strong face, although it was begrimed with dust and smoke. His surcoat was as bloody as a butcher's apron, but Arnaud-Amaury could make out the lilies on the blue field that designated its wearer as belonging to the contingent from the Ile de France, home to the Capets, the ruling dynasty of France.

"Do I know you?" Arnaud-Amaury asked. He could not place the young man, although he had been traveling with the nobles from the North for almost a month.

"Guy de la Beauce from Rambouillet, at your service." The squire bowed his head.

"And your knight is…?" Arnaud-Amaury raised his eyebrows.

"My knight, Bertrand de Rambouillet, is dead, alack and alas." He cocked his head to one of the bundles on the horse. "He fell in the fighting in the city. 'Twasn't as easy as some people would have you think. There was fierce resistance."

"'Twas well done, and I am grateful for your bravery and for that of you master, whose death I rue. Were you close to each other?"

"Yes. He was my mentor and inspiration."

"You must think him to be a martyr to his Church. But I'm intrigued. Why were you searching for me?"

Rambouillet nodded his head toward the man he was leading, who grimaced under the weight of his burden. "This *routier* was stealing a purse from one of our dead knights. Caught him red-handed. Had my sword out, fixing to dispatch him, when he came up with a story involving some monks in your order. Said he knew of something valuable that had been stolen from an abbey outside Narbona, and that you would know about it."

Arnaud-Amaury swallowed hard. Could that pitiful dreg of humanity bowed down by the load on its back know something about the scrolls? He crouched down beside the man, who kept his eyes on the ground. "What do you have to say? What do you know?"

Later that evening, Arnaud-Amaury sat on a stool outside his tent. Almost all of Besièrs was ablaze. Smoke swirled up in a towering plume that blotted out the setting sun and flames and sparks soared hundreds of feet into the air, their awful turbulence creating a thunderous roar. His new squire, Rambouillet, had bathed in the river and had changed his blood soaked hauberk and surcoat for clean garments. He now he stood awestricken beside his patron.

"'Tis a paradox," Arnaud-Amaury said to the squire, "we were going to burn the heretics anyway. At least, this saves us the trouble of burying all those dead. The Lord God has infinite ways to lend his faithful a helping hand."

Rambouillet nodded. "Forsooth, but 'twas dimwitted of those *routier*s to set the fires. There was more plunder than we could carry. Now 'tis gone up in smoke. What a pity."

Inside his pavilion, Arnaud-Amaury lounged with his feet resting on a saddle. His valet had brought him a horn of wine and he was about to ask for another. Through the open flap, he could see a pall of smoke hanging over the smoldering city. He jutted out his lower lip appreciatively.

Its rapid conquest and the ensuing massacre was precisely the stratagem the crusade needed to intimidate Carcassona and the other Trencavel strongholds. Terror was worth a thousand knights. He could now expect little resistance. The heretics would be cleaned out of the Midi and the French nobles would take control and prevent the heretics from regaining a foothold. No preaching had been necessary; not a breath had been wasted in pleading; force of arms and hardened hearts had done more in one day than ten years of fruitless persuasion.

Moreover, the *routier* had recounted the story of the scrolls and described how painstakingly he had worked to discover the name of the man who had given the scrolls to Castelnau.

Arnaud-Amaury now knew that in addition to the thief and the Jewish couple, only one other person alive knew about the scrolls, and that was a Provençal knight named Olivier de Mazan. Thus, completely by chance – or, more likely, by Divine intervention – the sack of Besièrs had killed two birds with one stone. Once he subdued Trencavel, he could easily hunt down Mazan. In the meantime, he would keep the thief alive just in case the goldsmith and his wife turned up among the Jewish refugees in Carcassona.

All in all, the good Lord had smiled on him, he gloated. Once he had finished mopping up the rest of Trencavel's holdings, he would be able to name his own price to the pope. He would ask for the Archbishopric of Narbona, the highest ecclesiastic office in the entire Midi.

For years, the pope had been trying to oust the sly old Archbishop, Berenger, but somehow Berenger had always managed to hang on, despite heroic efforts by the legates to remove him. He always found a way to get back into the good graces of Innocent, blaming Arnaud-Amaury and the other legates for conspiring against him. They were to blame for the diminished power of the clergy in the region.

Successes like the capture of Besièrs would eclipse any excuses Berenger could possibly make to the Pope, and Arnaud-Amaury was certain that it was only a matter of months until he would sit on the throne in the archbishop's palace. And after that, who knew? Innocent wouldn't live forever.

Carcassona

In the bright morning sunlight of a mid-summer day, with distant orchards already shimmering in a heat that promised to surpass that of the preceding days, Olivier Mazan stood watching thousands of crusaders assembling in the barley fields to the south. The parapet he was standing on was part of the battlements enclosing the densely built *castellare*, a suburb that crouched at the foot of the escarpment over which soared the high walls and towers of Carcassona. After two days of house-to-house fighting, the French had captured the surburb of St.Vincent that lay between the river and the city, and the following day, they had overwhelmed the garrison of the Bourg, a walled suburb built against the northern wall of the city.

Olivier had taken part in a bloody sortie into St. Vincent, and had lived through prolonged combat. It had been a terrifying experience, in which he found himself fighting just to stay alive. The helter-skelter blows he had struck against foemen had been virtually desperate attempts to stave off life-threatening slashes and thrusts meant for *him*. Killing and maiming the enemy became an utterly accidental result of self-preservation.

Now, manning the ramparts of the *castellare,* he stared as enemy hordes prepared, once again, to try to put an end to his life and those of his companions. To deprive him from ever beholding Micaela again, let alone holding her in his arms! As desperate and terrifying fighting at close quarters had been, the sight of the massed enemy was even more unnerving. Several thousand footmen were arrayed behind a few hundred knights sitting on gaily caparisoned mounts. He had never seen so many people in his life, and they were bent on killing him! It was a living nightmare that made his hair stand on end. A groan escaped him. Why?

Why was he here? How could this dreadful catastrophe be happening to him?

As unspeakable fear swept over him, a distant trumpet sounded and with a mighty roar, the French surged forward, brandishing their weapons. Long scaling ladders bobbed among their ranks. As they advanced, he gripped the hilt of his sword with white knuckles.

When the attackers came within bowshot, thick clouds of arrows and crossbow- quarrels flew toward them from the ramparts on either side of him. Although many stumbled and fell, the human wave came crashing onward. He looked right and left along the parapet, where cauldrons of boiling pitch and piles of heavy stones were stored in readiness, and except for the busy crossbowmen, his fellow defenders stood stock-still, awestruck by the sheer number of men attacking them. His muscles began to tremble uncontrollably.

Suddenly, somewhere off to his right, he heard a shout, "*Trencavel e Carcassas!*" He and his fellows took up the cry as loudly as they could. Somehow, the din put an end to the shaking fit and he felt defiance and strength surge through him. "*Viva Paratge!*' he bellowed with the rest. Now righteous anger swept over him, anger at these foul and rapacious foreigners from the north, invading *his* soil and threatening *his* way of life. Let them suffer; let them die like dogs! He would kill and maim as many as he could find. Fury swept away all other emotions.

The top rung of a ladder suddenly appeared in the crenel before him. Plucking a *ranseur* from a rack of pole arms, he jammed the rung with the hilt of the blade and furiously started pushing the ladder out away from the wall. As the ladder reached the perpendicular, the eyes of the *routier* clinging to its upper rungs widened in terror.

"Fuck you, you French cunts," Olivier cried and thrust the ranseur as far as he could. The ladder and its screaming

131

cargo plunged backwards toward the ground. Olivier felt a fierce joy. A quick glance through the crenel told him the ditch below was teeming with the enemy.

Throwing down the pole weapon, he gathered up a stone as big as his head and lurched back to the battlements. Holding it in both hands, he leaned out through a crenel and hurled it down onto the head of an enemy footman, who dropped in his tracks. His second stone missed, but the third crushed the face of a man who was craning his neck upward. As Olivier replenished his supply of stones, a quarrel hummed by his head, and he realized that he was exposing himself to French sharpshooters. He hid behind a merlon and heaved the next three stones over the wall blindly, hoping they would find a target in the crowded ditch. Looking sideways, along the rampart, he watched cauldrons being emptied and saw other defenders heaving stones over the wall. By the screams from below, he knew that at least some of the enemy were paying heavily for the attack and he found himself strangely elated at the thought.

A sudden howl of derision went up among those around him. Peeking through a crenel, he saw the French had abandoned the attack and were stampeding back out of bowshot, leaving scores of dead and wounded in the ditch before the walls. A torrent of relief, mixed with the pride of accomplishment, swept over Olivier, and he added his voice to the deafening jeers and cheers. '*Viva Trencavel*,' they bellowed, shaking their weapons scornfully at the retreating French. They had thrown back the cursed crusaders!

Inside the *castellare*, church bells begin to ring and soon the big bells of the cathedral within the city began to add their full tones to the paean of victory. The defenders slapped each other on the back and swapped stories of their exploits.

Looking up at the battlements of the city above him, Olivier could see that they were jammed with waving and cheering citizens. He waved back. He was certain that many of them were the inhabitants of the two suburbs that had fallen to the French, but who were now taking refuge inside the walls of the city. Carcassona had become a huge refugee center for people from villages and farms who had fled before the advance of the crusaders from the North. Small wonder that they were so jubilant at seeing the despised foreigners repulsed!

During the next two days, the French remained in bivouac, eerily inactive. Olivier joined with others who went out and dug a mass grave for the French left behind in the ditch by the castellare walls. Often, they threw the French wounded into the grave along with the dead, to Olivier's horror. When he objected to burying people alive, the others shrugged. "'Tis war," they said. The brutality of those on his own side caused Olivier to reflect on what he himself had done during the attack, and about the men he had killed in rage. Surely, the Devil had possessed him and everyone on both sides. War must be the very religion of the Devil, he brooded.

Was there any dispensation during battle that would protect his soul? He needed to know, and was anxious to find a Good Man to see if he needed to confess and repent. After talking it over with other Believers he had met on the walls of the *castellare,* he and three others used the lull to search out Good Folk within the city.

Inside the massive walls, they found the streets were filled with refugees living in makeshift tents, their belongings piled about or in tumbrels. Livestock clogged the space that remained and the stench of animal and human waste was overpowering. The heat wave and the number of refugees had depleted the water supply, they learned, and the wells were dangerously low. Despite the hope that had been kindled by the repulse of the French attack, they could see that the people of Carcassona were in desperate straits, their misery increased by swarms of mosquitoes from the marshes along the river.

The search for a Good Man turned out to be easy; one or two inquiries sufficed and soon they found themselves with three dozen other Believers at a service conducted by three Good Men and one Good Woman in the shadowy interior of a small house that fronted on the street running alongside the Cathedral. They performed the rite of *aparelhament* in which they asked and received the Good Men's blessing in a public confession and exchanged the kisses of peace.

Then one of the Good Men, a deacon, spoke: "I have a sermon, but I see you have a common need. 'Tis evident that you are defending the city with your lives. You realize that the blessing you asked for and received aimed at bringing you to a good end. And, forsooth, that should mean receiving the Consolation before you die. Yet, 'tis possible that you may receive a fatal wound so grievous that you cannot participate in the Consolation. In that case, an *Amelioration* may serve as a covenant that you fully intend to receive the Consolation ere you die, whether you can speak or not. Is that your intention?"

Olivier and the others hastened to agree.

134

"Then repeat after me. I hereby ask the lord to bring me to a good end even if I am unable to speak."

The men repeated the phrase and exchanged the kisses of peace.

The deacon cleared his throat and began the sermon.

"My brethren, today we see the result of cupidity and fanaticism, represented by the armies of the North and the Roman Church. Like a horde of ravenous locusts, they have swept down on us, slaughtering thousands of our neighbors, and forcing thousands of others to flee their homes. They've uprooted vineyards, burned fields, plundered dwellings and poisoned wells. Refugees crowding our streets face starvation and pestilence. Indeed, the entire population of Carcassona is in mortal danger. Except for a large contingent of Jewish refugees from Besièrs, most worship the Roman Church. And yet they are besieged by other Roman Catholics who covet their homes and land and would kill to get them!"

"This calamity is solely due to the Roman Church's desire to eradicate our faith, which threatens to supersede theirs among the people. The evil that the French have done has been inspired by the evil that is engrained in the Roman Church by its own dogma. They call us apostles of Satan. By my troth, 'tis true that we worship Jesus Christ by following the teaching of his apostles, which is the antithesis of the satanic evil preached by the Roman clergy."

"What does that signify for you who fight? How should you conduct yourselves? When you take prisoners, I beg you to act in the spirit of Jesus and treat them like your neighbors. Just as the population of Carcassona is caring for the refugees, so should you act like Good Samaritans,. Remember, in the end, all men will be saved, even the cruelest and most selfish among them."

"Remember the Good Samaritan? According to the scriptures, a master of Judaic law decided to test Jesus's knowledge. 'Rabbi,' he asked, 'what must I do to inherit eternal life?' 'What is written in the Law?' Jesus responded, 'How do you read it?' As a good Rabbi, Jesus was hinting that the answer was obvious to anyone familiar with the law."

"'Love the Lord your God with all your heart and with all your soul and with all your strength and with all your mind; also, love your neighbor as yourself,' the lawman recited."

"'You have answered correctly,' Jesus replied. 'Do this and you will live forever.' "

"But the master of law wanted to justify his original question, so he asked Jesus, 'And who is my neighbor?' "

"Jesus recited the parable, in which a poor Jew -- lies naked and battered in the road. A Jewish priest detours around him and goes on his way. A passing Rabbi also avoids the victim. Yet, the Samaritan delivered solace to the unfortunate Jew, whose own priests had passed him by!"

"Think what this means. 'Tis the way to heaven. Love your neighbor as yourself, though he be your enemy! What a concept! It says a Roman priest should go to the aid of a Jew. A crusader should help a Good Woman who has met with misfortune instead of dragging her away to be burned. A Saracen should succor a wounded Crusader, and we Good folk should do the same to one and all."

"The Friends of God believe that all men will be saved at the last judgment, whether they be Jew Saracen, or Christian. Yet, the Roman Church believes that hell and purgatory await those who do not follow its dogma. The Roman clergy see victims and pass them by, but when Good Folk see the same sufferers, we go to their aid. *We* do what Jesus taught. Today, *we* are his faithful apostles, and whosoever acts in the spirit of Jesus and the name of God shall not have to wait for the last judgment to attain the heavenly Kingdom. Ours is a faith of inclusion, whereas the Roman is a faith of exclusion."

"We are all poor wretches lying on the hardscrabble road to Jericho, by reason that an evil power has created our bodies and the rest of the material world, with all its misery. I say unto you, be a good neighbor, and walk in the steps of Jesus. When you do, you will be clothed in the mantle of the Good Lord of Heaven."

After the Good Man finished his sermon, Olivier took him aside and confessed his fears about the lives he had taken.

"Of course you should be concerned," the Good Man said. "Killing another human being is the Devil's work, and killing any animal is against our creed because we believe they may contain the souls of those who eventually will reach heaven."

"Are you saying that I shouldn't bear arms against the French and their Roman masters?"

"I'm saying that when a soul departs from one body and goes into another, it chooses bodies that are close by. These Northerners probably don't have possess any souls from the Midi. Therefore, when you slay a Frenchman, there is little chance that you are hindering souls of people who have lived and died in the Midi."

"Then may I kill the French with impunity?"

The Goodman shrugged.

On the way back to the castellare, Olivier worried about what he had been told. *Love thy neighbor though he be your enemy* seemed a very clear instruction, one which he was violating over and over again as the siege went on.

When he returned to the parapet of the *castellare* that night, Olivier found the air much less foul than in the crowded city, and although the mosquitoes still bothered him, they were tolerable. He fell asleep almost before he put his head down on his pack. He believed he had hardly closed his eyes when he was shaken awake the next morning.

"Up with you, Sir, the French are tryin' to undermine the wall, and we've got to stop 'em," a burly sergeant cried into his ear and he pointed along the wall. "They got a cat up against the wall yonder."

Still half asleep, Olivier was amazed to see a strange contraption that was standing against the wall three hundred paces away. It was a wooden shed on wheels that sappers rolled against walls to protect them while undermining the foundations. Its peaked roof was covered with hides and to get a closer look he started to lean through the crenel, but the sergeant pulled him back.

"They dug a trench out there last night. 'Tis filled with snipers waiting for someone like you to poke his head out. Unless you're throwin' a rock or pouring pitch or shootin', it don't make sense to stick your neck out, does it?"

"Thanks," Olivier grinned, feeling sheepish. "So, what can I do?"

"We're trying to set fire to the cat, but. 'tis covered by thick layers of cowhide. Flaming arrows haven't worked, so we're trying to break it apart with stones. We need you to gather up stones and tote 'em over to where we can throw 'em onto the cat."

"I'm your man," Olivier said, and sprang toward a pyramid of stones in a corner of the wall. "Can you find anyone else to give me hand?"

"Give me a moment and I'll send them over," the sergeant said, and he turned and hurried away along the parapet.

In spite of a rain of stones and fire-arrows, the roof of the cat held until the early afternoon, when it erupted in flames, but by that time, the wall had been undermined. Emerging from the cat and clambering over the piles of earth they had excavated, the enemy sappers were met with a volley of quarrels. A few staggered and fell, but many others made it back to the defensive trench unscathed.

During the night, although the defenders stood guard on the battlements above the smoldering wreck of the cat, the French sappers snuck back and managed to light the firewood and dry brush that had been stuffed under the foundation. By the time the sentinels smelt smoke, a plume of flame had risen where the cat joined the wall. Olivier and his comrades watched impotently while the French reassembled their large force just out of bowshot, a few hundred dismounted knights forming their vanguard.

Knowing that the weakened wall would soon collapse, the defenders rushed to erect a crude barricade of stone and wood a few paces inside the threatened section of the wall. They had succeeded in raising a barrier almost four paces high, when thirty paces of the wall and the parapet collapsed in a cloud of dust. The noise of collapsing masonry had not even subsided when the enemy hordes charged with a ferocious roar. Although the crossbowmen on the wall shot as quickly as they could cock and load their weapons, the flood of crusaders poured over the intervening ground and headed for the breach.

The first French knight to climb up over the piles of rubble and mount the makeshift barricade tumbled and fell with a quarrel through his neck, but dozens more came on behind him. Two more knights who had vaulted on top of the barricade were promptly skewered by spears, but other crusaders hurled their own spears at pointblank range, and several defenders went down. The enemy spearmen drew their swords and scrambled over the barricade.

Olivier stepped forward and swung his great two-handed sword sideways with all his might, and felt the bones of an enemy's leg crunch as he cut the man's feet from under him. He had just enough time to parry a sword blow by a knight who had just leapt over the barricade and butted his head against the man's chest, knocking him to the ground. After plunging his sword through the enemy's hauberk, he looked up just in time to dodge the lunge of a spear. Clinching the attacker with his left arm and dropping his sword, he drew his dagger and drove it up through the man's chin. The man dropped like a stone. Spying his sword lying beneath two bodies, Olivier snatched up the dead crusader's spear and fended off another attacker.

More than a dozen crusaders had successfully climbed over the barricade and as more and more followed, the men of the Midi slowly gave ground. Feinting a thrust with the spear, Olivier reached down with his other hand and pulled his sword from under the dead men. Fear that he and the other defenders were about to be overwhelmed gnawed at him. If his comrades fled, he didn't want to be left behind. He began to feel light-headed, as if he was dreaming.

Someone cried out, "Fall back into the streets! A few of us can hold off an army!" He and the men around him ran back into the roadways that pierced the blocks of houses in the *castellare* and turned to face the enemy. In the narrow alleys, three or four men were able to fight off several times their number, but fatigue began to take its toll. Olivier was finding it harder and harder to wield his heavy sword. He had even given up trying to land a fatal stroke. It would be just a matter of time before he could no longer parry a lethal blow or a well-aimed thrust.

"Comrade," cried a voice in his ear, "step aside and let me pass. We're your replacements." Hardly believing his ears, Olivier did as he was told, making way for knights in clean surcoats and unstained armor, and soon he and his companions reached the end of the alley and passed through a small gate in the lofty walls.

Inside the city, the din of the battle was strangely muted. Staring at each other, they saw so many grimy, dead-tired butchers' helpers splattered with blood.

"We made it," Olivier said and reached out his hand. "*Per lo Midi e lo paratge.*" The others clasped their right hands to his. "*Per lo Midi e lo paratge,*" they answered.

That evening, Olivier and his comrades climbed onto the ramparts to survey the scene of their combat the day before. Looking down at the warren of houses within the walls of the *castellare*, they noticed that the streets were full of Frenchmen carrying booty and streaming through the gate back toward their camp. Only half a dozen guarded the small gate that connected the *castellare* with the city. The suburb was ripe for the retaking! They hurried off to report what they had seen.

Two hours later, flames could be seen shooting up from the suburb, as house after house caught fire. When he learned that the French had left a skeleton force behind in the *castellare*, Trencavel had made a strong sortie into the suburb and set fire to the houses, so that just as in the Bourg, they could not be used to protect the invaders as they sapped the walls or set up siege weapons.

141

Seeking relief from the sickening stench of the city as the midmorning sun blazed overhead, Olivier stood on the towering ramparts. Down below, draft animals and livestock were dying and even though they were butchered for their meat, the remains spoiled quickly in the heat. The wells were running dry, and water fetched by midnight forays to the river was too precious to share with animals.

The crowded conditions, the breakdown of sanitary waste disposal, the decomposing animal carcasses, and the excessive heat combined to produce an overpowering miasma that sapped the morale of the besieged. The city consuls had finally organized teams to collect and carry away the offal, but from the start, it was almost a losing battle.

Olivier was sniffing in vain for the slightest hint of fresh air from the fields and orchards outside the walls, when a strident cheer drowned out the tumult in the streets below. It came from a section of the wall beyond the tower on his right. What did it mean? To find out, he loped along the parapet over to the tower and passed through its guardroom to the parapet beyond.

"What's up," he asked a man who was gazing out over the battlements at the French camp.

"See you not?" the man exclaimed, and pointed excitedly toward the French camp. "Yonder riders bear the arms of Barcelona and Aragon!"

Olivier shaded his eyes and peered at the enemy lines. Behind the French pavilions, a cloud of dust rose from a thousand hooves, and he could make out distant banners with the unmistakable red bars on a yellow background. Now he understood what the cheering meant. Trencavel's suzerain, the King of Aragon, was threatening the French from the rear! Relief was in sight and the siege might be lifted at any time! He found himself cheering along with the others. Their hard-fought defense had not been in vain.

Yet, as the cheering tapered off and the morning wore on, the expected attack on the French by the Aragonese did not take place. In fact, the newcomers had dismounted and seemed to be mingling with the enemy. The besieged looked at each other with disbelief crowned by dismay and a sense of dread. Could the King of Aragon be making common cause with the crusaders against his own vassal?

Midday came and went. In the distance, the horses of the Aragonese force were grazing on the shoots of young barley, and yellow and red banners were planted alongside newly erected pavilions. Hunger finally overcame curiosity, and Olivier left the ramparts in search of some gruel, the only nourishment that could be found within the city walls. As he entered the refectory reserved for the garrison, Olivier was accosted by one of Trencavel's pages.

"Sir Olivier, I'm so glad to have found you," the boy exclaimed, "I've been looking everywhere. The Viscount is hoping you can join him in the great hall. He is expecting a visit from King Peire of Aragon within the hour. Shall I tell him you'll be there?"

"Forsooth. But my garments are hardly fit for court."

The page shrugged. "Everyone is accoutered in the same fashion. 'Tis war, Sir." He touched his cap, and spun around toward the doorway.

'Aye, so 'tis," Olivier sighed, as the boy hurried from the room.

Aude's family had been vassals of the Trencavel dynasty, and after Olivier arrived in Carcassona with the Ravenels and

143

found them a place to stay, he had attended a reception that Trencavel had held for his vassals, and it had turned into a plenary council of war. Since then, he had seen Trencavel on the walls from afar, but had not had the opportunity to talk to him. What possible advice could he give Trencavel? It depended entirely on what King Peire of Aragon intended. Without his intervention, Olivier saw no hope for the city. Soon there would not be enough water to keep the population alive.

Would Peire's dynastic ambitions dictate his actions? His family were Counts of Provença and Montpelhier, and his brother in-law -- Raimond of Tolosa, his traditional rival in the Midi -- was now in the crusaders' camp! The Trencavel holdings in Besièrs and Carcassona linked Peire's feudal possessions in Provença to those in Roussillon, so that he commanded the entire Mediterranean littoral from Nice to Perpinhan, except Melgueil, which lay between Montpelhier and Nimes.

From the King's perspective, Olivier conjectured, it was imperative that Carcassona and Besièrs remained in the hands of Trencavel and not be ceded to a prince from the North, or even worse, ceded to Raimond of Tolosa. It seemed to Olivier that Peire had every motive to keep the crusaders from crushing Trencavel.

When Olivier reached the keep, the ramparts were crowded with people gazing at the French camp. Close by Arnaud-Amaury's distant pavilion, three men had mounted, and were walking their horses through the French lines toward the city. Their surcoats and bucklers were emblazoned with the red and yellow bars of the House of Barcelona and the Kingdom of Aragon. As they came up to the city walls, cheers broke out from the spectators lining the battlements.

"Long live King Peire," they shouted, "long live Aragon!"

144

At the entrance of the great hall, Olivier gave his name to the guards, who waved him through. Inside, he shook hands and made small talk with his acquaintances among the scores of peers. Like Olivier, most of them wore dirty surcoats over chain mail, and cradling their helmets in the crook of their arms. Tables and benches had been drawn up in a large semi-circle facing two thrones, a tall one with rich carvings and golden inlays and a smaller, less ornate one.

Raimond Roger had gone down to greet his suzerain at the gate, Olivier learned, and the formal reception would begin when they climbed back up to the great hall. An honor guard of two knights and two trumpeters stood at either side of the entrance to the stairwell. The peers began to form two lines leading from the stairwell to the thrones. Olivier found a place in the middle of one of the lines, next to one of the knights who had fought by his side in the *castellare*.

A sergeant emerged from the stairwell, and smote the floor three times with the butt of his *guisarme*. The trumpeters put their shiny instruments to their lips and blared a fanfare.

When the last notes faded, a page appeared at the top of the stairs and piped, "His Majesty, the King of Aragon."

The peers craned their necks as Peire II came up the last few steps and paused in the doorway. As a man, they fell to one knee and bowed their heads. Walking between the lines of bowing men, the king came up to the taller throne, then turned to face the peers and a beaming Raimond Roger, who had followed a few paces behind his suzerain, and who now bent his knee. After the Viscount rose, he shook hands with his host -- even though they had done so informally when they met below -- and embraced.

The two men were a contrast in many ways. Peire, at age thirty, was every inch the warrior, with a tall, muscular frame. A high forehead, straight chiseled nose, the boring eyes of an eagle and a rugged chin complemented his military bearing. It was clear that men would follow him anywhere. His spotless surcoat looked as if it had been put on for the first time, and his golden spurs and scabbard glittered in a shaft of light from a high window.

Raimond Roger, on the other hand, was short and wiry, and but twenty-four years old. His face was more that of a cleric, than a soldier's. Deep-set hazel brown eyes, a generous mouth with thin lips, and a square jaw set off his long nose. His surcoat bore the Trencavel arms: three yellow bars with stylized black beacons arrayed between them

In a ringing voice, Trencavel hailed his guest. "We welcome your royal majesty to our hearth and we devoutly hope that your formidable presence here shall dissuade the invaders from continuing their inhuman siege and convince them to return home, leaving us in the peace and tranquility that we here previously enjoyed. Our city is crowded with refugees from Besièrs and many other towns, and they are suffering greatly, along with our own residents. We long for the time when they can get back to their homes and rediscover the felicity of peace, thanks to your timely intervention."

Peire listened impassively, a forefinger crooked over his upper lip, and watching Raimond Rogier with baleful eyes. Removing his finger, he started to speak.

"I'm touched by the warm reception here at the hands of so many of my vassals. I must express my heartfelt thanks and gratitude for such loyalty. But I must also respectfully point to the folly of allowing the Cathar heresy to flourish here unchecked. 'Tis a canker not only in the flesh of our Holy Church, but in our body politic."

146

He rose from the throne, and began pacing back and forth in front of it. "Tis this heresy, pure and simple, that induced this crusade, a holy war that allows participants to confiscate property in the name of piety, an undertaking that, to be sure, feeds greed more than it preserves the faith. The crusaders fail to discriminate between the property of the heretics and that of those who follow the Holy Church. By my troth, this invasion is a disgrace to our mutual concept of *paratge*.

However," and he turned to glare at Trencavel, "you would not be in this plight had you heeded my advice to rid yourself of these heretics once and for all. I had expressly warned you to be quit of the heretics in your midst, and to root them out without mercy." He shook his finger at the young Viscount. "To say truth, you should have learned from watching Count Raimond reap the bitter fruit of his own foolish toleration of heresy in his domains. Indeed, at the very last moment, 'twas his conciliatory behavior that enabled him to redeem himself with the Mother Church, and so he saved his domains. Now he comes in the guise of a crusader, and threatening your very walls, by my troth! Methinks his imitation of a chameleon is a practical lesson that you, obviously, did not learn."

The Viscount winced, and as the King went on with his public reprimand, Olivier recalled Arnaud-Amaury's cold and pitiless, rebuff of Raimond Roger's conciliatory offer.

"This midday I dined with Count Raimond," the King continued, "sitting at the right hand of Arnaud-Amaury, the chief crusader. Both were adamant about continuing the siege. Had I not been there, I'm certain they would have discussed who will rule Carcassona, Besièrs, Albi and Razes. All four fiefs, I remind you, belong to me through you. Now, because of your stubbornness and refusal to heed my advice, these lands could become forfeit. The fall of Carcassona will be my tragedy as much as yours."

"They want to depose me and put a Frenchman in my place," Raimond Roger croaked in frustration.

"Forsooth," Peire added coldly. "What did you expect? You could have avoided it. Now they are hardening their position because of the facts on the ground. The abbot is threatening to do make Carcasonna into another Besièrs if you don't comply!"

"The untimely fall of Besièrs is difficult to comprehend!" Trencavel said, starting up from his throne. "'Tis uncanny. They could have held out forever, I trow." He clenched and unclenched his fists.

"Ah, of course," Peire said, observing Trencavel with widened eyes, and shook his head sadly. "You don't know. You haven't heard. The French aren't exactly proud of the way they took the city. The city militia made a sortie and this enraged some the *routiers* and camp followers who were setting up the crusader camp nearby. They grabbed the nearest weapons and went after the militia, following them through the open gates and into the city, where they went berserk."

Trencavel sat, stunned and several moments went by before he spoke. "Who could have foretold such an unlikely event?" he asked, with a shake of his head. "I was full sure that Besièrs would easily outlast the forty days that bound the crusaders to military duty."

"It didn't last a day," Peire replied.

Trencavel slowly shook his head. "My lord, I simply can't find it in my heart to turn over the heretics as you suggest. Some of them are close relatives. Most are my friends, my people. They have never harmed anyone. They're known as Good Folk, by their devout neighbors who attend Mass regularly. Together with their sympathizers, they

148

make up more than half of the population of my counties. How can I betray them? They are far less corrupt and far more honest than most bishops. Secondly, I have more than a thousand Jews to protect. I just can't leave them to the mercy of fanatics like Arnaud- Amaury."

"*I* would certainly have no problem if I were asked to choose between heretics or my fiefdoms," Peire said. "I wot well what I fain would do. I came here expressly to offer my services in arbitrating negotiations between you and the crusaders. But I don't believe that either party is ready to negotiate."

Raimond-Roger turned red. "Sire, I must needs acknowledge our gratitude for your presence here and humbly accept your offer to mediate a truce. We did not foresee —and methinks none could have—the awful fate of Besiers and the wanton cruelty of our enemy, especially that of its ecclesiastical leader. Simply put, we don't want a repetition here. The lives of my people are too dear to me to be wasted by any vainglorious posturing on my part. The people have reached the end of their endurance, and every day that passes brings us closer to catastrophe. Their suffering is too painful to watch. Unfortunately, the only bargaining ploy I have is to try to outlast the siege. If the French go home when their duty time is up, then the legate will have to raise the siege, because the Count of Tolosa doesn't know how to conduct a siege, or any other military maneuver."

"Forsooth." The King stopped pacing and took Trencavel's hands in his. "The legate is trying to create facts on the ground. If you surrender, you lose. If you outlast him, you win. Those are the simple facts. We came here with one hundred knights and two hundred squires. Arnaud-Amaury has ten times that number, plus thousands of foot soldiers. We are too few to break the siege. The best thing

I can do is to mediate a truce and help negotiate your surrender. Failing that, I don't think I can accomplish anything by staying here. Do you agree?"

Trencavel nodded. "Yes, your Majesty, you would be wasting your time. If you had more than a hundred horse, 'twould be a different story. As it is now, 'twill come down to which side caves in first. I'm forever in your debt for taking the trouble to come here, and I regret that my *paratge* forbids me to sacrifice heretics and Jews to save my possessions. You must put yourself in my shoes and understand why I must continue to resist."

"I shall try," the king said, "I shall try."

"Thank you your Majesty. I will not dwell upon what should or should not have been done in the past. Instead, let us strive to save the citizens of this city. Did Arnaud-Amaury propose any terms?"

"He did. And they are as draconian as you might expect from such as he. He claims your city is a nest of raving heretics. He said that your determined resistance against the army of God has cost him hundreds of casualties, and 'tis high time to re-enact the sack of Besièrs. As a Christian monarch who has fought the infidel in the name of the Holy Church, I argued with him. When I told him that the majority of your subjects are good Catholics, he scoffed at me. 'God will know his own,' he told me, 'just as He did in Besièrs.' However, after arguing back and forth, he said that, as a favor to me, he would give you the following terms: you and eleven companions will have safe passport out of the city, with all you can carry. The rest of the population will be at his mercy."

Raimon-Roger's face flushed red, and he held a fist up to his face. "Tell him to stick it up his arse! By God, we will sortie and cut down as many of his men as we can!

150

Bah!" The Viscount threw himself back down on his throne.

"'Twas my reaction, too," Peire said. "I told him that donkeys are more likely to fly than have you accept such terms."

"Forsooth!" Raimond Roger said, smacking the arm of his throne. "We will fight to the death, and he will rue the day when he allowed his priest's serpent tongue to hiss such an insult! God, how I'd like to meet him face to face."

"I'm sure it won't be necessary. I will take your refusal —couched in slightly more diplomatic terms—back to him. I trust I can exert some pressure so that he will give you better terms. Regrettably, if he fails to compromise, I cannot remain to see it through. I must start back to Barcelona tomorrow. I hate to leave you in such a situation and I hope we will meet again on a more propitious occasion.

"Thank you so much, your gracious Majesty," Trencavel said, "may your journey be safely achieved. Tell Arnaud-Amaury that every last person in this city must be given a safe passport. Tell him that my *paratge* will never settle for less."

Peire studied the ceiling of the refectory. If he had kinsmen and close friends who were heretics, would he give them over to be burnt? Especially if a refusal would mean the loss of two of the richest counties of his kingdom? He sighed and rose to his feet. "I will remain your friend, not just your suzerain." He took Trencavel's hand in both of his and shook it firmly. "Farewell and good luck."

Trencavel accompanied the king and his retinue to the stairwell, where they embraced. As the King swept down the stairs, Roger stamped off to his private quarters, without a word to his peers. After he left, a hubbub burst forth from the attending throng who had listened silently to the exchange. There was nothing but praise for Trencavel's performance. The mood was to fight to the death.

Following the rebuff to their terms, the French mounted repeated assaults against the battlements for three days in a row, but were driven back with heavy losses by the defenders' crossbowmen. The crusader's siege weapons failed to dent the walls, and his artillerists were decimated by sharp shooters in the fortress. Yet, while the military defense was as strong as ever, the health of the inhabitants steadily deteriorated.

Among the leaders of Arnaud-Amaury's army, there was dissension about what would happen if Carcassona would surrender. From the experience in Besièrs, which was set afire by mistake, many of the northern barons realized that excessive violence was counterproductive, and provided very little booty to the victors. In the final analysis, sharing the spoils was far better than sharing the slaughter, they argued.

Three days after King Peire's departure, Arnaud-Amaury relented and sent a message to Trencavel under a flag of truce. With so many of his people living in appalling squalor, the Viscount reluctantly agreed to negotiate. Under a pledge of safe conduct, he and eight of his leaders attended a parley in the Count of Nevers' pavilion.

Arnaud-Amaury proposed the terms suggested by Peire of Aragon. Everyone would have safe conduct from the city, but would not be allowed to carry any possessions besides the clothes on their backs. The defenders had little choice but to accept, and after putting his signature to the document, Trencavel and his lieutenants rose to depart. That was when Arnaud-Amaury's men surrounded and disarmed them, and put the Viscount in chains.

"Let's see if your heretical magic can undo shackles," Arnaud-Amaury taunted. "I wot full well that you'll feel right at home in your own cozy dungeon. Those who take arms against the church militant cannot expect us to turn the other cheek. Those who support and protect heretics must be aware that they are far more dangerous to the Holy Mother Church than the heretics!"

"Let's see how you reflect on your actions in the privacy of a dungeon cell where the passage of time and lack of disturbance may give you new insight. Consider yourself blessed that we provide you with the opportunity to think long and hard about the various advantages and disadvantages of both faiths, so that you can make an informed choice. I am confident that in time you will make the right choice. Goodbye, Viscount. I doubt that our paths will ever cross again." The legate's mantle swirled around his legs as he strode out of the pavilion.

Holding year-old Isadore in his arms, Olivier shuffled along behind Ruth Ravanel, who was leading seven-year-old Rebecca by the hand. They were part of a single-file of Carcassona's inhabitants that was snaking its way through the city gate and passing through a gauntlet of French sergeants poking fun at the people as they passed and who, now and again, would wrench bags or sacks of possessions out of their arms.

"Hey, Granny, only the rags on your back. The rest is ours." A French soldier said, and snatched away the bag an old woman was struggling to carry as she limped along.

When an attractive woman came by, a guard held up the bag and cried, "How now, my pretty, how about swapping granny's bag of stuff for the clothes you got on?" The other guards laughed and leered at the woman, making rude gestures.

Olivier seethed at their bullying behavior, and remembered the high hopes he had entertained when he left home a month before. There would be a battle and they would rout the French and send them reeling back up the Rose valley in disarray. But instead of a battle, there had been a siege. Instead of victory, there had been surrender. And now there was humiliation, too. He had come well-mounted and accoutered, but would return footsore and in rags. At least, he reflected, he would return; he was alive, and hadn't been wounded. And at last, he would be reunited with Micaela and his two girls. His heart ached at the thought of them.

When the surrender was made known, Olivier had gone in search of the Ravanels and finally found Ruth alone with her children. He was shocked by her appearance. The once beautiful woman was haggard and pale with dark circles under her eyes. Her skin was pale and blotchy, her hair dull and tangled. Between sobs, she told him that Jacob had been killed on the first day of fighting at the Bourg, and that his body had never been recovered. Her parents had died of dysentery during the siege, and now she and the baby were suffering from the same disease. The stench of excrement arose from the infant's swaddling.

154

Like most of the refugees, Ruth did not want to return to Besièrs, having heard it was a shambles, a city of ashes, ghosts, and fat ravens and dogs. She said she would only feel safe in Tolosa, a distance of thirty leagues to the northwest. Olivier, however, longed to turn east toward home, toward Micaela and the girls, but how could he abandon this poor woman whose fate had become so inexorably linked to his own? Besides, he needed to take the Tolosa road in order to make sure his mother got out of Fanjaus before the French arrived.

When he had volunteered to accompany Ruth, he feared that she would not survive the trip alone. Her gait was faltering and weak. Even Fanjaus, lay seven leagues away, an enormous distance for a sick woman with a sick infant. How in the world could she make it? And what about the baby, whose once plump face was gaunt, its skin stretched over its skull?

Nearing the gate, Olivier spied a familiar face peering at the outcasts, one by one, as they passed through the gate. He felt a knot in his stomach. Thibaut, the thief stood studying each passing face. A strong young squire stood at Thibaut's elbow, a hand resting on the hilt of his sword.

Olivier stopped and stood still, holding the baby in front of his face. With his other arm, he pulled Ruth aside. "Walk backward," he whispered. "Don't turn around. They are looking for us. Let the people behind pass you by." They began to walk backwards and people shuffling forward passed them on either side. When the street bent around a corner, he turned around and led Ruth to walk as briskly as she could along the wall of the ramparts until he came to a small wooden shed. He shepherded Ruth and Rebecca through its door and led them down a spiral stone staircase into a small vault with a massive door on one side. Lifting a heavy oaken bar from stone brackets on each side of the door, he put it aside and pulled on an iron handle. The door creaked open.

Turning to Ruth, he explained that they were going to use a tunnel that passed under the wall and into the cemetery of the Bourg, the suburb that had been destroyed early in the siege. He and others had used it to harass the French at night. It was about four hundred paces long and there would be no light until they came to its terminus. It might seem frightening, but if they just kept going, they would be through it in no time. The main thing would be to keep their hands clasped. Could she do it? She nodded, and took Rebecca's hand in hers. Cradling Isadore in one arm, he gripped Ruth's other hand and carefully felt his way down another spiral staircase in utter darkness. Then he crept forward until he bumped in to a wall, and felt along it until he found the tunnel opening. He slowly advanced, letting his left shoulder brush along the moldy wall.

It seemed forever before he finally saw a small beam of light far ahead. Moments later, they entered a tomb, dimly lit from a crack in its roof, where skeletons garbed in moldering clothes lay in niches on both sides of the room. Narrow shafts of bright light shone around the edges of a door, which was barred from the inside. He gently lifted the bar and eased the door ajar. At first, the daylight blinded him, but finally his eyes adjusted and he peered outside. The cemetery was deserted. He opened the door further and stepped out. The ramparts loomed a few hundred paces away, but on this side of the castle, they seemed to be abandoned. He beckoned Ruth and her daughter to join him, and soon they were trudging west across empty fields. Once they had put a league between them and Carcassona, Olivier figured, they would leave the fields and angle northward toward the road.

Thibaut couldn't meet the eyes of the Abbot who stood looking down at him, eyebrows lifted in anticipation. He glanced sidelong at the young French squire, who shrugged. The Abbot's unanswered questions hung in the air.

"You saw them not? Not the smith, nor the wife, nor the children, nor the man who you say impersonated a monk? What was his name?"

The thief's tongue seemed to stick to the roof of his mouth, but finally he blurted out, "Olivier de Mazan. No, I saw them not, your Excellence. They did not pass through the gate, full sure am I." He looked at the squire for support, and finding none, studied the pattern of the marbled floor.

"Be you full sure that you didn't miss them?"

"Yes, your Excellency. Mazan has blond hair, which is rare in this country. He would have stood out like a horse turd on a platter."

Arnaud-Amaury scowled at the man; his impulse was to turn him over to the French to be tortured to death as a pilferer, but then he would be quit of the only person who could identify those who had access to the scrolls. He pounded his fist on the table. "Then mayhap they didn't come to Carcassona at all. They could have gone north to the Black Mountain. Or south to the Donezan. Or west to the Lauragais." Sweat poured down his face. He poked Thibaut's chest hard with his index finger "If you had grown up here as a Cathar and wanted go to the closest stronghold of your people, where would you head?"

Thibaut's eyes darted about as if searching for a way to escape. "I wot not, your Excellency; there are many such places where Cathars congregate. Mayhap, Cabaret. Montreal, too, is close by. But a little farther along, there's Fanjaus. For years, it's been a regular beehive for Cathars. Even more than Montreal."

"Ah yes, Fanjaus. Interesting. Just a league or so away from Prolha, where my colleagues from Castille set up an abbey for lapsed Cathar women. Think you the town will submit to our cause? Or will it resist?"

"I know not, your Excellency. I am not a military man. But Fanjaus is far harder to defend than many other strongholds."

"Guy," Arnaud-Amaury said, "take our friend and find him some victuals and drink. Methinks we'll have to look for Mazan some other day," he sighed. "Besides, I've got my work cut out for me this morning," and waving a hand in dismissal, he lumbered to his feet.

The work at hand was to elect a new military commander to crush any or all resistance in the Midi. Someone who could assume Trencavel's title and properties. To Arnaud-Amaury, that also meant someone who could eventually strip Count Raimond and the Count of Fois of their possessions in order to rid the entire Midi of the heretical vermin. He had handpicked a college of electors comprised of two bishops and four knights who would follow his bidding.

On the surface, it seemed ridiculously easy. He had the most powerful barons in all of Europe to choose from. Yet, they seemed unwilling to serve beyond the forty days they owed their suzerain, Philippe of France. As he had come to know them during the campaign, Arnaud-Amaury realized that the really grand barons, such the Duke of Burgundy, or the Counts of Nevers and Saint Pol, were far more interested in acquiring spiritual, rather than material treasure. Their *quarantaine* had assured them they would go to heaven, and they were more than satisfied.

He'd also seen them bristle whenever he reminded them of their vows to achieve the pontiff's goal of eradicating heresy. They were just as concerned with the judicial ramifications of feudal obligations as King Philippe himself, and stood resolutely against having Raimond's lands broken up. They refused to take possession of fiefs that their king had not conceded to them, and they also fiercely defended Raimond against allegations of being soft on heresy. After all, he had ridden beside them during the campaign, all the way from Valence to Carcassona. He was a *copain*.

The situation with King Peire of Aragon was far more complex, Arnaud-Amaury brooded. Peire was Trencavel's suzerain. Whoever succeeded Trencavel would therefore become Peire's vassal, but only if Peire acknowledged him. And although imprisoned, Trencavel was still alive. His lands could not be forfeit as long as he lived. Peire had extremely strong relations with the pope, which he had consolidated by choosing Rome for his wedding.

As for the pope, the mere thought of him made the big Abbot seethe. Because of his legal training, Innocent was as cautious about trespassing on feudal rights as Philippe, which is why he was reluctant to discipline Raimond. Arnaud-Amaury kicked at a tuft of grass in frustration.

Almost as annoying were the three great barons; no matter how hard he had tried to win their friendship, his relations with them remained tenuous. While besieging Carcassona, they had made it clear that they did not want another Besièrs, where so many Christian souls were lost and where so much plunder had gone up in smoke. On the other hand, the lesser barons, while also motivated to join the Crusade for the indulgences it promised, were far more eager to wear the cross in hopes of gaining land as well as booty. But, no matter how much their greed coincided with his own hopes of dispossessing Raimond, Arnaud-Amaury worried about the ability of any of them to lead a united army against the Midi. To watch the crusade fail because of internal dissension and squabbling, let alone lack of baronial support, was not acceptable.

He locked his fingers together and cracked his knuckles. Pulling aside the heavy flap of his pavilion, the heat of the August sun struck him as if a firebrand had been waved in his face. He shielded his eyes with a hand and noted the position of the sun. He still had some time before his handpicked electors arrived. A pair of varlets lugging two benches appeared, and he waved them inside the pavilion and showed them where he wanted the benches placed.

No sooner had they left, than a voice said, "Sire, I'm back."

Arnaud-Amaury turned to find his new squire, Guy, standing in the entrance.

"I did as you asked, Sire. Thibaut is even now gorging himself."

"I don't trust that thieving scum as much as a viper," the Abbot answered. "Think you that he'll bide and help us search for Mazan?"

"Aye, he sees it in his best interest, to share the... er...uh... spoils, or whatever might come our way, I ween."

"Let me ask you something entirely different and in utter confidence. I have sounded out others about choosing military leaders, but I'd like to hear what a squire who was in the thick of the fight thinks. Among the French, does any leader stand out? Someone who's also pious and really dedicated to eradicating the heretics?

"When you put it that way, Count Simon Montfort is your man. He's got all the qualities you mentioned and then some."

"Such as?"

"He's extremely popular among all ranks, and he's courageous. He rescued Hugues d'Escaille who lay wounded in the ditch right out from under the volleys of the enemy crossbowmen."

"He sounds daring, forsooth, but can he lead?"

"His men would fain die for him, and methinks the rest of us feel the same way."

"Word has gone about that he's too impetuous, too impulsive."

"Decisive were a far better word. 'Tis said he regularly holds councils of war and heeds advice, then acts without further delay. With brutal force."

"Aha! Thank you for that, my boy. Isn't he from up your way?"

"Yes, he's a neighbor. But that's not why I like him. He's just so much more determined than any around him. He's a real soldier. A real crusader."

"I'm glad to hear it," Arnaud-Amaury nodded. "Now leave me while I prepare for the college. We'll talk about this later in the day."

As Olivier and the little family plodded along the road through the dusty heat, they could see knots of refugees in front of them and behind them. Here and there at the side of the road, local farmers sold melons, olives, cabbages, and barley to those with money and often gave their produce away to those who had none. Some had brought carts with demijohns of water.

At one cross roads, a rude tent had been set up and two elderly men administered to the lame and the ill. It was obvious to Olivier that he was in the presence of Good Men, even though they did not wear their customary black vestments. He looked up and down the road, and seeing no one but other refugees, he believed he could safely address the Good Men. He asked one of them to perform the *aparalhament.*

"Of course, my son," replied the Good Man.

Olivier knelt before him with both hands folded together, bowed forward to touch his forehead and hands to the ground. "Bless me, Lord, and pray for me." He genuflected two more times, each time asking the Good Man for the blessing and prayer. After the last genuflection, Olivier said "Lead me to a good end."

The Good Man bowed his head and said, "God bless you. In our prayers, we ask from God to make a good Christian out of you and lead you to your good end."

Olivier rose and he and the Good Man hugged and kissed each other. "Thank you, Good man," Olivier said. "My friend here," he nodded toward Ruth, who was sitting exhausted on the ground, "has dysentery. So does her baby. Can you help them?"

"No, but if you can get your hands on some coriander and make it into a brew, she should find some relief. Also, garlic will do much to help. Two or three cloves four times a day."

Olivier thanked him and helped Ruth onto her feet. She tottered along like an old woman and it seemed to Olivier that every refugee on the road was overtaking them. As they came by, he asked if they had any garlic or coriander, but to no avail. He looked at Ruth. How could she go on? What were they going to do, he wondered. To add to his despair, poor little Isadore began wailing piteously, and Olivier tried in vain to rock him to sleep. Ruth took the baby from him and changed its wrap, which was sodden with putrid smelling filth. That was the last clean wrap she had brought with her, he noticed, as Ruth tried to nurse the sick child while she staggered along.

Evening was approaching when Olivier spied a line of willows several hundred paces away from the road. He knew that it must mark the course of a stream. Carrying the baby, he led the woman and her daughter across the fields until they reached the rivulet, which was only two paces wide and a few fingers deep. Along its bank, he found a grassy marge, and handing the baby back to Ruth, he set about looking for firewood.

Although willows don't make good firewood, it was all he had, and after gathering a pile of dead branches, he took out his flint and steel, and soon had a fire blazing. Using his poniard to cut a few green branches, he fashioned two forked uprights that he poked across the fire from each other, then carved a spit. He had purchased a rabbit from one of the vendors along the road, and he sat down to skin and gut its carcass, through which he thrust the spit. The coals snapped and popped and the meat sizzled. The aroma of roasting flesh made Olivier's mouth water. He smiled at Ruth and her daughter. Ruth smiled weakly in return, and Rebecca laughed, licking her lips in pantomime.

When they had finished the meal and nibbled the bones clean, they drank from the stream and walked out of the firelight and into the dark in opposite directions to answer the calls of nature. Making his way back to the fire, he found Rebecca snuggled between the roots of an old willow a dozen paces away, while her mother nursed Isadore.

While trying to decide whether to find a place on the other side of the tree or sleep nearer the fire, Olivier sensed, rather than saw, something move in the darkness on the other side of the rivulet. In the dim glow of the coals, he made out three shapes, three men. Daggers in their belts glinted in the firelight.

Olivier froze in shock, as first one and then the others sprang across the rivulet. The man in the middle, wearing the leather curaissse of a foot soldier, pointed at Olivier.

"Ne bougez pas!" he growled. Nodding toward Ruth, he told the man on his left, *"Pierre, enleves l'enfant de cette garce, et si-t-elle resiste, casse lui la gueule."*

These were French *routiers*, perhaps deserters, Olivier realized. They were going to take the woman's baby and probably use it as a hostage while they raped her or worse. Perhaps they would rape the little girl. They would also rob him and...fear knifed through him...they would kill him.

"Vous!" the man leveled his finger at Olivier. *"Rendez-moi le poignard. Ne hésitez pas, ou nous ferons mal aux enfants,"* the man threatened.

Olivier understood that if he didn't give up his dagger, they were going to hurt the children. He also knew that once he was disarmed, the men would be able to do whatever they wanted. He could run, or he could fight. However, there were three of them. And if he fought, they might kill the woman and her children just for spite. Yet, if he didn't fight, the family might be killed anyway.

"Allez, allez vite! Rendez-le à moi." As the crusader angrily repeated his demand, Ruth began screaming as she tried to prevent the man called Pierre from taking the baby.

An image of wrestling flashed through Olivier's head, and stepping carefully around the fire, he approached the crusader. He reached to his belt and drew the dagger from its sheath.

"*La poignée d'abord,*" the man ordered, gesturing to Olivier to present the hilt first. Olivier put the blade in his left hand, the hilt pointing to the Frenchman. As the man took it in his right hand, Olivier gripped the crusader's wrist with his left hand and stepping strongly forward, threw his own right arm over the man's arm and reaching down into the man's crotch, thrust himself down and back with all his might.

The maneuver propelled the *routier* violently down onto his face, which thudded into the glowing coals. Lying along side of him, Olivier felt the man go limp Olivier extracted his leg from under the unconscious enemy, and rolled to his left, away from the fire. Snatching the dagger from the man's hand, Olivier rose in a crouch. Only paces away, the man called Pierre stopped struggling with Ruth, and stared open-mouthed at Olivier in surprise. Before Pierre knew what was happening, Olivier's dagger drove between his ribs and he died before he could scream.

As the man sagged and fell, Olivier turned toward the third routier, who had drawn his dagger and taken a step toward Olivier. Then, in an apparent change of mind, the Frenchman turned tail and jumping the rivulet, made off across the field toward the road. Olivier caught up with him in the middle of the field, tackled him from behind and stabbed him again and again until he no longer moved. Olivier rose and started off, then went back and searched the corpse. A purse was strapped to his belt, and Oliver used his bloody poniard to cut the man's belt in two. Picking up the purse, belt and all, he wiped the poniard on the dead man's tunic, and retraced his steps.

When he returned to the campfire, Ruth and her children were gone and the *routier's* hair was ablaze; for the second time that day, the smell of roasting flesh filled Olivier's nostrils, along with the stench of burning hair.

Olivier called into the darkness. "Ruth, 'tis me. Come on back! The French are gone! There's naught to fear!" While waiting for an answer, Olivier dragged the dead man out of the fire and hauled him over along side of Pierre. He rummaged through the men's clothes and found fat purses bearing evidence of their success at highway robbery. He felt a certain amount of relief. The bastards richly deserved their violent deaths.

At the sound of faint rustling, he looked up and saw Ruth and Rebecca approaching warily out of the darkness. He went to meet them, and Ruth, holding her baby, threw herself in his arms, sobbing while Rebecca clung to his legs. He explained that it was wise to find another place to sleep. Dousing the coals with handfuls of water from the rivulet, he led them along the stream for several hundred paces until they found another place to sleep. Olivier gave Ruth the purses he had taken from the dead men. She thanked him and shed tears of gratitude.

He went back to where the two dead men lay, and using his dagger, cut the clothes off their bodies. They would serve as wrappings for the baby and washcloths for Ruth and Rebecca. Returning to where the little family was bedded down, he lay down and curled on his side a few paces away from them.

How very lucky they were to be alive, he mused. It had been a very narrow escape. He had executed the wrestling hold flawlessly. He and Camille had both practiced it, but neither had ever succeeded in performing it against the other. Had the *aparalhament* played a part in protecting them? He lay awake going over and over the details of the ugly episode until he finally pushed the violence out of his head by conjuring up images of Micaela and his daughters.

Somewhere in his brain, the images switched off as he fell asleep, where he would meet them again in dreamland.

The next morning Olivier awoke to wailing. Little Isadore had died during the night. While Ruth and Rebecca wept inconsolably, he dug a grave with his poniard and buried the baby. When it came time to take to the road, he found that Ruth had soiled herself and had become too weak to walk. If she were to survive, she needed the care of a physician, he knew, but where could he find one? He looked frantically across the fields in every direction but saw no sign of habitation. A few refugees moved along the road a few hundred paces away, so he laid her down in the shade of the tree, took off his tunic and rolled it into a pillow for her head. Then, telling Rebecca to watch her mother, he ran to the road through the knee-high barley in search of help. But everyone he stopped pulled away from him, and no one he encountered was carrying coriander or garlic.

In desperation, he ran back to where Ruth was lying. She had become feverish and delirious, and her breathing was rapid and shallow. She couldn't respond when he spoke to her.

He decided to cool her off in the rivulet, but he balked at carrying her because of the excrement that saturated her kirtle. Reaching down, he pulled her up into a sitting position, and stooping behind her, thrust his hands under her armpits, clasped them together over her chest, and pulled her up almost to her feet. Half-carrying and half-dragging her, he moved to the stream. Lowering her into the water and cradling her head, he hoped to wash away the filth and cool off her fever at the same time.

The current was too weak to clean her kirtle. He would have to remove it, which meant passing it over her face, and he couldn't bear the thought of that filth falling into her face. He asked Rebecca to bring the three purses, and put them under Ruth's neck to keep her head above water.

Using his poniard, he sawed away at the neckline of her kirtle. Digging the grave had dulled the blade but finally the cloth gave way. He took the ends in both hands and ripped the kirtle open right down to the hem, which finally gave way to more sawing. Then he called Rebecca, and together they eased Ruth's arms out of the sleeves, and passed the kirtle down and out from under her body.

Her breasts, still full of milk, sprawled onto her arms, but the rest of her body was emaciated. Olivier gagged at the sight of her pudendum and thighs, which were coated with bloody excrement. He used the clean upper part of the kirtle to wash away the filth and when he was finished, he picked her up and carried her to a bed he had made of the Frenchmen's clothes. Her eyes opened slightly, fixed on his and then rolled toward Rebecca. She lifted her head slightly and started to speak, but then fell back, emitting a sigh that seemed to go on forever, her pupils dilating in a last look at her daughter. Olivier tenderly closed her eyes, and pulled Rebecca into his arms, hugging her tight. She was only a few years older than his own daughters, he guessed, and he was certain that Micaela would raise this child like her own.

Just as Arnaud-Amaury feared, all three grand barons, one after the other, refused the honor the electoral college wanted to bestow on them. Even worse, when it asked Simon Montfort to lead the crusading army, he also refused, on the grounds he was not competent and unworthy. Resorting to his authority as papal legate, the Abbot formally commanded the Count to accept the position in the name of the oath of obedience that every crusader had taken. Monfort accepted his new role only on condition that all of the assembled nobles pledge to come to his aid in case the crusade became endangered.

Once the other barons guaranteed their support and Montfort was finally invested as the crusaders' commander-in-chief, Arnaud-Amaury felt that a huge weight had been removed his shoulders. He would remain in overall control of the crusade, and serve as its spiritual leader. But now he had a single commander for the army in the field, and the lines of command would be far more efficient than before, when he had to get Raimond and the three grand barons to agree on every move.

The new arrangement would also let him concentrate on reducing Raimond's influence, while Montfort would finish the conquest of Trencavel's possessions. Of course, Milo was ostensibly the only legate with whom Raimond should deal, and although Arnaud-Amaury chafed at this papal whim, he knew it didn't really matter. He was still in absolute control.

Finally, now, there would be time to try to recover the scrolls. Maybe, just maybe, in the wake of Montfort's army, he could pick up their trail. If only he could get his hands on them! His mind reeled with the possibilities.

Fanjaus

Aude stuffed the last skein of wool yarn into a woven basket with the others, and set it down besides the loom while she adjusted its straps. If she had been stronger she would have dismantled the loom to take along, but she knew it was too much to carry. Faye and Raimonde waited outside the doorway, their belongings strapped in baskets on their backs.

News of the sack of Besièrs and the fall of Carcassona had traveled fast. Now word came that the Crusaders had chosen a French baron, Simon de Montfort, to lead the crusade against the Good Folk. The fact that the crusaders had spared the population of Carcassona had encouraged the leaders of Fanjaus to send emissaries to Monfort, declaring the people's willingness to open its gates to him as their new liege lord. Both the Roman majority and the True Christian minority agreed that the Good Folk should evacuate the town, for their own good, as well as for that of the town as a whole.

Many of the Good Folk had already departed, some going north to the Black Mountain, and others heading south to Montségur, where Aude and her friends had decided to go. It was high time, too, for Fanjaus – only seven leagues from Carcassona -- was definitely a plum ripe for the picking.

As Faye and Raimonde were helping Aude slip her basket onto her back, a familiar voice boomed behind them.

"Ah, my Good Women, you weren't going to leave without saying goodbye, I trow." Camille the smith thrust his head inside the door and winked at them. "'Tis well I came by just now. 'Twill make my heart glad to load all your belongings on my mule. It can carry almost ten times what the three of you have on your backs, and 'tis tethered right outside."

"Master Smith," Aude replied, "'tis a fair, fair thing that you propose. We had been minded to leave most of our possessions, including our loom, but if your mule can take the weight, then we fain would accept your boon."

"Allow me," Camille said, and helped the women put down their baskets.

"Where are you heading?" Camille asked, as he stooped down and began helping Aude disassemble the loom.

"We deem 'tis safest to go south, to Montségur. 'Tis not too far."

"A bonny choice. Lord Pereille is building a citadel up there."

"I wot that well. Some Good Folk have been dwelling up there for years. You'll see when you get there."

Camille had just taken the base of the loom apart, when he looked up and saw a gaunt, bearded stranger standing in the doorway, holding a little girl by the hand. "You've got company," he said to Aude.

Aude looked up at the ragged man, and her eyes lit up. "Olivier! Olivier, my boy," she cried out in delight, and she flew to the stranger and hugged him as tightly as she could. Then she released him, and bent down to take the girl's hands in her own. "And who are you?"

"Her name's Rebecca, Maire. Her parents are dead, so I'm going to take her home with me. But first I would fain make full sure you are safe and sound..."

Camille sprang up to crush Olivier in a bear hug. "Didn't recognize you, Ollie! I can scarce trust my eyes. You've come in the nick of time. These early birds are about to fly south."

"So I gathered when I came to the door, and..." Olivier broke off as Faye and Raimonde embraced him in turn. "It gladdens my heart to see you Good Women again, I fain the occasion were more auspicious and I were more presentable," he said.

"'Tis well done, indeed,to have two big strapping men to help us." Faye said. "But first, let us help you find some clean clothes. And we have basins of water in the next room that you can use to wash off that..." She blushed because she was going to say "stench."

"I've got clothes for Ollie, Dòna, don't worry," Camille said to Faye. "'Twill be some time before I fetch them, for I fain would try not to lose any parts to this loom," he added, as he sat back down and resumed his task.

"Rebecca, my darling child, you come with me," Aude said putting an arm around the little girl, who was a bit bewildered by all the ado. "Raimonde and I will tend to you. You will love to have your hair washed and combed," she said and led the girl into the next room.

After washing, and pulling on the clean garments Camille had brought him, Olivier stepped outside and looked south, where the snow-capped massif of St. Bartholemy gleamed white in the bright afternoon sun.

"Aye, 'tis where we're headed," Camille said, coming up behind him. "Well, actually, a league or so closer. Montségur's nowhere as high, so we can't see it from here."

"I wot it well. We could see St. Bartholemy clearly from the ramparts of Carcassona. 'Twas like a banner; you can scarce believe how it lifted our hopes. How many folk dwell on Montségur?"

"Belike a few dozen, I trow, but they are forever coming and going, hither and yon, and are mostly Good Men and Women. Gilhabert de Castras -- remember him? Word has gone out that he bides there all year round," Camille said.

"Yes, I met him at my mother's Consolation. I was there, remember?"

"How could I forget? You had your lovely wife with you. What are you doing here? And who's the little girl?"

"Tis a long story. I'll tell you on the road, by reason the French are coming and we can't let them catch my mother and her friends. Will they be safe at Montségur?"

"Safe? What else can Montségur be?" Camille chuckled. "'Safe Mountain.' 'Tis well named. You'll see for yourself."

"I hear 'tis quite a fortress."

"Well, they've been building it ever since that big to-do at Mirapeis."

"When was that?" Olivier asked.

"About five years ago. About six hundred Good Folk attended."

"Ah, yes; I call to mind that my mother wrote about Innocent's revival of the old Lateran Council ordinance."

Camille looked blank. "What was that in heed of?"

"It proclaimed that the property of heretics and their supporters were forfeit, and that heresy was the equivalent of treason."

"Methinks treason is a capital crime."

"Forsooth!" Olivier nodded in agreement. 'Tis the basis for the crusade. 'Tis why the Good Folk are trying to make Montségur a refuge from the invaders. But hold your peace, here come the ladies and Rebecca."

Guy ambled up to the table where Arnaud-Amaury was enjoying a cantaloupe, and bowed.

"What news, my boy," the Abbot said.

"Good day, Sire. Do you call to mind our talk about Fanjaus yester morn? Believe it or not, a party of merchants from Fanjaus just rode in, looking to speak to you. They must needs give you the keys to the city."

"'Tis well! There's naught like the mention of Besièrs to make other towns throw open their gates. Fetch 'em here. I've got some questions to ask them concerning Thibaut's information. After I'm through with them, take their leader to meet with Montfort."

Alzeu de Fanjaus wiped his brow. Although it was the third week of a blistering August, and Carcassona was just as hot as Fanjaus, his forehead was clammy with *cold* sweat. Despite the legate's friendly demeanor, Alzeu had heard rumors about his heartlessness at Besièrs, which was one reason he and his fellow townsmen had dared everything and flung themselves on the mercy of the crusaders and the Holy Church. The lives of his wife and children, and indeed the rest of the population of Fanjaus, depended on the Abbot's benevolence. Alzeu also prayed that his own life-long devotion to the Roman Church would count for something.

In answer to Arnaud-Amaury's questions about the heretics, Alzeu explained that they had fled in small groups, going in every direction except east, toward Carcassona.

174

But when the legate asked him if he knew anyone with a Provençal accent, Azeu almost lost the power of speech. His neighbor, Aude, had a son from Provença who had shown up the day before just in time to flee with his mother and other Good Folk.

Alzeu fought the impulse to lie to the legate, who, as though he had read the merchant's mind, warned, "don't try to protect these people, no matter how well you know them, by reason they are Satan's apostles and they are experts at hoodwinking innocent Christians. I asked you a simple question. Do you know anyone, resident or visitor, in Fanjaus who speaks with a Provençal accent."

His eyes downcast, Alzeu said, "Nobody in town. But yesterday a stranger who spoke with a Provençal accent visited one of the Good Women —er, I mean Perfects — and then left town with them. They feared for their lives."

"As well they might," Arnaud-Amaury cried. "This stranger, what was the color of his hair?"

"Blond."

"Be you sure?"

"Full sure, Sire. 'Twas dark blond."

"Was he alone?"

"No, he had a little girl with him."

"How old was she?"

"Mayhap five or six."

"Hair?"

"Darkish brown. Curly."

"What about the heretic that he was visiting. What's her name?"

"Aude."

"Has she always dwelt in the village?"

"She was born here, but moved away when she married."

"Do you know where she went?"

175

"Provença. Her husband was a noble from the Comtat Venaicin."

"Then what was she about, there in Fanjaus?"

Azeu shrugged. "After her husband died, she moved back here to be with her mother, who was still alive. And about three years ago she became a Goo—she became a Perfect."

"Who accompanied her?"

"The other two Perfects she lived with, and the blacksmith and her son."

"Mayhap you saw which way she went?"

"South."

"Toward Mirapeis, or Limoux?".

"Mirapeis."

"Mounted or afoot?

"Afoot. They carried their possessions on the smith's mule."

"'Twill do for now, good sir. Thank you and may the Good Lord protect you."

Following the man outside, he found Guy conversing with the sentinels. "Our quarry is almost in sight. Saddle our horses, and find Thibaut," the abbot cried. "I'm going to ask Montfort to lend me some knights to help us hunt down these heretic swine."

Mirapeis

The seven-man troop reached Mirapeis a few hours before nightfall. The knights and their squires had left their hauberks and surcoats behind and like Arnaud-Amaury himself, wore merchants' clothing. Because none were fluent in the *lenga d'oc,* they bivouacked outside the walls a bit beyond where horses and pack animals were tethered.

The legate and Thibaut entered the town in search of their prey. The streets were packed with refugees, and here and there they saw the tell-tale black robes of Perfects. Many people were sitting or lying on their bundles in the street. As discretely and casually as he could, Arnaud-Amaury inquired about "his old friend Camille, the smith from Fanjaus," to no avail.

As darkness fell, with no sign of the fugitives, Arnaud-Amaury broke off the search and signaling Thibaut to follow, trudged back to join the others. On a whim, he hailed the watchman at the gate, and described the man whom he was looking for, including a mule laden with pieces of a loom. His heart leapt when the guard said that such a group had spent the previous night bedded down not far from where he was standing. He had no idea where they had gone, the guard said, although many Good People seemed to be heading for Montségur, which was about two or three leagues south of Lavelanet, which itself lay only a bit more than eleven leagues away.

Arnaud-Amaury rubbed his hands together in glee. The hounds had picked up the scent of the hare, which in this case, moving at the pace of women, was more like a tortoise! If they rode all night, they could probably catch up with their prey somewhere near Lavelanet. 'Twould be two knights, three squires, one thief and himself − against one knight and a blacksmith. The odds favored him auspiciously.

Lavelanet

It was market day in Lavelanet when Camille led the mule up to the ramparts, and tied its bridle to the rope that ran through iron rings in the wall. Although it was only midmorning, some two dozen donkeys and mules were already tethered there. The three Good Women fussed among the baggage and pulled out several bolts of cloth that they planned to sell in the market. Camille put the bolts under his arm and followed the women through the gate, while Olivier tended to the animals.

They had traveled at least eight leagues the day before and had camped barely three leagues from town when the women, exhausted and footsore, had refused to take another step. Nearing Lavelanet, the forest defiles had become narrower and narrower and they had often lost sight of the snow covered crests of St. Barthelemy that had beckoned to them most of the way. But as they came up to the village, they beheld a green peak capped by a white fortress jutting up in the distance. Montségur!.

Olivier yawned and stretched his arms above his head, then took a comb out of a saddlebag and started currying the mule. As he was just finishing the job, he spied a small cavalcade of merchants approaching from the direction of Mirapeis. There was something about the way they sat in the saddle that caught Olivier's attention. They halted a good eight hundred paces from the ramparts, and all but one dismounted. The lone rider, accompanied by one of the men on foot, urged his mount forward at a walk. What was it about the man on foot that made him uneasy, Olivier wondered.

As they came closer, Olivier suddenly realized that the man on foot was Thibaut, the thief! He ducked behind the mule, and then briskly worked his way through the other pack animals to the gate, where he stepped behind the stone jamb of the archway. The presence of the thief could not be a coincidence; evidently, they had picked up his trail. He watched the rider dismount and tether his horse. The horseman was a big man who also seemed somehow familiar. Who was he? He racked his memory. Then he remembered Montpelhier, three months ago, when Viscount Trencavel begged forgiveness from the crusaders. The rider, he realized with a shock, was Arnaud-Amaury, the papal legate, the Abbot of Citeaux, the leader of the Crusade!

What in the world was he doing here, and what was he doing consorting with a thief? Lavelanet lay in the County of Fois, which was a major fief of the king of Aragon. The Crusade had no authority here. The fact that the legate and his men were disguised as merchants proved that this was definitely not official business. As the legate and Thibaut neared the gate, Olivier flung himself down in the far corner of the gateway and pulled his mantle up over his head, hoping they would take him for a homeless beggar. Through a small gap in the cloth, he watched them walk by into the town. Getting back to his feet, he followed them, keeping well back as they entered the thronged market place. As he went, he tucked his hair locks into his cap. His blond hair would be a dead giveaway.

In the middle of the market, the two men stopped and conversed. Arnaud-Amaury craned his neck this way and that, as Thibaut was pointing up at the battlements. Then the legate nodded, and began to amble around the market place, while Thibaut made a beeline to the wall and climbed a flight of stairs to the parapet, where he disappeared into a *garderobe* built into the wall.

Aha! The thief wants to piss, Olivier deduced. Another flight of stairs was but paces away, and he took them two steps at a time, then slouched along to the *garderobe*, keeping an eye on the Abbot below, who fortunately was looking everywhere but up.

Thibaut was standing with his breeches down and shaking the last few drops from his foreskin when Olivier came up behind him and clamped one hand over his mouth and thrust a poniard beneath his testicles with the other.

"Hands against the wall, and don't make a peep," he hissed, "or off comes your manhood."

Feeling the cold steel on his scrotum, Thibaut hurried to do as he was told.

"Remember me?" Olivier whispered.

Thibaut nodded.

"Remember what I said about keeping away from me and mine?"

The thief shook his head, then nodded frantically when the hard blade pressed upwards.

"Know you my name?"

Even more vigorous shaking of the head.

"Forsooth?"

Vigorous nodding.

"The horsemen you came with. They're French?"

More nodding after a hesitation.

"Let me guess. They don't speak Occitan."

More nodding.

"What do you mean? That they do?" He lifted the blade a bit.

Thibaut's eyes bulged and he violently shook his head.

"Ah, they don't. 'Tis why they bide outside?".

"Thibaut nodded and let out the breath he had been holding.

"You're not going to mention our little talk to anybody, are you?"

Violent shaking.

"Good, and just to make sure…" Olivier pulled the poniard away from the thief's pudenda and plunged it into his abdomen an inch or so below his sternum and thrust it upwards through his heart. The thief slumped forward onto the lip of the *garderobe*. Olivier tipped him headfirst the rest of the way into the cavity. He had not meant to kill Thibaut, but disgust and rage had overcome him at the last moment. He did not rue what he had done.

Instead of taking the same staircase back down to the market place, Olivier kept walking along the ramparts until he came to the gate tower, where he took a spiral staircase to the street level. He went over to where the watchman was lounging at the gate. "By my faith, I fain wouldn't impose on your duty, but methinks some French spies are watching you."

"Frenchmen? You're joking. Why would they be spying on us?"

Olivier shrugged. "I wot not. Thought *you* might be know."

"The Crusade's against Trencavel. Our lord is the Count of Fois, and his liege lord is King Peire of Aragon."

"Forsooth. Therefore, what are French knights dressed up like merchants doing here in Lavelanet? Doesn't that seem odd?"

"'Twould, if I could see them. Where are they?"

"Right over there. See?" Olivier pointed at the group of horsemen.

"Seem like ordinary merchants to me."

"Ask yourself: if they really are merchants, why aren't they in the marketplace instead of dawdling around out there Why not try talking to them? I'm telling you, they don't understand a word you say!"

The watchman's eyes shifted from Olivier to the five horsemen and back.

"Wait here. I'll be back," the guard said, and sped away into the town.

After a short interval, Olivier hurried back to the market place in search of his friends. He spotted Arnaud-Amaury, who was a head taller than anyone else. Working his way through the crowd, Olivier was startled to find Arnaud-Amaury talking to his mother, who was showing him a bolt of cloth. It suddenly came to him that his mother didn't know whom she was talking to, and that her only value to Arnaud-Amaury was to lead him to her son. He bent his knees slightly to lower his profile and snuck away, desperately looking about for Camille. After traversing the entire market place, he finally found Camille chatting with a pretty cheese merchant.

"May I have a word in private with my friend here?" Olivier asked, and putting his hand on the back of Camille's head, propelled him away from the table piled high with cheeses toward the shelter of a vintner's tent.

"Just don't make it too long," the woman called as they disappeared behind the canvas flaps.

"Camille, did you notice the big guy talking to my mother?"

"No, I was more interested in sampling the local cheese."

Still using his hand to steer Camille, Olivier turned him around to look across the market place. "See that great big galoot over yonder?"

"The one in the purple cap?"

"That's the one. Guess who he's talking to?"

"How the in the name of Peter should I know? I'm a stranger here."

"My *mother*, that's who. He's talking to my *mother!*"

"Do you want me to go over and tell him to piss off?"

183

"No, you anvil head, *hearken* to me! Does the name Arnaud-Amaury call aught to mind?"

"You don't mean the Abbot in charge of the whole fucking Crusade? The papal legate?"

"I do."

"What's he doing here?

"You would fain not know. I've got something he wants bad enough to trail us here. And he's got a couple of knights and some squires waiting outside the walls. I need to create a diversion, so that I can steal his horse and ride to Montségur, make a delivery, and be back by sunset. Trouble is, I need a guide."

"Maybe my friend knows a boy who will take you."

"What friend?

Camille rolled his eyes toward the cheese stall.

A dozen Pater Nosters later, Camille and Olivier emerged from the gateway with a young boy in tow and sauntered over to where the legate's horse was cropping the sparse grass. Across the way, a small crowd had gathered. The watch, with its pole arms, had swelled to a dozen, and a number of other town officials and onlookers surrounded the Frenchmen, who were flailing their arms in frustration.

"There's naught like a standoff between people who don't even speak the same language," Olivier said.

Camille grinned. "You can say that again!"

Olivier swung up into the saddle and Camille handed him the reins, then lifted the boy up onto the pommel as if he was a light sheaf of barley. "Have a nice ride and say hello to Bishop Castras for me," Camille said. "If all goes well, we'll be there tomorrow."

Olivier waved to his friend and put the horse into a canter toward the snowy peaks ahead.

Sweat beaded on the legate's brow. He had found the three women Perfects, and had passed himself off as a merchant from Limoux. He had gone so far as to buy bolts of cloth from them as he stalled for time, waiting for Aude's son and the smith to show up. From snatches of the women's conversations, he gathered that the two young men must have found an alehouse. He stifled a groan. Where was Thibaut when he needed him? Finding and identifying Mazan was the only reason Arnaud-Amaury had brought the thief along. How long does a man need to empty his bladder, the Abbot raged. Or his bowels, if that were the case? By the Holy Rood, he should never have trusted the thieving bugger. When he got back to Carcassona, he would bury Thibaut in a dungeon so deep that it would make the one in which he had imprisoned Trencavel seem like a tower.

In the meantime, there was nothing for it, but to wait for Mazan to show up. The women had made it plain that they were going on to Montségur, so he didn't dare let them out of his sight. They were the bait he needed to catch Olivier de Mazan and finally get his hands on the scrolls.

Arnaud-Amaury leaned unhappily against the stairway leading to the battlements, his buttocks partially supporting his weight. The Good Women were still hawking their wares, but there was no sign of either Thibaut, or Mazan, or the smith. The shadows were lengthening as the afternoon wore on. Where could they be?

As if in answer, a sudden commotion off to the right caused him to look over his shoulder, where a couple of well-built men edged their way through the crowd. The man in the lead had golden locks protruding from his tight cap, while the other had a heavy beard and a dark tangle of hair that fell to his shoulders. Aude of Fanjaus looked up at them and smiled.

"There you are at last! You gave us cause for grief," she cried, as Olivier came up to her and hugged her. "Where have you been? "

"Just hither and yon. Are you ready to push on? I fain would be quit of this town."

"Why, what's the matter?"

Olivier shook his head in disgust. "Someone picked my pocket," he said in a loud and indignant voice, and looked around as if searching for the culprit. "We spent the whole time combing the town for him."

"You saw him do it?" Aude said, her eyes like saucers.

"No, forsooth, but I know full well who did it. Mind that I told you that I was taking an important document to Montségur? A thief tried to steal them from me once before, but this time he succeeded. I'm full sure 'tis the same man. Come on, let's get out of here." The two men helped the women gather up the few bolts they had not sold and moved off toward the gate.

The legate fumed as he watched them go. So this was how that thieving scoundrel Thibaut repaid him! He ground his teeth. He would fetch his men. It no longer mattered that they didn't understand the *lenga d'oc*. It only mattered that they knew what that sneaky bastard Thibaut looked like, so they could hunt him down. He would go to the ends of the earth to apprehend the man who had so cunningly gulled him. He removed the bolts of cloth from under his arm and dashed them onto the ground before making for the gate.

The Abbot became even more enraged to find that the town authorities had arrested his men for trespassing. It took him almost two hours to explain that yes, although they were French, their main interest was boar hunting. As a textile merchant looking for bargains, he had offered himself as a guide to the Ariège where wild boar abounded and so he was mixing business with pleasure. He toyed with disclosing his real identity and using the tremendous power of the Holy See to cow them into subservience, but his presence in the County of Fois with a handful of crusaders would have seemed so bizarre that he decided against it. Although they did not take the boar-hunting story seriously, the authorities were appropriately mollified when he opened his purse and made his generous amends.

There was naught for it but to ride back to Carcassona, his mission unaccomplished. He could scarce believe that a petty thief had made a fool of him. 'Twas a hard matter to swallow, and he rode away in silence, furious with the way things had turned out.

Montségur

Guilhabert Castras warmly welcomed the three Good Women and had summoned one of the women in residence to show the newcomers to their quarters. Then he shook hands with Camille and at last turned to Olivier, who was holding Rebecca's hand.

"I see everything went well, my friend, and you have come back safe and sound. Who is your little companion? What's your name, child"

"Rebecca," the little girl said, hiding behind Aude's mantle.

"She's the goldsmith's daughter," Olivier said "You've already heard what happened in Besièrs and Carcassona, I trow. Both of Rebecca's parents, along with her poor little baby brother, died in the siege of Carcassona."

"Ah, so that means that Rebecca is the last of the line?"

"Olivier shrugged. "As far as we know."

'Tis a sorry matter."

"Forsooth! To have been spared the fate of the citizens of Besièrs only to lose their lives in Carcassona!"

Castras nodded. "Aye, and 'tis a terrible time for our Midi, but we shall overcome. Your mother says she'll bide with us for a while, and that makes me glad of heart. But what about your wife and your children? Are they back in Provença? They're well, I trow?"

"'Tis over a month since I left home, but yes, they were in the bloom of health when I last saw them."

"Good. I wish them the best. What are *your* plans, now?"

"To get back to them as soon as I can, by my troth! I fain would have Maire safely installed here before I go home."

"What about the child?"

"I'm taking her back with me."

"I see. Know you that your mother and the other Good Women would be only too happy to have her stay here, I trow. 'Twould make your journey so much easier. When the crusade is over, you can come back and fetch her."

"The thought has crossed my mind," Olivier nodded.

Castras looked around. Camille was climbing a staircase to the battlements, bent on admiring the countryside and the big peaks to the south.

Lowering his voice, Olivier said, "What about the scrolls? Did you get a chance to look at them? I'm sorry I couldn't tarry yesterday, but I explained to you why I was in haste."

Castras patted his mantle. "Both copies are here," he said, "and yes, I studied them and I am eager to have you go over them with me. Then I'll put them where they'll be completely safe from prying eyes."

"Belike they're safer here than any place I can think of."

"I hope and trust you are right," the Good Man said. "Thank you for everything you have done to bring them here. But now, let's go up and join your friend on the tower." He led the way up the stairs to the top. "Up here, we are very high, but see there, the mountains across the way are three times higher."

Looking out over the vast panorama, Olivier looked toward the east, away from the setting sun, trying to determine which valley might lead him back toward Provença.

As if reading his mind, Castras said, "Your best way home lies a few leagues down that valley there." He pointed. "That would take you through the gorge of the Fright – the name of that mountain over there — and then across the plateau of Soult to the Aude, and... well, I'll draw you a map."

"That's awfully kind of you Good Man, 'twould be most helpful."

"And I meant what I said about tending to the little girl. She would slow you down considerably, and although eventually you'll use the Via Domitia, the way I'll send you avoids the routes used by the invaders," Castras said. "Tis also tough going for a little girl, even if faring on horseback. Later, we can go to the stables and you can take your pick of the half dozen steeds there."

"By my troth, 'tis too kind. I don't…"

"Nonsense. Especially after what you've done for us. So we'll keep Rebecca until you come again. 'Twill be better for everyone.

"Methinks you're right, and I wot well that my mother will be delighted to have a child around. Especially one so well behaved.

Olivier hugged and kissed his mother one more time before he started to lead his horse through the gates of the south barbican. He had pressed one of the purses of the French *routiers* into his mother's hand, despite her protests, and had given another to Castras as a contribution to the Friends of God on Montségur. The third he needed for contingencies. On horseback, he easily could cut a whole week from the time it would take him on foot. Camille was walking alongside him, holding the halter of his mule. They would descent the pog together; then, when they reached the valley, Olivier would turn south and the smith would head north to Fanjaus.

They had just started to descend, when a man appeared before them, on his way up and leading a mule laden with comestibles. Olivier stepped aside to let him pass.

"Good day, and thank you," the man said, as he stopped and wiped his forehead with his sleeve. 'Tis a bit of a climb."

"Good day to you, too." Olivier said. "What news?"

"The French took Fanjaus and Mirapeis and were headed toward Pamias, last I heard."

"Was there any resistance? Any fighting?" Camille asked.

"Oh, no, they gave up without a fight. They didn't want to end up like Besièrs, now, did they? Although I hear that a lot of Fanjaus got burned down anyway."

"What? The French set it on fire?" Camille asked, his face livid with concern.

"Don't rightly know. But if you're asking about the Good Folks, they was all long gone when the French got there. In fact, I hear that Fanjaus was completely deserted.

"D'you hear that, Olivier? Maybe they torched my smithy!"

The anguish Olivier read in his friend's face went to his heart. After all that Camille had done to help him and his mother reach Montségur, how could he just let him go his own way?

"We'll find out. We can make it by sunset if we hurry."

" *We?* You mean…?"

"By my troth, I'm coming with you. 'Tis much faster than the southern route.

"Are you full sure? You wanted to go south to avoid the crusaders."

"Forsooth, but I've changed my mind. Now let's get going!"

Fanjaus

"Shit!" muttered Camille as he reined in his mule, and Olivier pulled up along side of him. A half-league ahead, the walls of Fanjaus were gilded by the setting sun, and over the tower of the main gate, a bright banner with a gold rampant lion on a red field was flapping in the early evening breeze. It was the Montfort crest. Either the French had come back, or the merchant was wrong and they had never left.

"What now?" asked Olivier.

"I'm going in alone, Ollie. I'm not only a resident, but I'm a smith to boot, and they have every reason to need me. You, on the other hand, are a different story. They might get suspicious. So, let me take a look around and then I'll come out and tell you what's happening."

"Shall we meet here?" Olivier asked.

"Remember that shepherd's hut we passed about a league behind us? I'll meet you there around *compline*."

"See you then. Good luck and be careful."

Camille urged the mule forward, and Olivier turned his horse back the way they had come.

When the distant church bells rang *compline*, Olivier was curled up asleep on the floor the tiny hut. The not-too-gentle prod of a chain-mail boot on his ribs woke him. In the darkness of the hut, he was unable to see the face of whoever was poking him.

"Camille?" He started to get up, but the pressure on his ribs intensified.

"Who are you? What are you doing here," boomed a gruff voice in Occitan. "Olivier of Mazan, of Provença," he said, scrambling to his feet and reaching for the hilt of his sword. "Who are you?" As he spoke, he felt the tip of a sword press against his chest."

"Ah-ah, don't touch that hilt if you want to live."

Olivier put his hands in the air. The swordsman had backed out of the hut into the moonlight, and Olivier glimpsed the crest of Fois, which had three pallets instead of the four of the House of Aragon, on his surcoat. But for the sword point boring into his sternum, Olivier would have heaved a sigh of relief. At least he was not dealing with a Frenchman.

"Who are you?" he repeated.

"I'm asking the questions," the man said. "What are you doing here?"

"I'm on my way home," he said, and gingerly pushed the sword point to the side with the flat of his hand. "I have no quarrel with the Count of Fois."

"Let's put it this way, then. What're you doing here in the Lauragais so far from home?" The sword still hovered near Olivier's left shoulder.

"My mother dwelt here. After the fall of Carcassona, I came to make sure that she got away from the crusaders."

"And what did you do at Carcassona?"

"I helped defend it against the crusade."

The man lowered his sword and sheathed it in his scabbard. Then he extended his hand. "My name is Pons de Pamias, and I'm at your service. We had to make sure that you weren't a spy. If you'll come with me, I'm sure the Count will be glad to meet you."

193

Olivier's eyes had adjusted to the dark, and now he saw dozens of horsemen standing in the roadway. Pamias led him over to a circle of dismounted knights, one of whom was questioning Camille, whose arms were being held by a knight on either side. He prayed that Camille would not decide to fling them off him. .

"Ah, Pons, you found another one?" exclaimed Camille's interlocutor.

"Sire, permit me to introduce Sir Olivier of Mazan from Provença. Says he fought with Trencavel at Carcassona." Olivier surmised that he was in the presence of the Count of Fois.

"Delighted, Mazan," the Count said. "Do you know this fellow standing here? He says he's the town smith and farrier, but we found him lurking about. Can he be a French spy?"

"Sire," Olivier said trying to keep his face straight, "he is who he says he is and he's a good friend of mine. Up on Montségur, word had gone out that much of Fanjaus had burned down, and thus we had cause to grieve about his smithy. We planned to meet here at *compline*, after he found out what had taken place."

The Count gestured at the men restraining Camille, and they released him. Then he stepped up to Camille and shook his hand. "Glad at heart to meet you, Master Smith." he said. "So now, we are all in anticipation. What did you find out?"

Camille flexed his shoulders and scowled at the two men who had been holding him. "My lord, I am glad to report that my smithy is undamaged. Most of the houses haven't been harmed. Unfortunately, the French reoccupied the town yesterday, after they got back from attacking Pamias and Saverdun."

"'Tis why we're here. We didn't come up here to play patty-cake with these French cunts," the Count said. "We plan to attack them tonight. We've got ladders to scale the walls. And if you know their dispositions, Master Smith, 'twill be a big help. 'Tis high time we taught this Montfort a lesson."

Camille shook his head. "I rue it well, my lord, that I only heeded my smithy. Had I only known you were here and what you wanted, I would've accounted for every last one of those foreign whoresons."

"Belike 'twill be the same," the Count said, "no matter what we know. After *matins* sound at midnight, we shall scale the walls. Our men will split up in bands, each of which will advance along parallel streets in order to mount a coordinated assault on the citadel. I'd be grateful if you'd come along as a guide," he said to Camille.

"Be glad to serve you, my lord."

"Make that the two of us," Olivier said.

Lit by the moonlight, the large bulk of the citadel loomed into sight as they came to the end of the dark street. Its portucullis was down.

"What about those doors up there?" said the Count in a low voice, pointing up to the doors on each side of the citadel that gave egress onto the ramparts.

"Dunno," Camille said. "The French might have barred them."

The Count motioned to Pons. "Take your men and get up there and see if we can get in from the ramparts."

Pons nodded and dashed off around the corner with his men at his heels. From that direction, came a shout, "*Qui va là?*" and then repeated shouts of "*Aux armes, on attaque!*" and the sounds of a scuffle with the clanging of steel.

"The fat's in the fire," the Count said, then yelled, "Death to the French!" and rushed toward the sound of the fighting, with Olivier, Camille and the rest of the men surging behind him, roaring "Death to the French!"

By now, the square was filled with men from Fois, and to the right of the citadel's gate, a handful of Frenchmen were fighting with their backs to the wall. As Olivier watched, the French threw down their weapons. He grinned at Camille and shrugged. "I guess we won't be needed."

No sooner had he uttered those words, when the sounds of a bitter skirmish broke out to his far left, and many of the Count's men ran to their comrades' aid. Camille punched Olivier's arm. "Come on, let's take 'em in the rear." and set off back down the same street they had used to get to the square. Several nearby men-at-arms from Fois guessed their purpose, and joined them as they pelted through the dark street after Camille.

Camille led them into a narrow passageway that was pitch dark and suddenly the noise of the fighting seemed just ahead. As they debouched from the dark alley, the moonlight revealed a gaggle of French spearmen, oblivious of the danger from behind, weaving and lunging at some Fois men, both sides taunting each other and hurling insults.

Olivier sprinted ahead and swung his sword in a deadly arc that chopped through an enemy's shoulder and crunched into his spine, dropping the man in his tracks, spurting great gouts of blood. Olivier barely had time to avoid a spearman's thrust, but a moment later, the tumult died down, and the Fois men picked their way past the blood-soaked bodies of their foes to embrace each other.

The men were excitedly boasting of their own roles in the fight, when a large shout from the direction of the citadel announced that the night's battle had taken yet another turn. The men surged off toward the fighting, but Camille put the palm of his hand on Oliver's chest. "Ollie, let's go the long way around. Maybe we'll be more helpful, *Oc*?"

They were retracing their steps through the narrow passageway, when Olivier, who had taken the lead, banged into someone coming full tilt the other way. "Please, please, I surrender," cried the man who fell to his knees, blubbering in anguish.

Recognizing the Ariège accent, Oliver pulled the man up to his feet and gripped his surcoat. "Get a hold of yourself. What's wrong?"

"The French..."

"What about them? What about the French?" cried Olivier.

"They – hundreds of them—charged us from the Citadel. We didn't have a chance.'

"Where are your mates?"

"They ran. I figured we were goners, so I ducked in here"

Olivier spoke over his shoulder to Camille. "Hear that? 'Tis a rout! The French sortied from the citadel, and everyone panicked. Can you get us out of here in one piece?"

"Just stay close, and we'll be outside the walls in a jiffy. Hopefully, our new friend here can keep up with us."

197

Bram

Riding with the Count at the head of the column, Olivier tried to overcome his misgivings as they approached the Via Aquitania, the ancient Roman road between Tolosa and Narbonne. After the debacle at Fanjaus, he had agreed to accompany the men of Fois on their raid for a few more days before he turned homeward. He knew that it was foolish to risk his life on what might be a wild goose chase when he could be well on his way to holding Micaela in his arms again. A few more days would not make so much difference, he rationalized, but down deep, he knew it was madness.

Although he had lost twenty men in Fanjaus, the Count was determined to get revenge for Montfort's foray into Fois. His plan was to trail Montfort's army, picking off any laggard elements or supply trains and restoring hope in the countryside that organized resistance was not only desirable, but highly feasible. As they progressed, *faidits* and other disgruntled local knights joined the cavalcade. Soon, he had as many horsemen as when he left Fois.

Coming to the walled village of Bram, they were denied entry by fearful sentinels watching them from the gate tower. The highly nervous men explained that only a week before, Montfort had captured the town after a three-day siege, and then committed horrible atrocities and forced the survivors to swear fealty to him. They dared not open to the Count and his men for fear of reprisals even worse than those inflicted so far, they explained. By this time, many of the townspeople, mostly women, were lining the battlements, listening, and now and again putting in a word or two, and often all speaking at once.

When Montfort had passed that way two months before, the village had opened its gates to him and paid him homage. Montfort had appointed the village priest as mayor, and had ordered him to run the town in the name of the Church. The priest was also charged with rounding up and imprisoning any heretics. But when Montfort's forces left, the priest turned administration of the town back to the secular authorities.

Unfortunately, when Montfort returned with far fewer men, the town consuls decided to resist, which turned out to be a horrible mistake. When they finally surrendered, Montfort had the priest defrocked, tied to the tail of a horse and dragged through the streets before hanging him.

Obviously intent on using terror to intimidate his foes into surrendering without a fight, Montfort then committed an even more monstrous atrocity. He had his men gouge out the eyes and cut off the noses and lips of all except one of the hundred or so men who had defended Bram. That person was blinded in only one eye so that he could lead his sightless and hideously deformed comrades to the Cathar stronghold of Cabaret, a dozen leagues away toward the northeast. Montfort defended his action, saying that Giraut del Pepios Besièrs had similarly disfigured two French knights, and that this was literally an eye for an eye. Olivier calculated it was more like twenty-fifty eyes for one.

If *he* had been one of those unfortunates, Olivier tried to imagine, would he have been able to face Micaela? Even if she loved him, as he believed she did, wouldn't she push him away in horror? And if she didn't, even if he couldn't see the revulsion in her eyes when he embraced her, wouldn't he sense it was there? How could he even kiss her, if his lips were gone? Not to feel her lips against his, not ever again, no matter his longing? Jesus Christ! For her, it would be like kissing a grisly skull. Even worse, he would never look on her beauty again. Never see his daughters again. He had to wrest his mind away from the very idea of going on living after such disfigurement.

199

Breaking into Olivier's daytime nightmare, the Count excitedly related some intelligence that pushed the fate of the wretched men of Bram out of his mind. A large force of crusaders from Allemania had taken the road to Castras, obviously intent on catching up with Montfort and providing him with much needed reinforcements. If the Count had a guide who knew the country, he could overtake the crusaders on parallel roads and get ahead of them in order to lay an ambush. The only trouble, cursed the Count, was that the people seemed too frightened to show him the way.

But when he told the people of his intention to ambush the Allemands, several women whose husbands had been mutilated volunteered as guides to help them waylay the crusaders and a riotous clamor arose as every last man of Fois vied with each other to have a woman ride with him on his horse. Finally, it was arranged to have two women join them as guides, and to avoid any appearance of favoritism among his men, the Count announced that one woman would ride behind Olivier and the other behind Camille. On hearing the news, Camille leaned over and nudged Olivier.

"The luck of the draw-strings," he quipped, pointing at the knot that held his trousers up.

Olivier chuckled. "At least she'll won't have to put up with any folderol as long as she's sitting *behind* you."

"You obviously don't know the penetrating power of my farts."

"Sorry I mentioned it. Poor woman. I pity her."

"I've got to keep her entertained, don't I?"

That night, as they rode through the darkness, it was Olivier's drawstrings that felt a tug. The woman guide who had mounted behind him at Bram was a plump, lusty woman of thirty-five or forty named Simone who told him her whole life story after they had only gone two or three leagues.

More angry than saddened by the cruel fate of her poor husband, she bitterly extolled his virtues. He was not only an *allodial* landowner, whose land was free from any feudal ties, but an expert farmer and a good provider, she chattered. In fact, he had just planted adjoining orchards of almond and fig trees, which would provide hard cash. They were going to be rich.

Now that he was incapacitated, who was going to do the pruning and the picking and all the other things that needed to be done to ensure the yield of the orchards, not to mention their staple crops? She'd heard how the crusaders took savage pleasure in the uprooting of vineyards and olive groves. What would she do if they destroyed her orchards?

No, she didn't have any children, she didn't know why. Maybe she should have been more friendly with the priest or her brother-in-law, she joked, but she wasn't very devout and besides the priest was a horrid drunk. And so was her brother-in-law. But she really didn't need kids, she said. She had hired hands when she needed them.

Her father had farmed land for a small nobleman, and had been killed in a silly land dispute with men from a neighboring castle. Her mother had been a seamstress for the Baron d'Alzonne. It had been her mother's savings that provided her with an attractive dowry, although that, of course, was not all that her husband saw in her, and she laughed and tickled Olivier's ribs. She, herself, was also a good seamstress, and once a week she sewed for the Baroness. As a matter of fact, she said, she was good at everything she put a hand to. And she giggled.

What about him? She was sure he was a knight. Yes, he answered, and told her that he was from Provença, that he

201

was married and had two daughters. That his mother-in-law came from Fanjaus. Is that why he was here? To see his mother-in-law? Yes, that was why he was here. And his friend, who had her townswoman riding behind him, is he the smith in Fanjaus? After he answered in the positive, he lapsed into silence and listened to the clopping of hundreds of hooves behind them as they rode on in the dark.

At the top of a hill, Simone tapped him on the shoulder.

"Stop here," she said.

"What's the matter?"

"Look back over there," she said pointing to the southeast. "See all those lights? 'Tis the enemy camp."

By this time, the Count had come along side, and Olivier pointed to the distant campfires.

The Count touched his cap. "Beldam, how do we get back to the main road?"

"About two leagues up ahead." Simone answered. "'Tis a goat path, but 'tis an easy ride."

"All right, then, we'll camp there tonight and get up early to keep ahead of them. Carry on, Sir Olivier."

"As you wish, my Lord," he answered and urged his mount forward at a walk.

The night sky had clouded over, and Olivier found it difficult to see along the narrow track, and he left it up to the horse to avoid any obstacles. Simone had been riding with her hands clasped around his waist, and it reminded him of the many times Micaela had ridden behind him and of the thrilling, yet comforting touch of her hands. He shivered and then realized that Simone's right hand had stolen slowly down to his crotch and was stroking its bulge. Could the goodwife be actually...? Yes, she was, and as he became tumescent, her fondling became less casual. Taking one hand off the reins, he pushed her hand away. Like a flash, she used her other hand to pull open the knot of his trouser drawstrings and clasp his erection. He winced from the intense shock of pleasure that racked his body.

He couldn't believe it. Here they were on horseback, trying to outflank a dangerous enemy, and he was literally in the hands of a woman for the first time in months and it was as delicious as it was ridiculous. He was thankful for the dark of night, or he could never live it down. As she caressed him with both hands, he groaned involuntarily. Then came that familiar rush that paradoxically seemed surprisingly new every time it happened. Racked with spasms, he pulled back on the reins and almost caused the horse to rear. Simone would have fallen off were it not for the tight grip she had on the slippery organ that was rapidly becoming flaccid.

"Is all well up there?" cried the Count, a few horse lengths back. "Something in the road?"

"A fox, methought," Olivier answered hoarsely, having gotten his horse under control again. .

"I *told* you I was good at what I put a hand to," Simone hissed over his shoulder, and gave him another hug.

Countercurrents of emotion ran over him. He was furious because she had taken advantage of him virtually in public, but on the other hand he hadn't stopped her. He had tried, but...not really. Had he betrayed Micaela? Not really....well, yes, really! He was disgusted at his weakness and ashamed...because he had enjoyed it so much.

When they reached the cross roads, he pulled on the reins. The riders behind him had already begun to dismount.

"Time to get down," he said, over his shoulder, "we're going to bed down here."

"Here?" she asked, looking at all the riders removing their saddlebags and their saddles from their horses. "Why here? Wouldn't you fain go somewhere where we can have more privacy?" She hugged him and rubbed her chin on his back.

He felt himself being aroused again. Of course he wanted to go somewhere where they could fornicate the night away, every fiber in his body yearned for it.

"No, methinks right here will do. Ah, but see," he said, "here comes my friend with your townswoman." He inclined his head to his left, where a dozen paces away, Camille was leading his mule, with the other woman from Bram at his side. Olivier helped Simone slip off the horse and then swung out of the saddle.

"Camille, over here," he called, and waved.

"'Tis that you, Ollie?" came the answer. "Let me get settled and take care of the mule. Then let's break bread together. I'm starved."

"'Tis a fair thought," Olivier answered. He unsaddled the horse and laid the saddle and the saddlebags on the ground. "Dòmna, there's food and blankets in the bags. Mayhap you and your friend can serve it up while we're tending the horses. There's also a flint and steel if you want to start a fire."

In answer, she gave a toss of her head. Holding the bridle of his horse, Olivier moved away, trying to catch up with Camille. Soon he made out the forms of horses and men and his shoes crunched on the stubble of a recently reaped barley field. Once their mounts were securely tethered, the two friends helped each other curry the horses, and then headed back toward the women.

"Camille, I need a favor."

"Ask, and ye shall receive."

"The woman riding with me is feeling amorous. Is there any way…"b

"…you want me to take her off your hands?" Camille asked.

"I mean, perhaps you have something going with the other one," Olivier said.

"Fret not, my happily married man, 'twill do me good to help you remain virtuous. Consider it done. 'Tisn't the first time I've had to deal with two at a time."

"Thanks, old friend. Mayhap I can get some sleep tonight, after all."

"Take a couple of winks for me, then; belike I'll be busy all night long."

Montgey

They broke camp before dawn and moved up the road toward Castras, trying to stay four or five leagues ahead of the allemands. As they passed through villages, townspeople and peasants joined them, bringing along their scythes, pitchforks and homemade pikes. Just before the village of Montgey, the Count had called a halt. On both sides of the road, thickets of scrub oaks, shrubs and junipers sprang from slopes that rose fifty paces or more above the level of the roadway, and stretched for hundreds of paces.

"Perfect. You could hide an army up there," the Count told Olivier and Giraut del Pepios, who had joined the column with a contingent of *faidits* from around Besièrs. "I think I'll have the stone throwers take the lowest tier and put the javelineers on the next tier, and the archers and crossbowmen shooting from the top. How does that sound to you?"

"Where are you going to put all those village people?" Pepios asked.

"Methought I'd put half of them in front and the other half in the rear, to keep the enemy from escaping. 'Twill be like a wine press." As they talked, the bells of Montgey rang *terce*. The Count grinned and rubbed his hands. "They won't get here before *none*, Mazan? "

"At least. But while we're waiting, we should make full sure that everyone knows what's expected of them."

"Forsooth. But first we must hide all the horses well beyond the village. Once 'tis done, we'll hold that council of war."

The time passed more swiftly than Olivier anticipated. Picketing the herd of horses had taken a long time, and then the council of war, followed by instructions to every fighting man, took at least as long.

206

Scouts sent out to report on the enemy's advance came back with the news that they were still more than a league away. Men began seeking places on the hillsides where they could conceal themselves. They were still finding their hiding places when the village bells rang *sext*.

The plan called for the Count to signal the attack by shouting "Bram!" At that moment, all the missiles would be loosed to produce the greatest amount of shock, followed by a steady barrage of stones and arrows, and then by a second volley from the javelineers and the crossbowmen. After that, the knights and sergeants would attack the survivors hand-to-hand, while the villagers would rush out and seal off both ends of the road to prevent escape.

Bracing his feet against a small boulder imbedded in the hillside, Olivier shifted his weight to even the pressure on his haunches. In the dense underbrush to his right and left, he knew that other men were staring down at the road below waiting for the approach of the enemy. When he looked hard, he could make out a man here and there in the thicket across from him. The waiting was almost painful. Olivier kept reminding himself to stop holding his breath and to inhale. Then a lone runner loped around the bend, motioning behind him. "They're coming," he hissed and disappeared into the bushes.

From the direction of the village, came the faint sound of men singing. Olivier had heard that the allemands sang as they marched, but dismissed it, but now, as the volume of the voices increased, there was no doubt about it.

A lone, helmetless knight on a big warhorse appeared on the roadway. His spotless surcoat was adorned with a cross, and more knights and squires rode forward in what seemed to be an endless column, three and sometimes four abreast. They were still singing. That was when Olivier realized that not all of the enemy would be inside the ambush when the signal was given.

Which way would they flee when they realized they were trapped? Forward or backward? Or would the ones in the rear ride forward to help what would seem to be an attack on their van?

Just then the shout "Bram!" resounded in the dale and Olivier realized what fain would be, fain would be. He drew back his arm and hurled a fist-sized rock at the crusader nearest him. Javelins, arrows, quarrels and rocks flew toward their targets. There was a moment of unreality when the unsuspecting foe were still lustily bawling out their song, and then a mad upheaval of men being swept out of their saddles, horses rearing and plunging and screams of agony and outrage. Those who remained in their saddles were fighting to control their wild-eyed mounts, while those on foot fell under the thrashing hooves of animals crazed by their wounds.

Along with those around him, Olivier found himself shouting with defiance as he threw a stone at an Allemand who had drawn his sword in a futile gesture of resistance. The stone hit the man squarely in the chest, but he managed to keep his seat and disappeared behind a riderless horse with an arrow in its flank that was bucking and kicking.

Fresh riders picked their way forward over the dead and dying, trying to avoid the maddened horses, but the shower of stones and arrows, toppled them into the roadway, where iron shod hooves stove in skulls and broke limbs and ribs and ruptured intestines in the blink of an eye. The lead horseman, his charger prancing on its hind legs, blew a blast from a horn, and waved the survivors forward. Those who tried to obey his command now became victims of well-aimed missiles that felled them row after row. Every mounted crusader with a crossbow became a prime target for stones and arrows.

Oliver sucked in his breath. It was happening. Those in the rear were being summoned forward into the trap. It was too good to be true. Each javelineer still had his reserve weapon and the crossbow men had reloaded.

Close on the heels of the horsemen, several hundred foot soldiers bearing pole weapons crowded forward, bellowing guttural, incomprehensible curses, and jamming the road. It was this closely packed mass of men that received the second volley of javelins and quarrels that winnowed their ranks as if a huge rake had passed through them. Staggering to a halt and bewildered about which way to run, those still standing were struck with more stones and arrows. Then, with a mighty roar, the knights and sergeants from Fois and the Minervois charged them on both flanks.

Olivier leaped down the slope, whooping as he went and brandishing his sword. His first stroke severed the arm of an Allemand foot soldier who had engaged one of the Minervois, then he parried a spear thrust, and grabbing its shaft, pulled its wielder toward him and stabbed him in the chest. Although the sword didn't penetrate the enemy's hauberk, the Allemand fell backwards writhing in pain. Out of the corner of his eye, Olivier saw a giant young crusader begin to swing a war axe at his head; bobbing under its swing, he drove his blade up into the man's crotch. The man dropped his axe and whirled away in agony, the motion wrenching the sword from Olivier's hand. Howling in pain and fright, the big man bent forward awkwardly at the waist and tried to ease the blade out of his body, but Olivier picked up the axe and almost severed the man's head in a spray of blood.

Next, he confronted a knight on foot, whose surcoat carried three golden eagles on a light blue field. Circling each other, they struck and feinted, weaved and bobbed, blades clanging together, or whistling through the air. Olivier's brow beaded with sweat, and he started to pant as he parried and riposted. His youthful foe showed no sign of tiring, and shouting taunts in his guttural language, began a frenzied attack that Olivier desperately tried to ward off. Suddenly, the Allemand stopped and grunted. The shaft of a javelin vibrated in his rib cage. Bright red blood bubbled out of his mouth and he was trying to speak when he crashed to the ground.

"Methought you needed some help," a javelineer from Fois cried, as he leaned down and yanked the spear free, releasing a torrent of blood.

"I'm forever in your debt, my friend!" Olivier grunted, wiping the blood and sweat from his face, and glad to be alive. The mayhem around them was coming to an end. The few crusaders who remained on their feet were enveloped by howling villagers who were attacking them with their homemade weapons, egged on by the men-at-arms from the Ariège.

He took a deep breath. He had survived unhurt. The deafening outcry had died down to a hum of excited voices. The villagers were giving the *coup de grace* to the wounded enemy, and stripping them of their clothes, their armor and their weapons. Others were mutilating the dead and dying. Aghast at such savage depravity, he turned away to search for Camille. There was such a crowd, that he was despairing of finding his friend, when someone clapped him on the shoulder. It was Camille.

"Glad to see you're still in one piece." Camille said.

Olivier shook his head. "'Twas a slaughter."

"'Twas a perfect ambush."

"That I trow, but why butcher the dead? There'll be reprisals for sure, I'll wager. Besides, just look. They're but boys."

Camille looked down at the naked bodies strewn in the roadway. "Forsooth. Just think, coming all this way to end up like so much carrion for the crows."

"They were told their sins would be washed away," Olivier said.

"What plainly needs to be washed away is their blood. And especially their guts."

The sound of laughter erupted behind them, and they turned to see some villagers looking at a corpse whose hands had been joined as if in prayer. As they watched, the peasants moved from body to body, chuckling and joking as they arranged the dead into attitudes of prayer. Others joined in on the sport.

"I wonder what old Montfort will think when he sees all these stiffs with their hands folded?" Camille asked.

Olivier looked into his friend's eyes. "'Twill not augur good, methinks." Then, putting his hands on Camille's shoulders, he said, "old friend, now I must needs be off for home. I'll try to find the Count and make my farewell, but I want you to know how much I appreciated all your help. I couldn't have done it without you."

"Say no more, Ollie. If it hadn't been for you," Camille said with a chuckle, "I couldn't have done those two women last night, either. I guess that means I owe you one."

"One woman, or one favor?"

"Take your choice."

Olivier laughed and hugged his friend. "Let's go find our horses."

"My mule."

"Your half-ass!"

211

Tolosa

Standing in the reception hall of the Castel de Narbona, Artaud de Roussilon, Arnaud-Amaury's emissary to the Tolosa city consuls, could not believe his ears.

"What do you mean you have no heretics? What is this?" he cried, tapping a list of names with his index finger. "Your own Bishop supplied these names. Are you accusing him of lying?"

"No, no," the Chief Consul said in a placating tone. "Forsooth not. We are merely saying that we can't turn the people on that list over to the French because they've *already* been burned at the stake. They no longer exist! You must remember that the old Count, the father of the present Count, was very severe on heretics and confiscated their property along with that of their protectors, and so when we found them, we burned them. Poof, they're gone!"

"'Tis not what the bishop says. If I heard you correctly, you're not going to turn a single heretic over to us. Is that right?" The emissary glared at the Chief Consul.

"We're saying that we have none to deliver." The Chief Consul shrugged.

"I take that as a refusal."

"You can take it any way you wish."

"Let me repeat my demands. We want all suspected heretics to be delivered to the French authorities, who will judge them according to the customs that apply in the *Ile de France*."

"And *we* say that, even if we *did* have heretics living among us, we would not hand them over to any secular authority. Instead, we would turn them over to you, as a bona fide representative of the Holy See, in compliance with canon law as practiced by the Holy Roman Church, if not by the inhabitants of the *Ile de France*." The Chief Consul smiled thinly.

"Again, that is a refusal, pure and simple." Artaud's face flushed crimson.

"We are complying with canon law, and not the secular, unlawful customs of foreigners. Surely as a representative of the Church, you should agree with such action." The Chief Consul bent his head to the side, indicating a patient tolerance of errant nonsense.

"Then we have nothing more to discuss," Artaud fumed, and turning on his heels, he stamped out of the room.

Avinhon

Pacing back and forth in the study of the Bishop's Palace, Arnaud-Amaury was in a foul mood, but his mind was racing. He was still smarting from Thibaut's treachery, but now he had to refocus on the Count of Tolosa. He wanted to make sure that Raimond never pulled the wool over his eyes again. At St.Gilles in May, the Count had sworn to follow what the Church had prescribed, but had not made the faintest effort to fulfill his promises. Yes, he had joined the Crusade, but obviously, that was a stratagem to protect his land and gain time. He had no intention of fulfilling his pledge to root out heresy.

But almost worse than Raimond's duplicity, the legate seethed, was Innocent's annoying and inexplicable pandering to the backsliding Count. The Holy See wanted to absolve Raimond and grant him total immunity, even though long experience had shown he could not be trusted. If Arnaud-Amaury pressed on with his prosecution, Innocent was insisting on all the legal niceties, such as producing an accuser. Also, Innocent insisted on a duly recorded charge to initiate an investigation, including testimony from both parties. In Arnaud-Amaury's opinion, such a prissy policy was doomed to failure. Give Raimond a chance to put himself in the clear, and he would find a way to do it.

Why couldn't the Pope see that the Count was toying with him? Instead of applying the scourge, the Holy See pampered him like a baby. It was stupid! So far, the crusade against Trencavel had been executed perfectly, and now Trencavel's vassals were tumbling over each other trying to ingratiate themselves with the crusaders. At long last, the real persecution of heretics was at hand.

It was also annoying and even demeaning that the Pope forbade him to treat directly with Raimond, and that Milon was responsible for carrying out the negotiations.

There was a knock on the chamber door. The legate turned and barked, "Enter!"

Guy of Rambouillet stepped inside the room and bowed. "The Council awaits, sire."

With a curt nod to his squire, Arnaud-Amaury brushed past him and marched into the large audience room, where his fellow legates, Milo and Thedisius presided at the head of a long table, on both sides of which sat nineteen bishops and four archbishops. A dozen abbots were seated in rows at the foot of the table. Arnaud-Amaury took his place in the empty chair between his colleagues.

Ostensibly, the Council had been convened to reform the negligent ecclesiastical mores in the Midi, using the recommendations of the 1179 Lateran Council as a basis for proceeding. In his opening remarks, Arnaud-Amaury made it clear that restoring the Church to its former dignity could not take place without restoring its authority. It was high time that the bishop in every diocese wielded his full power boldly and relentlessly. How this could be achieved was the subject of twenty-one canons that the legates had prepared and that his colleague, Thedisius, would now read to the council.

Among other measures, the canons insisted that a bishop must compel the local nobility to exterminate heretics; that excommunicated parishioners must pay their proper amends; that Jews were forbidden to hold any administrative roles; and that nobles must swear to uphold the Peace of God. In regard to the suppression of heresy, the bishops were to administer justice firmly, equitably and rapidly and their zeal should produce the timely prosecution and punishment of heretics.

The deliberations crawled on all day, but at last, the council unanimously adopted every one of the canons. As the meeting came to an end, and Arnaud-Amaury bustled about congratulating and flattering the participants for their foresight, his squire tiptoed into the room and whispered into his ear. The consuls of Tolosa had refused to deliver a single heretic of the over two hundred names they had been given. The chief legate's face turned black with rage, and he abruptly declared the council adjourned. Without waiting to mingle with the participants, or thank them for their roles in accomplishing such important work, he beckoned to his two colleagues and stalked back to his chamber.

Inside, he turned and harangued them. "The Holy Father asks us to be circumspect in treating with Raimond, and then thumbs his nose in our faces. I've just learned that the consuls of Tolosa have not turned over a single one of the two hundred heretics on our list. Can you believe it? We are asked to coddle that snake, and in return, all we get is a poisonous bite."

"Milo, prepare a writ of excommunication for the consuls of Tolosa and issue an interdict against the entire city. Let them sweat, let them see how they can live and die without the Holy Sacraments. I would fain watch them suffer, every one of them, from the preening, obnoxious nobles to the haughty merchants who dare to look down their noses at the clergy. Let all those so-called 'free' townsmen with their precious liberties take their anger out on the prime cause of their misery, their own Count Raimond. And when he feels cornered from all sides, let him come crawling."

He bustled over to the table and plucked up a sheet of parchment from among the documents lying there, and waved it aloft. "I scarce believe that His Holiness could have written such tripe, urging us to either absolve the Count or to allow him to justify himself. As long as I'm in this office, neither will come to pass." He slammed the table with his fist.

"'Tis a hard matter," Thedisius agreed. "His Holiness minds us to excuse the Count's misdeeds, and also stipulates that only he, not us, can find the Count guilty."

"Theres only one way out," Arnaud-Amaury said. "We have to prevent Raimond from presenting his justification and thereby putting everything in question again. 'Twould destroy what we've just accomplished here in Avinhon"

"I wot not why the Pope turns a blind eye to Raimond's failure to carry out his oath," Milo said. "Yes, Raimond has knocked down some of his border castles, but he has failed to remove the fortifications from the churches he despoiled; he hasn't reinstated the bishops of Carpentras and Vaison; and he's still exacting tolls; still employing mercenaries; and naming Jews to administrative positions."

"Forsooth! By each of these foul deeds, he forswears the oath he made at St. Gilles last June, thereby mocking the Holy See, and especially us, his legates!" Arnaud-Amaury was boiling with anger.

"Methinks I might have a solution to our problem," said Thedisius, and rummaged through the documents on the table. He pulled out a page and ran his finger down it. "Ah, listen to His Holiness's precise instructions: 'While the Count awaits his hearing before the council, we expect him to execute our orders.' Did you hear that? *We expect him to execute our orders!*"

The Abbot glared at him incomprehensibly. "You call that a solution?"

"Yes, though I never marked it 'til now, my Lord Abbot. The major accusations that hang over Raimond, those that we would fain pin on him, are abetting heresy and the murder of Castelnau. Being the primary grounds for prosecution, they will be judged by a council subject to all

217

His Holiness's legal niceties. But there are also these secondary grounds, the papal orders mentioned earlier. We must insist that these orders be carried out!"

"What do you mean?" Arnaud-Amaury frowned.

"Let me explain," said Thedisius. "In his Bull, the Pope states that while waiting for the council to convene, he expects the Count to execute our orders. Now, as you wot well, the Count has not executed *any* of these orders. Ergo, he violated his oaths on the secondary points."

"We wot that well. So what?" The Abbot said.

"So," Thedisius said, "if he has broken his oath on the *minor* charges, how can his word be trusted on the *major* charges? What scruples would keep Raimond from perjuring himself over the two enormous crimes of abetting heresy and murdering Peter Castelnau?"

The Abbot raised his eyebrows. "Aha! I divine your meaning."

"In other words, in accordance with pontifical instructions, Raimond's justification is unacceptable, right from the start, unless he carries out the orders."

"By my troth, 'tis brilliant!" Arnaud-Amaury cried, beaming at his colleague.

"But wait a moment," Milo interjected, as he looked over Thedisius' shoulder. "That quote may well be taken out of context, and we may be interpreting His Holiness's words in a sense he didn't mean."

"Now what?" Arnaud-Amaury said, as if he had bitten a rotten apple.

Milo took a deep breath. "His Holiness goes on to say, 'we have decided that the fact of not having executed all the clauses of the contract should not jeopardize his property rights. We have therefore enjoined the Holy Christian army, which operates according to instructions against the heretics, not to touch the Count's domain."

"That admonition is of little weight here," Thedisius said. "We're not talking about property rights, we're talking about his blatant failure to obey the orders of the Holy See, which is totally different."

"My brothers in the Church," said the Abbot, raising his hand with palms outstretched, "let's not complicate things. 'Tis not for us to try to interpret what his Holiness may or may not mean," he simpered with false humility.

"I will summon a council at St.Gilles in December, ostensibly so that the Count can reconcile himself with the Church on the two major charges. And at the council, I shall announce that we have no objections to his swift reconciliation. 'Twill be your cue, Thedisius, to rise and read the line from the Papal Bull and declare that no evidence can be heard on the major charges until he has complied with the minor ones. And that, my friends, should cook his goose!"

As he said this, the simper turned into a fiendish smirk that caused the Abbot's associates to turn away, their spines crawling as if threatened by a frightful serpent.

Montpelhier

At long last, Abbot Arnaud-Amaury told himself, he had Raimond of Tolosa by the balls, and he almost chuckled out loud as he struggled to keep a straight face. He had convened the four principals who could determine the outcome of the crusade, and here they were, in the sacristy of Nòstra Dòna deis Taulas in Montpelhier.

There was the dashing King Peire of Aragon, a favorite of the Pope; Simon Monfort, the brilliant commander- in-chief, whose crusaders had overrun most of the former Trencavel lands; crusty old Raimond Roger, Count of Fois, whose resistance to the Crusade was a constant nuisance; and finally, Raimond VI of Tolosa himself, whom Arnaud-Amaury now believed had backed himself into a corner.

The Abbot listened as his fellow legate, Bishop Raimond of Uzès, relayed Pope's Innocent's conviction that a permanent peace was possible in the Midi, if and when heresy was exterminated, and how it behooved the four leaders to cooperate to achieve this common goal.

Out of the corner of his eye, the Abbot watched the King, who was in a tight spot. As Trencavel's suzerain, he still had not recognized Montfort as his *de facto* vassal. Earlier that year, Monfort had knelt before Peire and begged to be accepted as his vassal, only to be rejected. But with his recent victories, Montfort had solidified his claim to be Trencavel's successor, and it was entirely possible that he might renounce Peire and seek out Philippe of France to be his suzerain. Arnaud-Amaury had met with Peire in private and implored him allow Montfort to pay homage to him and become his vassal.

The Abbot also knew that Peire had more than just the Midi on his mind. As part of a Holy Alliance with Castille and Navarre, Peire was preoccupied with the great counter offensive to repulse the latest invasion by North African Muslims. With war brewing to his south, Peire needed Montfort on his side, not against him. Therefore, Arnaud-Amaury had taken the precaution of arranging for the crusader to repeat his request during the course of the meeting.

When the Bishop finished speaking, the Abbot nodded at Montfort, who rose on cue and moved around the table to where Peire was sitting. Bending down on one knee, he took the king's hand in both of his. "Sire, I humbly beseech you to take me as your vassal, and to ratify me as the Viscount of Carcassona, Albi and Besièrs, as well as Minerva and Tèrme. In return, I pledge to serve you faithfully as long as we both shall live. Please lift up my spirit by telling me that you accept my honest service to you and our Lord Jesus Christ."

Peire remained silent for a moment, then pushed his chair back and rose. Arnaud-Amaury could barely restrain himself. The king was finally going to take the step that would change one third of the Midi forever! It was an incredible moment in history, and he wondered if any of the others appreciated its significance. He looked across the table at Count Raimond, who was scowling. Yes, fret away, you two-faced cheat, the Abbot gloated silently, just hark to what's coming.

Grasping Montfort's hand, Peire spoke. "My dear Viscount Montfort, in the presence of the witnesses here assembled, I hereby accept your homage, and as your suzerain, formally ratify you as Viscount of Carcassona, Albi and Besièrs, as well as Minerva and Tèrme, including all of the fiefs previously answerable to the late Viscount Trencavel. Our future relationship shall include all the responsibilities, commitments, and services that exist 'twixt suzerain and vassal. May the Good Lord bless and sustain the confluence of our efforts. Please rise and give me your hand in a pledge of eternal fealty."

Montfort stood, and shook the king's hand in both of his. "Thank you, my lord; I am honored and very proud to be of service to you. I shall endeavor to fulfill my duty for the rest of my life as your faithful servant. In the name of our Savior, may the good Lord bless and keep us."

A beaming Arnaud-Amaury led them in repeating the Lord's Prayer, and they sat once more.

Before the Abbot could begin his humbling of Count Raimond, Peire rose again. "My dear friends, in the interest of the peace we all long for, let me propose that our esteemed friend and loyal vassal, the Count of Fois, enters into a mutually beneficial pact with my new friend and vassal, Viscount Montfort, a pact that will provide both parties with certain benefits and will be balanced by reciprocal concessions. If Count Raimond-Roger swears to obey the orders of the Holy Church and to stop defying the crusade, we would expect Viscount Montfort to restitute any and all lands that he has taken from the Count, except for Pamias. How say you my Lords, are you with me?"

He looked from Montfort to Raimond-Roger. After a few long moments of silence, Montfort nodded. "I am with you, and I've naught to add."

All eyes turned to the Count of Fois, who frowned and said, "But I cannot."

"In that case," the king went on, "here is my decision, over which I have thought long and hard. I, myself, will guarantee the peace. I will garrison the Count's castle with a troop of my knights. In that way, if he should take any hostile action toward the crusaders, then his castle will be immediately forfeit to Viscount Montfort." He turned to Montfort. "Here are letters patent transferring the property to you, my lord Viscount, if such a thing befalls." He handed a sheaf of parchment to Montfort, and then turned back to the Count. "'Tis no idle threat, my lord Count," he said to Raimond-Roger. "You have everything to gain and your castle to lose." He sat down and raised his eyebrows in expectation, but Raimond-Roger refused to meet his gaze.

Arnaud-Amaury turned to the king, saying, "Thank you, your Majesty, in the name of our Holy Church, in taking this initiative to preserve the peace. 'Tis a simple plan that, if followed, will work to everyone's benefit."

"I myself have a similar plan that I would fain propose to Count Raimond. As he wots well, the Church has asked him to hunt down and exterminate the heretics in his lands. If he does that, the Church is willing to let him keep all the goods of his personal property. He would also keep all of his rights to heretics' properties in all of his fiefs, and finally, he would be able to confiscate a third of all heretical property located outside of his fiefs."

"Thus, he will benefit not only from a reconciliation with the Holy Church, but also from the assurance that the French will not usurp his power, and still more, he will have a great opportunity to enrich himself with spoils from the heretics and thus enlarge his domains."

"In exchange for this generous offer, what do I ask in return? Merely, my Lord Count, that you engage yourself in the fight against heresy. I ask not for an oath. I ask not for a promise. Forsooth, I ask not for a reconciliation. I ask only for action. Show us that you are persecuting the heretics. 'Tis all I need to see."

Through narrowed lids, the Abbot watched the Count struggle to answer. He knew that Raimond hadn't the slightest desire to eliminate heresy, or he would have done it long ago. Besides, hunting down heretics was far easier said than done. Throughout Raimond's land, the Good Folk mixed with Roman families, and they had sympathizers everywhere. The Abbot knew that Raimond had no stomach for attacking his own villages, or punishing his own people, let alone hanging them, burning them at the stake, or destroying their crops, or pulling up olive trees or vineyards. He had put the Count's back against the wall. The others at the table would see it as a magnanimous offer that Raimond could hardly refuse.

"No. I won't do it." The Count said

"Pity," said the Abbot, reaching for a sealed document that Thedisius handed him across the table, "because in that case, we have prepared a charter for you, which you can read at your leisure. Basically it commands you to observe the Peace of God; disband your *routiers*; restore to the clerics the rights which have been denied them; lift your protection from Jews and heretics; eliminate your tolls, and finally, you must reimburse those who have been illegally taxed."

He looked at Raimond, whose face had clouded in anger, and after pausing to let his words sink in, he went on. "Your countrymen shall share the following restrictions with you: the eating of meat shall be limited to twice a week; the wearing of good quality clothes is forbidden; all castles and fortresses are to be demolished; all land and goods must be surrendered at the discretion of the crusaders; all knights must dwell outside the towns; and every year, every household need pay a tax of four deniers."

The Abbot winked at Thedisius. They had discussed the various measures of penance thoroughly days before, and decided that it would take collective punishment to break the back of the merchant class, as well as that of the nobility in the Midi. They were far more dangerous protectors of heresy than Raimond.

224

"Is that all?" the Count asked sarcastically. "Full sure am I that you have something else up your slimy sleeve."

"To say truth, I do. You, yourself, must go to the Holy Land and stay there as long as the Roman Curie wants. You have to join the Templars or the Hospitaliers. After you do all that, they will give you back your castles, et cetera, et cetera. If you refuse, you'll be hunted down like a wild animal and you will have nothing left."

"Did you hearken to that?" Raimond asked the king. "Have you ever heard its like? The monks have lost their wits."

. "Tis so utterly overmuch that only God Almighty can sort it out," Peire agreed.

Raimond pushed his chair back from the table and stood up. He glared at each of the legates, bowed to the king, and stalked out of the room. Resisting a triumphant snicker, the Abbot winked at Thedisius again. He had outfoxed the fox.

Narbona

Steaming with fury, Arnaud-Amaury waved the Papal missive that had just arrived in the faces of his colleagues, Raimond d'Uzès and Thedisius. "Whose side is His Holiness on?" he roared. "If he wants to get rid of heresy here in the Midi, he's got to get rid of Count Raimond. The Pontiff blows hot and cold depending on the person with whom he last consulted. He's like a reed in a swamp, swaying at every trifling breeze."

His eyes roamed around the room, one of three private apartments in the Archbishop's palace, flanked by ornate gold and silver sconces. Magnificent tapestries from Flanders covered the most of the wall. Gilded curules and ornately carved side tables bearing silver candelabra were arranged along the walls.

Four months before, having at long last succeeded in hounding old Berenger out of office, Arnaud-Amaury had been elected Archbishop of Narbona, the highest ecclesiastical office in the Midi. At the same time, he had usurped the vacant throne of the Duke of Narbona, which gave him secular power over fiefs in a vast swath of territory from the Aude to the Rose.

His suzerain in the west was Peire II of Aragon and in the east, at least theoretically, Raimond VI of Tolosa. Arnaud-Amaury's claim to the ducal office collided with Montfort's own ambition to become Duke of Narbona. The two leading figures of the Crusade were now bitter rivals, if not enemies.

"Lend an ear to this," the new Archbishop said, and read a portion of the Pope's letter aloud, deliberately mincing its words. "The Count has neither been convicted of heresy nor of involvement in the murder of Peter Castelnau, even if he is a strong suspect. We have therefore decreed that if he were the object of a legal

226

accusation, we would be authorized to act in the manner prescribed by our instructions to you, where we reserve to ourself the right to pronounce the definitive judgment. However, our mandatories have not yet proceeded with the justification."

"Can you scarce believe it?" the Archbishop said. "He keeps on insisting that we didn't give Raimond a chance to vindicate himself. 'Tis simply not true."

"Begging your pardon, your Excellency," Raimond of Uzès said, "'tis true in part. We never let the Count proceed to justification because we deemed that he hadn't complied with the Holy See's own demands."

"I care to say. How can anyone, whether or not he is the Holy Father, continue to trust someone who scorns the commands of the Holy See?" The Archbishop flapped the letter above his head.

"What else does the letter say?" asked the legate.

Arnaud-Amaury held the letter in both hands and read aloud. "We therefore fail to see on what ground we can transfer the Count's land to another, since neither he nor his heirs have yet been dispossessed of it. We are determined not to give the impression that we used a ruse to extort those castles from him."

"Have you ever heard the like of it?" The Archbishop said. "And he goes on. Just listen to this: 'The Apostle prescribed not only doing away with evil, but even the appearance of evil. If, on the two main accusations, the judgment doesn't conform with the procedure prescribed by our mandate, it should be, incontestably, considered as null. See what I mean? He keeps going back to the two main charges, without even mentioning our grounds for refusing to listen to the Count's pleas."

"Forsooth. He has never acknowledged the rectitude of our judgment and excommunication, and yet he authorized me to expropriate the Count's castles in Melgueil," the legate Raimond answered.

"Which is totally inconsistent with what he is saying here in this letter. How can he act on the consequences of our action and then later on try to deny it or water it down?" Arnaud-Amaury rolled his eyes and handed the letter to Thedisius.

"Because he deems that the Count will repent and will scourge the heretics out of his lands," Thedisius said, shrugging his shoulders. "Just listen to this: 'The Count has shown himself to be guilty of many things, toward God and toward the Holy Church; he has proved his disobedience and his rudeness to the legates; that is why they excommunicated him and exposed his land in the hope that such rigor would make him listen to reason.'"

The Archbishop put his chin on his chest and shook his head in disgust. "On one hand, the Holy Father agrees that it was legitimate to punish the Count for past faults, as long as it forced Raimond to repent. But he refuses to see it as grounds for taking his lands, which is the only step that will ever get rid of heretics in the Midi."

"So the goal of the Holy See is repentance, rather than dispossession, clearly contradicting the way it treated Trencavel," Thedisius said.

"Exactly! His Holiness refuses to apply the same reasoning to Raimond. He fain would give the Count still another court hearing and yet urges us to act promptly. Here's exactly what he says: 'See to it that when executing Our orders, you *do not show yourselves to be as lukewarm and snail-like as you've been up to now.*' That's adding insult to injury, if ever I heard it."

Thedisius nodded "His Holiness is, after all, a lawyer, and had carefully constructed a legal trap for Raimond, but now that the trap is sprung, he refuses to apply the law to the facts."

"Right, whereas Montfort sees the facts as the law." The Archbishop said.

Thedisius threw up his hands in frustration. "In the statutes of Pamias, Montfort recognized King Philippe as the only suzerain involved. Then King Peire of Aragon protested to Rome and as a result, instead of acting on Peire's claim, the Holy See orders Monfort to surrender the lands he conquered!"

"I can scarce believe it!" The Archbishop cried.

"What I don't understand is why His Holiness waited so long to get tough with Montfort," said Thedisius, slowly shaking his head.

"No?" Arnaud-Amaury raised his eyebrows. "Methought 'twas obvious. After the fall of Carcassona, Montfort informed the Holy Father that he was restoring the property rights of the Roman Church by collecting quit rents from every household in his domain. But, then there was a hitch. The collection system had fallen in disuse and 'twasn't until Montfort restored it that the Church started collecting." Arnaud-Amaury stared at his colleague and slowly nodded his head to indicate that he had caught the Holy See pursuing its own venal ends.

"Are you saying that the influx of hard cash caused the Holy Father to ignore the ultimate goal of eliminating heresy?" Thedisius had let his jaw drop open.

"No," the Archbishop said, "but he couldn't help seeing how profitable the Crusade could be to him. Stopping the conquest would have dried up all that income! And 'twas only after Montfort's collector, Pierre March, sent all the arrears to Rome, that the Pope called off the Crusade." The Archbishop shrugged. "The Holy See had a vested interest in the Crusade, forsooth!."

"Think you that's why he gave Montfort free rein for so long? So the Holy See could profit?" Thedisius asked, in disbelief.

"Do you see any other reason?"

Thedisius frowned. "If His Holiness were really greedy, he would try to continue the Crusade instead of bringing it to an end."

Arnaud-Amaury shrugged again. "He is akin to a reed blowing in the wind."

Montségur, a year later
Olivier looked out over the battlements of the keep at Montségur, and watched a flock of choughs perform their acrobatic flight, swooping, zooming and even looping at breathtaking speeds. He was sitting at a small table that Guilhabert Castras had asked some varlets to carry up to the tower platform. The late August sunshine produced such a blinding glare on the snow-covered peaks to the south that Olivier had to look away.

Castras chuckled. "Dazzling, isn't it?"

Olivier nodded He had arrived that very morning after a six-day ride through the Aude valley, the route that he had not taken the year before. His mother had been working at the loom when he appeared in her doorway and she had flung herself into his arms. He had spent a long time telling her about the lives of her grand children down to the slightest detail, and then she took almost as much time telling him about Rebecca, who called her Nou-Nou, why, she didn't know. The girl and the other children and their mothers had gone to pick berries down near the Tor, at the opposite end of the *pog*, and would probably linger there for a while.

After the sun had traveled halfway across the sky, Aude had taken him to see Castras, who suggested they go up in the tower and drink some mead. Aude had begged off because of her work, and the two men had climbed the steps to the top of the tower.

"When I contemplate those birds," the Good Man said, "I sometimes feel that they might be the exception to the rule that the Dark Power made the material world."

"I agree. They're angelic. They seem to enjoy the sheer joy of flying as much as I enjoy just watching them."

"Exuberant innocence, I call it. They are not feeding or nesting or mating. They're simply playing. If only people would do that instead of making war. Here we are, with the Crusade into its third year, which is cause for much grief. What news do you bring?"

"Minerva has fallen."

"Ah, that is a heavy sorrow. I hear many Good Folk had sought refuge there. "

"That's true, and, alas, it gets worse. After the garrison surrendered, the French burned one hundred and forty of the Good Folk alive."

Castras bowed his head and slowly shook it. "Once again, the Romans demonstrate their moral superiority. But will Montfort be satisfied with conquering Minerva?"

"Apparently not. He was besieging Tèrme, the last I heard. Apparently, Peire Rotger of Cabaret almost captured his siege train, but was beaten off at the last moment, so there's no telling how long the siege will last."

Castras frowned. "We've heard terrible tales about Montfort's atrocities."

Olivier nodded. "He's pitiless and uses terror as a weapon. When he took the town of Bram, he put out the eyes of one hundred prisoners, cut off their noses and their lips, and left a man with only one eye put out to guide them on the road to Cabaret."

"We heard the same tale Last year, in my home town, his men captured two True Christians, one was a Good Man and the other a Believer. Both men refused to abjure their faith, so Montfort condemned them to the stake. The Believer then decided to abjure after all, but Montfort had him burned anyway, claiming that if the Believer had really repented, then the fire expiated his sins, whereas if he had merely pretended to repent, then he deserved his punishment because of his perfidy. Heads I win, tails you lose." Castras shrugged.

"Tis strange, because back in Provença, we heard the same story, with this twist: supposedly the recanting Believer actually survived the fire safe and sound with absolutely no sign of burns. Thus demonstrating God's infinite mercy and the power of repentance."

"Pure fantasy," Castras said. "'Tis ironic! According to canon law, heretics must be prosecuted in an ecclesiastical tribunal presided over by a bishop or his representative. Only after the tribune condemns him, can the accused be remanded to the secular arm for the appropriate punishment. Therefore, in my hometown, with no bishop or legate at hand, Montfort took on the role of prosecutor, judge and executioner. He's an outlaw, even within the rotten Church to which he gives so much lip service."

Olivier cleared his throat. "About the scrolls, Good Man…"

"They are safely hidden away," Castras said.

"I've been wondering. Have you thought…?"

"Are you asking about what effect they will have on our dogma?"

"Well, 'tis not my business, I trow, but…"

"'Tis a legitimate question and I will try to answer you, because you are in the almost unique position of knowing their significance. I trust that you will share this with no one," Castras said.

"Of course, Good Man."

"I have said naught about them to my colleagues. I fear that such revelations might have a detrimental effect on the Church of the Friends of God at a time when our faith is under tremendous strain from the Crusade. Even though it does not negate our basic dogma, it alters our perception of Christ, and so might awake doubts about our faith. That, like enough, could leave us powerless to persevere in the face of this evil Crusade. Once we are quit of this scourge,

I will share this knowledge with the other bishops, and I trow they will agree to adjust our dogma. Now is not the time. Faith can be more important than truth, don't you agree?"

As far as the dogma of the Church of the Friends of God was concerned, Olivier was loath to agree with Castras. In his opinion, those faced with being burned alive should have the benefit of knowing the twists and turns of dogma and make up their minds with all the truth revealed. Or was ignorance really bliss? But instead of voicing his reservations, he nodded. "I stand by your decision, Good Man, and will never breathe word of it again. The subject is closed."

Castras sighed, then looked at the choughs. "How I envy those birds. They have no questions, no qualms about their ability to fly. They have absolute faith in their wings."

When Rebecca burst into Aude's room with two big baskets of black berries, it took several seconds before she realized who the big man sitting next to Nou-Nou was. Olivier stood and picked her up and swung her around his head. She shrieked with pleasure and hugged him around the neck. He was infinitely relieved that he would not have to build up the relationship all over again.

They spent the next two days exploring the fortress and the terrain it stood on, and at night, after she went to bed, he spent hours talking to Aude about her new life at Montségur. She had become attached to Rebecca, but she knew that the girl would be happier back in the Comtat

Venaicin with her two little granddaughters and many more potential playmates than she had up on the *pog*.

On the eve of Olivier's departure, mother and son walked up onto the ramparts and watched the sun gild the snowy crests of the mountains.

"My heart is glad that you're safe and sound, up here, Maire," he said pulling her close to him. "The French are committing horrible atrocities."

"So I've heard. But look," she said, waving a hand at the golden peaks in front of them, "they seem to be protecting us. They look so close."

"How was the winter?"

"Twas bitter cold with heaps of snow and ice, if that's what you mean, but we managed. In truth, we had all we needed. And by reason of being shut in, we spun and wove every day. You would have been amazed to have seen all the cloth we loomed. After the spring thaw, we took it down to market in the villages roundabout."

"Tis hard, the weaving and all?"

"Not to speak of. We spend much time carding and spinning, too. Then there's the dyeing."

"Take care when vending your wares and making your pastoral rounds, these days, when the French can appear where you least expect them."

"We do. If the French ever come this far south, we won't venture from the *pog*."

"'Twill make me sleep sounder if I know full sure you are safe. Also, from now on, you won't have the burden of caring for Rebecca."

"'Twas no burden at all. We'll all miss her dreadfully."

"Micaela has been fussing for me to fetch her home for a whole year. I have my marching orders," he said. "I'm looking forward to paying Rebecca heed myself. What befell her parents haunts me still."

"Bethought you ever to find a foster mother among her own people?"

"Forsooth. But after thinking about it, we deem she will be better off with us. She can always take up the Jewish faith when she comes of age, which isn't that far off. How did *you* guide the religious aspect? "

"In the first place, there are no Jews up here, so there was no way to give her instruction. At the beginning, we worried about it, but when we asked her if she wanted to practice her religion, she just shrugged. She seems to enjoy the deacon's sermons."

"Interesting. Mayhap she would fain attend the monthly *aparelhament.* 'Twere well to make sure that she feels loved and is part of a family. And obviously, from what I've seen, you gave her a great start up here."

"As I said, we were all delighted to take care of her and I only hope we didn't spoil her. As you are apt to do," and Aude squeezed his hand.

"Like you did to me?" he said, squeezing her back.

"Forsooth!"

The next morning, when it came time to say goodbye, Aude held Rebecca in a long embrace, then brushed her own tears away with a kerchief that she then used to wave as Olivier led the horse down the tortuous switchbacks that were worn into the steep slope. From her perch in the saddle, Rebecca waved back energetically.

Looking down from above, Aude felt as if she could drop something right on their heads as they slowly zigzagged downhill. When the path finally began to level out, they looked unbelievably tiny before she lost sight of them in the trees. If only, she sighed, if only they could have stayed for one more precious day.

Part III

Rome

Leaning back on the cushions lining his throne, Pope Innocent III savored the wine his valets had brought him. It had been a long, hard day and it was not over. The tendentious issue of the division of territory as a result of the Albigensian Crusade had been resolved in his own mind, but here in the audience room of the Lateran Palace thronged some two hundred clerics, princes, nobles and magnates, as well as the ambassadors of the Kings of France and England. Most of them, he sighed, would argue against his position. At least, it was a relief to be out of the press of the Lateran Basilica. During the plenary session, more than fifteen hundred prelates had been packed together so tightly that a bishop had died of suffocation.

At the plenary, his secretary had read out seventy-one canons, most of which would reform the church and make its operation more efficient, including increasing its revenue, and combating clerical corruption. The battle against heresy was re-enforced, as were the restrictions against Jews, and the plan for a Fifth Crusade in the Holy Land was approved. All in all, much had been done.

Perhaps, because of the crush in the Basilica, there had been very little dissent and even less discussion when the canons were presented, so that they were quickly adopted. Nevertheless, reading them – some of them went on for two full pages — had taken much time, as did the adoption by vote of each and every canon. At the very least, Innocent knew, he had put his minions on notice that the Church would no longer be a sinecure for lazy and corrupt clerics, no matter what their rank.

The business at hand –the disposition of the lands won by Montfort -- was daunting. There would be disappointment and even anger when he made his decision known, but it was the result of years of discussion and his knowledge of law, both canonical and feudal. It was, of course, a political decision as well, and a momentous one at that, but he had never shrunk from making judgments, no matter how unpopular.

He looked out at the audience. In the first rank stood Raimond VI of Tolosa and his son, who would someday be Raimond VII, as well as the two English bishops who represented King John of England. They were flanked by Viscount Montfort's brother Guy, and Raimond-Roger, the Count of Fois.

The presence of Montfort's brother evoked the great triumph of the Church in defeating those lords who had supported, or at the least, permitted heresy to flourish. Yet Innocent felt like wringing his hands. Was the Count of Tolosa really guilty of heresy? In spite of the serious charges lodged against him, Count Raimond's presence personified the legal case for due process. Was it legal, let alone fair, to give Raimond's lands to Montfort, even though the Count himself had never been accused of heresy? Moreover, Raimond could not be dispossessed of his land without the consent of his suzerain, King Philippe of France, who had never faltered in upholding his vassal's rights. After all, Raimond's mother was Philippe's aunt.

As for Raimond's son, who was soon to attain his majority; why should he, who had never threatened the Church in any way, suffer the loss of his inheritance? Innocent felt the same way about eight-year-old Raimond Trencavel, who was only two years old at the time of his father's death. Was depriving him of his father's lands a greater crime than denying Montfort his just rewards for a victorious crusade? Can compromise ever satisfy opposing parties?

The pope cleared his throat. "My lords, fellow prelates and distinguished colleagues including our two honored guests who represent the throne of England, once more we bid you welcome to our private residence.

"We are met on a momentous occasion, both for the Holy Church and for those who rule much of Christendom. Our Crusade against the Albigensians has broken the satanic grip of heresy that has threatened the souls of untold thousands of our Christian brethren. There is a scarcely one village between the Rose and the Gironde, that has not welcomed men-at-arms wearing the Cross of Redemption.

'Tis difficult to find words to express our gratitude to those who have accomplished this miracle, but it is not at all difficult to single out the one man whose valiant and determined leadership has brought us this triumph. We are proud to hail Viscount Montfort as having embodied the will of the Holy Church in this endeavor. In the name of the Father, Son and Holy Ghost, we thank this soldier of Christ and give him Our blessing. And we wish to reiterate our earlier confirmation of his titles. I regret that this athlete of Christ was unable to attend, but we are honored by the presence of his brother, Guy. "

The audience broke into applause, and Guy Montfort bowed stiffly.

The Pope smiled and nodded. "We would also fain to acknowledge Count Raimond and praise him for taking part in the Crusade at the outset and for his persistence in trying to reconcile himself to the Church and satisfy the demands placed upon him by the Holy See."

"We also recognize that, although the Count has lost most of his domains in battle, we insist they be restored to him along with the appropriate titles, given the fact that he himself is innocent of heresy. Moreover, his suzerain refuses to accept the fealty of the current possessor of those domains that were won in battle." The Pope paused as an angry hum ran through the crowd, and here and there were loud protests, especially from the eighteen bishops from the Midi.

After order was restored, the Bishop of Albi stepped forward and remonstrated that the rabid heretics had faded away, thanks entirely to the Crusade and to Montfort. Moreover, he continued, the Holy See had promised that those who took up the cross would be entitled to the domains of any who supported the heretics or resisted the Crusade. Clearly, by those criteria, Raimond's lands were forfeit to Monfort.

When the Bishop finished, the Pope countered, saying that while Monfort was qualified on such scores to take deed of the lands and titles of heretics, Raimond himself had not been accused or found guilty of heresy. In fact, he had joined the Crusade, and later on, when Montfort had invaded his lands, it was only natural that he defended them. In any case, feudal law dictated that the disposal of Raimond's domains depended entirely upon King Philippe, who had absolutely rejected the idea of enfeoffing Montfort in place of Raimond.

Thedisius, the former papal legate who had become Bishop of Agde, spoke up, reminding the Pope of the wide sway that the Cathars had once enjoyed in the Midi, a force that had threatened the very foundation of the Church. He pointed out that Montfort had chased away the nobles who had belittled the prelates who served them, and who had refused to contribute the tithes they owed the mother Church. He reiterated how Raimond had not carried out the orders that the Holy Father himself had issued, including those asking him to assist the League of Provença. Although Raimond had never been shown to be the author of Peter Castelnau's murder, Thedisius said, nevertheless he had made public pronouncements that were tantamount to issuing a death warrant, and that he could be considered an accessory to murder.

Innocent replied, trying to keep his temper, that they had covered this ground before and that after extensive consideration of Count Raimond's behavior, the Holy See had duly notified Thedisius and the other legates that the Count was as innocent of heresy as he was of murder. He said that it was shocking that the decision of the Holy See was under question.

When he finished, all the bishops began shouting and Innocent realized that the very men he had appointed to bishoprics in the Midi were the most vociferous in their opposition to his policy. It had been an exhausting day and now this. He had never experienced such tumultuous opposition to his policies. If protecting Raimond on a legal basis meant fomenting a rebellion within the Church, he would have to give in.

Narbona

At first, Sir Guy de la Beauce from Rambouillet and his fellows had shrugged their shoulders and joked about the news that the young Count Raimond and his father had returned from Rome and had debarked at Marselha to the great acclaim of the Provençals. Chauvinistic displays were nothing new in the Midi. But when they heard that the massive rally to the colors of Tolosa had metamorphosed into a full-fledged attack on Beaucaire, it became cause for alarm. The French garrison had been driven out of the city and had taken refuge in the adjacent castle, besieged by thousands of Provençals.

The disaster couldn't have arrived at a worse time, Rambouillet groaned. Monfort was still in Paris, where he had gone in triumph to do homage as vassal to King Philippe. Indeed, the outcome of the Lateran Council and the huge victory that Philippe of France had won in Flanders over the armies of the English and Emperor of the Holy Roman Empire had finally persuaded the king that it was advantageous to accept Montfort as his vassal. But while Montfort was savoring the monarch's long awaited acknowledgement, his army was dispersed throughout the Midi, totally unprepared to relieve the siege of Beaucaire.

Nevertheless, Rambouillet was confident that upon hearing the news, Montfort would lose no time in marshalling his forces to march on Beaucaire. Hesitation was not a trait of Simon de Montfort. And so the young knight pestered the armorers whom he had paid to work on his accouterments and repeatedly visited the farrier to make sure that the hooves of his charger were properly trimmed, balanced and shod.

Beaucaire would be his first major battle since Muret, where he had ridden with Bertrand de Marty's squadron and had crushed the Aragonese knights. With a veteran's pride, Rambouillet recalled the course of the battle. That paragon of chivalry, King Peire II of Aragon, had clad himself in the armor of an ordinary knight and joined the front ranks of his army. When the concentrated force of the French charge exploded into the Aragon horse, Peire was one of the first to die. Thanks to Montfort's decisiveness, it was a great victory.

So, too, was the battle the year before, when Rambouillet had won his spurs in the hot and dusty Sierra Morena. There the crusaders had shattered the Muslim infidels at Las Navas de Tolosa and driven them out of the northern Iberian peninsula. They had discovered a pass through the mountains and surprised the enemy at dawn. The battle had turned into a rout and a slaughter that reminded him of Besièrs, except this time there were no women and children. But just as in Besièrs, his surcoat had been soaked with the blood of the men he had butchered.

His patron, Arnaud-Amaury, who had organized and led the contingent of French crusaders, had knighted him on the field. At the time, Rambouillet was eighteen years old. Now he was four years older, with a wife and a baby son back home in the Beauce and a pair of mistresses in the Midi. In the meantime, the pope had elevated Arnaud-Amaury to Archbishop of Narbona, and once established in that office, the erstwhile Abbot had also assumed the title of Duke of Narbona, a rank invented by Raimond of Tolosa's grandfather.

In the midst of preparing for battle, Rambouillet was summoned to the Archbishop's Palace. He donned his finest garments and hastened to attend his great patron. Gaping about at the magnificent furnishings in the Archbishop of Narbona's private cabinet, Rambouillet realized for the first time just how high his patron had advanced in the world. Up to that moment, he had believed that as the chief papal legate in the Midi and the overall leader of the Crusade, Arnaud-Amaury's importance had been vastly superior to that of an archbishop. However, upon seeing the opulence of the archbishop's palace, he had changed his mind.

Entering the room, the archbishop waved his hand at the tapestry-covered walls. "A lot better than a campaign pavilion, isn't it? Tis hard to become used to all this, but that's a burden one must assume in any high office, I ween," he said, and smiled at Rambouillet. "How do you find your quarters?"

"Never had better, Your Eminence," Rambouillet said. "You sent for me?"

"Forsooth, my fine young fellow. Do you call to mind that blasted scroll that I was after? Only two people beside you and me know of its existence. One is that whoreson thief, Thibaut, who gave us the slip in Lavelanet; and the other is that knight from the Comtat Venaicin, Olivier de Mazan, the one we were following in the first place."

"Ah yes, Thibaut, the thief who stole the scrolls from Mazan ...."

"I've received word that a man's decomposed body was found in a *garderobe* in the *castrum* of Lavelanet. I have reason to believe 'tis Thibaut, and none other."

"Really? Why?"

"Because one of dead man's pockets contained a crucifix that I used to wear. Remember how I looked high and low for it and thought I lost it?"

"Yes, now that you mention it."

"Well, apparently Thibaut nicked it from me, else how did it end up in his pocket? The last words he ever said to me were that he had to take a piss. That's when he ran up to that *garderobe*."

"Maybe someone robbed him."

"Then why didn't they take the crucifix, too? 'Twas solid gold and silver."

Rambouillet shrugged. "Maybe the scrolls are still in the shit."

The Archbishop shook his head. "They drained the whole *garderobe* and found nothing."

"But didn't you hear Mazan say that someone had picked his pocket?"

"Clear as a bell." Arnaud-Amaury nodded. 'Twas a mighty shock, by my troth."

"*Clear as a bell?* Is that what you just said?"

"Yes, 'tis my recollection."

"Wait." Rambouillet put his hands on his head. "*Clear as a bell*. In that case, mayhap Mazan would fain have had you overhear what he said. Mayhap he *wanted* to make it look like Thibaut had stolen the scrolls. Mayhap 'twas *Mazan* who pushed Thibaut into the *garderobe*!"

"You're saying that Mazan killed Thibaut and kept the scrolls?"

"Why not? How else did Thibaut end up in the *garderobe*? Why would Mazan blame Thibaut out loud unless he wanted you to hear it?"

The Archbishop saw that Rambouillet's explanation was plausible. 'Twas like enough that Mazan may have made fool of him. But 'twould not do to admit he had been gulled. He slammed a fist into his palm. "I've been thinking along the same lines, but I wanted to make sure my suspicions were well founded. Methinks we're right. I want you to travel to Provença."

"I intended to join Montfort when he comes."

"I don't want to wait that long. Besides; his offensive may complicate recovering the scrolls."

"Sire, tell me what you want me to do. Your wish is my command."

Arnaud-Amaury ground his teeth in fury. In effect, the Pope had wrested the Duchy of Narbona away from him and awarded it to Monfort! 'Twas outrageous! The angry Archbishop felt he had clearly earned the right to the fiefdom because he had led the crusading army when it passed by Narbona on the way from Besièrs to Carcassona. The Pope's high-handed decision was nothing short of betrayal, an abject concession by the Holy See to secular power.

Back then, he -- Arnaud-Amaury -- *not* Count Raimond of Tolosa, the nominal Duke, and certainly *not* Montfort, had dictated harsh terms to the Viscount and Archbishop of Narbona, forcing them to turn over their fortifications to the crusaders and to supply him with financial and military aid. He also made them promise to turn over any refugee heretics who had fled from Besièrs, and to tighten up their suppression of heresy in Narbona.

And who was Montfort at the time? A nobody. Just one of the many barons under his command. Since then, had the people of Narbona come to respect Montfort for his military prowess? Or put him on a pedestal as the Athlete of Christ? Hardly.

The archbishop snickered as he recalled his consecration at Narbona, at which Montfort was represented by his young son Aimery and his brother Guy. Arnaud-Amaury had used their presence to spread a rumor that the boy had forced his way into the Viscountal palace. As a result, mobs poured out into the streets around the Templar

Commandery where Aimery was lodging. The deadly riot killed several crusaders, including two of Montfort's personal squires. Montfort may have been a hero to the French, but to the people of Narbona, he was but a foreign villain, the archbishop gloated.

He rose and began to pace about the room. The Holy Father was plainly losing his grip and had outlived his usefulness. His behavior had become personally insulting and his decisions nonsensical. It was time for Innocent to step down, but unfortunately, Arnaud-Amaury knew of only one Pope who had ever resigned, and that was the dissolute Benedict IX, who actually had resigned three times. On the other hand, he mused, violent death had ended the papacy several times over the centuries. There was no reason in the world why such a pattern should not repeat itself. And soon.

Mazan

Micaela's hand rested lightly in the crook of Olivier's arm, as they strolled in the garden that she was so fond of tending. He inhaled deeply. The scent of roses at this time of year was intoxicating. To his right, beyond the low garden wall, the dark green vineyards stretched away to where they met the light green of the barley fields. Up ahead, their young daughters shrilled and whooped as they played tag with some of the stable boys of their own age. Isabel was almost ten and, and Margarida was already eight. Where had the time gone? He sighed.

"Melancholy on a day like this?" Micaela remarked. "What sort of sad swain has taken my arm?"

"One who utterly adores you."

"I should hope so!"

"Methought how quick the years have passed," Olivier sighed.

"'Tis why we must delight in the present. And, speaking of time passing, maybe we should be more diligent in finding a suitor for Josetta." Micaela nodded toward the young woman on the garden wall watching the children. "She's going on seventeen."

"I wot it well. But she is very particular."

"She's very keen on Alain de Lavaur."

"Is she?"

"Yes, and now he's off besieging Beaucaire with young Raimond. 'Twould be a sorry day if he gets killed," Micaela said, and stopped walking.

"Don't say that, my darling!" Mazan said, and put an arm around her shoulder.

"Superstitious?"

"Forsooth!"

"My heart is gladdened that you are keeping your sword in its scabbard this time," said Micaela, squeezing his arm. "I wot well that you're doing it for love of me. When young Raimond came to Avinhon, I could see how you yearned to join him, yet here you are, by my side."

"Oh, fie! By my troth, you were no less eager than I to hail the young Count."

"How could I have remained still? Everyone was in the streets, shouting for the French to go home, and *viva el Comt!* Who would have imagined that people in Provença would champion a Count of Tolosa?"

"Aye, what a difference a few years have made," said Olivier, shaking his head in wonder.

"'Twas Montfort's own cruelty and cupidity that have worked against him, I trow," Micaela said. "At first, many of the Church of Rome deemed that the crusaders were redressing heresy. Now they see it differently."-

"Especially when Peire of Aragon went to Raimond's rescue. No one, especially Innocent, could accuse Peire of being of anti-Roman. After crushing the Muslims in Spain, who could have ever imagined that the great warrior would be vanquished and slain by Montfort?"

"Forsooth. 'Twould have been quite different if Peire had won at Muret, or, at least, if he hadn't been killed, think you not?" Micaela said.

"Yes, but now look what's happening right here in Provença. People have risen up against the French and are flocking to young Raimond's cause."

"'Tis all the more a brave deed to resist the urge to put on your hauberk. That means so much to me. Seven years ago, I died a thousand deaths," she said, and gave his hand a squeeze.

Olivier raised her hand to his lips. "Yet, 'tis maddening, the way they try to force their laws and customs on us. In many ways, 'tis worse than seizing property. Satan himself must have written those vile statutes of Pamias."

251

"I know full well how much this occupation chafes you, and that's why I keep repeating how grateful I am that you're staying here with me. But please, let's get back to Josetta and Lavaur."

"Are you changing the subject?" He pressed her arm.

"No," she said, squeezing back, "we were talking about Josetta before you mentioned the siege. She's been a wonderful addition to the family, think you not?"

"Yes, and therefore, I trow, she needs an appropriate dowry."

"I care to say. 'Tis a pity that the occupation virtually puts Maire's properties in the Lauragais out of question," said Olivier.

"What about the old chateau in Vaison?"

"It needs some renovations."

"Should we get started on seeing that they get done? Methinks you'd enjoy supervising the work." Micaela arched an eyebrow.

"You're irrepressible. Of course we shall." Olivier patted her hand. "But if they do wed, what kind of a service should it be? We changed her name from Rebecca to hide her identity from that villain Arnaud-Amaury, but should we consider a Jewish service?"

"'Twould be asking for trouble, I trow. Rightly or wrongly, we've raised her in our belief. Besides," Micaela said, "know you that Alan's grandparents on his father's side were both Good Folk?"

"'Tis true?"

"Yes, but, sad to say, they were burned alive with 380 other Good Folk after Montfort took Lavaur back in 1211"

"'Tis a foul deed! How did you find that out?"

She turned a troubled face to him. "Josetta herself told me just yesterday. Isn't it awful? They refused to abjure their faith."

"'Tis hard to envisage. Methinks I could not suffer it. I would abjure."

"Forsooth, you're a good and faithful Believer, but full sure am I that you'll never become a Good Man," she laughed. "That would mean giving you up, my darling, and that I'll never do."

From within the shadows of an old stone garden shed, Rambouillet watched the two girls playing on the paths of the garden outside the Castel de Mazan. They were laughing and shrieking boisterously as they rolled their hoops back and forth over the gravel surface. A handsome young woman, who he assumed was their older sister, sat on a nearby stone lintel, busily crocheting. For days, he had been watching them emerge from the castle, bringing their favorite toys and dolls with them, and rarely standing still. Whooping with pleasure, they ran helter-skelter about the garden.

When Olivier joined in their games, their joy knew no bounds, and they piped with glee when he swung them through the air in big circles by their ankles and wrists, or bore them on his back crawling on all fours. He also taught them how to skip flat stones in the pond and coached them in the archery that they practiced with the grooms. But their favorite pastime was riding their ponies out on the fields, or on mountain trails, alongside their father.

Because they never went out without their sister or parents in attendance, Rambouillet despaired of being able to carry out the Archbishop's plan, which called for the abduction of one the girls and demanding the scrolls as ransom. Clad like a merchant, he had hoped to blend into the market activity of the town, but somehow he stood out like a sore thumb, and he knew he was drawing suspicious glances from the villagers, particularly because he was reluctant to speak and give away the unpopular fact that he was one of those dreadful foreigners from the North.

For that reason, he lurked in the copses and behind outbuildings where he could observe the girls at play, completely unaware that he himself was the object of surveillance by more than a score of warders in the community, as well as by the mother of the two little girls. They knew where he tethered his charger and the location of his favorite hiding spots. Therefore, he was the only one who was surprised when Olivier interrupted his morning ride by turning his horse aside and approaching the garden shed, where he spoke.

"Good day to you, Master Merchant! Olivier de Mazan, at your service. I feel flattered that you take so much interest in my daughters. Perchance are you intending to offer them some of your wares? In which case, why don't you call on her ladyship?"

Rambouillet, flustered by Olivier's directness, racked his brain for a reply that would seem offhand and innocent. "Forsooth, good sir, I beg your pardon, but I stand guilty of admiring your eldest daughter yonder. I really have naught to offer her but my heart." As he spoke, Olivier's eyebrows rose. He's onto my French accent, Rambouillet cursed silently.

"Well said, Master Merchant, and full sure am I that at one time such frank sentiments would have charmed my daughter. Alack, she is betrothed and hence, although such expressions of esteem might not fall on entirely deaf ears, they would certainly fall on a cold heart, a heart hardened,

I might add, by the death of her loved ones at the hands of people like you." Olivier's eyes had narrowed as he spoke.

"I am truly sorry, my lord, and had I known these circumstances, I would not have disturbed your lives. I am but a merchant," Rambouillet said.

"That falls far short of the truth and you wot it well. I have seen you in the company of that Cistercian shit who led swine like you to pillage and despoil our lands, where they mercilessly..."

"You dare call my lord and master a   " Rambouillet interrupted angrily. "You, who consort with heretics and abet them in their satanic pursuits? Let us settle this with steel on steel. For I am Sir Guy de la Beauce from Rambouillet, knighted on the field of Los Navas de Tolosa."

"I don't give a fig if you were knighted in the Holy See itself, but I accept your challenge." Olivier snapped his fingers, and several warders stepped out of their hiding places. "By masquerading, trespassing and spying on my daughters, you have forfeited the privileges of chivalry, but I will waive the rules in your case."

"You'll let me retrieve my weapons, I trow? You see they are not on my person."

"My men will fetch them from your lodgings; in the meantime, I'm locking you in the dungeon. I fain would not have you change your mind and run for it. Tomorrow morning, justice will be done."

Twisting and turning on a pallet of straw in his narrow cell, Rambouillet ruminated about the day to come. *Vespers* and *compline* came and went, and he still couldn't sleep.

When he finally dozed off, *matins* woke him. He rolled over and just as he was about to drift off again, something poked him.

"Pssst. Wake up," hissed a woman's voice. In the pitch-black cell, it was impossible to see anything. "Grab the staff, and I will lead you to the stairs. Once you have ascended, you'll be able to see. 'Tis but thirty-five steps "

"Then what?"

"I'll show you a postern gate with your horse tethered outside."

"Sorry, my lady, but I have a matter of honor to settle tomorrow. Running away is out of the question. I must bide."

"If being buried alive is how you want to settle a dispute, then stay, by all means."

"Buried alive? What are you talking about?"

"'Tis the fate the *castellan* is planning for you. Why would I risk being blamed for your escape, if it wasn't so serious?"

"But he agreed to settle our differences through mortal combat, by wager of battle..."

"'Tis just what he told the others. They're presently feeding the roots of a bed of roses. But suit yourself. I don't have all night."

Rambouillet had heard that this horrible fate was a favorite means of execution in the Midi, and he shivered. "Then of course, I accept your offer. But who are you?"

"Someone who doesn't believe in cruelty. Are you ready?"

"Yes."

"Then take hold the end of the staff and I will guide you. We must act quickly."

Micaela slipped back under the covers. Olivier had turned onto his back and was snoring. The sleeping potion she had put in his wine had apparently lost none of its potency since she last used it herself during her bout with mastitis. On re-entering the bedchamber, she had been careful to replace the key to the dungeon in Olivier's mantle pocket.

Rambouillet's miraculous flight from the field of honor would be met with scorn and he would be branded a coward. Olivier would quite naturally be furious and beside himself that the Frenchman managed to escape, but he would also live the day out, which might not have been the case if she hadn't acted. As her mind groped toward sleep, Micaela couldn't help smiling. Her husband's life infinitely outweighed the contents of the scrolls that he and others believed to be so precious. The sheer satisfaction of having acted so decisively carried her across the border between waking and sleep, and soon she was gently snoring in harmony with her husband.

Olivier squeezed his eyes shut and set his jaw. To be sure, many might blame Rambouillet for running away from a trial by combat, but Olivier was convinced that others might believe that he himself had freed the young knight in order to save his own skin! It not only debased his *paratge*, but it was maddening to have Rambouillet escape, just when neighbors were flocking to Raimond VII's colors. More and more, Olivier felt obligated to join them, particularly when word had gone out that Viscount Montfort had assembled an army and was counterattacking the Provençal army at Beaucaire.

Montfort had hurried back down the Rose valley from France, scraping up knights along the way and hiring as many mercenaries as he could. Joining his brother Guy, who had pulled together forces from Tolosa to Montpelhier, Montfort launched a massive assault on the Provençal fortifications, trying to overwhelm his foe with one decisive blow and so avoid a drawn-out siege. But despite the valiant sacrifice of dozens of knights and scores of routiers and sergeants, the attack was repulsed. At the same time, the Provençals tightened their grip on the Frenchmen holding out in the castle. The decisive battle remained to be won, and Olivier was convinced that he could contribute to that victory.

Again and again, he racked his brain; who could have unlocked the door? The key was still in his trousers pocket when he woke. He thought of the servants, but dismissed their participation because they had no motive to free the prisoner and had not taken part in his incarceration. The warders who actually took Rambouillet to the dungeon did not live in the castle. Who had access to that key?

There was Micaela, of course, but why would she free the Frenchman? What could have been her motive? That very day, she had praised him for staying out of the war and not joining the Provençal army besieging Beaucaire. If she was so thankful for his refusal to fight…if she…?

Wait…. Micaela had been overjoyed because he *hadn't* gone off to join the siege! Did this mean that she would be overjoyed when he stayed out of any fight, including a trial by combat? Thinking back on it, she had always opposed every one of his military efforts. She had discouraged him from ambushing the bailiffs of the Count of Tolosa; she had pleaded with him not to go to the aid of Trencavel; she had scorned the political reasons and she had argued that his *paratge* would be better served by staying home than by donning armor and taking up arms.

Mayhap his pious mother had exerted too much influence on her? The thought of his wife risking his reputation by stealing into the dungeon and releasing the prisoner was hurtful. He kicked a stool across the scullery floor.

It was virtually betrayal. If he confronted her, and she denied it, what could he do? There was no way to prove it. And if she said yes, which would feel like a hammer blow, what was he to do? How could he ever trust her again?

Knowing that he had to find out one way or the other, he sought her out in the sewing room where she was teaching Isabel and Margarida how to hem gowns. He kissed her on the cheek and then hugged his daughters.

"Children, please leave me and your mother alone for a time. Mayhap Josetta will play some games with you."

The girls looked at their mother, and after she nodded, put their sewing away and ran out of the room, their voices piping Josetta's name.

"Are you going to make love to me right now before I have a chance to remove my thimble?" Micaela smiled up at him.

"'Twould be a fair thing, but I have a question which I find very difficult to ask."

"That might make it even more difficult to answer."

"My dearest love, did you… did you help that French swine escape? I have to know if ….Are you the one who

259

unlocked the door to the cell? I don't want to falsely blame any of our retainers."

"Yes, forsooth. I could not bear the thought of you being hurt or killed. I took the key and let him go. 'Twas my doing. If you must needs blame someone, blame me."

Olivier felt as if the wind had been knocked out of him. Micaela had betrayed him and jeopardized his *paratge*! And the fact that Rambouillet had fled was incomprehensible. "He fled of his own accord?"

"By my troth! He even thanked me!"

"He knew who you were?"

"To say truth, he had no idea 'Twas pitch dark."

"I scarce believe that he complied. He seemed so eager."

"Methinks the matter overtaxed him." Micaela did not tell him about her ruse about being buried alive.

"But, my darling, know you not what you've done? Full sure am I that people will think I helped him escape by reason I was afraid. "

"Let them think what they will. Here you stand, alive, without a scratch."

"That's not the point. 'Tis not your place to countermand decisions I have made."

"'Tis my place to try to make sure that my daughters' father stays alive. 'Twould gladden my heart if you were to mind that prospect, too."

"If you persist in opposing me, there'll be consequences. Besides, now Monfort has laid siege to the besiegers. Raimond needs my help," Olivier said.

"And so do I. So do your daughters."

"If Montfort wins, 'twill not go well for us."

"And if you die, 'twill go even worse."

"Fighting against injustice always involves risk."

"A risk that's unjust to your family."

"Let us put quit to this argument. I have made up my mind."

"Then, methinks, I'm wasting my breath. Excuse me while I attend to the girls," Micaela said, as she rose and swept out of the room.

Olivier sank onto a curule, and putting his elbows on his knees, cradled his head in his hands and sighed. If only Micaela had listened to reason, and he had made a better case! She had defied him once again. Now he would have to go to war without her support, which was the last thing he had ever wanted to do.

Avinhon

As the knights and squires of the Legion of Provença rode into Avinhon on their way to the Ardèchan, a tumult of tolling bells echoed through the narrow streets. Who could have died, Olivier wondered. Someone important, it was certain. Could it be old Philippe, the King of France, who was crowned more than two score years ago, when he was still in his teens? On the other hand, French monarchs were hardly popular in Avinhon at the present time. What about Archbishop Arnaud-Amaury, who was about the same age as Philippe; that would be good riddance, indeed. Then there was the possibility that the Bishop of Avinhon himself might be dead, although he was much younger than the other two. As he racked his mind trying to divine who it could be, he heard shouting over the din of bells mixed with cacophony of hundreds of iron-shod hooves striking cobblestones.

"The Pope! The Pope is dead!"

Ah, Pope Innocent! Of course! He was the same age as the King and the Archbishop. Olivier felt no remorse. In fact, the Pontiff's death seemed more like a cause for celebration. It was Innocent, not Philippe or any other monarch, who pushed for the Crusade that transmogrified into an unending war of conquest and occupation that had cost countless lives and treasure. The Crusade was Innocent's creation and therefore his responsibility, even though after it started, he had tried ineffectively to mitigate the tide of conquest.

One of the unintended consequences of the Pontiff's actions, Olivier reflected, was the loss of the Holy See's most pious ally, Peire II of Aragon, the most devout and dedicated Catholic monarch in the entire region. Peire had actually paid homage to the Pope as his suzerain before unpredictably losing his life and much of his dominions to

Simon Montfort, an upstart baron from France. Peire's earlier and decisive victory over the Muslim hordes at Navas de Tolosa had removed the threat of infidel hegemony on the Iberian Peninsula, a tremendous triumph for the Roman Church and the only truly successful Crusade thus far.

In contrast, Montfort's defeat of Peire at Murat set back the Catholic cause and may even have served to increase the numbers who believed in the Church of the Friends of God. Time will tell, Olivier mused, and right now, both time and the tide of war seemed to be on the side of young Raimond VII of Tolosa.

By the time they began crossing the bridge over the Rose, the details of Innocent's death became known. He had been hale one day and dead the next. Apparently, while traveling in Tuscany, he suddenly developed violent dyspepsia, and died shortly afterwards. Observing the drawn faces of his comrades as they took heed of the loss of the only pope they had ever known, Olivier couldn't help reflecting on the even hand with which the Dark Power struck down both the powerful and the powerless. It called to mind the satanic leers that stone masons carved into the faces of gargoyles on cathedral portals. *Mors vincent omnia.* Death conquers all.

On reaching the far shore, he shivered and spurred his horse into a trot. Hopefully, the Dark Power would overlook him in the combat that lay ahead.

Narbona

The Archbishop of Narbona was neither surprised nor dismayed when news of Innocent's sudden death reached his palace. After all, he had planned it so meticulously, he would have been surprised and dismayed if it *hadn't* taken place. Better yet, there was not a hint, not a whisper of the possibility of foul play. *Usus est magister optimus.* Practice makes perfect, he grinned. 'Twas his master stroke!

The death of Innocent would come to be seen as a great blessing, Arnaud-Amaury assured himself. In the struggle against heresy, Innocent had become a liability, not an asset, and he had failed to realize that the ultimate enemy were the feudal dynasties that could challenge the Church and compete for its funds. The Church had succeeded in establishing its supremacy, but its role was tenuous at best. That is why the heretics, with their backing by various feudal factions, threatened the very foundation of the Church. The Pontiff's off-again-on-again policy toward Raimond VI was a case in point, and now the insurgency led by the young Count of Tolosa proved the error and even the inanity of the Pontiff's ways. What had been decided at the Lateran Council was now in shambles. The young Raimond might even give Montfort his come-uppance, an outcome that the Archbishop would hardly mourn. After all, unchecked, Montfort himself might found a dynasty that would compete with the Church for power.

For a moment, Arnaud-Amaury rued that Innocent had died before suffering the chagrin of seeing his policies fail. Then the Archbishop's mood brightened again. Out with the old and in with the new! In his lofty role as the Archbishop of Narbona, he would be able to mould the new pope into a leader more to his liking. He might even become a candidate himself, and be elected to the Holy See. It was only what he deserved. If he could get his hands on those scrolls, there would be no preventing him from becoming the most powerful man in all Christendom. *Christen*dom? The *very name* would have to be changed!

Mazan

Olivier eased himself out of the saddle as carefully as he could to avoid aggravating the pain in his side. Otz, his squire, helped him down, but still he gasped involuntarily as pain knifed along a shattered rib.

Olivier and his comrades from the Legion of Provença had ambushed one of Montfort's supply trains coming down from the Ardecha, and at the outset, a well-aimed shot from an enemy crossbow had almost knocked him off his horse Had it not been for his hauberk, the quarrel would have killed him. As it was, it broke a rib and the point penetrated his chest cavity to the depth of a fingernail.

Despite the acute pain, he had gone on fighting, but by the time they had captured the wagon train and pack animals, every breath had become torture, and almost every movement with his left arm was agony. After helping escort the supply train across the bridge to Avinhon, he and Otz had ridden homeward, alternating cantering with walking, because trotting significantly exacerbated the pain.

Adding to Olivier's misery were his misgivings about his homecoming and its reception. Three weeks earlier, he had left home for the first time in his marriage without embracing Micaela. They had quarreled about his decision to join the Provençals fighting the French invaders, and Micaela had gone so far as to leave the conjugal bed and set up a pallet in the children's room. He had longed to set everything right before going off to fight and possibly die, but his attempts to talk had been met with icy responses. He knew that she would not relent unless he gave up the idea of defending his *paratge*, and this he would not do.

Now, standing in the courtyard and exhausted from the grueling pain, he sent Otz to fetch Petronilla, the aging housekeeper who doubled as a midwife, to treat his wound. After delivering the message, Otz was to inform the *castellane* that her husband was back home. Otz nodded and hurried off, while Olivier gingerly sat down on the edge of the horse trough by the well, clenching his teeth in an effort to keep from moaning.

Hardly any time elapsed before Petronilla appeared at his side, and while she stood listening to him describe his wound, Micaela rushed up and threw her arms around his neck. He jerked in pain, but returned her kisses. Then Micaela asked Otz to help Olivier walk to the cook room, where Petronilla had gone to fill a large kettle with water and stoke the fire.

Inside, Micaela and Otz cut off his surcoat and began loosening the ties of his heavy hauberk. Once the long and careful process of removing the chain mail was over – with Olivier trying to stifle his groans as they eased his left arm out of the heavy sleeve -- they unlaced his *gambeson*, the padded jacket worn under the armor, and carefully slid it off of him. By the time they cut away his shirt to expose his torso, he was in agony.

Micaela gasped when she saw the large purple bruise and the swollen, blood-encrusted margins of the wound. Clucking her tongue, Petronilla dipped a cloth into the kettle and gently began to clean the site of the puncture. Olivier flinched, trying not to move or scream. He began to cough, and each cough was excruciating.

"Darling," she said, as she wiped the sweat off his brow, "what is the name of that Jewish physician in Carpentras? Methinks he should come and see you, don't you agree, Petronilla?"

"Valabrègue," Olivier muttered, trying desperately to keep from coughing. He didn't seem to be getting enough air and he began to pant.

"Otz, ride like the wind and fetch Senhor Valabrègue. Tell him my husband will die if he doesn't come. "

"And where will I find him?"

"Ask anyone, but now be off."

By the time Otz came back with the physician, Olivier's condition had changed for the worse. His cough had turned into short barks and his breathing had become increasingly rapid. He was sitting up in bed, propped up by pillows. Valabrègue, a man in his sixties, pulled away the covers and gently palpated the area around the wound. Then he laid his ear on Olivier's chest, first listening to the left side and then listening to the right side, and then moved once more to the left side. He nodded to himself and then turned to Micaela.

"Just as I feared from what Otz told me. I must extract some air from his chest or he will die. It happens in many cases like this with penetrating chest wounds or broken ribs. I have an apparatus that can help me accomplish this."

He rummaged in a small wooden traveling chest that he had brought with him, and drew out a box about as long and wide as a man's forearm. Opening it up, he pulled out a large syringe with a hollow glass needle and removed the plunger. "Mistress," he said to Petronilla, I think you said you had a kettle of boiling water. I would like to soak this pyculus in that water. I always try to work with clean instruments. Do you have a large clean bowl?"

Petronilla fetched a bowl, and Valabregue carefully laid the disassembled syringe in it and helped her pour boiling water from the kettle into the bowl. After a few moments, he decanted the water and when the glass was cool enough to handle, he picked up the barrel and moved to Olivier's bedside.

"M'lord, I am going to place an instrument inside the wound in order to extract some air. Please remain absolutely still when I do this, *Oc?*"

"*Oc,*" Olivier grunted.

Valabregue inserted the needle in the wound and there was a hissing sound as air escaped through the empty barrel of the syringe. He watched Olivier, whose breathing was becoming less rapid.

"Feel better?" Valabregue asked.

Olivier nodded.

When the noise stopped, Valabregue removed the syringe, inserted the plunger, then placed the syringe into the wound, and drew back on the plunger. He repeated the process two more times.

. "How do you feel now," he asked.

"Much better, thanks," Olivier said, "except it hurts every time I take a breath."

"I fear you are going to have to live with that for some time. I will mix a potion that will help you sleep. 'Twill do you a world of good." I am also going to sew up your wound to help prevent air from entering your chest and then bind your rib cage. 'Twill help with the pain."

As Olivier lay sleeping, Micaela took Valabregue's hands in hers. "I can never thank you enough, Senhor,. Methinks you saved his life."

"Possibly, Dòmna, but he's a pretty tough bird. And most important, he's still a tough *young* bird. How does he seem to be sleeping? Any coughs, any rapid breathing?"

"No, he seems to be sleeping like a baby."

"Good. I'm returning home, but if there seems to be any problem, send for me, and I will come."

"I have never seen a device like the one that you used. 'Tis a new invention?"

The old doctor smiled. "Ah, no, forsooth. 'Twas blown in Granada, where I studied, almost twenty years ago."

"So you've done this many times before."

"To speak truth, I commonly use it to suck pus out of wounds, or cataracts out of people's eyes. That's what it was invented for, centuries ago, by a great physician named Ali al Wawsili, although some say the ancient Romans were the first to use them."

"And on how many patients like my husband have you used it?"

Valabregue looked down at his feet, and then raised his eyes to hers and smiled, the crow's-feet working at the corner of his eyes.

"Today was the very first time. My mentor in Granada once performed it on a similar patient, and explained about the trapped air. Since then, I haven't had the occasion, because all the others with this complication died before I got to their bedside. Methinks we both have cause to celebrate."

"I can't tell you how very grateful I am for your good services," she said, and handed him a heavy purse.

"Thank you, my lady," Valabrègue said, "he should get out of the bed three or four times a day, even though he'll feel weak. Many patients get the lung fever if they lie abed too long, and we should avoid that at all costs."

With Petronilla sitting with Olivier in the afternoons, Micaela found she could easily manage nursing him back to health. Within two weeks, he was strolling in the garden with her, admiring the roses and the other flowers.

As he convalesced, Olivier tried to keep abreast of the news from Beaucaire. During July and early August, young Raimond's trebuchets pulverized the castle towers and his men smashed down walls with a huge battering ram. As summer lengthened into August, the garrison of the castle finally capitulated, and Montfort was forced to withdraw.

The jubilation that followed this ignominious defeat of the great French warrior was infectious, and spurred countless uprisings against French overlords throughout the Midi. Monfort marched back to Tolosa, which was nominally in his possession and razed its walls. When the citizens took arms against him, he rounded up and banished its most distinguished residents, taking over their property, and exacting stiff reparations and other financial obligations.

By the time Olivier could move around without pain, Montfort had pounced upon the Count of Fois' possessions in the far off bvalley of the Ariège, even though the Pope had reinstated the Count as their rightful lord. Ignoring the fact that the Count had gone out of his way not to provoke the crusaders, Montfort had no qualms at thumbing his nose at the Holy See, and raised his banner over the walls of Fois.

With the Ariège pacified, he hastened all the way back across the Midi to invade the March of Provença, where he conquered town after town along the Rose until he was threatening Avinhon. That was when he learned that young Raimond VII had entered Tolosa to great jubilation and that the populace had risen up and butchered every Frenchman they could find.

Part IV

Narbona

Throngs of joyous people were dancing in the streets to the rhythms of cymbals and drums that were almost drowned out by the pealing of every bell in the city. From a balcony of the Archbishop's palace, Arnaud-Amaury waved at the delirious crowds chanting *El ei mòrt, el senhor Montfort,* and he couldn't help wondering how the citizens of Tolosa must have reacted to the death of the hated foreigner. After almost ten months of besieging Tolosa, Montfort had been hit in the head with a huge piece of masonry flung by a trebuchet manned by women inside the city walls. The missile broke every bone in his skull and reduced his face to an unrecognizable bloody pulp. A month later, Montfort's son Amaury had burned his siege weapons, and moved the crusader army back to its base in Carcasonna.

On the balcony, Arnaud-Amaury danced a few steps of a jig celebrating the death of the man he had once lifted to great power, only to judge him to be an ingrate and a false friend. Instead of applauding or at least tolerating his clerical colleague's assumption of the title and privileges of the Duke of Narbona, Montfort had opposed him with invective and claimed the title for himself. Furious at this lack of gratitude, the Archbishop had excommunicated Montfort on the spot. Not to be denied his prize, the Frenchman had taken the dispute all the way to the Holy See. As a result, Pope Honorius had sent a new legate to make peace between the two principal figures of the Crusade.

The legate, a cardinal from Rome named Bertrand, had been immediately reviled by the Provençals, who ridiculed him and went so far as to attack him and his entourage with crossbows. When he learned about Bertrand's reception in Provença, Arnaud-Amaury had chortled. That should teach that smug Italian of the difficulties the Holy See had made for itself throughout the Midi, he gloated.

However, much to Arnaud-Amaury's chagrin, the Provençals' excesses drove Bertrand to support Montfort's claim to the Duchy of Narbona. Now, with Montfort out of the picture, Arnaud-Amaury mused, there was no reason for the Holy See not to award him with the duchy, and he sent off a letter to Honorius, pleading his case.

If only he could get his hands on those purloined scrolls, he could turn the tables and dictate to Honorius, and even become his successor. The scrolls still wore on his mind. With the lifting of the siege of Tolosa and the retreat of the crusaders to Carcassona, Rambouillet might be eager to help him persuade Mazan to surrender them. There is nothing like a threat to one's family to motivate a devoted father, and through the ecclesiastical network, he had succeeded in identifying and locating all three of Mazan's grown daughters. The oldest would be perfect prey for Rambouillet. He rubbed his hands together and smirked in anticipation.

Mazan

The chain of dancers snaked back and forth across the floor of the great hall, the dancers' feet moving with the beat of the tambours, their faces flushed with pleasure and excitement. Musicians playing recorders, rebeks, flutes and harps were providing a lively tune. The newly weds, Alan and Josetta, broke away from the head of the line, and joined their hands in an arch through which the next couple ducked to form a second arch, and so on until the entire chain had changed into a tunnel of arms.

A sudden change in the beat and the tune, and the arch broke up into rings of four couples performing an *estampida*, with lively hops and rhythmic stamping, with frequent changes of partners accomplished by swinging each other in turn by the crooks of their elbows.

Having just left the floor, Olivier and Micaela were watching the spectacle from their table, drinking beakers of water, and thankful to get some rest. Olivier was sweating profusely from his exertions, and Micaela fanned herself with a kerchief. Both Isabel and Margarida were dancing, often with young men they had never met before as well as with old acquaintances from the Venaicin.

How fast they grow up, thought Olivier, only yesterday they were playing with their dolls. In only a few more years, they will be wed, with babes of their own. He glanced at Micaela, and smiled, slowly shaking his head at his daughters' apparent maturity. She read his thoughts and put her hand on his.

"They are beautiful, aren't they?" she murmured.

"Yes, indeed," he said, watching Isabel swirl by with a handsome young man, probably a *faidit* like Alan with probably the same poor prospects. Isabel had his fair hair and blue eyes, whereas Margarida was the spitting image of her mother. He craned his neck trying to catch a glimpse

276

of his youngest daughter. At fourteen, she was on the threshold of womanhood, but to Olivier, Margarida was still but a girl. Then suddenly there she was, whirling along on nimble feet, dancing with one of his companions from the League of Provença, a man of his own age! He caught Micaela's eye and raised an eyebrow, but she merely shrugged. It was only a dance, she seemed to be saying. Looking about for Isabel in vain, Olivier waved his empty beaker at a varlet, who went to fetch a flagon of wine. He was eager to rejoin the dancers with Micaela on his arm.

Gerard de Castèlnòudari stood outside of the keep, inhaling the fresh air and intoxicated with the moonlight, the dancing and especially the pretty young woman by his side. He had led her out of the Great Hall by the hand, and he thrilled to its touch. He raised it to his lips and brushed it with a kiss. He longed to make love to her, but he tried to control his passion by making small talk.

"You are a wonderful dancer," he told Isabel. You must excuse me if I seemed clumsy."

"Oh, no," she said, "'tis not for you to apologize. You're an excellent dancer. I couldn't wish for better." She was grateful that he had spoken, for she was tense with ardor.

"Well, I'm from the Lauragais, and we've always heard that you Provençals excel at dancing."

277

"The Lauragais? My grandmother comes from Fanjaus," Isabel exclaimed. "'Twas she who taught me to dance, so mayhap I dance more like you than like a Provençal!"

"Fanjaus? 'Tis but a few leagues from my hometown, Gerard cried, and shook his head over the coincidence..

"But what brings you here, then? Are you related to the groom?"

"Aye, that I am." Gerard's eyes glowed as he marveled at Isabel's beauty.

"'Tis a goodly journey, I trow."

"To say truth, but today, 'twas only from Uzès. When Montfort took Castèlnòudari, my mother moved to Uzès where my aunt lives, and I'm visiting them."

"Think you to return to Castèlnòudari, now that the French surrendered?"

"I've already done that. I've been living in my ancestral home, and when the war is over, full sure am I that my mother will return. I'm biding here just for the wedding."

"Like enough, the war is drawing to an end."

"Forsooth, the young Montfort is no match for his father, thank goodness."

"Yes, my father says the French seem to have lost interest. 'Tis astonishing that their king gave up his campaign so quickly last year." Isabel said, surprised that she could make this small talk while her heart beat out of control.

"'Twas certainly a stroke of good fortune," he said. Then he took a deep breath. "But nowhere as great as the one that brought me here to meet you." He lifted her hand to his lips again.

"Your good fortune is mine, sir."

He gently cupped her face in his hands, and put his lips to hers. Their tongues met tentatively and then strove with each other in frenzy. He put his hands in the small of her back and she threw her hands around his neck and pulled him to her.

When their mouths separated, he ran his lips across her cheek and onto her ear, and then sank them onto her neck. Isabel shuddered. A mounting need had taken over her body, and when he put his hand on her breast, she moaned with pleasure.

"Where can we…?" he whispered.

Now it was her turn to take his hand and lead him to the shed where the heckled flax was stored, ready for spinning, and where she surrendered herself, body and soul.

Isabel had hardly re-entered the great hall, when Micaela accosted her. "Wherever have you been, child? Is aught wrong?"

"No… well, yes, methinks I've had too much wine. I had to vomit."

"Oh, you poor thing. Are you feeling better? Do you want to go up to bed?"

"Yes, 'twould be wonderful. I hope you're not angry with me, Maire."

"Of course not. Come, let me take you to your chamber."

"Please, Maire, I can find my own way. Besides, you mustn't leave the dance because of me."

"Nonsense, I won't hear of it. I'm going to make sure that you're properly tucked in."

When Micaela returned to the Great Hall, she slipped onto the bench beside Olivier. "'Tis strange, Isabel drank too much. She's never done it in the past."

Olivier shrugged. "There's always a first time for all things, my sweet."

"Yes, but usually wine has less effect when one exerts oneself. Dancing helps sober people up."

"There are exceptions to every rule."

"Excuse me, my lord and lady." A young man with a boyish face had come up to their table and was standing before them. "You may not remember me, but I'm Christophe of Entrechaud. We met in Carpentras in March."

Olivier stretched out his hand and grinned. "Of course, how nice to see you again. I know your father well."

"Are you enjoying the dancing?" Micaela asked.

The young man looked crestfallen. "'Twould be more enjoyable if I could find Isabel. I was hoping for another dance with her, but she seems to have disappeared."

"'Tis true. She isn't feeling well and I just got through putting her to bed."

"Oh, I deeply rue her discomfort. 'Tis hapless to be ill on such an occasion. I was looking forward to dancing with her. We danced together at the start of the evening and then she was monopolized by another."

"Really? And who might that be?"

Christophe shrugged. "Someone from Castèlnòudari, I forget his name."

Micaela smiled sweetly. "Well, full sure am I that she'll rue not to have seen you again before retiring. Why don't you call on her in the next few days? I fain she would be delighted, as would I and my husband."

"Thank you a thousand times, Dòmna, and by my troth, 'twill make me glad in the heart to see you soon again." Christophe bowed his head to each of them and then wandered back toward the music.

"That's a pleasant young man," Micaela said, "think you not so?"

"Yes, he seems very agreeable. His father is an excellent castellan."

"Somehow, my love, I like not what I heard about Isabel spending so much time with one dance partner. Did you see who 'twas?"

"I saw her dancing with someone, I trow, but I paid no heed."

"Think you they went off somewhere together?"

"Aught is possible my darling. 'Tis a beautiful evening and young people have hot blood. However, didn't you say the wine had sickened her, and did you not put her to bed? Could she have been pretending?"

"Methought not. But now I'm not so sure."

"Well, let's join the dancers one more time. Are you up for it?"

"Of course."

As May lengthened into June, Isabel missed a menstrual period, which was strange, because she had always been regular, from the very onset. She pined for word from

Gerard, who had left for Castèlnòudari the day after the wedding, but heard nothing. In the meantime, news came that young Amaury Montfort had besieged Castèlnòudari, greatly adding to her anxiety.

When they had parted at the flax room that night, she had explained to him how to reach her sleeping chamber and that he should be careful to wait until he knew she was alone, because her mother would probably insist on putting her sick daughter to bed. To her delight, Gerard had appeared in her room shortly after her mother left, and they had lain together until cockcrow, when he crept away, avowing how much he adored her.

Because she had always enjoyed robust health, Isabel was surprised when she woke with nausea one morning. She found that eating crusts of bread provided relief, but it recurred the next day. And the next. What was wrong? On market day, she consulted an old crone from Mormoiron who told fortunes. She told the hag that she had a friend who was nauseous every morning, but otherwise seemed healthy. Was there something the matter with her? Was she seriously ill?"

The crone's eyes grew crafty, and her lips parted in a leer that revealed rotted teeth.

"Be your friend regular with her bleeding times, or has she missed one or two?"

"She has missed one."

"Well, if she misses the next, you can tell her that she is with child. Puking in the morning is one of most common signs of pregnancy. She doesn't need a fortune teller, she needs a midwife."

Isabel decided against seeking a midwife, because she feared that her mother would learn about her condition. She tried to continue her daily pastimes, which included many that she performed in concert with her little sister.

282

She longed to tell Margarida what seemed to be going on, but she was afraid that her sister might be angry with her for jeopardizing her *paratge*, although Margarida had always doted on her almost to a fault. Why would she change now? Isabel decided that if the blood flow from her womb did not come on schedule, she would definitely share her problem with Margarida. After all, when her sister's bleeding began, she had gone to Isabel for advice.

If only Josetta lived close by! She would have known exactly what to do, but a week after the wedding, she and Alan had departed for Lavaur, which Raimond VII had just liberated from the French, along with dozens of other towns throughout the former Trencavel domains. To Isabel, Josetta might as well have lived in England or Jerusalem.

The day after her talk with the fortuneteller, Isabel was getting ready for the daily ride that she and Margarida enjoyed together. Olivier had taught them to ride astraddle like a man, both with and without saddles, and Micaela had taught them to ride sidesaddle. They had become expert riders and usually ended their daily canter with a gallop back to the stable.

While changing into the trousers she usually wore for riding, she noticed spots of blood on her shift and down her legs. Her menses had begun! For the first time she could remember, she was glad to see it.

Upon reflection, she realized this was the first day she had not been nauseous in several weeks. If the fortuneteller was correct, then the onset of menses and the lack of nausea would mean that she was not pregnant. She covered her loins with a folded napkin and swaddled it in place. Then she pulled on the trousers and a pair of leather leggings. She hummed a tune as she slipped into a boy's jerkin.

But at the stables, as she took the reins of the horse from the waiting varlet, a sudden onset of cramps doubled her over.

"What ails you?" called Margarida, who had already mounted.

"Oh, dear, I don't know...oh...oh ...." Isabel moaned.

In a flash, Margarida had slipped down from the saddle and was standing beside her, holding her in her arms.

"Tell me what's ailing you," she whispered.

"Methinks my bleeding time is upon me," Isabel gasped. And....oh...Oh!" She bit her lip. "I must needs visit the *garderobe*," she whispered to her sister, and tried to run, even though every step was a nightmare.

She made it as far as the stable, and ducking into an empty stall, she untied and stepped out of her trousers, pulled away the bloody napkin and squatted over the straw. She strained until the tears came, then suddenly the pain was over. She looked down at what seemed to be a piece of liver the size of a fingernail lying among the blood and urine.

By this time, Margarida had dismounted and raced to her sister's aid. She helped Isabel clean herself up and pull up her riding trousers.

"How do you feel?" Margarida looked at her sister with concern, and gently brushed some stray hairs back under Isabel's cap.

"Much better!" Isabel shrugged and smiled. "I trow I could ride, but methinks I should not."

"Forsooth. Let's go back inside. 'Twere well you repose a while."

"Oh, no, please go ahead and ride. Don't let me spoil your morning. I don't need any help."

"That's what *you* say. Come along, my sweet, I am going to put you to bed." Margarida handed the varlet the reins of their horses, and arm in arm, the two sisters walked toward the large gate that led into the keep.

Castèlnòudari

Known as Rambouillet to his peers, Guy de la Beauce sat astraddle a curule in Amaury Montfort's pavilion, two bowshots from the walls of Castèlnòudari, while several of his fellow barons were animatedly discussing the merits of different types of siege artillery. He was studying a scrap of parchment that he held in his hands.

The previous day, an enemy courier bearing a bundle of correspondence had been captured, and Rambouillet had skimmed through the pile to see if he could glean any intelligence about the enemy's strengths and weaknesses, or if they expected an attempt to raise the siege. After more than a dozen years of campaigning in the Midi, his command of the *lenga d'oc* was adequate for the task.

The note that preoccupied him was a highly personal love letter. He would have discarded it with the others, but the name Mazan had leaped out at him and opened an old wound. Could *Isabel* have been the name of one of the little girls he had spied on? She would be in her mid-teens now, and easily old enough to marry or carry on an affair. If so, her father, Olivier de Mazan, was not only the man that Arnaud-Amaury had tried so hard to find, but even worse yet, he was a false knight who had planned to bury his challenger alive, instead of facing him on the field of honor!

Smarting anew at the memory, Rambouillet crumpled the letter into a tight ball and was about to throw it into the embers of the brazier that smoked at his feet, when he stopped. Was there aught in the letter that he could use to get back at Mazan, something that could possibly help him get even? He smoothed out the parchment and re-read it:

My darling Isabel,

No hour goes by that I don't think of you and treasure every sweet memory of the precious moments we spent together. I love you far more than these poor words can express. If I had wings, I would fly to your side and remain there forever.

Alas, no sooner had I returned home, than the French invested the city and we have been under siege ever since. 'Tis my first opportunity to sit down and tell you how much I love you. Writing materials are very scarce, so please excuse the brevity of this letter.

I adore you,
Gerard.

Nothing in the letter suggested anything more than an ordinary romance. Nevertheless, Rambouillet decided, it might turn out to be useful. Particularly if he could capture the fellow named Gerard.

Giggling like school children, the young couple ducked into the shepherd's hut to escape the force of the Mistrau, which had filled their mantles like sails and propelled them before it at a run, in spite of their attempts to dig in their heels. They threw themselves down side by side on the log that served as a bench. The wind whistling through the chinks in the stone structure almost drowned out their laughter.

"I feared 'twould blow us right up to the top of the mountain," Christophe gasped, "and I weigh a lot more than you."

"You were afraid? And all along I was depending on you to keep me from being blown away," Isabel panted, as she leaned back against the wall.

"Now you wot why knights wear armor. 'Tis what anchors us to the ground when the Mistrau blows."

"Brrr, I'm freezing." Isabel said and drew her mantle tight around her shoulders.

"Here, let me tend you" Christophe said, and putting his arm around her shoulder, pulled his mantle around both of them.

She nestled into him. "Aahh, that's better, "she said, as she felt his body warmth. She also felt safe. For more than six months, he had been in virtually constant attendance on her and her family, and had become a fast friend. There was none of the awkwardness that often characterizes courting.

At first, because she was so blindly in love with Gerard, she couldn't abide Christophe's presence, but he was attentive to her parents and to Margarida, and had proved to be a friend and neighbor, as well as a helpful and undemanding companion. There was something very solid and reassuring about his constancy. So, little by little, in spite of herself, she found herself welcoming his company. He often joined the two girls on their daily rides and also went hunting with their father.

He lacked Gerard's strong, keen features that had turned Isabel's head, but his jovial, boyish face was handsome in its own right. She noticed that her parents listened to his views on land use and husbandry. Margarida adored him.

Now, with her head resting on Christophe's chest, she remembered the feel of Gerard's body, and was overcome with guilt. She had heard nothing from him since their one night together and, apparently, it was not his fault, because the French had besieged Castèlnòudari right after he arrived there and he obviously could not communicate with anyone. Had he really surrendered his heart the way she had given hers? Alas, there was no way to know.

In the meantime, she had come to enjoy Christophe's company. What would he think of her if he knew she had been Gerard's lover? What if Christophe was actually paying suit to her in a low-key manner? Was she leading him on? She was ready to fly to Gerard the moment he returned. Aye, that magic word, *return*. What if he had been killed during the siege? What then? Almost worse, what if he survived, but did not want to return to her? What if he loved another?

She had never had a male friend like Christophe before. He made her laugh. He and her father had uproarious times together, and her mother doted on his jokes and story telling. In contrast, what did she know of Gerard? Was he as merry as Christophe? She knew his body, aye, that she did. As she sighed in remembrance, she felt the blood rush to her face and she was glad Christophe couldn't see her blush.

"Comfortable?" he asked, as she stirred against him.

She nodded her head. "Very."

"May I ask you something personal, Isabel?"

"Yes, but I know not if I can answer."

"Understood. You and your family list not the Holy Mass, is that right?

"We do not follow the Roman ways, but methinks you do."

"And so I do, but to say truth, mainly on holy days." He thrust out his lower lip and shrugged.

"And the other days?"

"Oh, marriages, baptisms and funerals. And once in a while, the occasional mass."

"That's hardly a strong declaration of faith."

"I believe in moderation. What bethink you?"

"Of moderation, or faith?" She said, trying, but failing, to twist her head around far enough to see his reaction.

"Faith. Or, mayhap, both."

"We're Friends of God, or True Christians, as you wot well, I trow. Compared to you Romans, we're very moderate, I ween."

"Forsooth, but that's not how the Church regards you."

"'Tis true, and its notion of us would be silly, if it wasn't so spiteful."

"I wot well what you say. Let people deem what they list. 'Tis not my affair if others don't share my belief," he said, and shrugged again.

"By my troth, the Good Folk would never dream of persecuting Romans for their beliefs."

"Does that mean I have nothing to fear from you? You won't even try to convert me?"

"No. When the time comes, methinks you'll come to us on your own accord," she said.

"Here I am."

"What do you mean?"

"I came on my own accord and I would fain be shriven."

"Shriving is not necessary to join our church, and the only sacrament you'll ever need is the *consolation*, which is usually administered on your death bed, unless you want to become a Good Man."

"What about marriage?"

"Tisn't a sacrament, either, 'tis more like a pledge of love and duty."

"And you, would you ever deem to marry a Roman?"

"I'd fain do it, if he allowed me to worship as I please. You wot full well that mixed marriages are frequent enough."

"What about the ceremony itself? For a Roman, it must take place in a church."

"For a Friend of God, such vows might be a sticking point. However, 'tis like an ordinary person could accept them. They're like our pledges, I trow, but more binding. We can't abide oaths. But how came we to this subject? Think you of marriage?"

"I'm always thinking of marriage. Of finding that woman with whom I can spend my life."

Isabel looked up in surprise. She had meant to tease him, but Christophe had taken her seriously. "Do you mean a woman of great family, or great wealth?"

"A woman of great beauty and intellect."

"And where would you find such a paragon?" Isabel freed herself from his mantle and turned her upper body to face him.

"Why not right here in Provença?" Christophe shrugged, and craned his neck right and left as if the lady of his dreams might appear at any moment.

Although Isabel knew she had no claim on Christophe's affections, his confessed interest in other women vaguely annoyed her. In spite of her infatuation with Gerard, she had been flattered by Christophe's attention. "Do you have someone already in mind?" She tried not to sound jealous.

"I do."

She felt a pang in her breast. "I see. Do you see her frequently?"

"Oh, yes."

Her heart sank. "Have you wooed her?" she asked in a small voice.

"Not properly. I was hoping you could advise me how I should go about it."

"What experience do I have? I am but a maid." She blushed as soon as she said it, as she realized that this was no longer the truth. "How can I coach you on how to charm your elegant and sophisticated lady? You are very musical, I ween. Why not write her a song? That might win her heart."

"A song? Forsooth, I have already done so. Like to hear it?"

"Shouldn't your lady be the one to hear it first?"

Christophe laughed, then began to sing:

The glance that my lady darts at me must slay,
Born of her sweet eyes amorous and gay.
If I have none of her let me die always;
The glance that my lady darts at me must slay.

On my knees I shall beg of her today;
The glance that my lady darts at me must slay.
Humbly before her then I go to pray;
That she solace me, one sweet kiss I'd weigh.

The glance that my lady darts at me must slay,
Born of her sweet eyes amorous and gay.
Her body's white as snow that on glacier lay,
The glance that my lady darts at me must slay.

Fresh is her color as a rose in May,
The glance that my lady darts at me must slay.
Her hair, red gold, pleases in every way,
Softer and sweeter than a man can say.

The glance that my lady darts at me must slay,
Born of her sweet eyes amorous and gay.
God made none so beautiful nor may,
The glance that my lady darts at me must slay.

Her body I'll love, forever and a day,
The glance that my lady darts at me must slay.
And long as I live I'll not say her nay,
And die for her if I can't have my way.

The glance that my lady darts at me must slay,
Born of her sweet eyes amorous and gay.

When he finished, Christophe looked into Isabel's eyes and smiled. "Think you she'll like it?"

Although the song had enchanted Isabel, a wave of envy washed over her. If only she herself had been the subject! She struggled to find an answer that didn't sound peevish. "'Tis lovely. How fortunate your lady is to have such an ardent suitor! 'Twill definitely win her heart."

"Have I won yours?"

"How can I dare reply when clearly you meant it for another?"

"But there is no 'other.' "

"What are you saying?"

"I wrote this for you, fair lady, and 'on my knees, I beg of you today, And if I have none of you, then let me die away.'"

Isabel felt her heart would burst. Christophe was in love with her, something she now realized she had longed to hear, but how could she answer him, she who was a maid no more and whose body and soul belonged to Gerard in faraway Castèlnòudari, and who might even have lost his life in the siege? How could she spurn either of these knightly men?

"You take me by surprise, sir. 'Till now, I have taken you as a dear friend, no more."

"But 'tis what I have most at heart: a dear friend and companion for life. All I ask is for you to consider my offer of marriage and permission to speak to your parents."

"Gladly would I render you the answer you seek, Christophe, because I esteem you so highly, both as a man and as a friend. However, months ago, I pledged my heart to someone else. But for that, I would be yours forever."

"Methought that might be a possibility. 'Tis that knight from Castèlnòudari at your sister's wedding, I trow."

"Aye, 'tis he. "She could not hold back the tears. "And ever since, he's been under siege, unable to betroth me properly."

"Said he aught about wedding you?"

"He told me he worshipped and adored me." Now she was sobbing, and Christophe held her close.

"But naught about taking you for wife?"

The question was like a knife in her breast. Gerard had not proposed marriage. Of that, she was sure. "I can't recall," she lied. "Why are you pestering me with all these questions?"

"My sweet Isabel, 'tisn't an inquisition. I would fain learn what he pledged. When young men make love, they usually speak of love and worship. But oft they plight troths and speak of marriage. Did he?"

294

If only, she grieved. "I told you I can't recall. Why is it so important?"

"Because, if you two plighted your troth, then I must beg your forgiveness for presuming you were free to marry. But if you didn't, then 'twere not ill of me to have asked for your hand."

"Twere not ill at all. You are the kindest, most agreeable man I know, but I fear I love another, and if I did not pledge in words, I pledged in deed." As she spoke, she dreaded his reaction. Now he would treat her like a leper.

"Dearest Isabel, whether by word or by deed, I now wot well that you and your friend did not plight your troths Therefore, I fain would make you my wife, and fain would have done so since the first time I clapped eyes on you."

If only Gerard were here, everything would be clear, thought Isabel. "I cannot tell you how much your words mean to me. Alas, I cannot give you the answer you seek, and probably never shall. I am ever so much honored by your affection for me. I hope we can remain friends, no matter what happens."

"'Tis my most devout wish, dear Isabel, whomever you choose to wed."

Isabel wished she could be alone and think over all that had been said. Could she even trust her own heart? "Hark," she cried, "it seems the Mistrau has lost its strength. 'Tis time to ride home."

"I'm at your command," he said, as he rose and helped her to her feet. "Let's go out and see if the horses really were too heavy to be blown away."

Castèlnòudari

Rambouillet sat looking into space and tapping Gerard's letter against the palm of his hand. Somehow, he knew, the letter could provide a means of getting even with Mazan. But how? It was a love letter written to Mazan's daughter, and there were two possibilities; either the two lovers were betrothed, with Mazan's blessings, or they were not, in which case its exposure might create an unpleasant rift between father and daughter by informing Mazan of his daughter's clandestine love affair. The odds of possibly injuring Mazan were therefore no better than flipping a coin.

If, on the other hand, he put aside his vendetta against Mazan, was there anything to be gained by using the letter to entrap Gerard? If he could get his hands on Gerard, then collecting a ransom might be possible, and Mazan might be the one who would pay it, which would be an added bonus.

How could he bait the trap? What if he wrote a reply as if it were coming from Isabel? Or from her father, for that matter? What would induce Gerard to try to sneak through the French lines? News of Isabel's death? Even better, what if she lay dying? Desperate to see his beloved one last time, Gerard might risk capture. Using this ploy, Rambouillet would have the same odds as before in making Mazan's life miserable, but there would be an added monetary advantage.

Rambouillet stuffed the letter into his pocket and rubbed his hands together. Mazan would rue the day that he tried to cheat a knight from the Ile de France.

Making his daily inspections of the battlements, Gerard was chatting with a lookout when his squire, Henri, appeared at his elbow.

"Sire, a courier from Provença arrived shortly after dusk, and he had a letter for you." Henri held up a small note that was folded and sealed. "I've got it right here."

"Thank, you Henri," Gerard said, "for coming up here to find me." He took the letter and stared at the seal. It bore the arms of the Mazan family. Good news or bad news? His heart seemed to race. He excused himself to the lookout, and stepped a few paces away and broke open the seal. Unfolding the letter, he read:

To Gerard de Castèlnòudari
Sir,
Isabel was delivered of a stillborn child five days ago and is gravely ill. She is calling for you. Perhaps your presence can save her. As her devoted father, I beg you to make haste. I treasure her life more than my own and bear you no ill.
  Olivier Mazan

Gerard read and reread the letter and hung his head. Months ago, he should have taken the action that he knew had been necessary. Now he must fly to her side and leave the defense of his city to others. Apparently, there was no time to lose if he wanted to see Isabel alive. He thrust the letter into the pocket of his mantle and beckoned to Henri.

"You and I have to leave for Provença this very night!"

Carcassona

Gerard had slowed his mount down to a walk, so it could blow, and Henri followed suit. Once they had slipped through the French lines in the dark, they had ridden hard and their horses were lathered. Gerard felt that if they could elude detection or pursuit at the outset, the rest of their journey would be uneventful.

They dismounted, and as they led their horses along the ancient Roman Via Aquitania, the dark mass of Carcassona rose in silhouette before them. If all went well, they could hire fresh mounts, and reach Mazan before midnight the next day.

"Hark," hissed Henri, "there's a troop of riders behind us." Gerard stood still and listened. Many hooves were pounding the road behind them. Should they mount their spent horses and try to outrun those coming up behind them, or should they leave the road and make off through the fields? Gerard hesitated.

"*Qui va la?*" rang out ahead of them. The starlight revealed a dozen men with leveled pole weapons blocking the road.

As Gerard put his foot in the stirrup, intending to make off across the barley fields, some one shouted, *"Ne bougez pas, si vous voulez vivre!"* Then, the same voice cried in rough Occitan, "Three crossbows are trained on you. Throw down your weapons."

Gerard glimpsed more shadowy figures in the field he had planned to use as an escape route, and put his foot back on the ground. He nodded at Henri, and unbuckling his sword belt, let it fall to the ground. The squire followed suit.

A large knight came up to them and spoke in Occitan. "My name's Guy de la Beauce from Rambouillet and methinks you're Gerard de Castèlnòudari. Shouldn't you be defending your town instead of running away from it?"

"Forsooth, I am on an errand of mercy. A young noble woman is dying in childbirth in Provença, and I must be at her side. I give you my word as a knight that I will return here and give myself up if you allow me to continue my journey. Please, Sir Knight. There is no time to spare."

"Ah, a love story. Indeed! Belike you should have stayed with your beloved instead of resisting those who would stamp out heresy and overthrow the wicked lords who support that vile creed. By breaking the Peace of God, you have forfeited your right to knightly courtesy."

"Are you refusing my request?"

"Forsooth," Rambouillet answered, and commanded his men to bind Gerard's and Henri's hands behind their backs. "I promise to release you just as soon as someone pays your ransom, such as the father of the expectant mother. I have prepared a letter, and all I need is your signature. Do you have your seal with you?"

"In my purse, but I wouldn't dream of sending such a letter to Sir Olivier, and I have no idea whom I would ask to pay a ransom."

"We have accommodations in our dungeons that are astonishingly effective in helping our prisoners come up with the names of potential payers," Rambouillet said, then turned to the men-at-arms standing by. "Now, men, let's march these two into Carcassona and show them to their new quarters."

Mazan

As Christophe d'Entrechaud arrived for the chess game that had become a ritual between the two men, Olivier was flustered. The night before, he had received a letter from one Gerard de Castèlnòudari, who had apparently been captured during the siege. The stranger was asking him to pay a ransom of 100 melgorien pounds. He vaguely remembered meeting a young man with that name at Josetta's wedding, and it had turned out that he had been acquainted with Gerard's late father when that nobleman was still alive. What he could not comprehend was why *he* was expected to pay money for the freedom of this relative stranger? Who was this Baron de la Beauce to whom the ransom was to be paid? Could he be related to that scoundrel called Rambouillet?

As he started to set up the pieces on the board, he told Christophe about the strange request that he had received.

"I know Gerard, he's a friend of mine," Christophe said after Olivier finished his account. "Give me the letter, and I'll take care of it. As you say, 'tis no concern of yours. Perhaps de la Beauce confused our names."

"How could that be? They couldn't be more dissimilar!"

"To the French, all Provençals are the same, I trow." Christophe said, and smiled when Olivier pulled an eyelid down in mockery. "In any case, please let me handle this."

"As you wish," Olivier said, and went ahead placing his pieces on the board. "'Tis an enormous relief not to deal with that rogue, Rambouillet."

"Give it no further thought. However, I hope you will indulge me in discussing a much more serious subject that is as close to your heart as it is to mine."

Olivier raised his eyebrows. "Of course. What is it, my friend?"

300

"I have been very grateful for the warm welcome you and your family have extended to me over the past year and I want you to know how much I treasure your friendship."

"The feeling is mutual, my dear fellow. I feel as if I've gained a younger brother."

"I would fain confess that by seeking you out, I was not entirely without guile. At your oldest daughter's wedding, I was quite taken with Isabel."

Olivier laughed. "Forsooth, I thought you'd never get around to having this conversation. My wife and I deemed that you had forgotten what had attracted you in the first place."

"I will not deny that I am extremely fond of all of you. As our friendship has ripened, it strengthened me to ask you to give me Isabel's hand in marriage and thus make me an official member of your delightful family."

"By my troth, you have dissimulated your ardor very successfully. You never acted like a lovesick swain."

"That's because when I'm alone with her, I've always striven to behave as I do when in your company."

"Have you made your intentions clear to her?"

"Yesterday I asked her to consider me as a suitor."

"And what was her reply?"

"She believes she loves another."

"*Believes?*"

"'Tis more than a half year ago since he was besieged at Castèlnòudari, and she has received no news of him.

Olivier stared at Christophe. " Castèlnòudari? Are we talking about your friend Gerard?"

"One and the same."

Olivier scowled. "I like this not. I fain would talk to her. 'Tis but a passing fancy, I trow."

"Methinks 'tis more serious than you say, but I deem you know best. She considered my suit very seriously, and she's fond of me, I trow, but she feels obligated to Gerard."

"I must needs talk to her and get to the bottom of it. Mayhap she'll listen to reason from her father," Olivier said with a frown.

"I hope so."

Carcassona

The jailer announced, "Castèlnòudari, you have a high ranking visitor." The key squeaked in the lock, and light flooded into the cell. A large silhouette temporarily blocked it off, but when the visitor raised a lamp, Gerard recognized Rambouillet.

"Good day, good sir,' Rambouillet said, "I hope you've found the accommodations to your liking. I've come by reason that fortune smiles on you. Your ransom has been paid in full and you are now free to go."

"But who…?" Gerard asked, perplexed because he hadn't solicited anyone.

"I wouldn't worry, if I were you," Rambouillet said. "'Tis unwise to look a gift horse in the mouth, but if you insist on knowing the identity of your benefactor, his name is Christophe d'Entrechaud. The sooner you get your gear together, the quicker you'll be on your way and breathing fresh air again." Rambouillet stooped under the lintel and stepped into the corridor.

Gerard slung his wallet over his shoulder and shuffled along the dark passageway. Now he could finish his journey, but would he be too late? By the time he reached Provença, Isabel may have long since died and been entombed, which would make it painful to meet with her family, presuming they knew that he had gotten her with child. Either way, 'twas like the same; he must hie his way to Mazan. Afterwards, there would be time enough to seek his strange benefactor and thank him appropriately.

Entrechaud

A valet led Gerard into Christophe's private apartment just off of the great hall, and then took his place at the door. The room was fitted with one of the new-fangled chimneys built into the wall, in which several logs burned brightly. Christophe, rose from a curule, and came forward to greet his guest.

"Welcome to Entrechaud," he said with a smile, "I'm glad to see you at liberty. We met almost a year ago at Josetta Mazan's wedding."

"Yes, of course." Gerard said, and blushed deeply. "It seems like years ago, but 'tis my liberty and how 'twas purchased that I desire to talk about. I am completely in your debt and I find it hard to find words adequate enough to even begin to thank you, let alone broach the subject of repayment." He tugged at his collar nervously.

"I understand," Christophe said, touching the fingertips of both hands together, "'Twas presumptuous of me to buy your freedom, but when I explain my motives, I hope you will agree that the end justifies the means. But mayhap we're galloping when we should walk. Come, take a seat. You must be tired, and perhaps some wine might help you revive." He waved to the valet. "How was your journey?"

"Nothing special, except that I was in a hurry to get to Mazan."

"Ah?"

"During the siege of Lavaur, I received word that Isabel was deathly ill, and that I should hurry to her bedside. I did so forthwith, but on the way here, I was captured and imprisoned in Carcassona. You can imagine both my surprise and joy when you ransomed me, but that still left the great anxiety over Isabel's fate, so I made haste, and I'm afraid I wore out three mounts on the way."

"And?" Christophe lifted his eyebrows.

"Well, when I got to Mazan, I asked the first person I saw about the health of the castellan's daughter -- fearing the worst -- and the woman told me she had seen them out riding with you *yesterday!* You can imagine my great relief after deeming she lay mortally ill, or worse."

"Did you visit with the family?"

The valet reappeared with a tray holding a flagon and two beakers, and set it on the table before them. "No, I was so flustered, that I deemed it would be better to come here right away. I wanted to thank you and find out how I can repay you, and at the same time learn about Isabel's well-being from you, since you saw her just yesterday."

"I believe 'twas the wise thing to do. Come, let me fill up your beaker," Christophe poured the wine for them both. "Let us drink to Isabel," he said, "may she outlive us both." They both lifted their beakers and drank.

"Apparently, she made a surprising recovery, if the information I received was accurate," said Gerard.

"My friend, what intrigues me is that someone told you that she was sick at all."

"But the letter was from her father.... I have it right here."

"May I see it?"

Gerard hesitated. If Christophe read the letter, then he would know that childbirth was involved, which would not only compromise Isabel, but would reveal Gerard's involvement. But in light of what Christophe had done for him, how could he refuse? He pulled out the letter and handed it to Christophe. Christophe read it over twice, and then looked at the broken seal. He apposed the two halves, then shook his head.

"My friend, you are the victim of a forgery. The seal is a poor imitation of what the real one looks like. The hand and the signature are not those of Sir Olivier

"But why would anyone try to hoodwink me?"

"That depends. Did you leave Lavaur precipitously?

"Forsooth."

"How were you captured?"

"'Twas an ambush. A trap."

"Traps. Ambushes. Belike they had foreknowledge of what you would do and of the route you would take."

"That would make sense." Gerard said and leaned his head on his fist. "I hadn't even thought of that."

"Methinks this letter was the bait to set the trap. Do you have any sworn enemies?"

"Not that I know of."

"Well, then, we have come to a blank wall. But, let's get back to the purpose of your visit,"

"Aye, 'twas to thank you and to see how I could pay you back."

"Let me ask you: are you in love with Isabel? Do you want to marry her?"

Gerard stared at Christophe as if he had grown a tail. What kind of question was this? Yet it was a very simple, straightforward question that he should be able to answer! Even worse, he had often asked himself the same question over the last long months and had failed to answer it decisively. He blushed with embarrassment.

"I don't rightly know." It was the truth, but it was so lame. "I met her at the wedding and methought I was in love with her. She was so appealing. I had never met anyone like her. But…"

"But what?"

"'Twas a long time ago. I don't really know her. Sometimes I can't even recall what she looks like. Why do you ask?"

"Because," Christophe said, his eyes probing Gerard's, "I am in love with Isabel, and have been ever since the wedding. In the last six months, I have seen her almost every day, I enjoy her company and she enjoys mine, and I think I know her heart. I want to marry her."

"Then why don't you?"

"Because she thinks she's in love with you."

"She does?" Gerard couldn't help breaking into a smile.

"Yes, she does, after that night last year when you two were intimate."

Gerard blushed. "Belike I made a good impression."

"You did, I trow, but you put your *paratge* at risk, and *hers* too! You were not betrothed. You showed a total lack of respect for her position in society and that of her parents. I'm not blaming you; I'm trying to put your behavior into perspective. What I *do* find reprehensible, is that you turned your back on her."

"I had to defend my property and my town from the French," Gerard cried.

Christophe shook his head. "There is no siege on earth that can stop a man who is hopelessly in love. You could have gone to her at any time, not just when you learned that she might be dying by reason of your unbridled act of passion. Methinks 'twas shame that drove you, not love."

"Bethink you that I haven't regretted not going earlier more than a thousand times?"

"What if she had actually been with child? What if you had been killed in the siege? What kind of match could she have made under those circumstances?" Christophe's eyes bored into Gerard's.

"Don't think I haven't gone over and over the same ground myself" "Gerard said, shaking his head. "'Tis not that I wouldn't marry her, given the chance. 'Tisn't that I don't respect her. As I remember, she is as true as a person can be."

"Truer, I trow. I know no maid, no woman who is her equal in truthfulness.

"Look, Christophe, I must needs do the right thing by Isabel."

"Aha! You want to do the right thing? Then *do* it. Tell her that you release her from her pledge of passion."

"'Tis a difficult thing to do."

"Nowhere as difficult as 'twill be for me if I don't spend the rest of my days with the one I adore. Why think you that I paid your ransom?"

"You are buying me off. Or, more like, you are buying her."

Christophe decided to ignore this slur to his *paratge*. "Can't you see, that had you remained in prison, she would have gone on deeming that she loved the one evening with you more than she loved life itself? She might have joined a convent."

"You say she thinks she loves me; does that mean that she thinks she doesn't love you?"

"She loves me like a brother. She cares for me like a friend. She respects me. She's told me so. That's the major difference between the ways she regards us. The fact that I haven't touched her carnally, that I haven't even tried, is of lesser importance. I have too much respect for her and her family. You have to understand that her parents and I are friends and I cannot abuse that friendship."

"But I do respect her now and I respected her then." Gerard cried.

"By my troth, your way of showing respect, of acting respectfully, is far from mine."

Gerard regarded the other man and shook his head. "I may sound insincere, but I mind my *paratge*, believe it or not. You have freed me from prison at your expense, and in exchange you want me to tell Isabel that what existed twixt us was not love but passion, and she should regard it in that way."

"Forsooth, and if you repeat what you just said, I wot well you'll own 'tis true."

Gerard took a deep breath. "I do. 'Tis true, by my troth! I hadn't looked at it that way before. But you must believe that I would have made it right. What little I know of her, I could not have asked for a better wife."

"That last is true, but God only knows how many have married just to make things right, when it should be the other way around. When things are right in a courtship, when people are in accord, that's when a marriage makes sense. But when a maid is seduced, she innocently pledges her heart.

"But I pledged mine as well!"

"By galloping off to Lavaur? Tell me truly, during the siege did you make love to anyone else?"

Gerard blushed again and after hesitating, spoke out. "Aye. I was lonely."

"*You* were *lonely*? How deem you *she* felt after her lover abandoned her? Did she seek carnal pleasure elsewhere, or throw herself at other men? No, forsooth! She remained faithful to the pledge she made, one that must be withdrawn, my friend. Can I rely on you to see that 'tis done?"

Gerard had kept his eyes on the ground, but when he looked up, they were glistening. "That I promise," and he gripped Christophe's hand and shook it until Christophe pulled him into a hug.

"Thank you, Gerard, old man," he said, "you are saving my life."

Isabel was thrilled and hurt. Thrilled, because who should appear in the great hall but Gerard de Castèlnòudari in the company of Christophe! Gerard was as handsome as the last time she saw him, as she lay in his arms. His keen, aquiline features contrasted with Christophe's boyish good looks, and she felt her heart skip a beat. He had come at last! Then immediately, she felt a pang of remorse. She would have to forgo her relationship with Christophe, whose daily visits she anticipated with such joy, although if she were to marry Gerard, perhaps Christophe would dedicate his life to her, like the hero of a troubadour song.

All these thoughts were running through her head as she stood on the threshold of the hall watching Christophe present Gerard to her parents as if he were his best friend.

Then they turned to Margarida, who was also at the table, and as the introductions were made, Isabel noticed how Gerard's eyes widened in admiration. For Margarida was a beautiful young woman, and although Isabel had always been proud of her sister, at this moment she would have preferred Margarida not to be so striking.

It was then that the men spied Isabel standing in the doorway. She nodded at them, and walked toward them, trying to look demure, although she was atremble. Would Gerard turn to her father and ask for her hand? Would he rush over and take her in his arms? Or would he be stiff and formal, and pretend that nothing had ever happened between them?"

"Isabel," her father said as she came up, "I think you remember Gerard de Castèlnòudari from Josetta's wedding."

Isabel blushed. "Of course, how nice to see you again, Sir Gerard. I thought Lavaur was still under siege."

Gerard's face flamed red. "There are times when the enemy can be foiled. And I am as enchanted to see you as the last time we met."

"Come," Micaela said, "let us salute friendships, old and new. Please sit with us and tell us news of the Lauragais, Sir Gerard."

He told them about the hardships involved in a siege, and how Amaury Montfort was not the soldier his father was.

"Would you young people fain take a turn in the garden while we try to sort out what we can do to visit Josetta and Alan.?" Oliver asked.

Isabel looked at her father in gratitude, and rose, fully expecting Gerard to take her proffered hand, but her sister had already looped her arm through Gerard's and was steering him to the door. Christophe raised an eyebrow, and offered Isabel his arm. "I suppose to some, we no longer belong to the young people," he chuckled, and then quickly added in a low voice, "But fret not, I'll see to it that you have an opportunity to talk to Gerard in private."

Although angry with her sister, Isabel realized that the maiden had acted in innocence, particularly since more and more, she had become accustomed to seeing Isabel arm in arm with Christophe. Fifty paces ahead of them, Gerard and Margarida were gaily laughing at something one of them had said. What's so amusing, Isabel asked herself bitterly.

As if he read her mind, Christophe patted her arm. "Let me handle this," he whispered, and called, "Margarida!"

Margarida turned and looked back at Christophe.

"Remember the new bridle I promised you? I left it in the stable, but if you'd like to see it now, I can show it to you before I forget. I think Isabel is equally qualified to show your guest the garden."

"Of course I want to see it. What about you, Isabel, do you and Gerard wish to come with us?" Margarida asked.

"No, thanks, we'll just continue to stroll and you can catch up with us later."

"'Till then," Margarida said, and went off hand in hand with Christophe.

Gerard took Isabel's hand in his. "'Tis been a long time, Isabel. I am so sorry that 'tis so."

"So am I. Alas, what's done is done. I would that you had come before now. I waited and waited."

"I have no excuse. And I feel that I wronged you."

"Perhaps so, but still I waited."

"You really didn't know who I was, nor did I know you."

"Methought I knew, so I waited."

"What existed between us was not love, but passion, deem what you list."

"Back then I deemed it love, didn't you?"

"Forsooth, but 'twasn't."

"How do you know?"

"Because I failed you, and now I see that I am unworthy of your love."

"Isn't that for me to judge?"

"Forsooth, but we were mad with passion. 'Twas in the dark of night, without the approbation of your family, or your friends. And on top of that I failed you." He hung his head.

"Aye, by failing, you proved unworthy of my love. More than that, methinks you failed yourself."

"I know. My *paratge* is stained. I must redeem myself. As a start, please withdraw the pledge you made to me, as I clearly failed to keep mine to you. You deserve far better than me, and should feel yourself free to find someone worthy of you."

"Thank you. I bear you no ill will. But, if ever I make such a pledge again, full sure am I 'twill be for love."

Later, after Christophe had left and Gerard rode off to visit his uncle in Uzès, Isabel felt somehow cheated. She had not known how she would react to Gerard. If he had taken her in his arms, she might have declared she was his forever. When he failed to do so, she had been torn between throwing herself into his arms anyway, or treating him with icy reserve.

At the same time, she was annoyed with Christophe for his apparent role in bringing Gerard to Mazan in the first place. Had it been coincidence, or had it been planned? Whichever it was, the matter had been brought to a head. A union with Gerard was now out of question. The bittersweet yearning for a faraway lover had been replaced with the empty hurt of rejection.

With a start, she suddenly realized that now there was naught to keep her from accepting Christophe's suit. All of his attentiveness and acts of caring came flooding into her heart. Suddenly she hungered to see him, to look upon his open, guileless face. To hug him and kiss him. Yes, kiss him! She had never done it before. She fain would gallop all the way to Entrechaud to tell him, not just that she agreed to be his, but that she loved him. Yes, she *loved* him! With her heart pounding, she hurried off to the stables.

313

Uzès

Isaiah Valabrègue was highly agitated as he explained the terrible predicament his people were facing. Along with four leaders of the Jewish community in Uzès, Isaiah had called on the Castèlnòudari's town house that afternoon, hoping to find its owner, but instead found himself talking to the nephew, who looked younger than his twenty-two years. Isaiah himself had just turned twenty.

Gerard knew Isaiah was a scion of one of the oldest Jewish merchant families in Provença. His uncle was a well-known and respected physician. During the French occupation of the Gevaudan, Isaiah's father and Gerard's uncle had engaged in clandestine resistance and had become fast friends. Now, in Isaiah's hour of need, Gerard offered to help without blinking an eye, acting as he knew his uncle would have done had he been home and not away in Bagnols on an errand of mercy.

Isaiah recounted what had led to the desperate situation of his people in Nimes. With the precipitous withdrawal of Prince Louis's army of crusaders from the Midi, the young Count of Tolosa, Raimond VII, was leading a triumphant reconquest of territory that had been in French hands for more than fifteen years, his forces gaining one victory after another. He was hailed as the legitimate sovereign, but a few pockets of Montfort power still remained. Even worse, Isaiah said, certain rogue elements had abandoned the Montfort banner to enrich themselves through brigandage. They were totally merciless and had sacked and pillaged villages and towns from Tolosa to Nimes, without regard to allegiance or religious preferences.

While the consuls of Nimes were wavering about which side to back, a notorious band of French freebooters led by Jean and Foucaud de Berzy had presented themselves as emissaries of the King of France's vassal, Amaury Montfort.

314

Using this ruse to gain entry to Nimes, the brigands put the town militia to the sword and took control of the city. Holding the consuls hostage, the de Berzys were demanding an indemnity of twenty thousand marks, plus the fortune of its Jewish community of merchants and bankers. The Jews had responded by barricading the entrances to the Jewish quarter, and in response, the de Berzys threatened to break down the barricades and massacre its population if they didn't surrender all their possessions including the gold and silver in their treasuries and on their persons.

To the Jews, Valabrègue explained, it seemed a miracle that the city had not been sacked and that their population had not been slaughtered. The priests who rode with the de Berzys preached that Jews were the original heretics and should be treated with the same draconian punishment meted out to the Cathars. The Jewish elders believed that fleeing was the only way to save peoples' lives. According to Valabrègue, such a flight could be carried out.

When he was a boy, Valabrègue recounted, he and his friends used to play in the *castellum divisorium*, the ruin of an old Roman collecting basin that distributed water throughout the city twelve hundred years before. Located within the Jewish quarter just inside the present walls, the *castellum* was still surrounded by the old Roman wall that had been built when Nimes was three times its present size.

The boys had also explored the abandoned aqueduct that ran for twelve leagues clear across the valley of the river Gard and all the way to Uzès. Most of it was roofed with heavy slabs of masonry, just as in Roman times, but, here and there, the duct was open to the sky, the slabs having found their way into someone's wall or house. When he was fifteen, Valabrègue said, he and another boy had packed some food and spent hours walking inside the duct with a pair of torches. After about eight leagues, they came to a place where a roof slab had been removed. and they hitched themselves up for a look. Three hundred paces below them, the blue-green Gard flowed on its way to the Rose, a sight he'd never forget. Although the aqueduct continued to Uzès, he'd never completed the trip.

"What if the Jews of Nimes, all 614 of them," he asked, "were to file into the *castellum* and escape through the aqueduct to Uzès? That would enable them to avoid any patrols on the roads." The main problem, as he saw it, was shelter once they arrived in Uzès. With their treasury, purchasing food was no problem.

"Ah," Gerard said, "then we could house all of you in the *Plaça deis Herbes*, in the center of town. You would need tents. How long would you stay?"

"Only as long as the de Berzys remain in Nimes. They usually raid towns randomly, and take the easy pickings-- only what they can carry on horseback – then ride off. They really couldn't hold Nimes against a strong force, and if one were to show up, I think they would pull out without a fight."

"*Show up?* Hold on, mayhap there's an entirely different option here," Gerard exclaimed. "Why should your people, including women and children, trek leagues and leagues through a dark and dingy tunnel if 'tis unnecessary? What if we reverse the flow? Instead of you fleeing from Nimes by the aqueduct, why couldn't a relief force use the aqueduct to show up inside Nimes and rout the brigands at night?"

Valabrègue and the others stared at Gerard with mouths agape. "A foray into the *castellum*? But..." Valabrègue began.

"Why not?" Gerard met their gaze. "Methinks I can gather thirty or forty knights without too much trouble. Also, maybe 100 footmen. How many do the Berzys have?"

"Maybe 50 to 60 knights, and 150 footmen and assorted camp followers. They're holding the city consuls and their families hostage, but they are dispersed about the various gates."

"Where are the hostages?"

"In the dungeons of the arena."

"Is there any way of getting inside the arena without passing through the main gate?"

"There are several entrances, but they are well-guarded."

"No matter, we'll make do. I will rally my men and help you take back the city. I promise. We will use the old watercourse. Is that feasible?"

"Forsooth! I can't tell you how grateful I am for your support," Valabrègue said. "I wot well that I'm asking the impossible, but there's absolutely no time to lose. Mayhap the Berzys are attacking my people as I speak. Can you make it tomorrow night?"

Gerard grimaced. "'Twill be difficult, but a few less won't matter if we catch them by surprise. You say they are dispersed among the different gatehouses?"

"Yes, and they're watching the Jewish quarter as well, but at least half of the knights are quartered in the Arena. I can lead you to them."

"Consider it done." The two young men shook hands.

Valabrégue started off, and then turned back. "I have to get back to Nimes and alert the elders. Is there a place where we can rendezvous?"

"Let's meet at Marguerittas. You're familiar with the village?

"I could get to it blindfolded," Valabrégue said.

"Be there at midnight. Good luck!"

Nimes

Gerard's force of *faidits* assembled at the hamlet of Marguerittas, a half league from Nimes at midnight. There were thirty-three knights, nine squires, and forty-two footmen, each of whom had ridden to the rendezvous mounted behind a knight or a squire. Leaving a squire and five footmen behind to care for the horses, Valabrègue led Gerard and the others to the ruined aqueduct and the ancient water course. Before entering, Gerard used a flint to start a flame and light an oil lamp to make the going easier through the tunnel.

Even so, following Valabrègue through the tunnel made Gerard's skin crawl. Even with the flickering lamp light, it was like walking through a tomb. He wasn't sure what he would do if he stepped on a rat or some other moving creature. He found himself holding his breath as if he was under water, even though the air was not particularly damp, nor did it have an unpleasant odor. As the leader of the attacking force, he knew he had to set an example, and he clenched his teeth and thanked God that no one could see the fright in his face. He was grateful that Valabrègue was moving along swiftly and that his ordeal would soon be over.

After an elapse of time that seemed far longer than it actually was, they emerged into the old Roman *castellum* where a score of armed men from the Jewish community awaited them. The oil lamp was extinguished and the Jewish contingent led them through dark, narrow alleys, avoiding the principal streets and ending up on the other side of the city where the ancient Roman arena hulked above them like a cliff. At this point, the Jews in the vanguard beckoned to Gerard and Valabrègue. They whispered that two sentries were guarding the entrance to the arena, which led to the apartments that had been constructed on sand that once had been saturated with the blood of gladiators and wild animals.

Gerard proposed that both of them walk into the street fronting the arena, and shoot the sentries at close range. Then the rest of his force, guided by Jews, could fan out and surprise the French as they slept. Making sure that his crossbow was cocked and loaded, Gerard motioned to Valabrègue and they stepped away from the wall of the arena and walked into the middle of the darkened street, heading toward the entrance to the arena, their weapons dangling behind them.

Because the sky was overcast and visibility was poor, they didn't see the sentries until one cried out, "*Qui va la?*"

In that split second, they spotted their targets and Gerard hissed, "I'll take the one on the right." The sentries had scarcely leveled their *guisarmes*, when they crumpled backward, quarrels protruding from their chests, their weapons clanging on the cobblestones. Gerard turned and waved to the waiting men to join him. He gave both sentinels the *coup de grace* with his sword, virtually beheading them, and after wiping his blade clean on the dead men's' clothes, he waited for the rest to come up to him.

Their guides said the French knights were dispersed among 13 different apartments, so Gerard divided up the men into squads of eight, with at least one Jew assigned as a guide in each squad. With Valabrègue leading the way, Gerard and seven others followed in single file toward the hotel that the de Berzys had requisitioned.

As they stole along to the end of a wall, Valabrègue paused, and pressing himself against it, held up one finger. Gerard nodded. A single sentry guarded the de Berzys' apartment. Gerard cocked and loaded his weapon and crept

319

forward to where Valabrègue stood in the shadow of the wall. Valabrègue pointed and following his arm, Gerard strained his eyes and finally made out a sentry leaning in a doorway some fifty paces away. Concealing the cross bow behind him, Gerard strolled up the dark street,. When the sentry caught sight of Gerard, he grabbed a spear leaning against the door, and pointed it at Gerard, but Gerard had already swept up his cross bow and from a distance of 15 paces, put a quarrel into the sentry's right eye, dropping the man in a heap as the spear clattered to the ground. The sound was unnerving in the silence, and Gerard ran to the door and hurriedly felt for the door latch. It was locked. After a frantic search of the dead man's body, he found a large key on a ring attached to the man's belt.

By the time Gerard drew his dagger and cut through the belt to remove the key ring, the rest of the squad had come up. Inserting the key in the lock, he turned it as quietly as he could. The latch moved and he slowly eased open the door and tiptoed inside. As Gerard stood trying to adjust his eyes to the dark, Valabrègue took his arm and led him to a spiral staircase. Gerard drew his sword and stealthily ascended. Valabrègue had whispered that once he was up, he should turn left and head toward a doorway at the end of a hall. Again, he felt Valabrègue's hand pulling him forward until they reached a heavy curtain that hung in the doorway. Behind the curtain, Valabrègue had told him, was an antechamber with two open doors on either side.

The lack of windows meant that they were almost totally blind in the dark. Gerard decided to light the lamp they had brought along, so again he took out his flint and steel, laid down his tinder on the stone floor and soon had a small flame that enabled him to relight the lamp. The flickering light revealed four other rooms along the hall, and from one of them the sound of snoring could be heard.

Gerard selected his good friend Jules Souchon and two others to overpower the occupant of the room on the right, while he, Valabrègue and Raoult Conza would see to the one at the left. The two other men would stand guard in case someone woke up in the other rooms.

Gerard stepped into the room and held his lamp at arms length. Robert de Berzy lay asleep on a bed of furs, one arm flung over the neck of a young woman who was struggling awake in the lamplight. Her eyes filled with terror as she saw the drawn swords, but before she could scream, Valabrègue clapped one hand over her mouth and placed the index finger of his other hand in front of his pursed lips. She looked about wildly and Gerard tossed her a blanket that had slipped off the bed, and beckoned her to get out of bed. Winding it around herself, she slid out bed, and stood up, shaking with fear in Valabregue's arms.

The movement woke, de Berzy, who started up only to lie back down again as the point of Gerard's sword pressed against his Adam's apple. "*Que voulez-vous?*" he gasped, his eyes round with alarm.

Gerard understood that much French, and answered in the *lenga d'oc.* "We want you and all your men out of Nimes. You will release all prisoners and hostages. You will surrender all your weapons and any booty you might have acquired. And if you ever return here, we will display your head on a pike from the walls, and I will personally use your scrotum as a money pouch, do you understand? Translate that for him, Isaiah."

Isaiah was winding up his translation when there was a bellow from across the hall.

"*Au secours, mes gars, au secours!*" followed by a scream of pain, then moans.

"Sounds as if your brother doesn't understand our language either." Gerard couldn't resist a smirk. "Don't try

321

to follow his example, because if he got hurt, he had it coming. Isaiah, tell de Berzy to turn over on his belly and cross his hands behind his back. Jules, hand me his belt. We are going to tie him up good and proper. Cutting some long strips from a blanket, Gerard trussed de Berzy's wrists together behind his back and then wound the belt around them. He was pulling it tight, when he heard a clamor out in the hall.

"Keep your eyes on him," he said to Isaiah, and turned to Raoul. "C'mon, let's see what's happening," he snapped, and drawing his sword, stepped through the door way holding the lamp up with his other hand. In the dark antechamber, swords clanged and rasped as Gerard's two men thrust and parried, trying desperately to repulse an attack by four French knights in varying degrees of undress who were trying to fight their way into the antechamber from the hall. As Raoul jumped into the fray, Gerard put the lamp down, and ducked back into the bedroom. He pulled hard on the belt around de Berzy's bound wrists, and when the Frenchman screamed in pain, Gerard cried, "On your feet, you bastard," and pulled de Berzy erect, lifting the Frenchman's arms behind his back until he had to stand on tip-toes to avoid the pain. From behind, Gerard clamped his left forearm across de Berzy's neck, and still pushing up on de Berzy's wrists with his right arm, frog-marched him into the antechamber. "Get the lamp, Isaiah, and hold it high," he called to Valabrègue. "Tell them to throw down their weapons if they want their chief to keep his balls and pecker."

In the lamplight, de Berzy's men saw their stark naked chief in the grip of a knight holding a poniard underneath a shriveled scrotum. As they gaped, Isaiah told them to drop their weapons, else their leader's genitalia would become dog food. Then de Berzy himself repeated the command.

As the French knights looked at each other trying to decide what to do, two of Gerard's men emerged from the other room and thrust Foucaud de Berzy, naked as the day he was born, alongside his brother.

"*Faites ce qu'on demand, ces gars sont fous!*" he cried, one hand trying to staunch the blood from the wound where his ear had been. Swords clanged to the floor and the French knights raised their hands in surrender.

Gerard had his men bind the prisoners' wrists and tied the ankles loosely together. Then they hitched the ankle ties to the wrists and to a loop around their necks. When they snugged the rope taut, it forced the prisoners to bend forward as they shuffled along.

By the time the sun came up, Gerard had marched Robert de Berzy to the other twelve apartments inside the arena, and obtained the surrender of their occupants, while Valabrègue led another force to the dungeon, where he had Jean de Berzy order the guards to release the prisoners. After locking up 48 knights in the arena, they marched the naked brothers to each of the city gatehouses in turn and effected the surrender of the rest of the band.

The town council, the Jewish elders and the other freed prisoners had been ill treated during their short captivity and bitterly denounced their captors, asking that their erstwhile captors receive the same treatment. Gerard told them that as far as he was concerned, the brothers and their entire retinue were now prisoners of the consuls of Nimes and what happened to them was no longer any of his business. He was ready to go home.

The consuls would have nothing of that, and insisted that he and his men stay on to help celebrate their liberation. Gerard agreed to stay, on condition that he and his men be provided with sleeping quarters; he was suddenly dead tired and assumed his men were similarly afflicted.

323

And so it was that Gerard found himself in the same bed that Robert de Berzy and his inamorata had vacated only hours before, and in his exhausted state, he was especially happy that he had the whole bed to himself.

Uzès

Two weeks later on a bright sunny day, Gerard bid farewell to his uncle and aunt in Uzès, and passed through the gate on his way home to Castèlnòudari. Amaury Montfort had finally lifted the siege of Castèlnòudari and retreated to Carcassona. His possessions were shrinking daily, and he desperately needed to shore up his base of operations.

As Gerard rode up to the crossroads, he noted the stone marker pointing toward Nimes, but there was another pointing toward Remoulins. *Remoulins*! Avinhon lay only four or five leagues east of Remoulins and Mazan was not even ten leagues beyond. If he paced his mount, he could be there before dark. Whether he arrived home in three days or three months made no difference. On the other hand, when would be the next time he'd be so near to ...yes, near to Mazan and near to Margarida, Isabel's charming younger sister? How long had it been since he had seen her? At least three months. His horse turned its head to look at him, as if it had read his mind. Gerard gave it the spurs and away they cantered toward Remoulins.

Mazan

Olivier was pleasantly surprised when his valet told him that Gerard de Castèlnòudari was asking to see him. News of Gerard's exploit in Nimes had spread through Provença, and Olivier told the servant to bring the visitor up at once and ask the *castellane* to join them in the great hall. In the meantime, he went to look for a good Gigondas.

Over a serving of sautéed chanterelles sprinkled with truffles, Olivier and Micaela welcomed Gerard with uplifted beakers. When he asked after their daughters, Micaela told him that Isabel was betrothed to his friend Christophe and they would be wed in two months. As for Margarida, she was probably in the spinning room, Micaela told him, adding that Margarida would surely be delighted to see him again. With that, Micaela excused herself and went to fetch her daughter.

Waiting until she was out of hearing, Olivier asked his guest if it were really true that he had threatened de Berzy's nether parts, and roared with laughter on learning the details, commenting that he had done the same thing years ago When the ladies arrived, Olivier announced that Gerard had consented to bide with them for a week. Although Gerard initially said he was just passing by, the eagerness with which he accepted the invitation to stay did not slip Olivier's attention; yet, he had to admit, he himself was looking forward to the young man's company

After a highly animated evening meal, the Mazans brought out their musical instruments and discovered that not only was Gerard a good tenor, but he could also play the harp. Out of the corner of her eyes, Micaela noticed how Margarida's eyes shone while she listened to Gerard sing and play.

As the days went by, the two men went hunting when Gerard was not riding with Margarida. Sometimes Christophe joined the hunting party, but for some reason, Olivier noticed, the young couple never visited Isabel and Christophe at Entrechaud. He and Micaela began to wonder if more than flirtation had taken place at Josetta's wedding. On the other hand, Gerard seemed to enjoy the company of Margarida's parents, and most evenings the family spent making music with Gerard. Olivier even quipped that Gerard was paying more attention to the mother than the daughter, and Gerard shot back that such a courting strategy was every bit as pleasant as it was certain to succeed.

The invitation to stay was renewed, one week after another. Neither Olivier nor Micaela was surprised, when one evening the young couple asked their permission to wed. Permission was granted and the nuptials were set for nine months ahead.

Giddy with the prospect of marriage, Gerard set off to attend to his property at long last. His uncle accompanied him, but found his town house so badly damaged from the siege, that he abandoned the idea of rebuilding it. Instead, he proposed exchanging his property in Uzès for Gerard's in Castèlnòudari, a trade that would allow Margarida to dwell much closer to her parents. Gerard accepted with almost indecent alacrity.

Saissac

Alan de Lavaur stood just outside the canopy of a huge old oak tree. Its limb span measured at least 60 paces, so that its broad leafy crown formed a spacious vault over the two hundred or more members of the Friends of God who had gathered for an *aparelhament*, the group confession that usually contained a sermon by the local deacon. Although it was still light out in the open, under the tree it was already dusk.

For more than a dozen years, the Crusade had greatly disrupted these traditional, monthly services throughout most of the Midi. Not only was it dangerous to assemble, but so many of the Good Men and Women who conducted the ceremonies had been burned at the stake, that it was extremely difficult to find one to perform the ceremony on a regular schedule. Although the successful partial reconquest of the region by Raimond VII, the "Young Count," had made it much easier for some Believers to congregate, many areas were still under control of the crusaders. The service had to be conducted as surreptitiously as possible, and with armed guards to provide some protection to the faithful. Even then, it was touch and go because betrayal was always possible. All that was needed was one disgruntled person to whisper to a priest the location of the ceremony.

Over Josetta's objections, Alan had volunteered for this guard duty along with his father, and now he stood scanning a wooded hillside. The other members of the guard, including his father, had taken positions along the lane on the opposite side of the tree, where it was deemed an attack was more likely.

Under the leafy canopy, he heard the deacon, a Good Man from Saissac, clear his throat and begin to speak. "Good evening, dear Believers. I am touched that so many of you braved arrest and hardship to come together for our

328

ritual Group Confession. Your attendance here confirms the faith and teaching of the Church of God as the Holy Scriptures tell us. For, in former times, the people of God separated themselves from the Lord their God. And they abandoned the will and guidance of their Heavenly Father through the deceptions of the wicked spirits and by submission to their will."

"Today, 'tis the Roman Church and its clerical minions who wickedly carry out those same deceptions by posing as intermediaries between the people and the Heavenly Father, when in reality, they are serving the Devil, the worldly power of evil to whom they pray.

Our Church suffers persecution and tribulations and martyrdom in the name of Christ, for He Himself suffered them to redeem his church and show them by deed and word that until the end of the world they must suffer persecution and contumely and malediction. In the Gospel of John, He says, *If they persecuted me, they will persecute you.* He also says, *blessed are they that suffer persecution for justice's sake, for theirs is the kingdom of heaven. Blessed are you when they shall revile you and persecute you and speak all that is evil against you, untruly, for my sake. Be glad and rejoice, for your reward is very great in heaven. For so they prosecuted the prophets who were before you. Behold, I send you as sheep in the midst of wolves, and you shall be hated by all men for my name's sake; he that shall persevere unto the end, he shall be saved. And when they persecute you in this town, flee into another.*"

"Now all these words of Christ contradict the wicked Roman Church, for it persecutes and kills all who refuse to condone its sins and its actions. It flees not from town to town, but rules over cities and towns and provinces, and 'tis seated in grandeur in the pomp of this world; it is feared

329

by kings and emperors and other men. Nor is it like sheep among wolves, but rather like wolves among sheep, and above all, it doth persecute and kill the Holy Church of Christ, our Church of the Living God, which bears all in patience like the sheep, making no defense against the wolf."

"In contrast, the shepherds of the Roman Church feel no shame in portraying themselves as the sheep and lambs of Christ, and they declare …"

A shrill whistle interrupted the deacon. In a twinkling, the crowd disappeared, running out from under the tree, away from the clash of steel and angry shouts that had erupted from the direction of the lane.

Drawing his sword, Alan rushed toward the sound of combat, only to find a phalanx of spearmen lunging toward him. As he instinctively recoiled, and started to turn around, he realized that his comrades had been overwhelmed and that he was alone and surrounded. He laid his sword at his feet and extended his arms to the side in surrender. At least his brother and the congregation had got away, he sighed. Perhaps the short-lived resistance had not been in vain. What about the other guards; were they still alive or had they been slaughtered? Looking at the hatred in the faces of the crusaders around him, he feared they would kill him instead of taking him prisoner.

Out of the corner of an eye, he saw a burly French knight with fleur de lis on his blue surcoat stride forward and the next thing he knew, he was on the ground, his cheek resting on a tuft of grass while a large foot encased in mail and tipped with steel came into focus. As he tried to orient himself and understand why he was lying there, his eye exploded with almost unbearable pain. He reached up to feel if the eye was still in its socket, and his hand was smashed by another hard kick. He pulled himself into a fetal position with his arms protecting his head as the kicks continued.

"*Levez-vous, espèce de sal cathare! Debout*!" boomed the knight.

Struggling to his knees, his arms still protecting his head, Alan felt an excruciating blow to his side as the French knight kicked him again. On his feet at last, he crouched with his forearms joined in front of his face.

"Tis but a taste of what we mete out to scum who dare take arms against those who seek to eradicate heresy," the knight said in the *lenga d'oc*. "If ever we are finished with you, I wot you will come crawling to repent your foul sins."

Alan spat out a tooth along with bloody sputum. The French knight must have knocked him unconscious with his mailed fist.

"Now that I see that you heed me, tell me the name of the Perfect who delivered the sermon."

"I don't know. I'd never seen him before." A backhand blow made Alan see stars, and blood dripped down his chin from his lips.

"I repeat, what is his name?"

"You can beat me to death, but I can't to tell you. You've burned so many Good men, that those still alive are complete strangers. No one knows their names. They keep anonymous precisely to avoid what you are doing here. "

"What's your name?"

"Alan de Lavaur. *Sir* Alan to you."

"If you expect me to treat you with knightly courtesy, pray think again. You have broken the Peace of God, and warred against my King and the Holy See and defended heretics. Back in Carcassona, we have a dungeon for your kind. You'll have plenty of company, you Cathar swine," the French knight said, and kicked Alan in the groin.

331

Mazan

Margarida and Gerard were visiting her parents. A whole year had gone by since they wedded and had gone to live in Uzès, and Margarida was now expecting a child. Micaela had bid her to bide in Mazan for the confinement, and Margarida had eagerly agreed. So when – out of the blue -- Josetta rode into the courtyard with a small retinue of servants, Margarida was the first to reach her side. The unmistakable bulge under Josetta's traveling cloak, evoked squeals of delight from Margarida, and then the rest of the family arrived. After much affectionate kissing and hugging, Micaela led Josetta inside, where she found her a room and arranged accommodations for her servants while Josetta refreshed herself after the journey and took her ease in the garderobe.

As they eagerly awaited her in the great hall, Micaela whispered to Olivier, "Something's not right. She doesn't look well."

When at last Josetta entered the great hall, the family gathered eagerly around her. What she related was shocking.

"Alan's in prison," she blurted out. "He was captured while standing guard at an *aparelhament* that was held near Saissac, and he's been charged with breaking the Peace of God and aiding and abetting heretics. I went to the French commandant in Carcassona and also to the Bishop to ask for his release, but they almost laughed in my face. They won't even let me visit him. So I have no idea about his condition."

"What about ransom?" Olivier asked. "Did you ask them about that?"

"Twas one of my first questions, and they turned me down. They said he committed a crime that didn't involve a courtesy of war. Instead of treating him like a prisoner of war, they are punishing him like a criminal.

332

"'Tis not meet," Micaela cried in indignation. "We should appeal to Montfort himself."

"The worst is not being able to visit him. 'Tis cruel and heartless of those foreign devils," Josetta said, close to tears. Micaela and Margarida rose and went to put their arms around her. "I wot not how he fares. He might have been wounded when they took him prisoner." In spite of her efforts, she broke into tears and her mother and sister hugged her close.

"'Tis customary to pay the ransom to the knight who took him prisoner. Do you know his name?

"De la Beauce, I think," she said. "But belike he is no longer in Carcassona. Methinks the garrison there is rather small, and most of Montfort's men are in the field."

Olivier stared at Josetta with opened mouth, and fought to control himself. Out of the corner of an eye, he saw Micaela wince, and Gerard grimace at the sound of Rambouillet's name. At that very moment, a beaming Christophe burst into the room.

"Look who's here, Josetta," said Margarida. "The proud father of your nephew, Odon."

Christophe embraced Micaela and Olivier, then hugged his two sisters-in-law and Gerard in turn.

"We have good tidings, my dear," Micaela said, "Josetta is with child. Soon I will have three grandchildren."

"I am so happy for you," Christophe said. "Come, give me a kiss." They embraced again, and for the first time since she arrived, Josetta smiled. Then she frowned. "But where's Isabel?"

"Back home, nursing the baby. You must come see him. By my troth, I'm the proudest of fathers."

"Alas, my son," Olivier said, "We also have very bad news. Alan is in prison in Carcassona, charged with breaking the Peace of God and aiding and abetting heretics."

"But how…?"

"He was taken while standing watch at an *aparelhament* near Saissac."

"I can't bear the thought of what he's going through," Micaela said.

"And just as you came in, we learned that the man who captured him may be the same one who took *me* prisoner," Gerard said. "Josetta, did you say Guy de la Beauce?"

"Yes, Guy was his first name. But his men called him something else…"

"Rambouillet?" Micaela asked, in a hushed voice.

"Aye, that's it."

"Rambouillet?" Olivier cried. "Are you sure?"

"Forsooth! 'Tis easy to remember because 'tis the home of the Montforts."

"If the knight who captured me is the same man who took Alan prisoner," said Gerard, "then there's a good chance for a ransom."

"He told me there is no such chance, so he must've had a change of heart. A change for the worse, I trow," Josetta said, jerking her head in frustration.

"Let's not discuss Alan's situation now without ordering the matter. We must take it up in all seriousness later. Right now let's have some fripperies to celebrate Josetta's homecoming.

"Estève," Micaela said to the valet, "please set out a platter of crudities as well as two flagons of Beaume de Venise."

"Of course, Dòmna," Estève answered, and disappeared toward the kitchen.

As the three daughters and their mother settled into an animated discussion of the domestic arrangements they would have to make for Josetta's confinement, Olivier beckoned to Gerard and Christophe to join him and walked outside onto the parapet.

"Belike 'tis no coincidence that Alan and Gerard were taken by the same man," Olivier said. "Rambouillet and I are blood enemies. At one time, I had something that he wanted very badly. Like enough, he deems I still have it."

"Bethink you that he is trying to use Alan to bargain with you?"

"It has crossed my mind, but as yet, he has made no demands on me. However, he's a devious scoundrel, and I would put naught past him."

"Know you aught of him?"

"Only that he was the long-time squire of Arnaud-Amaury, the Archbishop of Narbona, back when that old scoundrel was the chief papal legate and leader of the Crusade before Montfort. Rambouillet also squired Arnaud-Amaury when he led the French crusaders who helped defeat the Muslims at Las Navas de Tolosa. In fact, that's where Rambouillet won his spurs. More to the point, some years ago, I caught him spying on me, and I feared for my children. I challenged him to trial by combat, but he fled, with Micaela's help."

Christophe looked at him in astonishment. "The Dòmna helped him?"

"'Tis strange, I wot, but she feared for my life," Olivier said. "And since then, I've never seen him again."

"Can we turn the chess table around, and trick him into releasing Alan? Make a replica of whatever secret you have?"

"Perhaps. 'Twould take time and an expert scribe. And there's no doubt in my mind that Rambouillet would have his own expert in ancient scrolls to determine its authenticity."

"An ancient scroll?"

"Aye, but promise me you'll never discuss this with anyone, not even Isabel or Margarida."

They both promised.

"As to obtaining Alan's freedom, methinks we have no other choice than to offer a higher ransom. As you said, like enough Rambouillet was merely haggling."

"'Tis worth a try."

Carcassona

Josetta paused as she reached the top of the stairwell that led up from the dungeons. She leaned against the smooth stone portal and blew her nose in the handkerchief that was damp from her tears. She had returned to Carcassona, and after six months of constant and futile pleading, she had finally received permission to visit her husband in his dungeon cell. She had found that his living conditions were beyond anything she could ever imagine.

A turnkey had led her down two flights of stairs into a dark gallery between two rows of cells. The stench of shit and piss in rotten straw took her breath away. At each end of the gallery, a small lamp provided dim light that scarcely penetrated through the narrow arch with steel bars that marked each cell. The turnkey pointed at one of the arches. "That's 'im," he said.

She moved next to the bars and peered into the shadows. "Alan," she called softly, "'tis me, Josetta!"

There was no reply and the turnkey picked up a pewter pan lying on the floor and beat it on the bars. "Hey, you! Lavaur! Your honey is come t' see ya. C'mon 'n give 'er a kiss afore I do," he cried, leering over his shoulder at Josetta.

She pressed her head against the bars, and peered into the deep shadows. A form hobbled toward her and suddenly Alan stood before her and reached through the bars with trembling hands to embrace her. As she thrust her arms past the bars to return the hug, she was shocked at the way his vertebrae and ribs protruded under his skin. He smelled like an old dog that had rolled in its own excrement. They kissed, and his breath was foul. In spite of herself, she burst into tears and realized that he, too, was sobbing. It had been almost two years.

She had no idea of how long they stood there weeping, but finally she managed to ask about his health. He was lame in one leg, he said, his hip joint ached, probably because of the damp cold floor. She recounted her efforts to have him released and how the jailers had refused her requests to see him, and then, just as arbitrarily, had permitted her this visit. She told him how caring for their infant, Miranda, was the only way she had retained her sanity.

He begged her forgiveness for his filthiness, explaining that he received only enough water to drink, and even that was given grudgingly. They thrilled each other with caresses as they talked, despite the smirking lout slouching against the opposite wall. Then, much too soon, the pan rang against the bars.

"Time's up, ducky!" the turnkey cried, breathing his garlicky breath in Josetta's face. "Yer man is fagged and needs his rest. But I'm not, and..."

Alan shot an arm through the bars but couldn't reach the man. "How dare you speak to your betters," he cried, his face contorted with rage.

"Ooh, taking on airs, are we?" the turnkey snarled, revealing a gap where his incisors should have been. "Maybe we should ask the Missus who's better; me out here, or you sitting in your own piss and shit?"

"Don't let him vex you, my darling," she whispered, and kissed Alan passionately. "I will return as soon as they will let me, tomorrow cannot be too soon."

"I wouldn't count on it, love," the turnkey said with a scowl, "not after he done tried to take a poke at me. Fact, he ain't gonna eat much at all tomorry."

"Heed not his drivel, Josetta," Alan whispered. "All's well with me. Come when you can. I understand."

They exchanged another long kiss that ended when the turnkey banged the pan on the bars again. Their fingers touched once more and then she was briskly mounting the stairs, as much to avoid letting the cruel jailer see her in tears, as to get away from his bullying presence.

As she tried to pull herself together, she heard footsteps coming up the stairs behind her, and she hurried out into the courtyard and headed for the gate as fast as she could walk, dreading the thought of that awful man catching up with her. A tall French knight coming in the opposite direction slowed down, turned around and stared at her as she passed. At the same moment, the turnkey emerged from the stairwell and set off after her.

The knight grabbed the turnkey's forearm and spun him around. "Tell me, varlet, who's the woman who just passed by?" he asked in a heavy French accent.

The turnkey grimaced, seething with frustration. The foreign knight was using his rank to take the woman for himself, and that would be the end of his own chances at a coerced dalliance with Lavaur's woman. On the other hand, if he lied, the knight might find out and then it would go bad for him.

"She's the wife of Alan de Lavaur, a prisoner, yer Lordship."

"What's he in for?"

"He was escorting a Good Ma…I mean, a Perfect …to a meeting of heretics and the bailiff collared him."

"How long ago?"

"More'n a year, fur's I can tell. He come down to the lower level 'bout five months ago."

"Thanks for your trouble," the knight said, and made for the gate. Of course! He had seen the pretty woman before. She was the one he had spied on while she was watching Mazan's younger children just a few years ago.

340

Best of all, she was his prisoner's wife! He rubbed his hands at his good fortune.

Up ahead, Josetta was just turning a corner and he ran to catch up with her. When he was a few dozen steps behind her, he slowed down to avoid arousing her suspicion. After a few more twists and turns down narrow alleys, she stopped in front of a doorway, and fishing a key from a pocket in her mantle, she turned it in the lock. As the door swung opened, he strode forward and thrust his arm across the opening.

"Excuse me, fair lady, permit me to introduce myself. I am Guy de la Beauce, from Rambouillet. "I know your problem and I think I can help you."

Startled, Josetta stepped back. Incredibly, here was the very man who might hold the key to Alan's freedom but who also might be the one who prevented his release. Was he talking about Alan? Perhaps it was best not to let on that she knew who he was. "Please sir, you are blocking my door," she exclaimed. Then, when he didn't move, "I don't know what you're talking about. Please let me by."

"I'm talking about your husband's situation."

"What about it?" she said, casting her eyes to the ground.

"I can arrange to have him transferred to a proper room instead of a cell," he said.

"Yes?" she cried, looking up at him for the first time. He was a handsome man with light brown hair and blue eyes. There was something about him that wasn't quite right. Was it his crooked smile? His intense stare? "How can that be?" she asked.

"Connections," he said. "Knowing the right people."

Josetta was flustered. If only it were true; if only Alan could live like a human being instead of like a dung beetle! But why was the Frenchman trying to help now, when he had done nothing but hinder them in the past?

341

"But why… I mean, you don't even know me," she stammered. "And you're a foreigner. I don't understand…."

"Let's just say that I would fain be a friend of the family and gladden your heart." He smiled.

"But I…" She furrowed her brow as she tried to understand.

"Not a little would you give to have your husband out of the dungeon, I trow. Wouldn't that gladden him?"

"Oh, yes, but…" What in the world was he talking about?

"And 'twould gladden you, too, I trow."

"Of course, but…"

"Then, if I can gladden you both, mayhap you can gladden *me*," he said, leering at her.

"But how…?" As soon as the words left her mouth, his meaning struck her. She shivered with repulsion. "Please sir, let me pass," she said, and stepped toward the doorway.

He removed his hand from the jamb and backed away, sweeping his hand toward the open door. "As you wish, Dòmna, but please consider what I have said. I am a man of my word. Your husband is miserable. You are desperate. I am lonely. You hold the key to happiness for three people. I will come again next week. Until then," he said with a bow, and walked away.

That night, as her daughter Miranda suckled at her breast, Josetta tried to come to grips with hard reality. Her options were limited. In fact, there were only two, and she could not fathom accepting either. She longed to ask Margarida, or Isabel, for her advice, even though it repelled her to think of anyone – particularly Micaela – knowing where the one choice would lead. Nevertheless, who else could help her? Three heads might be superior to one, yet tragically, her sisters were leagues away! If only they were close by! When she thought of it, even Micaela, and perhaps *especially* Micaela would be able to tell her what she must do.

All through the following week Josetta tried to see Alan, and everyday she was turned away. She could hardly think of anything but Rambouillet's proposal. Was her chastity more important than Alan's well-being? Which was the greater sin, leaving Alan to die in his own filth or consenting to commit adultery with this scoundrel? On the seventh day, she trudged home and found Rambouillet lounging against the door.

"Have you considered my offer?" He raised his eyebrows in lewd anticipation.

"Yes," she said, looking away. "Will you please come in?"

Rambouillet beamed. "I wotted it well! You are as sensible as you are fair, after all," he said, and followed her inside. She closed the door and stood with her back against it.

"If..." she faltered, "if I agree to...make you... glad..., then you must promise that my husband be transferred to his former quarters *before* we..."

"That may be difficult," he frowned. "What about the day *after?*"

"No. The day *before.*"

"'Tis done!"

"And I may visit him *every* day. In his room. And bring him a change of clothes."

"I wot not..."

"Then we'll all just continue to be miserable."

"I will see what can be done. "

"One more thing. I have a daughter. A toddler. She is around the corner, where a friend looks after her while I am visiting Alan. You dast not stay here beyond the time I am allowed to spend with Alan. The time it takes to say twenty Our Fathers."

Rambouillet made a face and threatened to call off the arrangement, but she could tell that he was bluffing and she persisted in her demands.

"Now I have to fetch the child," she said, and held the door open. "Come at midday tomorrow if you agree with my terms."

Rambouillet's word had been good. When Josetta visited the prison two days later, the turnkey took her to a street level chamber with a heavy door. Its vaulted ceilings were high and light flooded in through arrow slits in wall. There was a pallet and two basins, one for body waste and one for washing. Alan had cleaned himself as well as he could, but his clothes remained in tatters. Josetta had brought a bag of clean clothes and scissors, and a razor.

She stripped away his rags and scrubbed him clean. She toweled him off, and began to pull a clean tunic over his head, when he stayed her hand.

"Darling love," he whispered, "I've dreamed of this moment for a year and a half. Come, let me…" And he untied the strings of her wimple and removed it. Her hair cascaded down to her shoulders. As his fingers moved down to her bodice, she hurried to help him remove mantle and kirtle. His lips found the tender spot below her ear and she moaned as his fingers moved onto her breasts. She was aroused, and at the same time she agonized over her shame from the previous day.

On that day, Rambouillet had bulled his way into her without waiting for her to undress. He simply pulled up his surcoat, dropped his trousers around his knees and pushed her down on her bed, thrusting her garments out of the way. Pain had knifed through her as he drove into her, and the pain became worse with every thrust he made. She closed her eyes and gritted her teeth and tried to imagine she was going through child birth. As bad as this was, birthing was worse. Finally, he spent himself and groaned.

"You women of the Midi have the driest cunts I've ever encountered," he panted, his full weight on top of her. "'Tis hardly worth the effort. Next time, we'll use some oil. By the way, what's your name?"

"Dòmna Lavaur."

"I mean your first name."

"No." She would never let this fiend use her name, never!

He leered at her, then studied his fingernails. "Let's see, could it be *Josetta?*"

How did she find out, she asked herself with a shudder and remained silent. .

"Well then, Josetta," he said, as he pulled himself away and sat on the edge of bed pulling his trousers back up around his waist. "I have another proposition for you. Your father has something I want. If I could procure it, I would have your husband set free. And our little trysts would come to an end, sad to say."

She gaped at him. If it were true and if he were true to his word, then her prayers would be answered. However, he was asking her to betray her father, as she had already betrayed Alan and herself.

345

"I don't know. I must have time to think."

He stood bolt upright and holding her wrist in a grip of steel, yanked her off the bed onto her feet and pulled her into the cooking room. "Let's see what you have in your pantry," he growled. In a wall niche, he found a ewer of olive oil and sniffed it. "Perfect! A bit stale, but we don't need the virgin kind, do we?" He laughed uproariously and dragged her back to the bedroom.

."Undress," he said, and released her arm.

"But my daughter…"

"We still have time for several Our Fathers," he said. "I like precision. Now get on with it."

Josetta's heart sunk. Her crotch burned like fire. "Please. I don't think I can, you've hurt me." she said.

"'Tis what this oil is for," he said swirling the ewer in his other hand. "Take 'em off, or I'll rip 'em off," he snarled, and tugged at her kirtle.

Once she was naked, he told her to lie on the bed. "Spread 'em!" he commanded.

She moved her legs apart.

"More," he ordered.

Shivering, she shut her eyes and complied. She had seen streaks of blood on her inner thighs and was terrified. She felt the cool oil pour over her vulva and then it burned as it penetrated her bruised labia. Then his rough fingers were massaging the oil into every crevice they could find. She froze in pain and fright.

Abruptly, she felt his oily hands move to her breasts, slithering across her nipples, under, over and across. She remembered how Alan had anointed her in the same way and her gorge rose at the Frenchman's violation of her body. Yes, she had agreed to his despicable terms, but the reality was worse than her fears and the loss of *paratge*. She

346

thrust his hands away in disgust, and received a stinging slap across her face that made her eyes run.

"We can do it the easy way or the hard way, your choice," he snorted. She felt him recoil from the bed and opened her eyes. He was pulling off his trousers. She closed her eyes and crossed her ankles as she listened to him undress.

Suddenly, she felt him yank her legs apart, then put his arms under her knees and lift up her calves above her head. There was a stab of pain as he entered her and the pain intensified as he drove into her again and again. She didn't know if she could endure the pain any longer and she whimpered aloud.

Rambouillet took the sound as encouragement and redoubled his efforts until his orgasm made him cry out. Lying on top of her and breathing heavily, he asked for a kiss.

"Only when I know you've kept your end of the bargain," she said with a grimace. "Besides," she said, "'tis time to fetch my child."

Yesterday's torture haunted her as she and Alan made love for the first time in over two years. With Alan, it was almost as painful as it had been with Rambouillet the previous day, but she did everything she knew to give him pleasure, no matter how much it hurt her.

The following day, when she went to the jailers, they refused to admit her. She returned home in apprehension, and sure enough, Rambouillet was waiting for her. "Do I get my kiss? I was true to my word."

Josetta looked up and down the street. "Come in," she said and unlocked the door. He followed her inside and she stopped. "Here it is." She closed her eyes, tilted her head and pursed her lips. Rambouillet took her in his arms, and tried to force his tongue between her teeth. She tried to shove him away, but he overpowered her, and put his nose against hers.

"Understand, my little Josetta, that our bargain isn't just for one day or for one kiss. 'Tis for as long as I list. Lavaur can go back to his old cell, 'twill be the same to me. It hangs on you."

"Then let me see him. Why can't I see him today?"

"Because, my sweet, today's my turn. Tomorrow's his."

"I never consented to a continuing arrangement."

"Didn't you? Then we can call it off and let your husband rot in the dungeons below."

"You'd do that, wouldn't you," she hissed.

"And you'll do as you did to save him, correct?" She didn't answer. "Look, Josetta, we're making ourselves miserable. Why can't we be glad? All three of us. You and I still have more than ten Our Fathers left for sport."

"Sport?" she cried, "can't you see you disgust me? I can't abide your very touch! You are vomit!"

"Aha," he cried "you've got temperament! Well, so do I." He grabbed her, slung her over his shoulder kicking and scratching, and took her into the bedroom, where -- despite her all-out resistance -- he brutally raped her again.

"Till the day after tomorrow. I trow you enjoyed it as much as I did," he taunted on his way out.

She gagged and then vomited. When she was through retching, an urge to geld Baron Rambouillet and then plunge the gory knife into his black heart overwhelmed her. The only thing stopping her was fear of what would become of her child. If it weren't for Miranda, she would do it with the greatest relish.

That night, Josetta was in more pain than ever. The bleeding was almost as strong as a menstrual flow and she constantly needed to pass foul smelling urine that stung as if it was scalding hot. The symptoms were familiar. She had experienced them long ago when she had first lain with Alan. Abstinence and rest had cured it then.

When she visited Alan the next day, she told Alan about her discharge, and he was understanding and held her close and made no demands on her for the rest of the visit. The day after that, she kept Miranda home and locked and barred the door.

At midday, Rambouillet rapped on the door. Josetta didn't answer. Incensed, he pounded on it. He tried smashing it with his shoulder, but the bar held. Fuming with anger, he stomped off toward the keep. He would show this Midi bitch, he seethed.

The following morning, Josetta arrived at the keep to find the jailer talking to the turnkey, and when they noticed her, they winked at each other and smirked. Josetta's heart sank. They were going to refuse the visit. To her surprise, however, the turnkey beckoned her to follow him down the stairs to the dungeon. Of course! Alan had been sent back to the hellhole where she first saw him, thanks to Rambouillet. She tried to keep back her tears as she descended into the dim light of the lower dungeon. She flew to the bars of Alan's cell.

"Oh my darling," she cried, "what have they done?"

Alan's saddened voice broke the silence that followed. "What have *you* done? Ah, Josetta, if only you had told me!" His face came close to hers out the gloom. "There was no *need*. I could have survived." In the dim light, tears glistened in his eyes.

So he'd learned about Rambouillet. Her heart sank. Shaking her head, she reached inside the bars. "You were wretched and starving. I had to save you. How can I live without you?"

When she reached through the bars to touch him, he pushed away her hands. "They put me back down here shortly after midday yesterday. There was a French knight who claimed he had…that he…" Alan's voice quavered "…slept with you. Then he offered to put me back in upper cell if I would…"

"Would what, my love?"

"…if I would share you…with him…as *before*,' " Alan sobbed. "Oh, Josetta! How could you? I can't bear it. If only …." He was blubbering, and she placed her hands behind his neck and rested her forehead against his.

"Alan, he put you back down here because I rebuffed him. But if I can keep you healthy; if I can be with you, yes, I will put up with that monster," she whispered. "I love you too much to lose you."

"Never, Josetta. I'll never agree. I cannot share you. I'd rather beat my brains out against the wall."

"But I want you to live, for me. For us. Don't you see?"

"No, my love. 'Twould kill me. I can't abide it."

She kissed him through the bars, and his tears felt salty on her tongue. There was a large clang that made both of them jump, and they looked around to see the turnkey with the pewter pan in hand.

"Time's up, my turtle doves," chortled the turnkey. "Your wife has another rendezvous, Lavaur. You wouldn't want her to be late, would you?"

"Don't listen to him," she whispered in Alan's ear, "I'll come tomorrow. I see well how this hurts you, but I need to have you survive! Yet, if you insist, I'll never see the Frenchman without your permission." Josetta kissed him hard, and stumbled up the stairs, blinded by her tears.

The next day, however, she was turned away and everyday after that. A week went by, and then Rambouillet accosted her in the street.

"Ah, Madame Lavaur," he said. "Isn't it a shame about your husband? I wot he pines for you." He fell in step beside her, when she changed direction.

"Leave me alone," she said between gritted teeth.

"And so do I. *Pine* for you, I care to say."

"Would you fain have me make a scene in the street here?"

"Go ahead. I will tell people I was haggling over your price."

She walked ahead almost at a run, her lips pressed together in a scowl. He quickened his own pace.

"Two men pine for you. You could make both of them very glad, just as before."

"I never wish to see you or talk to you again, unless...." Josetta stopped and looked at him in the eye. "Unless my husband agrees with your bargain. And I must hear it from his own lips before I hear it from yours. Is that clear?"

"I'll see to it," he said. "Au revoir, Madame."

Every day for a fortnight, she went to the jailer and was turned away, and then came a day when suddenly the jailer called over to the turnkey, "Madame Lavaur fain would visit her husband. Take her to him," he said with a wink.

The turnkey returned the wink. "To say truth, Dòmna," he said to Josetta as they wound down the stairs, "your husband ain't much for talking today. Nor eatin,' nor drinkin' far as I can tell. Maybe you can liven him up," he chuckled.

Peering into the gloom of Alan's cell, she made out a body stretched out on the filthy floor.

"That's 'im, and he needs livenin' up real bad," the turnkey nodded.

The reality struck Josetta as if someone had knocked the wind out of her. It was Alan, and when she stooped and reached through the bars to touch him, his skin was as cold as the stone floor. He was dead. Her Alan was dead! She staggered to her feet and reeled against the wall. Moments passed before she could breathe.

"I will send someone to fetch my husband's remains," she told the turnkey, amazed that she could speak at all. "When did he die?"

"Can't rightly say. He was alive at sundown last night, but was stiff as a board this morning. Last couple of weeks he hardly touched his food. Skimped on his water, too."

Josetta slowly dragged herself up the steps as if she were memorizing every flaw in the stonework. All her sacrifice and degradation had been all for naught.

On her way to the apothecary in Lavaur, Josetta walked along the river that coursed briskly through the town on its way to join the Garona. At this time of year, the Tarn was clear and from the bank, she could see its rocky bottom. She herself needed to be hard as rock for what she intended to do. However painful it might be, it would be nothing like the day when she arrived at the house of Alan's mother, Anaïs, and broke the news of why she was there and what was in the cart that stood behind her in the street. That had been sheer misery and once again, Josetta had been faced with the utter finality of Alan's death as she watched Anaïs break down in endless tears.

After the burial, she had decided to stay on with her mother- in-law for a few weeks before undertaking the long journey to Provença. Caring for Miranda would help them both get through each day of aching heartbreak. In addition, Anaïs was just ending her two year probation and she would be become a Good Woman within the month. Josetta wanted to attend the Consolation ceremony now that she was in Lavaur.

Just as she became reconciled to spending time with Anaïs, she learned she was pregnant, which presented her with a dreadful dilemma. Whose child was it, Alan's or Rambouillet's?

If it was the Frenchman's, she did not want to bear it. She knew she would loathe the child, all the more because it might grow up to behave like the father.

On the other hand, it could be Alan's, in which case she would lavish it with love and tenderness. She dared not confide her intentions to Anaïs – how could that poor soul even comprehend the torment she had gone through?

In her depressed state of mind, the chance that she might give birth to another Rambouillet, plunged her deeper into the depths of despair, until it threatened her sanity. She imagined giving birth to a fiend that would crawl out if its cradle and devour its older sister Miranda.

More and more, she began to think about removing the problem by doing away with herself. There, too, Miranda was the sticking point. How could she possibly abandon her baby?

Was there an alternative way out of her problem? What about abortion? She had heard that certain herbs could end pregnancies, and after days of weighing her options, she made up her mind. She would consult the apothecary in Lavaur, choose the most effective potion and double the dose to make sure that the evil that lurked in her womb would never survive to plague the world.

In his gloomy little room filled with various vessels of all sizes and small bundles of dried herbs, the old apothecary listened to her gravely as she explained what she wanted: a foolproof means of ending her pregnancy. It also had to be safe because she had a child to care for. With a nod of understanding, the old man set out concocting a solution of tansy, and as he worked, he cautioned her that it would make her sick and that it was important not to exceed the dose he recommended. Too much at once could even be fatal, he warned. He handed it to her in a stoppered ceramic beaker and repeated the warning. She nodded and paid him his fee. For the first time in weeks, she felt that life was worth living.

As Josetta returned along the river, she swiveled her head to make sure no one was around, then swallowed the contents of the beaker and threw it into the fast-moving water. She knew she was taking a risk, but she didn't want the medicine to fail, just as she didn't want Anaïs or anyone else to know what she was doing. Besides, she reasoned, the apothecary would hardly have given her anything that would really kill her. She was prepared to be violently ill, but she would welcome that as a sign that she had purged any trace of Rambouillet from her body.

However, she wasn't prepared for the excruciating muscle cramps that she began to experience an hour or so after she entered her mother-in-law's house. They were agonizing and kept increasing in strength and duration. She began to whimper and groan and Anaïs ran to her side and coaxed her into bed, then ran out to seek help. When she came back with two Good Men and one Good Woman, the cramps had changed into convulsions, and Josetta had lost consciousness. Her teeth were clenched and her eyes had rolled up under the lids. No matter what the Good Folk tried, the convulsions continued to rack Josetta's body.

When they finally stopped, so did her breathing. Miranda had become an orphan. .

Mazan

When the news of the deaths of Alan and Josetta reached Mazan in springtime, Olivier proposed that he ride to Lavaur and bring back Miranda to live with them in Mazan. Micaela disagreed. Anaïs had written how Miranda had become the center of her life and was more important her vocation as a Good Woman.

"She's all alone, and Miranda is all she has, therefore it might do more harm than good to suggest that Miranda should leave to come to us. It would be the height of selfishness to take away the one joy Anaïs had left.

"But she's a Good Woman," Olivier insisted. "She has taken vows to live ascetically and she has pastoral obligations. Surely 'tis difficult to raise a child in those circumstances."

"'Tis difficult to raise children in any circumstance," Micaela declared. "Methinks Anaïs will not force her privations onto the child, and she sorely needs the child, far more than we do. We already have grand children to pamper. Why should we deprive her of the same joy and privilege?"

Olivier threw up his hands. "Please, hold your peace, my love! I wot well when I've been bested," he said with a sheepish grin.

"Besides, the war is over," Micaela, said with a shrug. "Amaury Montfort has gone back to France like a dog with its tail between his legs, and Raimond of Tolosa, the Trencavels and the Count of Fois have reconquered their lost dominions. Vineyards have been replanted and walls and bridges have been rebuilt. We'll be able to travel back and forth to Lavaur without fear of running into foreign brigands."

"Mayhap, but methinks the reconquest might not be permanent."

Micaela frowned. "Why do you say that?"

"By reason that belike Amaury Montfort is offering those very same dominions to Louis of France, and I'm afraid Louis is a lot shrewder than his father Philippe."

"But how can he offer what he doesn't possess?"

Olivier shook his head. "In the minds of the French, those possessions are not really lost. Besides, if he's really smart, Louis knows that by reinvading the Midi, he can outflank the Plantagenets and overrun Gascony and maybe Aquitània itself."

"Why didn't the French do that before?"

"Because, to say truth, the Capets were trying not to confuse a holy war with a war of conquest."

"Think you that Simon Montfort's ravages didn't amount to a war of conquest? Even when the Pope confirmed him in Trencavel's possession and titles?"

"Forsooth," Olivier said, "but King Philippe never really supported him, and never took advantage of Montfort's conquests to attack the Plantagenets from the rear. Methinks his son will seize that opportunity."

Again, Micaela looked at her husband in puzzlement. "But, wait; didn't I hear you gloating a month or so ago that the Pope actually opposed another Crusade to the Midi? And that he deemed a Crusade to the Levant was more important at this time?"

"Aye, that I did."

"And a few days afterward, didn't you tell me that Louis had announced that he was abandoning plans to lead a Crusade against the Midi?"

"Forsooth," Olivier said with a sigh, "but just today I learned that all the Roman Bishops in the Midi went to Rome to complain that the wicked lords of the Midi are sapping their influence among the people."

"But the Pope..."

"Pope Honorius has appointed a pro-French Papal legate. Methinks Louis will leap at the chance to enlarge his holdings at the expense of the Plantagenets. 'Tis like that the Plantagenet's themselves are aware of this danger, by reason that they have sent an English army to Gascony. Why else would they do that?"

"But in the last few years, the war has gone against the French."

"They were fighting under Montfort, and then under his much weaker son," Olivier said. "If an invasion is led by the King himself, 'twill outnumber anything the French have put in the field before. Methinks the people of the Midi are so war-weary that they will not resist."

"Well, if they do, I sorely hope that you, my darling, have decided not to take up arms against them this time, or any time in the future."

Part V

Narbona

It was a pleasant surprise for Arnaud-Amaury to see how the towns of the Midi responded to news that the King of France had taken the cross and was invading the Midi with a huge army. The town consuls had enjoyed two years of peace since Amaury Montfort had finally given up and gone back to France, but this new threat of invasion found them ready to accede to the crusader's demands. Most towns hastened to cut their ties to the Count of Tolosa and pledge allegiance to the king. In fact, most people in the region believed that after so many years of warfare, the King's presence might bring peace to all at long last. Many of the towns sent emissaries pledging allegiance to the French King before the crusaders had even started out. At last, the Archbishop chortled, his grand scheme to rid the Midi of the protectors of heresy was to come true, and Raimond VII would be isolated and marginalized.

In advance of the invasion, Arnaud-Amaury himself proceeded to accept the surrenders of towns in the name of the Crusade and had the consuls pledge allegiance to the King. When he reached Nimes, however, he fell ill, and decided to return to Narbona, where he could rest up and wait for the Crusade to come to him.

Even in his palace, where he could lounge in leisure, he frequently had to sit to catch his breath. The slightest exertion made him gasp for air. Because of his breathing difficulties and his swollen ankles, his leeches decided he was suffering from dropsy, and that only increased his anxiety. He had lived long enough to know that most victims of dropsy become bedfast and die. Were his days on earth numbered? After all, he was an old man of sixty-three. Death itself didn't frighten him; the real problem was his eternal salvation, the redemption of his soul. Those were real worries.

He had not been honest with his confessors. The deaths of Pascau, Raoul and Castelnau had been politically expedient and had been carried out in God's name and for the sake of the Holy Church. So too, was the poisoning of Innocent. They were completely justifiable and necessary. Indeed, Castelnau's death had sparked the Crusade and garnered the Church a massive influx of wealth and power. Surely, the All-Merciful Heavenly Father would see these deaths as enabling the Holy Church to achieve its ends, which are to worship and glorify Him above all. Surely, the end justified the means.

Nevertheless, would the Heavenly Father see it that way? Therein lay the rub. The Archbishop groaned aloud. *Murder* -- a word that theoretically described his sins, but which his own conscience had strenuously denied as being applicable – must always be construed as a mortal sin, even when it helped strengthen, not weaken the Church. There was no escaping the fact that technically, he had committed four mortal sins. He, himself, had always said the Heavenly Father was an Absolutist, not a Relativist. By refusing to accept God's mercy by confessing and repenting his sins, the Archbishop knew his soul was in the danger of Hell's fire.

There was nothing for it, but to stop putting it off, and summon his confessor, an old priest who had served in the same role for his predecessor. To humiliate oneself before one old man was an infinitely small price to pay to avoid eternal damnation.

He was pulling on the oars with all his might, but the current was too strong, and the boat was being carried downstream, below the landing place. Redoubling his efforts and panting as he rowed, the old archbishop fought the river as if his life depended on it.

The man standing in the stern was deliberately rocking the boat; he laughed scornfully when Arnaud-Amaury begged him to sit down. There was something very familiar about the man, and suddenly it became clear that it was Peter Castelnau, which was impossible because Castelnau was dead. Suddenly Castelnau, or whoever it was, lurched, and the boat capsized, throwing Arnaud-Amaury into the torrent.

Dragged under water, he held his breath until he thought his lungs would burst. When he reached the surface he gulped for air, but his throat filled with water instead. He was drowning!

Arnaud-Amaury woke up, fighting for air. Liquid was gurgling in his throat! He spat it out and sat up, coughing and sputtering and wheezing, trying to inhale. Rigid with panic, and with sweat pouring down his face, he found every inspiration too pitifully small to satisfy his hunger for air. His chest was painfully tight. He tried to call out for his valet, who slept in an adjoining room, but he couldn't make himself heard. He didn't trust his legs to carry him in search of help. Was death upon him, he shivered?

For some weeks, he had been meaning to make his confession, but had put it off, day after day. Now it might be too late! Leaning forward and gasping for breath, he heard the bells ring *matins*. It was misery. By the time his valet looked in after the bells rang *prime*, he was exhausted. The valet immediately ran off in search of the leech, who, after what seemed an eternity, finally came limping back into the archbishop's bedchamber. He and his assistant, a monk from Frontfroide named Aurelh, set to work at once. Aurelh sent the valet back out to fetch more pillows to help the archbishop sit up, while the leech opened a vein in the archbishop's forearm.

"Do you want us to send for your confessor?" Aurelh asked, as he held a bowl to catch the blood.

Arnaud-Amaury nodded. Better late than never, he shuddered.

"Is he near by?"

Arnaud-Amaury shook his head. "There are (gasp) other priests... here...in the palace."

"I'm ordained as a priest," Aurelh said. "Would you like me to shrive you?"

Arnaud-Amaury nodded again. He would much rather have this stranger shrive him, than to confess to anyone he knew. After all, with or without the extenuating circumstances, great shame was involved.

The leech bound up the archbishop's arm and Aurelh set the bowl with its crimson contents on the bedside table.

"Please excuse us," Aurelh said to the leech, "but I must shrive the archbishop. 'Twill take some time, and I will call you when I've finished."

"Forsooth, there's little else that I can do," the leech shrugged. "Here, let me take this out of your way," and he picked up the bowl and limped out of the room, closing the door softly behind him.

Aurehl knelt by the bedside and joined his hands in prayer. "Now, Your Excellency, let us begin."

Arnaud-Amaury coughed and spoke in a husky voice not much louder than a whisper. "Bless me, Father... (cough) for I have sinned. 'Tis three months... since my last ... (cough) confession, but ..." he coughed again, ""twere ...well ... I be shriven."

"Are you contrite, your excellency? I need not tell you the gravity of your position."

"Forsooth.... I fear for... my immortal soul. I wot not if my... suffering... suffices as penance. Belike not... my sins...."

"Whatever their nature, your Eminence, if you be truly sorry, if you repent, then you are in a state of grace, and the Heavenly Father will forgive you and welcome you to His Kingdom. Methinks whatever venial sins you confess will require no further amends than those you have already made."

"Know you ...they be not venial, but *mortal*... I am sore afraid ... and deeply ashamed ... my rue is boundless. Can I be reconciliated ... with the Heavenly Father?

"Only you can make that judgment, Your Eminence. Only you can feel the grace of true repentance, whatever your sins may be. What is their nature?"

"I dread ... the word." Arnaud-Amaury studied the wall. "'Tis murder."

"*Murder*?" Aurehl repeated the word, dumbfounded.

"Aye, 'tis hard ... to conceive... that an archbishop .... I deemed it necessary ...and they blamed Count Raimond ...'twas the excuse for the Crusade. "

The Archbishop's meaning dawned on Aurelh. "You mean you are responsible for the death of Peter Castelnau? *Your own colleague?*"

"Alack, 'tis so."

Aurelh stared at the Archbishop as if he had seen him for the first time. "Tis grave indeed, no matter how noble your motive." He shook his head. "Forsooth, 'tis a mortal sin, and 'tis necessary to feel utter contrition in your heart. If you survive, you must do heavy penance. I wot well you understand."

"I do," Arnaud-Amaury answered, his eyes cast down again. "But I ...there's more."

Still stunned by what he had already heard, Aurelh frowned. "More what?"

"Murders."

Aurelh's mouth hung open.

"Two other colleagues ... obtained knowledge that endangered the Holy Church. They had to be silenced."

Aurelh could not believe his ears. "How?"

"Poison with one. The other was thrown down a well."

"They were my colleagues," Aurelh hissed. "You killed *my colleagues*! They were *unshriven*!"

"I had to ... to save the Holy Church. By my troth, I bore them no grudge."

"I can't believe it."

"There's still another I fain would confess."

"I suppose you are now going to tell me you murdered the Pope," Aurelh said, shaking his head in disgust.

The Archbishop's eyes widened. "How did you guess? Or did somebody tell you?" Arnaud-Amaury's voice broke apart from a coughing spell.

Aurelh's eyes popped in horror. "By my troth, 'tis beyond the imagination. 'Tis despicable, to say truth."

The Archbishop nodded and managed to smile. "Now, to make sure I'm shriven, can you give me the Eucharist? To ensure my entry into heaven?"

"Gladly." Aurelh reached into his wallet and pulled out the linen sac containing consecrated communion biscuits.

"The wine yonder...is consecrated." The Archbishop pointed a gnarled finger at a flagon of wine on a console.

"I see it." Aurelh said. "But I want to make sure that you are properly prepared." He unwound the bandage from Arnaud-Amaury's arm and laid it on the pillow

365

behind the archbishop's head. He went over to the leech's wallet standing next to the door and pulled out long strips of bandaging. Then he locked the door.

"Last year, we received instructions on how to ready penitents with mortal sins for the extreme unction," he told Arnaud-Amaury. "Their arms should be held rigidly in the sign of the cross." As he talked, Aurelh tied one of the Archbishop's wrists to a bedpost. "In this manner, the penitent feels closer to the passion of Christ, which helps him achieve repentance and contrition more readily." Then he tied the archbishop's other wrist to the opposite bed post. "You should feel helpless and vulnerable, like Christ on the cross."

"I do, but…"

"Now, if you would just open your mouth, I can give you the host. Can you open wide?"

The Archbishop opened his mouth, but instead of inserting a wafer, Aurelh snatched the bandage off the pillow and quickly stuffed most of it into the old man's mouth. He used another bandage as a gag to hold the other in place, and drew the ends taut around the back of the Archbishop's head and knotted the ends in front. The archbishop's eyes had first registered surprise, then anger, and now finally fear. Discerning the sneer on Aurelh's face and the malice in his eyes, terror gripped the old man, and he emptied his bladder and soiled himself.

He tried to call out, but only muffled sounds came forth, and he began to cough. He was choking. His eyes bulged with fright. He tried to tug his arms free, but he had no leverage. Sweat poured down his forehead. He wagged his head back and forth, hoping Aurelh could see a plea for mercy in his eyes.

Wearing a sardonic smile, Aurelh stared at the archbishop "I didn't really know our Cistercian brethren

Peter or Raoul, nor was I acquainted with the Pope, Your Eminence, but Brother Pascau was a friend of mine. He was a kind and decent man. He did not deserve to die the way he did. He had committed no crime. You, on the other hand, have committed dreadful crimes. Do you really deserve to die in peace?" Aurelh's tone was icy and full of hatred. "Methinks not," Aurelh said.

The archbishop's face was red as a beet, and contorted by a coughing and snorting fit as he fought for breath, his chest heaving with the effort. The whites of his eyes reminded Aurelh of those of a lame cow that he once seen when it was about to be slaughtered.

"I want you to know, Your Excellency, that Brother Pascau was a secret Believer in the Church of the Friends of God, and so am I. Yes, I've been ordained in your church," Aurelh nodded, "but if you believe I am a false priest, you also are aware that there are thousands of others who are far less pious. According to your Church, even a fallen priest can administer the Eucharist, as you wot well. So let's get on with it, shall we?"

Arnaud-Amaury shook his head desperately. He had been shriven, all right, but now that confession had been turned into a travesty, a nightmare! This false priest could not give him the reconciliation that he required. He needed a real priest; even a fallen one would do! Hell's fire was yawning before him. Hacking and coughing and gasping for air, he pled for Aurelh to send him a real priest, for the love of God, but the gag rendered his speech unintelligible if not inaudible.

"Belike you fear that I myself am not in a state of grace, I trow," Aurelh's voice now shook with rage. "Well, 'tis true, forsooth! I am in a state of anger! A state of outrage! Not just because you murdered my friend and murdered your own colleagues. 'Tis because you instigated a murderous war that has cost tens of thousands of lives. Butchery, pillaging, rapine, destruction of crops and property. Misery on a biblical scale. All because of your criminal actions at the behest of your so-called Holy Church."

Aurelh's voice dropped almost to a whisper as he spoke into the archbishop's ear. "Well, let me enlighten you. I deem your God to be *Satan* and that this sacrament of extreme unction is a *farce!* Only Consolation by a Good Man can get you to heaven, and I am not one of those holy men. Therefore, you wot well that this is a travesty of the sacrament you had counted on. You expected to be shriven of your mortal sins and to be admitted to heaven. Instead, you are doomed to burn forever in hellfire, according to your own belief and I am making sure of that. Take heed: I am not only a false priest, I am your executioner."

" So, let's go on with the sacrament. Here is the body of Christ," Aurelh said, as he stuffed the wafer inside the gag, while the archbishop moved his head around, desperately trying to avoid it, more for fear of choking on it than from fearing its blasphemy. "Don't fret, I've transubstantiated it," Aurelh mocked.

"Now for the blood," Aurelh said, and picking up the flagon of wine with one hand, he locked the other hand firmly in Arnaud-Amaury's tonsure, and tilting the old man's head back, poured the wine onto the gag. The archbishop feebly tried to jerk his head away from the smothering liquid, but found it was held in a grip like steel. As he struggled to draw a breath, he choked and aspirated the crumbled wafer. A violent fit of coughing convulsed his body. Wine trickled out of his nose and mouth. As his body flopped about, his face turned purple and his eyes rolled up in his head. After more convulsions, his body suddenly went limp and fell back onto the bed, its head lolling on a shoulder.

Aurelh put his ear on the Archbishop's chest and listened. Satisfied, he moved his hand across Arnaud-Amaury's eyes, and closed the lids. After removing the gag and untying the man's wrists, Aurelh used the bandages to clean the wine off the face of the corpse, and threw them into the wallet. He unlocked the door, and stepped outside where a small group of prelates had gathered.

"The Archbishop is dead," Aurelh announced. "He died in the act of confession, so alas, he was not shriven. 'Tis most unfortunate for a man of his stature and piety. I am sure that his soul can benefit from your prayers." Aurelh bowed, and with a sweep of his arm, he beckoned them to enter the Archbishop's bedchamber. If the prelates had not been crowding each other to get through the door and had looked back over their shoulders, they would have been surprised at Brother Aurelh's jaunty gait as he walked away down the hall.

Uzès

Watching Margarida nursing the infant Rainier, Micaela marveled at the progression of life. It seemed only yesterday that she herself was feeling the strong suction of Margarida's gums and tongue on her own breast. She resumed knitting the small blanket that would help keep little Rainier snug during the winter, and looked across the spacious hall where her son-in-law's aunts were busily weaving fine linen on their loom. They were both Good Women, and besides their skill in making cloth, they were excellent midwives, and had attended Margarida during Rainier's birth. They had also proved to be fine company during the months of Margarida's lying-in.

For Micaela, attending her daughter during the birth of her grandson and the postnatal period would have been sublime, had it not been for the gnawing worry and the pangs of separation from Olivier, from whom she had received no word for almost three months. Olivier had accompanied her to Uzès, and then gone back home to Mazan, intending to pass a few days with old friends in Avinhon on his way.

When he left, there had been no indication that Avinhon would be the target of a siege. Olivier had sent her a letter in early June, saying that because of his fluency in French, he was helping the Avinhon leaders negotiate with the French. Led by the newly crowned King Louis VIII, the French invaders had marched down the right bank of the Ròse, intending to cross the river at Avinhon on their way to Tolosa. For the people and leaders of Avinhon, the sooner they crossed the better, Olivier had written. Unfortunately, the St. Benezet Bridge was the only bridge across the river, he explained, and it could only be accessed from inside the city walls, and -- although willing to cooperate with the French -- the city fathers drew the line at having an unruly foreign army inside their walls. He added that the dilemma was being solved by building a bridge on rafts upstream from Avinhon, and that once the French were safely across, he would head for Mazan.

The letter arrived at Uzès almost simultaneously with the news that fighting had broken out between the French and the Avinhon militia, and that the French were now besieging the city. Since then, she had heard nothing from Olivier, and here it was, early September. In late August, word came that there had been fierce fighting, and the French assaults had been beaten back with heavy losses. This gave Micaela an additional cause to worry, and that was why she felt so ambivalent about attending her daughter and grandson. If only Olivier had remained with her in Uzès!

Her reverie was interrupted by one of the porters, who told Margarida that a French knight was below and wished to speak with the *castellane*. Margarida rearranged her kirtle and rose, handing Rainier, who had fallen asleep, to the nurse.

"Shall I see what he wants, my darling? Micaela asked. "I could tell him that Gerard is not home at present, and it might be better if he..."

"Excuse me for interrupting, Madame, the porter said, "but I already told him that the *castellan* was away and he insisted on seeing you. I could try to send him away, but – er- he has a whole company of mounted men with him."

"That won't be necessary, André, thank you." Margarida said. "Please show him up."

Turning to Micaela, she said, "I'll take care of it, maire," and patted her mother on the cheek. Turning to her aunts, she said, "My dearests, I believe it would be best if you would hide in the secret chamber while the Frenchman is here. Your black mantles advertise that you are Good Women, and that doesn't sit well with most Frenchmen."

Without a word, but blowing kisses to Margarida, the two women rose and disappeared through the doorway to the stairs.

"What in the world can he want? I wonder if it has anything to do with the siege of Avinhon," Micaela asked. She suddenly became agitated. Could the man be the bearer of bad news, the worst news? What if that was why they had come? She winced and tried to maintain her composure.

"We'll just have to wait and see, Maire," Margarida said calmly, although she, too, was on pins and needles. "We'll know soon enough." Did it have something to do with her father? She prayed not. Had the presence of her heretical aunts finally been wheedled or tortured out of a hapless neighbor? She hoped she could stand up to this foreigner, whoever he was.

"My lady?" André, the porter, had reappeared with a large French knight, with a cross emblazoned on his blue lily-spangled surcoat, "Baron Rambouillet has come to pay his respects," André said. Then he bowed, and left the room. Micaela and Margarida gasped when they heard the name, but after exchanging glances, recovered their composure.

Rambouillet gave Margarida a slight nod. "My lady... my ladies, I should say," nodding curtly to Micaela, "I know that this visit may be an inconvenience to you, but that is the nature of war, isn't it?" His Occitan was heavily accented but passable.

Margarida remained silent. Her face showed no emotion. Yet, both women were praying that he would not go on to tell them that he had come about a death.

"The siege of Avinhon is done," he continued. "The enemy, the Avinhonese, have capitulated. As we speak, their walls are being torn down to fill in the moat. Their reckless resistance has delayed us from getting on with our Crusade to wipe out heresy, once and for all, wherever people speak your hateful tongue," he sneered. Both women stiffened at the gratuitous slur.

"I have spent half of my life struggling to eliminate this scourge down here. I mean, the heresy, not the language, although 'twould be a good idea, too. 'Tis why we came sixteen years ago, and why we have had to return, again and again, by reason of the lies your people have told us, from one end of this Godforsaken land to the other." He paused and looked down his nose at them.

Micaela started to speak, but Rambouillet held up a broad hand.

"Ah, you might ask, what does this have to do with you? Isn't that so? Let me tell you. I have consulted the Holy Inquisition. Your name is on a list. You are harboring two so-called Good Women here. I am here to do what I originally came for: to eradicate heresy, and to punish those who have abetted those Apostles of Satan. Where are your aunts?" As Rambouillet spoke, he made it obvious that he was studying the looms. "Methinks that like most heretics, they like to weave. Where are they?"

Margarida reddened, and cursed herself for not hiding the looms, but remained stony faced. "You dare come into my hearth and insult me and my relatives? You dare bully women? What kind of man are you, what kind of country do you come from where manners are non-existent?" she burst out.

"Sir, my daughter is distraught. She ..." Micaela broke in, speaking in a conciliatory voice, but Rambouillet cut her off.

373

"Twenty years of acting Twenty years of tricks and stratagems, twenty years of pushing a boulder up hill, only to find it at the bottom again where you people have rolled it. Those days are past. We French are your overlords. Get used to it. Live with it! I want to see those two Perfects, now. Now! Understand? Or by God I will call in my men and have them dragged out. Which will it be?"

"I'm afraid you will have to call in your men." Margarida said, her eyes blazing with hatred. "My aunts are not here, they have gone out."

"Have they now? That's not what your porter told us. He must be lying, then, and the bible says the Lord hates a lying tongue." Rambouillet went to the stair well and shouted down, "Amenez le concierge!" Two men-at-arms dragged the porter up the stairs and into the room. André looked at his mistress, his eyes bulging with terror.

"*Foutes-le par terre, et coupez lui la langue!*" Rambouillet commanded. To the ladies, he reverted to Occitan. "His tongue will never lie again."

The men gaped at him. They both had engaged in many acts of violence and cruelty, but they had never cut out anyone's tongue before.

"*Etes-vous sourds, ou stupides? Foutes-le en bas, je te l'ai dit!*" Rambouillet roared at his men, and lunging forward, drove his fist into André's face. André's legs buckled and he fell to the floor. "*Le voilà!*" Rambouillet snorted. The men knelt and pulling out their daggers, worked at prying the unconscious man's jaws open.

Micaela and her daughter looked on with horror, and then looked at each other. What can we do, their eyes pleaded. Micaela looked around for a weapon. There was nothing. Then she screamed, "Stop, stop it! Stop it!" Margarida joined her and both were shrieking at top of their lungs.

"*Laissez-moi*," Rambouillet shouted over the women's screams and drew his dagger. He bent down, stuck it through middle of the porter's tongue, grasped the tip of the dagger with his other hand, and pulled. As he did, Micaela leaped on his back and sank her nails in his face.

"*Jules, tiens la tête, coinces-la!*" he roared, ignoring Micaela's desperate assault. As the man called Jules held the porter's head to the ground with both hands, Rambouillet drew the tongue out to an obscene length. "*Marcel, coups-la, vas-y vite, nom de Dieu!*" Rambouillet squeezed his eyelids tight to avoid Micaela's gouges, and the man Marcel quickly sliced off the tongue, releasing a gush of blood that welled up out of André's mouth and spilled onto the floor.

Rambouillet sprang up and whirled around, trying to throw Micaela off his back. She clawed at his face but slipped off. As she staggered to get her balance he grabbed her cap, and bending her head back, plunged his dagger into her abdomen. '*Putain!*" he snarled. She doubled up, and he pulled her erect by her hair and stabbed her in one breast and then the other. "*Espèce de putain du sal Midi!*" He spat out the words as she tumbled senseless to the floor, bleeding profusely. Margarida had been paralyzed with terror, but now she dove to her knees and cradled Micaela's head and shoulders in her arms, kissing her again and again between sobs. "Mama, Mama," she cried repeatedly. Micaela's head lolled lifelessly over Margarida's arm, while Rambouillet straddled them, with dagger raised, shouting to Margarida that she could be next.

His henchmen faced him aghast and stretched out their arms with open hands, gesturing for him to cool down. "*Seigneur, assez, assez, je vous en prie*," Jules cried. "*Allons chercher les deux heretiques*," Marcel pleaded.

Rambouillet backed away slowly and shook his bloody dagger in Margarida's face. "Bear it in mind," he rasped, reverting back to Occitan, "you can be next."

"No, that privilege will be yours, you hellhound!" cried a voice behind him, and Gerard de Castèlnòudari leaped forward, naked sword in hand. His first stroke virtually decapitated Jules, and the next disemboweled Marcel, who backed away, holding his intestines in his hands before sitting down on the floor, and regarding their glistening bulk with disbelief before toppling forward onto his face.

Rambouillet tried to parry Gerard's next blow with his dagger, but he slipped in the blood that spread across the floor tiles. The sword glanced off the blade of the dagger and cleaved a furrow from Rambouillet's left eyebrow to his chin, cutting through his nose and knocking out front teeth on both jaws. Rambouillet crashed down to the floor and his blood joined that of the others.

Gerard dropped the bloody sword and swooped down on his knees beside Margarida who, wracked with sobs and eyes swollen shut, was still rocking Micaela in her arms. "Is she …?" He asked.

Margarida looked up, her eyes streaming with tears, and nodded. Heartbroken, Gerard tried to think what to do next. They had to flee before the crusaders waiting outside found out what had happened and slaughtered everyone. He took Margarida's head between his hands and shook it gently. "My darling, flee we must and there's no time to spare. Where are your aunts? We must get down to the river and hide in the cave where the Good People meet. Do you understand? We have to fly!"

Margarida's eyes fluttered then shut again. "They're hiding in the secret chamber."

Gerard kept her head in his hands. "I'll go get them. I'm going to place Maire's body in the chamber, 'twill be as good a sepulcher as we can find. So please, let me take her from you. Mayhap you can fetch the other servants here." Scooping his mother-in-law's body into his arms, he bore it rapidly up the stairs.

Margarida remained on the floor for a moment more, then shakily rose and went over to where the porter lay dead, his mouth filled with coagulating blood. She hurried off in search of the servants. In a few minutes, she was back with three women and two men, who stared horrified at the four dead men.

When Gerard re-appeared with his wife's aunts, he quickly explained that they must flee through the same postern he had used to enter the castle scant minutes before. As he talked, a thought came to him that was as loathsome as it was practical, but he immediately put it into action.

"'Twould be best that these bodies never be found; 'twould lead the French to search for their missing leaders instead of looking for their killers. So the men and I will drag the bodies upstairs and put them in the secret chamber with Maire." Gerard grabbed one of the men-at-arms by the legs and started dragging him toward the stairs

Margarida thought she hadn't heard right and looked at Gerard horrified. "You can't, I won't stand...."

"I wot well what you're thinking, my love," Gerard interrupted, "and I agree, but I'm doing this to save our lives. Maire would have approved. Remember, these are but her material remains, not her immortal soul. When I come back down, I will help you clean up all trace of blood from the floor."

Roger, one of the male servants, who was standing over Rambouillet, exclaimed, "This one is still alive!" Gerard dropped the legs he was pulling and sprang over to where Roger crouched. It was true. Rambouillet was still alive, although unconscious. It would be simple to kill him now. However, that was far too kind, too merciful for this monster, who deserved to suffer bodily for his crimes here on earth!

Then it hit Gerard. They were turning the secret room into a de facto tomb, and the latch that opened it from the inside was skillfully hidden. If somehow Rambouillet *did* survive, he would find that he had been entombed among decaying corpses. He'd have no light, only darkness. The walls were so thick that even if he shouted as loudly as he could, no one could hear him. He would go mad before he died of thirst and starvation.

Gerard made up his mind. "Go ahead and drag him upstairs to the secret room. If he wakes up, he'll die a slow, lingering, horrible death. I want him to suffer."

When Gerard and his helpers came back down to the great hall, they found that the paving stones and the stairs had been scrubbed clean.

"Now," he said, "we really must hie ourselves to the cave. We'll leave by the postern door singly or in pairs and proceed as if nothing has taken place. Although the crusaders are by the front gate, one or two may be snooping around. Don't run; don't even *walk* hurriedly. Pretend you're out for a stroll. Don't look back. And try to take different paths to the river. Margarida and I will follow you with my horse. Aunties, strip down to your kirtles and stuff your black mantles up the chimney. I want you to split up, one with Roger, and the other with Margarida. Let's get going, there's no time to waste."

He turned to Roger "When we get to the river, take charge while I scout around and find out what the French are up to."

Olivier put his horse into a canter as he neared Argilliers, the seat of Gerard's property, only a long league from Uzès. It had been much more than ten years since he had been separated from Micaela for so long. His heart ached to see her and he was tempted to spur his mount into a gallop, but he resisted the urge, knowing that the horse was already badly winded.

He had used the country lanes to avoid the columns of crusaders who favored the main thoroughfares. As he rounded a knoll, and his daughter's castle came in view, he saw another horseman in the middle of the road. It was Gerard! He drew up beside his son-in-law, and leaning out of the saddle, started to embrace him. It was then that he noticed that Gerard looked pale and haggard.

"What's the matter, my son, why the long face? Aren't you glad to see me?" Olivier cried with concern.

Gerard then reached across and hugged Olivier, and broke into sobs.

Olivier's stomach churned. What could be wrong? Was the baby...? "What's wrong son? Whatever's the matter? "'Tisn't ...?" Olivier struggled with the words. "'Tisn't the baby, is it?" Gerard still clung to him, sobbing and shook his head. A shock hit Olivier. "Is...is Margarida...?"

"No, Paire." Although Gerard managed to recover his speech, every word he pronounced felt as if it was ripping his chest apart, "your daughter is healthy. Just before noon, a troop of crusaders came to the castle. I was on the way back from Nimes when they arrived and they began to mutilate André, our porter...."

'What did they do to him?" Olivier interrupted.

"They cut out his tongue." Gerard whispered.

"Oh, no," Olivier gasped, "No!"

"And as they were doing it, Maire intervened…" Gerard choked; the constriction in his chest made it impossible to continue.

"*Maire?* You mean Micaela?" Icy dread hit Olivier like a sledge hammer.

Gerard's tear-filled eyes met his and in their depths, Olivier saw utter despair. A mighty vice around his chest crushed his breath away.

"She…Micaela… she's…?" Olivier managed to say, wrenching the words out slowly, not daring to say that word that would take his own life away. Gerard nodded, sobbing, his arms clenched around Olivier as if were he to let go, both of them would plunge into a bottomless abyss.

Olivier was conscious of a roaring in his ears, and he seemed to be suffocating. He heard a shrill keening begin somewhere. He would have fallen from the saddle had not Gerard steadied him. Micaela! The person that he loved more than anyone or anything in this wicked world was dead and nothing would ever be the same. Micaela, the center of his universe. Without her, his existence was unimaginable. What would he do, how could he go on living…what was the use? The wailing became deafening and then he realized he was the one who was making the noise.

He knew that he should try to regain control of himself, but hopelessness engulfed him. Micaela had not even had the chance to be Consoled! Then suddenly it came to him. He knew what he had to do. He tried to speak despite the crushing pain in his chest.

"Gerard," he gasped, "I wot…well… what…I fain…would do." He stretched out his arm and gripped Gerard's shoulder.

380

"Paire, don't; you must rest." Gerard pleaded, his eyes desperately fixed on Olivier's. "Don't look for vengeance now, there will be other opportunities. There are too many of the filthy bastards."

"I don't …want…revenge," Olivier wheezed, digging his fingers into Gerard's flesh as if to make his point. "I know what…Micaela would have …wanted. And, by God, …'twill be done!. I will…take the Consolation. I…must needs…become…a Good Man."

The End

Historical and theological background

Those who are unfamiliar with the history of the early 13th century may desire an overview of its social, political and religious structures. I learned some of this lore literally at my mother's knee. Born in Carpentras, the capital of Vaucluse and the Comtat Veneissin, in 1899, she remained a devotee of Provençal life to her dying day. For her sake, I have tried to hew close to the historical record, although I have compressed dates and years. I have also attributed acts of violence to a historical figure that are pure conjecture.

When a major shift in history takes place, such as the extinction of a civilization with its traditions and language, few of those involved are aware of it because it usually happens over a progression of decades or even centuries. This was certainly true of the culture that thrived in the Midi (south)of what is now France, about eight hundred years ago. Its women were the most independent in Europe, and it had the highest percentage of people unencumbered with feudal obligations. It also had its own worldview.

Its people aspired to *paratge* (pronounced like *garage-eh)*, a non-religious ethic that calls for civility, tolerance, justice, balance, courtesy, excellence and nobility of soul. Related to the platonic idea of the kosmos, where heaven and earth, gods and men are linked by kinship, love, orderliness, temperance and justice, it is the antithesis of chaos and licentiousness. "Aspired" is apt because some residents of the Midi ignored *paratge* and engaged in as much duplicity and unbelievable cruelty as others in their time.

When exercising *paratge*, one is gently polite, even in face of disagreement, and receptive to opinions, practices, race, religion, gender and nationality that are different from one's own. One acts in a just way, instead cheating, or seeking unfair advantage. It means avoiding excess and seeking harmony with the universe; a person is honorable according to how well he upholds the other principles of *paratge*. Looking backward, I realize my mother was a whole-hearted practitioner of *paratge*.

From the eleventh through the thirteenth century, the Midi was renowned for its troubadours who produced poems and songs about love and the joys of living, which drew much of their inspiration and techniques from the rich Moorish culture on the other side of the Pyrenees. It was the center of Western European secular literature and music and gave rise to similar movements in France, England, Germany and Italy. In his Divine Comedy, Dante celebrated and even quoted its poetry. The troubadours spoke, sang, and wrote in the *lenga d'oc*, not French.

At the time, French-speaking people occupied the fertile plain stretching from the Vosges Mountains in the east to Normandy and Brittany in the west and from the Low Countries in the North to the Massive Central in the South. In the old French tongue, the word for yes was *ouil*, hence Frenchmen spoke the *langue d'ouil*.

In contrast, the people of the Midi spoke a different language closely related to modern Catalan that used the word '*òc*' for 'yes,' hence it was called *lenga d'oc* (*langue d'oc*), and, eventually, *Occitan*. Spoken from Aquitania in the west, to the Alps in the east, and from the Massive Central in the north, to the Pyrenees and the Mediterranean in the south, Occitan was the native tongue of Aliénor of Aquitania, and her sons, Richard the Lionhearted and John Lackland, who became kings of England.

Francophones didn't consider themselves as French, but as Nivernois, or Normands or Burgundians. Similarly, the inhabitants of what we now call Occitania thought of

III

themselves as Tolosans, Provençals, Albigeis, and so forth. (The term Occitania was not used until late in the 13th century.) The concept of nation states was still a long way off. Among its neighbors, France proper was one of the smallest realms, but arcane feudal ties dating back to Charlemagne had established its king as the ultimate suzerain and his more powerful neighbors as his vassals. The feudal practice of obligating liegemen to provide their liege lords with troops and military service on demand constituted the real power behind the French throne.

In the North, power was concentrated in a relatively few hands because of widespread adherence to the custom of primogeniture—where the oldest son is the sole heir to the estate—thereby strengthening existing estates possessing male heirs, or expanding them, through strategic marriages.

In Occitania, both customs were more honored in the breach: estates were divided among many heirs, producing political weakness and instability. A county, or a castle, could have a half dozen lords, and because liegemen did not feel obligated to their liege lords, it was difficult to raise armies or to achieve a unified political or military command. The County of Tolosa was probably richer than any in the North or South, yet its ruler was politically and militarily weak. Prized and fought over by the dukes of Aquitaine, the Counts of Foix and Tolosa, the King of Aragon and their respective vassals, Occitania was united only in speech and culture.

Like the rest of medieval society, life in the North was stratified and hierarchical, where lords who had gained power through violence or dynastic marriage became extremely wealthy from their vast holdings of rich wheat fields worked by powerless serfs. The upper crust got its cut, and the people at the bottom got the crusts, if they were lucky.

IV

Occitanian society also operated within a feudal framework, but with less de facto division between those at the top and those at the bottom; there was more upward mobility among the social strata than was possible in the North. Occitanian economy was largely based on cash and was far more trade-oriented compared to the largely agricultural North (Flanders was an exception). Cash crops like wool, wine, and olive oil were solid sources of wealth and industry in the Midi. Ports on the Mediterranean were gateways to the wealth of the Orient and crossroads like Carcassonne and St.Gilles were sites of international fairs.

Because of a wealthy merchant class, many Occitanian cities followed the Italian model, with consulates whose political power rivaled that of the feudal lords. Occitanian nobles often resided in the cities, a fundamental distinction between the life of those who used their castles and violence in the pursuit of power and pelf in both North and South. Rich merchants often achieved knighthood and joined the aristocracy.

No dynasty lasts forever

At the start of the thirteenth century, a major political confrontation was taking place in what would become France and England. The extremely wealthy and powerful Plantagenet dynasty based in Aquitania ruled more than half of what is France today and the British Isles as well, but was being slowly constricted by its arch rival, the Capetian dynasty, which was centered in Paris. A third dynasty, that of Aragon, was busy establishing fiefdoms all across the littoral of the Gulf of Lyon, from Barcelona to Nice.

As the novel opens, Richard the Lionheart, the Plantagenet Duke of Aquitania and King of England, has been dead for only a few years, and his brother and successor, John, is at war with the Capetian King Philippe August II of France.

V

While the Plantagenets would rule Aquitaine and England continuously for almost three hundred years, the main branches of the Capet family would rule France for 800 years. The last Plantagenet king, Richard III of England, died on Bosworth Field in 1485, but by that time, King Louis XII of France, a Capetian, had annexed Aquitaine, the wellspring of Plantagenet power.

The almost constant warfare between the two dynasties required them to concentrate on their contiguous borders, which helped the Midi develop its own political dynasties and keep the greater powers at bay...for a time.

By the end of the tenth century, the counts of Tolosa, whose family had roots in St. Gilles in Provence, had become the dominant power in the Midi. Including the March of Provença, their territory spread from the border of Aquitaine to the Alps. Although they were formally vassals of the Capetian kings of France, the feudal tie between them was weak. Count Raimond VI, who reigns over Tolosa at the start of the novel, had secured peace with England and Aquitaine by marrying Henry II's daughter Joan, thus becoming the son-in-law of Aliénor of Aquitania and the brother-in-law of Richard the Lion Hearted and John of England. When Joan died in childbirth, Raimond wed the sister of the King of Aragon, safeguarding his southern flank.

Because he was previously married to the sister of Viscount Roger Trencavel for twenty years, Raimond VI was also at peace with his major rival in the Midi. Trencavel's lands included Albi in the north, and Besièrs and Carcassona in the south, territories that are wedged into the heart of the County of Tolosa.

Along with the Trencavels, the Count of Fois and the Viscounts of Comminges and Narbona were vassals of King Peter II of Aragon, whose realm included the County of

Provença, the territory bounded by the Ròse (Rhone) and the Alps, and by the Mediterranean in the south, and the Duranca River in the north. Aragon also possessed the Gevaudan, a landlocked county bordered by Aquitania in the north and the County of Tolosa in the South. (See Figure 2) Aquitania itself was commonly called Gascony to the west of the Garonne, and Guiana to the east of that river, including Angouleme, Perigord, and Limoges.

As the suzerain of the Counts of Roussillon, Gevaudan, Fois, Comminges, Provença, and Viscount Trencavel, King Peire II of Aragon controlled as much territory as the Count of Tolosa, whose suzerain -- King Phillipe of distant France, -- was preoccupied with Aquitania and England.

The Crusades to the Holy Land distracted two excellent warriors from expanding or defending their domains in the Midi. Raimond IV of Tolosa was the leader of the first Crusade (1095) and never returned, breathing his last in Tripoli, in what is now Lebanon. In his absence, the Duke of Aquitania captured Tolosa for a short period. Raimond's sons had to fight off both the Plantagenets and the Kings of Aragon, and they lost Narbonne, Montpelier, Rousillon, Bearn and Bigorre. Because they preferred to live in Provença, Raimond and his heirs often found it difficult to rally the people of Tolosa.

Likewise, Richard the Lionheart saw his fortunes in Aquitaine and England ebb while he was away fighting Saladin in the Third Crusade(1187), and wiling away his time in prison after being captured in Hungary. (1192) Once ransomed, he won back most of his lost territories only to die from a wound from a rebel crossbowman.

A dissolution of faith

In medieval Europe, the high clergy of the Roman Church grew rich as they tithed the wealthy nobility and squeezed alms from the powerless poor. Society tended to be both materialistic and highly spiritual, ruled by the philosophy that might makes right, but, at the same time, weighed down by constant fear of eternal damnation. For Catholic parishioners of all ranks, excommunication was a fate worse than death. Life was a short, thorny road that led to hell, unless one coughed up the tithes and alms demanded by an insatiable Church, many of whose leaders were renowned more for their concupiscence and debauchery than for piety.

During the ninth and early tenth century, not only were weak Popes bought and sold, but the clergy itself was rotten to the core, from the bishops right down to the village priest. Parishioners and the pastoral clergy who demanded reform were therefore susceptible to a message that rejected most of the Roman dogma and advocated a return to the simplicity of the early church that did not emphasize trinitarianism or many of the sacraments.

A century later, Pope Gregory VII went out of his way to reform the clergy: he forbade them to marry and insisted on celibacy, working in concert with the powerful monastic movement. Gregory also buttressed the Holy See. He insisted that the church was founded by God and was therefore itself divine and supreme over all other institutions; that the Pope was the Vice-Regent to God and to disobey the Pope was to disobey God; and that clerical power was to be centralized in Rome, not in the bishoprics. By strengthening the papacy and attempting to reform the prelates, he antagonized bishops and priests alike, ironically weakening the church's hold on the faithful, who did not take kindly to clerical excesses.

VIII

By this time, many Occitanians had turned away from the money-grubbing, ostentatious, and fear-mongering Roman prelates in favor of a return to the simple worship of the early church. The Orthodox Church saw such a departure as heresy.

One of these heresies was a quasi-Christian faith that made no demands on the purse and that encouraged worship in the home, not in a church. Its practitioners called themselves Friends of God or True Christians; others sometimes referred to them as *Cathars*, or "pure ones." By the start of the second half of the twelfth century, a substantial proportion of Occitanians, whether of noble or common birth and including many former clerics -- particularly those interested in theology-- had taken up the new faith, and the Roman Church became concerned, particularly after Innocent III was invested as pope.

No one knows for certain how Catharism came to Occitania, but its appearance coincided with the corruption and immorality that was sapping the strength of the Roman Church. Such decay and dissension provided a golden opportunity for anti-authoritarian heresies to arise. Thus, Catharism may have been a spontaneous, homegrown pushback against a church divided.

On the other hand, there is evidence that it may have originated in Bulgaria, where it was called *Bogomilism*, Bogomil meaning *Dear to God* in Bulgarian. Bogomilism erupted throughout Bulgaria in the tenth century as a social and religious protest against the power and corruption of the Byzantine Church and state. Its roots, in turn, might go back to the Gnostics and Paulists, or even to Manicheism, a Persian dualistic religion founded by Mani in Babylon, around the middle of the third century AD, that spread throughout the Middle East and then found its way to China in the east, and to the lands bordering the

Mediterranean and Britain in the west. The great theologian Augustine practiced Manicheism before converting to Catholicism in the late 4th century and later used its precepts as straw men to advance his theology.

The old word for Bulgarian in French was *bougre*; however, because of its association with Bogolism and Catharism, which did not hold homosexuality as a sin, some etymologists say that *bougre* explains the modern day usage throughout the United Kingdom of the verb and noun bugger, meaning sodomize or sodomite, respectively. What was pertinent at the time was that many Roman Catholics believed Cathars to be sexual perverts regardless of their sexual preferences

In the city of Albi, northeast of Tolosa, True Christian adepts called Good Men actually debated priests in the mid twelfth century and the results were two-fold. First, the Good Men clearly proved themselves to be more adept than some of the best theologians in France, an outcome that was all the more unexpected because the some of the Albigensian debaters were simple weavers and artisans without seminary educations. The hypocritical prelates in their finery who praised the virtues of poverty became laughing stocks. Seminary students deserted the Church in droves to join the True Christians. The Church reacted in astonishment, then in rage. The prelates' conviction that the heretical upstarts had to be taught a lesson became the nemesis for the True Christians.

Another result of the debate in Albi was that the French began characterizing the heretics as Albigensians, a term that has survived down to the present.

Later debates produced the same results and in 1207, none other than Dominic Guzman, who would found the Dominican Order, was made to look ridiculous in a debate in Pamiers. However, Dominic came to realize that clerical

X

reform was at the heart of the controversy, and started an order of itinerant teaching monks to carry the Roman Church over its hurdles by riding the wave of reform.

The Heretical Dogma

The True Christians, or Friends of God, believed that the world is dominated by the opposing spirits of love and power. Power, which was believed to be synonymous with Evil, manifested itself through material things, thus matter itself is the opposite of love and is Evil. The creator of matter is an all-powerful force of Evil called Satan among other names, who is responsible for chaos and willfulness. This Evil force is opposed by the purely spiritual God of love who brings order and peace. For the True Christians, the aim of life was rejection of power and the physical world and the embracing of spiritual love instead. They beheld the wealthy Roman church with its sumptuous decorations and accoutrements as a living, tangible example of Evil's worldly sway, the whore of Babylon.

Since the fourth century Council of Nicea, Roman dogma has held that as God incarnate, Jesus died on the cross, was resurrected incarnate and so ascended to Heaven. This same God created the world, which is filled with Evil. To the True Christians, the Old Testament God was identical to Satan, and, therefore, if Jesus had been the incarnate son of God, he would be the son of Satan, which was unthinkable.

To the True Christians, the whole idea of the cross and the crucifixion was therefore blasphemy and obscene, even though they relied on the Gospel of John in their preaching. On the other hand, a totally spiritual Jesus sent to earth as an angel was compatible with worshipping a god of love. In contrast, the Roman Church, found – and still finds -- this concept of Jesus without the Trinity as heresy of the first order.

XI

Rank and file worshippers among the True Christians were called Believers; their mentors –Good Men and Good Women -- lived simple lives of great asceticism and frugality. Virtually all were self-sufficient because they were artisans, even though many had been members of the noble class. The Good Men and Women followed strict laws of chastity and dietary abstention; they avoided meat and other animal products. They abjured telling lies, the killing of any creature, and the swearing of oaths. This last was anathema to the mostly illiterate society of that day because business contracts and feudal allegiances depended on oaths given orally.

The Friends of God believed that after death, souls could be interchanged between sexes, and even species, hence a person's physical form was relatively unimportant. A believer's soul could be in a man in one life and in a woman in the next. The upshot was that men tended to treat women as equals and more than forty per cent of the church leaders were women. Therefore, the faith attracted women, who identified with its female leadership and desired social equality in contrast to the male hierarchy in the Roman Church. Occitanian women had always enjoyed a relatively higher social status than women in other regions, perhaps a vestige of their Ostrogoth origins, and because of such predilections, they had an affinity for the True Christians who clearly accentuated the equality between sexes.

Unlike the Roman Church's many repressive rules on sexuality, the Good People did not oppose contraception, or nonprocreative sex (fornication); instead, they frowned on procreative sex, because the progeny it produced were still more evil matter! Fortunately, for the growth of their religious community, they did not overreact when "accidents happened;" only Good Men and Women

XII

practiced chastity. Similarly, they did not proscribe masturbation or homosexuality because these sexual acts did not produce evil matter, whereas married couples engaging in sexual intercourse were risking the formation of still more evil. For this reason, marriage was not a sacrament, and the Roman Church considered this omission to be a major part of the heresy.

Good Men and Women were empowered to elevate Believers to Good Persons during a sacrament called the *consolation* –the wiping away of sin and any connection to the material world-- that involved a baptism performed by the laying on of hands. The *consolation* was also performed when a believer was dying, so that the believer's soul could enter heaven. The simplicity of only one sacrament, and that only at the end of one's life, was one of the many attractions to becoming one of the Friends of God.

In addition, the Friends did observe a few rites, such as the amelioration, by which a believer greets a Good Man or Woman with three genuflections, at the same time asking for a blessing. There was also the *aparelhament*, a public confession ceremony usually conducted by a deacon. All three rites are generally followed by a kiss of peace, the Believer kissing the Gospel and giving the Good Man or Woman a kiss on the lips if they are of the same sex, or laying their heads on the Good Person's shoulder if he or she is of a different sex.

If a Believer was in danger of death on the battlefield, he could arrange a *convenience*, which allowed him to participate in the consolation even if he was mortally wounded and could no longer speak. It was customary that the Believer would make a donation to the Church of Friends of God in return.

In the words of Michel Roquebert, the French historian who has spent his life studying and describing the Cathars,

"Catharism proposes a new relationship between a society and its church; and it is no longer a relationship between the exploited and the exploiters. On the contrary, the clergy and faithful live in total osmosis; far from being recluses or meditators, or like lords living off of their vassals and serfs, Good Men and Women participate in the collective life by performing the countless crafts that their rule imposes on them, and their shops and workplaces are natural places for people to come and listen to the good Word; there is absolutely no need for special buildings for preaching and ceremonies."

Spelling of names and places.

Wherever possible, I use Occitan spelling for names of people and places in the Midi, to make sure that the reader knows that she or he is dealing with Occitania, not France. I use French spelling for the names and places of the French characters, and use French only when a speech is attributed to a character speaking in French.

Expressions of time

Telling time in medieval days was terribly imprecise. Hence, the pace of life was much slower than our own electronic age. The hourglass, let alone mechanical clocks, had not yet been developed. The use of candle lengths to tell time was still to come. Sundials were available but impractical for anyone on the move, even though the pace of life was built around daylight. Estimating short time periods was almost impossible; one could have a rough idea by the number of Pater Nosters one could say for a given task. Church bells signaling church services did provide a rough notion of the passage of time, but the time intervals differed from day to day according to activity and especially to sunrise and sunset, which varied according to the season.

Canonical bells in 13th CenturyLondon

	Equinox	Midwinter	Midsummer
Matins	5:00 a.m.	6:40 a.m.	2:30 a.m.
Prime	6:00 a.m.	8:00 a.m.	3:40 a.m.
Terce	8:00 a.m.	9:20 a.m.	6:30 a.m.
Sext	10:30 p.m.	11:00 a.m.	9:40 a.m.
None	12:30 p.m.	12:20 p.m.	12:40 p.m.
Vespers	5:00 p.m.	3:00 p.m.	7:00 p.m.
(Sunset)	(6:00 p.m.)	(3:50 p.m.)	(8:20 p.m.)
Compline	7-8 p.m.	5-6 p.m.	9:20 p.m.

.Expressions of Distances

Long distances in this book are measured in leagues (*lègas*). One league is three miles. Short distances are given in paces of roughly 30 inches. The Occitan word for inch is *poce*.

Historical Figures

Most of the characters in this novel once lived and drew breath, including all of the Roman prelates (except for the Cistercian Monks Pascau and Aurelh) as well as the Counts of Tolosa and Fois; Viscount Trencavel; Simon of Montfort and King Peire of Aragon. By putting words in their mouths, the author follows the tradition of the 13th century authors of the *Cansó de la crozada (Song of the Crusade),* who created speeches for the crusaders and their Occitanian enemies.

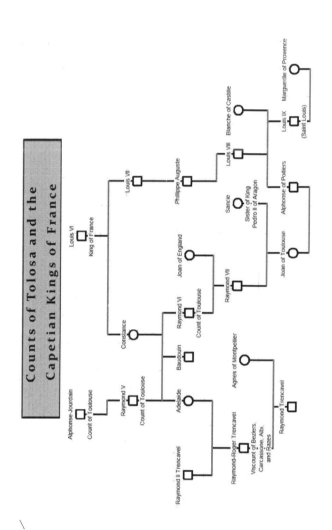

Counts of Tolosa and the Capetian Kings of France

XVI

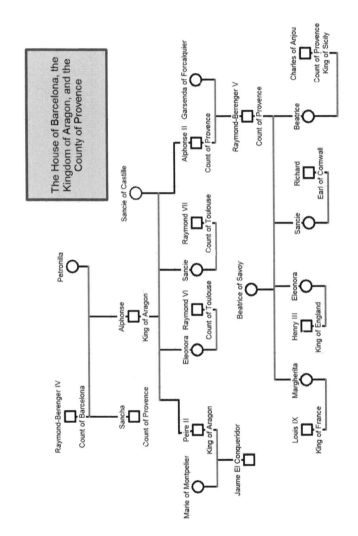

The House of Barcelona, the Kingdom of Aragon, and the County of Provence

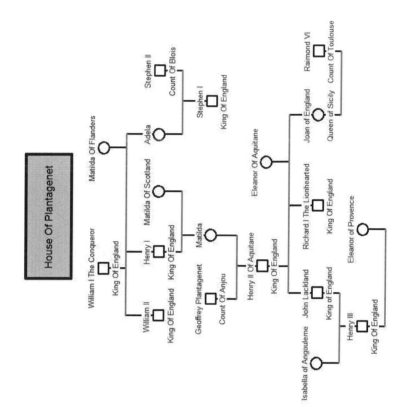

House Of Plantagenet

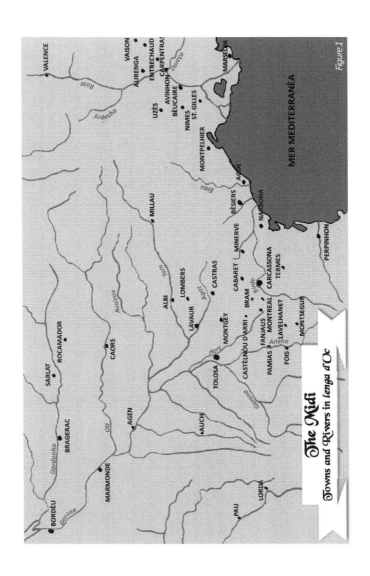

The Midi

Towns and Rivers in *lenga d'Oc*

Figure 1

XIX

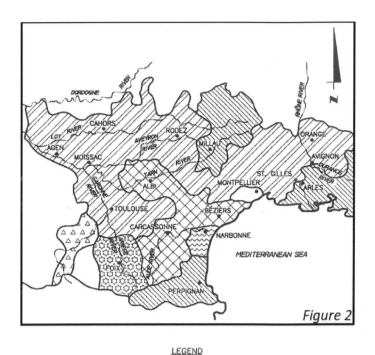

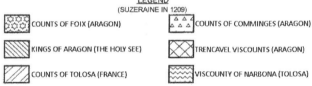

Feudal Possessions in the Midi, circa 1209

The Plantagenet (Anglo/Aquitaine) Empire, circa 1150

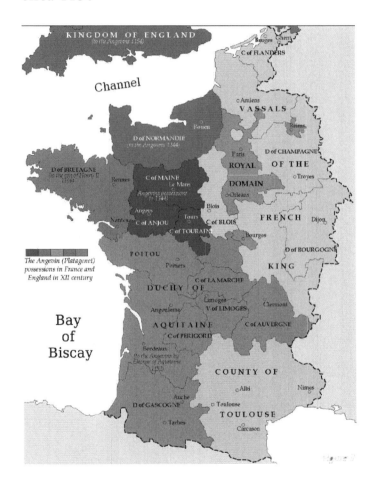

What's in a name?
Scott's father, Jack *Kimmich*, worked his way through college and medical school "F." stands for *Ferdinand*, the first name of the urologist who relieved his mother, Renée, of a painful kidney stone. She was also an avid reader of Sir Walter *Scott*. Born in Provence, she grew up reciting the works of Frederick Mistral, who did so much to re-establish Occitan as a living language. Scott passed on lore about the Albigensian Crusade to his children, who then badgered him, "when are you going to write the book, Dad?" And those little devils made him do it.